Conrad's Last Campaign

Book Eight
In the
Adventures of Conrad Stargard

By

Leo Frankowski
And
Rodger Olsen

Published by Great Authors Online

Cover Images From

text: Knight's Spur, (c) 2005, frielp, CC BY 2.0
text: Mongolian Steppe, (c) 2009, Marked Do, CC BY 3.0

Table of Contents

The Reluctant Crusader 8
Twenty Years Ago in China 12
Be Assured That Never Will I Try to Trick You 16
From the Secret Journal of Su Song, Part Two 28
"For God and Poland! We go to War!" 34
A Prince Among Men 43
Disaster in the Mountains 52
Moving up the River 61
We go Shopping 72
From the Secret Journal of Su Song, Part Three 96
Across the Sea of Grass 102
Betrayal. Dirty, Rotten Betrayal 105
The Second Betrayal 111
From the Memoirs of Duke Osiol 113
Wisdom from Conrad 129
Letter home from Captain William Orbitz 142
Conrad's Diary Continues 146
Su Song's Fourth Entry 155
Interlude in Uncle Tom's Control Room 160
The Trip to Karakorum Begins 162
From the Secret Journal of Su Song, Part 5 171
The War on the Tundra 174
Karakorum at Last 191
Captain Stanislaw's Tale 194
From the Secret Journal of Su Song, Part Six 204
Visitors are Coming for Dinner 205
Second Interlude in Uncle Toms Control Room 214
The Battle of Karakorum 215
Waiting for Our Visitors 224
From the Secret Journal of Su Song, Part 7 232
My Guests Arrive 234
The Waiting Game. 241
The End Game. 250
Post Game Highlights 258
Last from the Journals of Su Song 263
The View from on High 266
The Final Interlude in Uncle Tom's Control Room 271

Dedication

This book is dedicated to all those friends who, at our age, are slipping away. Leo Frankowski became one of those friends on Christmas Day 2008.

Acknowledgments

This book would not have been possible without the extensive help given by Chris Ciulla. He was a friend and help to Leo both before and after his death. His knowledge of the universe of Conrad Stargard is probably the best to be found anywhere.

Other Books

Mr. Frankowski's estate has republished *Lord Conrad's Crusade* and *Copernick's Rebellion*. Both are available in hard copy or Kindle format at [Amazon.com] and in EPUB format at [www.barnesandnoble.com].
Mr. Frankowski's co-author, Rodger Olsen, has published an apocalyptic novel, *The Empire of Texas*. It is also available at [Amazon.com] and [www.barnesandnoble.com]. Mr. Olsen's style of writing is very similar to Mr. Frankowski, so if you enjoy Leo's work, you may also enjoy the *Empire of Texas*.

Foreword

When Leo Frankowski returned from Russia in 2006, he considered the *New Kashubia* series to be finished and was willing to put it aside. He had published *Lord Conrad's Crusade* during his last year in Russia, but felt that Conrad's adventure was not resolved.

He began working on the final chapter of Conrad's life soon after his return to the States. His age and declining health made progress slow, but he was eventually able to complete the plot outline and write part of the final book. Leo and I had agreed that Conrad would grow and change a little in the last book and find a way to noble retirement or noble death. You will have to read the last chapter to know which path was chosen.

Unfortunately, Leo died before finishing the text. On Christmas Morning 2008, he died suddenly and peacefully from the effects of various drugs that he was prescribed.

I had been helping him with his writing for a number of years and had sat with him for many hours as he worked out the plot of the final book. At that point, virtually all of the writing had been done by Leo. At the time of his death, my only contribution was the opening prologue.

However, the book was well started and the plot known and Leo wanted everyone to know what happened to Conrad. I was familiar with Leo's writing style, having been coached by him to enable me to contribute to earlier writings, so I finished it.

I hope you enjoy it.

As those of you who have read the prior stories probably noticed, Leo was almighty careless in using his duodecimal system. The terms *gross* and *dozen* were used consistently, but Conrad often lapsed back into the base-ten numbers of his childhood. We were rarely certain if *thousand* was decimal 1,000 or 1,728 or whether *fifty* was 5*10 or 5*12. I have standardized the translations in this book. People using a base-twelve system would tend to think and build in *gross* and *dozen* and those terms have been preserved. All other numbers are now consistently base-ten, i.e. *fifty* is 5*10.

Prologue

It was still full dark when Megan whispered in my ear, "It is almost morning, your grace." She and Terry were pressing their bodies against mine and gently massaging my muscles to wake me. Gradually, I became aware of the sounds of a camp waking up. Muffled voices, the sounds of clattering pots, and footsteps filtered into the tent.

Soon they were dressing me in my armor. The golden armor gleamed this morning and under it my muscles were still hard and lean from the months I had spent in a slave pit. As my bodyguards dressed me, others were trying to feed me. I ate very little. A too-full belly can slow down a sword arm.

I had said my morning prayers, recited my oath and was ready to leave when the false dawn glowed outside. By the time full dawn came, I and my personal lance were approaching the battle lines.

I thought that I would be the first there, since the attack was not scheduled until almost an hour past dawn, but three companies of my men awaited my arrival.

The Africa Corps spread out on my left. They were battle-tested, but some of them were only months away from having been slaves in a medieval world. They were outfitted with our standard armor, but some had doffed their helmets, preferring to wear their brightly colored Mohawks into battle. Most held rifles or pistols, but some had drawn their swords instead and a few even preferred lances.

The Christian knights formed the right wing, the "place of honor." Most held modern weapons, but the profusion of armor styles, helmet plumes, and heraldry meant that they would never be mistaken for a modern army. We kept them as a favor to the pope. Actually, with their lousy training and poor discipline, they were the most useless part of the army. All you could do with them was to yell, "The enemy is that way: charge," then get out of the way. They had demanded and been granted the honor of leading the charge today.

A company of Wolves formed the center. Like the knights, they were noblemen trained from birth to be warriors. Unlike the knights, they went on to be trained as professional soldiers. They sat relaxed on their Big People and surveyed the battleground. Each of them held his shield close in front of him and rested his Sten gun or his sword on his pommel.

I didn't really want to attack Jerusalem, but they left me no choice when they had decided to fight rather than surrender. You would think they would have learned by now that everybody conquers Jerusalem. David took it from Canaanites and slaughtered the inhabitants. Then came the Egyptian pharaohs, the Assyrians, the Babylonians, Alexander the Great, the Ptolemies, Romans, Arabs, Crusaders, Saladin, and a bunch of others along the way.

Want to be a Boy Scout? Earn some merit badges. Want to be a scholar? Read some books. Want to be a conqueror? Sack Jerusalem. For extra points, send the inhabitants into exile for a few hundred years. It's tradition, and now it's my turn.

I had instructed the artillery to concentrate on the city walls only. If we damaged holy sites like the Church of the Holy Sepulcher or the Temple Mount, it would make it harder to govern the city later.

When the smoke from the last artillery barrage cleared, the knights would start the charge. However, Silver and I would be first through the wall, flanked by the Wolves. I reached down, clipped my Sten gun to my saddle, and drew my sword. This would be a historic battle, and history deserved to be written with a blade.

It was the early fall of 1263 AD. I was the Duke of Sandomierz, the Duke of Cracow, the Duke of Mazovia, the Hetman of the Christian Army, a Crusader, and a damned long way from home.

The Reluctant Crusader

Compared to the slave pit I had been chained if for the past year, my new home was a palace. In fact it was the Royal Palace of Jerusalem. It had become available when the old owner died suddenly and unexpectedly while charging a Christian Army line.

It had gilded furniture, rich drapes, grand halls, marbled floors, hot and cold running servants, and every luxury a man could want, except for a working toilet and clean running water. The Roman sewers hadn't been well maintained since the Byzantines left a few hundred years ago.

My office was on the third floor. From my balcony, I could see the Wailing Wall off to my left and, if I craned my neck to the right, I could see a little piece of the city walls between the buildings. For a second, I wondered if I was looking at the original city wall, the Roman city wall or the Crusader wall. There were lots of walls.

In the distance, work was proceeding on the twelve hexagonal snowflake forts that would ring Jerusalem. Each would be manned by a company of men, with their families. The pope, my old friend Father Ignacy, had wanted these very badly, to defend the Holy City. Five of them would be manned by our Jewish troops. That he didn't want.

The pope was becoming more conservative by the day. He was unhappy with my decision to allow everyone access to Jerusalem. He had expected the Muslim and Jews to be barred from the city or, better yet, killed. As I do not lead a Mongol army, I had declined the suggestion for mass murder. I guess I just don't have the proper attitude to be a crusader in this century.

I found myself staring down at the hand holding my whiskey. My right hand looked just like my left, but you could tell it was less grizzled and calloused. It took me a year to re-grow it after the slavers cut it off. Thanks to Uncle Tom's modifications, the hand grew back and my scars were gone, at least the visible ones were.

I had spent months as the engine of a piece of machinery, a water pump. How bad was it? The height of toilet protocol for pump slaves was to piss to the side so you didn't splash your fellow pumpmates. Your excrement you stepped over or walked in. That bad.

It's one thing to know slavery is an abomination and quite another to experience being sold naked at auction - at a discount, no less, because some Tuareg bastard had lopped off my right hand! The bastard who did it didn't know it would grow back and couldn't care less.

It wasn't the best time I've had in this century and for the first time in years, I felt homesick.

Home was my headquarters and palace at Okoitz, where my two formal wives lived.

Home used to be in 20th century Poland, but I once brilliantly managed to fall asleep, drunk, in a time machine. I woke up in the 13th century. It had been an interesting twenty years since then.

Now I was leading a Crusade. Not my idea. When Pope John Paul, formerly known as my friend Father Ignacy, ordered me to go on Crusade I had skipped town to avoid attacking innocent Muslims. That's how the damned slavers got me.

Fortunately, on my way home I met up with a crusading Christian Army. They were headed for the holy land and, since they were headed in my direction, I decided I might as well lead the Crusade as follow.

Before I even joined them, This Christian Army had conquered southern Spain and most of Northern Africa without much trouble. Since then, we had since taken the Holy Land, and were now working our way north on the Mediterranean coast on our way to the Christian city of Constantinople.

Mostly, we were just stringing the old Crusader States back together again. By accident, we were also protecting the Roman Empire and giving them an opportunity to reclaim a lot of lost land.

For now, I had time to relax and get back to being an engineer. For the first time since I broke out of Timbuktu I didn't have to fight anyone tomorrow and I was thoroughly happy sitting at a desk with papers scattered in front of me.

We were waiting for supplies and more manpower from Poland. We could probably finish off the Muslim states without it, since we had airplanes and machine guns and rifled cannon up against their swords, pikes and occasional muzzle-loading cannon, but there was no point in rushing to get men killed. War was exciting, but I preferred building to destroying and we were going to need a lot of building if we were going to hold the Middle East.

I was also secretly hoping that, given a little time to see how prosperous the former Muslim states got from being part of Europe, the Muslims might not fight so hard or at least would have armies full of men who saw an advantage in having railroads and light bulbs and access to European markets.

So, part of our war was building railroads. To take the region, we'd need to travel through some very difficult terrain. We'd have to build railroads as we went to move our troops and supplies. We were already laying tracks along the north coast of Africa, from Marrakech through Cairo to Jerusalem. From there, plans were to go north and west to Constantinople, and perhaps give those people a hand against their enemies.

To keep the territory we'd taken, we had to show the Arabs that they could prosper under our rule, and nothing contributes more to that than good transportation, although the lack of tariffs and low taxation helps, too. Shipping costs on one of our railroads were a tenth of what they were on a camel caravan.

To keep the prosperity rolling, I had just approved plans for the building of two Liner-class harbors, with housing, storage, and repair facilities, on the north and south sides of the Suez peninsula. A double railroad track would stretch between them, one going north and one south. They would transport troops, supplies, and eventually our trade goods. Our ships would still have to travel around the Cape of Good Hope, but they would only have to do it once!

After that, the crews would be rotated, but the ships themselves would stay in the Indian Ocean for the rest of their working lives, probably.

Working on the future also kept my mind off my pope problem. It was getting harder to maintain a relationship with a pope who was getting more fanatic by the day. Now he was pushing the concept of baptism by sword. He wanted the people we conquered to be baptized at the point of a sword or dispatched with the blade of one. It was only under discussion so far and I was hoping it would never come down as an order. I'm as good a Christian as anyone, but I won't kill a man for praying in the wrong church.

It also kept my mind of that nagging thought that kept bothering me. I'd always had a concern about the Mongols returning to Poland. We had barely beaten them twenty years ago, by dint of some modern organization and technology, nine years of hard work, and a little help from my time traveling Uncle Tom.

But what with all the slave girls they'd captured in their invasions, the average Mongol now had a half-dozen wives, and nobody there had ever heard of birth control. During a cold winter, sex just about was the only amusement available. If you assume four children from each wife, and half of them being boys, the next time, they might be able to hit us with a dozen times as many men as they did last time.

And all the lands they had taken gave them room enough to graze a sufficient number of animals to feed all of those people.

They were also more dangerous. The first time they came to Poland, they bypassed most of the fortified towns because you can't get much siege equipment on a horse. Places like Tver and Moscow held out if they kept their wits about them and kept the gates tightly closed. Of course, the Mongols still ruled the countryside and killed everyone not behind walls.

Now they would have Chinese engineers in the baggage train. They would probably have cannon and rifles too. They had captured an entire supply train of mine during the last battle, and they were well-known for developing any technology they came across.

In my own timeline they had come back about every twenty years and as we approached the twenty year mark I found my self thinking about them more often.

I walked down to the radio room, and had them get in contact with Sir Piotr, my "viceroy" in Okoitz, which was the Christian Army headquarters, and also my personal palace. Sir Piotr spent a quarter hour filling me in on various things.

Then I made my obligatory call to my main wives, Francine and Cilicia, and they later put me on to talk with some of my former harem girls who were living at the palace. It was a bit boring, but you have to talk to them to keep them happy.

It had been a long day, and I was getting hungry. I went downstairs, where my harem girls, fourteen of them just now, had a hot bath ready for me. Three of them were soon in the big tub with me, as nude as I was, scrubbing, shampooing, and shaving me.

I'd maintained a decent harem ever since we'd conquered Timbuktu. This tends to be a short-term occupation for the girls when you are traveling in wartime. You can't very well take a pregnant woman into battle. I'd made a practice of sending expectant mothers back to my palace in Poland, where they would get the best of care.

It's a good life.

Dinner was served western style at a big table that I'd found in the city. It had probably been left behind by the last bunch of Crusaders who'd owned this city.

The food was good, and the entertainment, music and dancing provided by my naked ladies, was very relaxing. Often, I had friends over, but not tonight.

Eventually, it was time for bed. One of my girls was new, and I was eager to try her out.

The Army used a twelve-hour day, with sunrise being at zero o'clock. Our hours were twice as long as those in my old time line. It might have been ten in the morning, long before dawn, when one of my stunningly beautiful, if not quite human, bodyguards shook me awake, a kerosene lantern in her hand, frightening the shy young lady that I was with.

"Please excuse me, my lord, but you have a radio call from Baron Boris Novacek. He says that it's very urgent!"

Boris Novacek commanded our Commercial Corps, and was in charge of the sales of all of the army's civilian products, across much of the world. He was also my secret chief of spies.

"Tell him that I'm coming," I said, grabbing an embroidered silk robe.

In the radio room, bleary eyed, I said, "Boris, this had better be good!"

"It's not, my lord. It's very bad. The Mongols are getting ready to move on Europe again. Their departure date is set for three months from now."

Twenty Years Ago in China

Polymaths, geniuses in multiple fields, are rare in history, but China in the tenth and thirteenth centuries, and the Ottoman Empire for a few centuries afterward produced more than their share. In a few rare lifetimes, more than one existed simultaneously. Su Song was a polymath working for the great khan.

In his younger days, Su Song had written an extensive book on pharmacology, cataloging hundreds of medicinal compounds and herbs. As with other polymaths, he also wrote books on engineering, metallurgy, military strategy, mineralogy, chemistry, and diplomacy. His most famous achievement was a forty-foot high clock built for the Song emperor. It was water powered, chain driven, regulated by an escapement four hundred years ahead of its time. In Conrad's home time line, it was famous a thousand years in the future.

As with most Chinese polymaths, he rose to prominence during the civil service exams and spent most of his life in Imperial posts. It was his diplomatic expertise and knowledge of history that caused him to end up in Mongol Imperial Service.

He was on a diplomatic mission to the Jin dynasty in 1237 when the city he was in came under Mongol attack. The city held out for two months, until captured Chinese sappers exploded nearly two tons of black powder under the city walls.

Because the city had resisted, the Mongols imposed the usual penalty; death to all inhabitants. However, the khan had learned by now that some people were as valuable as horses and land. The engineers who had sapped the walls and the gunpowder they used were, after all, Chinese engineers and a Chinese invention.

In spite of his fame, Su Song was kneeling in front of a raised sword when he was recognized and saved. It was an even closer call for his wife.

From the Secret Diary of Su Song

It has been five years now since I entered the service of the great khan. For the last three years, I have served the new khan, Ogedei, by improving siege machines, trebuchets, and gunpowder weapons and planning supply chains for his military campaigns, but today things became much more interesting. Early in the morning, two palace messengers summoned me to a meeting with the khan himself.

I remember that my wife fussed with my collar unnecessarily, her fingers lingering when they brushed the skin of my neck. I knew what she was thinking. When one was summoned by the great khan, one could return showered with wealth or wrapped in a shroud.

I tried to reassure her, "My dear, you have been fussing over my clothes for the past ten minutes. I'm more likely to be executed for keeping the great khan waiting than for wrinkled clothes". I immediately regretted the jest as her eyes teared over. Like most husbands, I am better at reading the stars than I am in reading my wife's mind.

Several of my assistants were waiting at the heavily guarded door to one of the grand halls.

Of course we dropped to our knees and began the ceremonial crawl to the throne. We had not gotten more than a few *chi*[^1] when the khan announced loudly, "Su Song, you and your men will have to stand to see what we have to show you. We have important business to attend to."

I looked up to an amazing sight. Ten crossbowmen stood on each side of the emperor. In all his years as emperor, the khan had strictly forbidden any deadly weapons in his presence He carried the only sword allowed in the audience chamber. Even his personal guard was not armed in the audience chambers or offices. Something momentous was going to happen, and I hoped that it would not involve the execution of several scientists.

The khan's moods always had to be judged carefully. Sometimes he was the regal Emperor of China who ruled wisely but would have you shortened for bowing too little. Sometimes he was the barbarian ruler who would drink and carouse with his men but kill them personally for disagreeing with him. Today, he was the working technocrat who would probably not have you killed for disagreement so long as it was said politely and backed up with facts.

We settled for bowing several times and walking with our heads down. "Su Song", he said, "Look around you. I have brought you some very expensive presents. Please look and tell me what you think of them."

At his gesture, servants removed the canvas coverings from three huge wagons and several tables around the room. The wagons were about four *bu* by about two *bu* wide. Two of the wagons had iron wheels and were mounted on some sort of iron strips. The third wagon was obviously some sort of war wagon with shield walls, similar to the Korean battle wagons, but with some sort of metal weapon mounted in place of the usual crossbows. The other wagons seemed to be primarily cargo carriers, but they also mounted weapons and on the front of one was a nozzle that looked like a fire lance. If the weapons were functional, that would explain the crossbowmen in the room. The khan would never take a chance that someone would use them on him.

Since the khan was looking at us expectedly, we wandered around the wagons and tables inspecting the contents briefly; very briefly as the khan's patience was famous for its absence. The cargo wagon held wooden forms covered with doped cloth, apparently some sort of war kite and a mechanism with a large propeller attached.

There were tin bottles and brass tubes in most of the wagons along with miscellaneous parts that looked like so much junk.

Sitting alone was a large mechanism as tall as a man and wider than it was tall that seemed to be driven by a rather inefficient looking water wheel. I had my doubts that the mechanism would actually work. Even though the water wheel had linkages that matched the bigger mechanism, I couldn't see how it could produce enough power to be useful.

The water wheel could be a paddlewheel from a warship, but those were normally powered by a treadmill and the linkage still didn't make any sense. The most interesting thing was the track system that two of the wagons stood on. The track was several times the length of each wagon, so I signaled two of my assistants to join me at one end of a wagon. As I suspected, the three of us could rather easily roll the cart forward in spite of its heavy load.

I spent several minutes inspecting the wheels and bearings and, more importantly, the iron strips they sat on. Their design was impressive. Wide flat tops and bottoms with a thinner vertical member gave them stability without using excess material. Somebody smart designed this system.

The khan's patience ended at the same time as the wine in his cup, "Well, Su Song, give your first impressions of what you see here."

"Your Imperial Majesty, it seems as if you have conquered yet another enemy and brought the spoils to us. What we can recognize is war material. The war cart reminds me of the war cart used by the Koreans. The weapons are some sort of fire lance, but I would have to experiment to know their power.

14

"The rail and wagon system is impressive and shows signs of long development. Such a system would cut the cost of bringing building material and supplies to the Celestial Palace by ninety percent or more. For now, we are limited to destinations on or near a very expensive canal. This would cost less than one percent of what a canal would cost, and could go anywhere.

"The engineer has also solved the problem of theft of the rails. They are made of the most cheaply manufactured cast iron, useless to blacksmiths, and each has a cast figure of a man in a noose. Apparently a warning to would be thieves.

"We will not know what the brass tubes are for until we open them and the water powered machine or paddlewheel will require work to understand. They do apparently use battle kites, as the Jin Dynasty did, to carry observers over the battlefield." I decided not to mention the incongruity of several large tree trunks stacked in a corner of the room.

The emperor looked pleased, "You did well for only having a few minutes of inspection. Batu, tell them what they missed."

An expensively dressed Mongol stepped out of the shadows and gestured to the items in the room. "Unfortunately, these are not the booty of victory. These items were dragged at great expense from a small country west of the Rus'. They are much more powerful than they first appear. With weapons and systems like these an army of farmers destroyed a million Mongol and Chinese warriors. The emperor himself has chosen to demonstrate the weapons."

With that, His Imperial Majesty descended the throne and walked over to a heavy table with one of the metal weapons mounted on it. On closer inspection, it looked somewhat like a crossbow stock lacking the crossbow and, strangely, carrying a small lit lamp on the side. The emperor pointed the weapon at the tree trunks and pulled the trigger. It sounded like a grenade going off. Then he pulled a lever back and forth and fired again, and again. Before he stopped, he had splintered several tree trunks in less than a minute. Eventually, he turned to us with his hand still resting on the weapon. "If we are not to be conquered by a nation of dirt grubbing farmers, we will need some of these. You will be moved immediately to a new facility about twenty *li* outside the city. Whatever you need in men and materials are yours for the asking. Use these weapons to strengthen our army or be killed by theirs."

Be Assured That Never Will I Try to Trick You

"Damn," I swore. "I knew that they would attack us eventually, but it sure could have happened at a better time! You are absolutely positive about your information?"

"I have had three independent reports come in during the last two days. I'm as certain as I can be, your grace."

"Holy shit! I'll see what I can do, but right now, half of our power is in the wrong place! Boris, get your people out of there! Tell them to try to find somewhere safe to hide! That goes for you, too!"

"I have already told them that, and I am safe enough. Good luck, your grace!"

"You, too, and keep in touch!"

I signed off. When I first got to this bloody century, I'd worked for Boris for a while, and I liked the man. A year later, he'd run into bandits on my land. He'd had his bodyguard killed, his fortune stolen, and both of his hands cut off. We'd saved him, and killed all of the bandits, but we had never found where they had hidden his treasure.

Boris soon married his nurse, a very patient young woman who didn't mind waiting on him hand and foot; services which he really needed. Without hands, he couldn't button his clothes, put on his shoes, or go to the toilet without help. But that man could sell sand to an Arab!

Since he was without his working capital, he couldn't continue as a merchant. Therefore, he had started to work for me as my commercial representative. He was very successful at this. Eventually, he had agents all over Christendom, profitably distributing our commercial products. Their reports often contained information about various political and military items, as well as commercial news. This function soon expanded into a spy network that had become one of the best in the world. We were selling our products, from hardware, plumbing, and farming equipment on up to and including whole factories, over a huge area now. Our salesmen, many of them, were also our spies.

Much of our profits supported a free school system that covered all of Europe now, from elementary schools to universities. We had a growing system of clinics, medical centers, and hospitals as well.

But for now, I had a serious problem. I had a major portion of our military might up here in the south on this *Crusade*, when they were soon to be badly needed thousands of miles down north of here!

For good and sufficient reasons, our maps had south at the top. Polack jokes are not permitted.

I went up to my office, telling my chief bodyguard, Terry, to have a cup of coffee sent to me ASAP, and whole pots of the stuff sent in at quarter-hour intervals.

"Yes, wake all the girls up. We have an emergency going on! The Mongol Horde is going to attack Europe in three months time, and we're all up here in the Middle East and Africa! Damn the pope and his silly Crusade!"

There wasn't any need for secrecy. The enemy already knew what they were going to do, and I wanted all of my men to know about it, too. A very old joke had it that there were three ways to spread the news quickly. Telegraph, telephone, and tell-a-woman. The last was the most efficient. Gossip travels faster than radio waves, I swear it!

I started writing up tentative orders.

All non-army fighting men were encouraged to leave for Eastern Europe. The army would pay for their travel expenses.

All garrison troops would be reduced by half, or down to one twelfth of the population of the city that they were guarding, whichever required fewer men. The rest of our warriors had to get to Eastern Europe to bolster our defenses there.

Work on army construction projects, including bridges, the railroads, the Suez project, and the Kuwait installation were to continue at the best possible speed.

Supplies were to be inventoried and reduced down to a reasonable minimum. The rest were to be sent back down north to Eastern Europe.

We would not have sufficient shipping to get everyone to the probable Mongol attack point in time. Therefore, many troops would have to take the North African and Middle East railroads as far as the Straits of the Dardanelles. The railroad should be completed to there within a few weeks. Ships, lighters and barges would be made available to ferry our forces across, from which point they could travel overland to their destinations.

It was a start, but it wasn't enough. I looked at the pot of coffee to my right and the girl waiting on me.

"Melissa, run down and get me a glass and a pitcher of that Shangri-La brandy I brought up from Africa. And Terry, go wake up Sir Wladyclaw and Sir Vladimir, and tell them that I want them both here in a quarter of an hour. Somebody have some hot coffee ready for them. Vanessa, go to the radio room, and have them get Baron Piotr out of bed. I want to talk to him soonest."

The three of them scampered out, leaving me alone except for the other five nude girls up there.

I took a drink of brandy and pondered the problem. We needed more time. If we could somehow delay the Mongols, it would be a Godsend.

17

Slowly, a plan started to emerge in my head. The Mongols had to travel on horseback. The average Mongol needed at least two spare horses, and some took along a string of six or eight. If we could kill enough of their horses, they wouldn't be able to attack Europe. Maybe not for years.

I didn't like the idea of killing all of those dumb animals, but it was better than having the Mongols kill millions of Christians.

We needed to organize a raid, a large, fast-moving group all mounted on Big People, with an awful lot of small arms ammunition along. We'd have to carry all of our food along with us, too, and we'd be living off of iron rations for several months, because we wouldn't have time to waste on cooking. Carrying all of these supplies might need all of the pneumatic tired carts the army had, and about as many Big People pulling them as we had human troops along.

I would take the remainder of my African Corps with me. They were not mixing well with the rest of the army, but they were very good fighters and fiercely loyal to me. The Jews would want to stay here in Jerusalem, and the Blacks were already well on their way back to Timbuktu, but the rest of them, Christians and a few Arabs, were almost a battalion strong. We'd fill in with warriors from the regular Mobile Infantry.

A battalion of Wolves was needed, as was a battalion of mounted infantry. Add to that three komands of artillery, because we wouldn't have time to be delayed by obstacles in our path. We'd have to just blow them out of the way.

And that meant more Big People to haul the cannons and ammo along.

And six companies of engineers would be a very good thing to have along, along with plenty of bridging equipment. From what I'd heard, many of the roads down there were passable by caravans only. Taking our carts through would be a challenge.

Word came that Baron Piotr was waiting for me.

In the radio room, I said, "Piotr, what I was afraid of will soon come to pass. The Mongol Horde will attack Europe in about three months. We have to get much of our supplies and more than half of our warriors back to Eastern Europe as quickly as possible."

"Yes, sir. Has the pope been informed?"

"No one has been informed yet, except you. Don't keep this a secret. Let everybody in on the news," I said. "I'll let you inform the pope and King Henryk. I might be rude to them at this point."

I could hear the grimace in his voice when he said, "Oh, thank you, sir."

"Hey! This Crusade was not my idea!"

Then I read my tentative orders to him.

18

Sir Piotr said, "Very good, sir. I'll have all of our ships at sea return to Europe by the quickest routes, unload their passengers and cargo, and head to Africa as fast as possible under ballast."

I said, "I still want the construction machinery and supplies to get here. I want work on the railroads and the Suez project to continue at full speed."

"Yes, sir. We'll get it sorted out. How good do you think your chances are of delaying the Mongols with this raid of yours?"

"I have no idea. All I can say is that we'll try our best. You should proceed with defending Europe as if I had no chance of accomplishing anything at all, and that they will be hitting you with all of their forces. If I can't stop the Mongols, I'll be following behind them, harassing their rear."

"Yes, sir. I'll have all of the land-based aircraft brought back home, too."

"Good. And until the enemy actually attacks, I want those planes disarmed. We need them for observation, with the longest range possible. If they have guns, they won't be able to resist making a few strafing runs, and they will get pin cushioned with arrows."

"The Eagles won't like that, sir."

"To hell with what they'd like. There's a war on. Conrad out."

I got back to my office to find Sir Vladimir and Sir Wladyclaw waiting for me.

Sir Vladimir was one of my oldest friends, and been with me for eight years before we defeated the Mongols the first time. For many years, he had been in command of our Reserve Forces, until we had time to build enough snowflake forts to house them all in. About the same time, we finally had enough Big People to mount them all. Sir Vladimir now commanded the Mounted Infantry, the biggest unit in the Christian Army.

Sir Wladyclaw was the son of my old friend Sir Miesko, and his wife, Lady Richeza. He had once taken two reductions in rank so that he could take command the Wolves, a cavalry unit made up of the scions of the old nobility. These men were too proud to do honest work, so they had become one of our few full-time fighting units. Most of our warriors spent most of their time being productive. But that political move on Sir Wladyclaw's part had made him one of the most powerful men in my army.

Sir Wladyclaw said, "The Mongols will be attacking Europe in three months time? What is your source of information on this?"

I said. "As to your second question, you don't have a need to know, except that I can assure you that the source of the information is reliable."

"I imagine that we must abandon this war in the south, and all get back to Europe," Sir Vladimir said.

"I don't think that we have to go quite that far. For one thing, I don't think that we have the transportation available to move everyone back to Eastern Europe fast enough. Many of our people must remain here, although more than half of our troops will be heading north. We will be leaving small garrison forces in the cities we've taken, and I want our construction projects, particularly the Suez installation, to be completed as soon as possible. No matter how it turns out, our war with the Mongols is likely to be a short one. I think that we will win it, and after that, we will still have the Muslims to contend with."

"If our garrison forces in the cities we've taken up here are too small, the Arabs will be tempted to revolt against us," Sir Vladimir said.

"Our garrison commanders will be instructed to use all available force against any possible revolts. They will have to be brutal. They won't have any alternative, being under strength," I said.

Sir Wladyclaw said, "Yes sir. Will you be going to Poland, or staying here?"

"Neither. Sir Piotr will command in Europe, Sir Vladimir will command our forces here, and you, Sir Wladyclaw, will be coming with me, into Mongolia. I'll need a reliable second in command and you can take charge of the Mounted Infantry."

They both just stared at me, so I continued.

"The Mongols can't attack Europe without a sufficient number of horses and other draft animals. I plan to lead a raid into Mongol territory, the purpose of which is primarily to slaughter animals. I'll be taking my battalion of the African Corps with me. They haven't been blending in with the rest of the army as well as I'd hoped."

"Well, what did you expect? They don't speak proper Polish, and they all wear those weird haircuts like yours," Sir Wladyclaw gestured toward my mohawk hairdo.

That had happened one night in Timbuktu, when I had fallen asleep with an inexperienced barber cutting my hair. She'd seen an Arabic travel guide that showed a Polish nobleman wearing a mohawk, so that's what she gave me. It started a fad among my men, and when they were all copying me, I'd felt obligated to continue with the style myself. It was good for unit morale, and I'd gotten to like the looks of it. I had the feeling that it scared people, and sometimes, that was useful.

The regular Christian Army already had their own weird haircut, similar to a modern military crew cut. At least it was weird for the [13]th century. They had felt no inclination to adopt a new one.

Every good army seems to need a strange haircut. The Mongols shaved a rectangular area on the top of their heads, for reasons best known to them.

I said, "Be that as it may. I'm also taking along a battalion of Wolves, a battalion of Mounted Infantry, some artillery, some engineers, and a whole lot of Big People hauling ammunition, bridging equipment, and canned food."

Sir Wladyclaw said, "Let's make it two battalions of Wolves. I have them available in this city, and this is the sort of mission that the Wolves were made for. They're good fighters, but they aren't very good as garrison troops, you know."

"Very well, two battalions of Wolves it is, and we'll take Sir Grzegorz to command them. I'll still need the Mounted Infantry, and everyone else I mentioned. We're also going to need some guides who know the way to Mongolia."

Sir Vladimir said, "I met an Arab looking for just such a position a few days ago. He said that he has sixty men working for him. But I'm not sure if I'd trust him enough to put him in charge of anything. It's nothing that I can prove, you understand. I just had a strange feeling about the man."

"Get him. We don't have much time. I want to leave in two days, in the early morning."

Sir Wladyclaw said, "Two days! That's rushing things, isn't it?"

"Yes, it is. We must get going soonest, and then we'll have to push very hard for many months."

We soon got down to the details of exactly who would go, and what we had to take with us. Then we had to figure out where we could get all of that stuff, and how we could get it all here in time.

After a while, Sir Wladyclaw glanced out the window, and said, "Whoops! Sunrise."

The three of us went out onto the balcony that faced east. We raised our right hands to the rising sun, and recited the Army Oath:

"On my honor, I will do my duty to God, and to the army. I will obey the Warrior's Code, and I will keep myself physically fit, mentally awake, and morally straight.

"The Warrior's Code:

"A Warrior is: Trustworthy, Loyal, and Reverent. Courteous, Kind, and Fatherly. Obedient, Cheerful, and Efficient. Brave, Clean, and Deadly."

Every warrior in the Christian Army recited that oath every morning of his life. Around and below us, we could hear thousands of other warriors reciting the same oath.

Then we went back to work.

By noon, we had a staff of over two hundred people working on our problems. I ordered for some food to be sent up to them, and then I broke for lunch, or rather breakfast, come to think of it. I took my two main men with me.

We were well into a decent meal when Terry, one of my eight bodyguards, announced that I had a visitor.

My bodyguards had much in common with the Big People. They were both bioengineered creations that had been produced in the same labs, owned by my Uncle Tom, the time traveler. But while the Big People were designed to look like horses, Terry and her ancestor Maude were designed to be bodyguards, dancers, housekeepers and child care workers. They looked like very innocent young women, school girls, with small breasts and thin flanks. But they weren't! They were in fact unbelievably strong and fast. They had been trained to be absolutely deadly, when the situation required it.

Reproducing by voluntary parthenogenesis, they had a sort of racial memory that emerged when they were four years old. At that point, they remembered everything that their mother knew up to the time of conception. They had all of her deadly knowledge of the martial arts, and all of her nice ones, like singing, dancing, taking care of children, and making marvelous love.

They had their quirks. The most obvious of these was their refusal to wear clothing, except for the smoothest and loosest of silk dresses, and then only under protest. They said that clothes were confining, scratchy, and made them itch. And every one of them always carried a small, hiltless sheath knife, very thin and sharp, resembling a kitchen knife.

"He said that he is Ali Mohammed Ahmed bin Maimed, but that we should just call him Ahmed," Terry said.

I said, "That's some relief, anyway."

Sir Vladimir said, "He's the guide I told you about."

"Well, send him in."

A swarthy fellow came in and bowed very low. His clothing had once been expensive, but it was showing a lot of wear. A bath and a haircut wouldn't have hurt matters either. He was working very hard at pretending not to notice the twenty-two stunningly beautiful naked ladies around him. The four men in the room were fully clothed, of course, since I wasn't one of the sort who takes equality too far.

I think that he tried to say that he was honored to be in my august presence, but his Polish was atrocious.

"Perhaps it would be more convenient to speak in Aramaic," I said in Aramaic.

"Indeed, my gracious lord. You are truly as well-educated as rumor has said," he answered in the same language.

"Thank you," I said. I didn't feel like telling him that I had learned his language when I was a slave in Timbuktu. "Now then, I intend to go into Mongolia, leaving early, the day after tomorrow. I gather that you have been there?"

22

"Several times, my noble lord. My men and I have often acted as guards and guides for the caravans traveling the ancient Silk Road."

"Good. I am primarily concerned about finding the proper passes through some of the intervening mountains. We can discuss the route later. First, we will have to see that you and your men are properly armed and armored. You will have to be introduced to our Big People, who will look like horses to you, although they are not. They are people. If the Big People accept you, you are in. This is important, because they can travel seven times farther in a day than horses can. Without them, you could never keep up with us."

He didn't reply, so I continued, "All of you will be well armed, armored, and fed the same food that I will be eating, at army expense. Tentatively, your pay rate will be that of a knight banner, some sixteen European pence a day. Six of your men at your choosing will be paid as knights, at eight pence a day. The rest of your men will be paid as pages, at two pence a day. I'm not sure how much that is in the local currency."

"Ah, but I do, my generous lord. What you suggest would be most acceptable."

"Good. Have your men in the courtyard at mid-afternoon. But for now, are you hungry? I mean, have you eaten lately?"

"It happens that it has been a most busy morning, your grace, and …"

"Girls, get him a plate, silverware, and a cup. Set him up at the end of the table."

He watched us very carefully while we ate and used the silverware unfamiliar to him, but in the end, he ate quite a bit. Obviously, Ahmed had been going through some hard times lately.

After lunch, Ahmed went to collect up his men, and I sent a few of my household messengers out to find at least sixty-one unattached Big People for the testing.

My African friend Juma had a strange, perhaps psychic talent for seeing what he called *manna*. Everyone in his tribe could do it. It seemed to be something like the aura that some psychics said that they saw around some people. Observing a person's aura, Juma claimed to be able to tell much about a person's character and about any crimes that the person had committed. I'd found it hard to believe, but I'd seen repeated proof of it.

Weirder still, the Big People seemed to be able to the same thing, only better. And my bodyguards had been created in the same facility that made the Big People.

I called Terry over.

"Terry, the Big People can look at someone and tell if he is good or evil. Can people like you do the same thing?"

"Yes, your grace."

"Interesting. How do you do it?"

"Well, you look at them, and you know."

I said, "That doesn't tell me much."

"Well, how do you know if something is black or white or red? You look at it and you know!"

"You are saying that you can't explain it to me anymore than I could explain colors to a person who had been blind from birth?"

"Yes, your grace, I suppose that I am."

"Humph. Anyway, we are going on a raid into Mongolia, to see if we can slow down their invasion of Europe. I will need you and your sisters with me, although I will be leaving the human girls here behind. Is this all right with you?"

"Of course, your grace."

"Good. Ahmed says that he and his people can guide us there. I want to see what the Big People think of him and his men. If they are not trustworthy, we are better off without them. I'll also want the opinion of you and your sisters. If they are truly evil, we might have to kill them. Please have all of your sisters in the courtyard when Ahmed gets back with his men."

"Yes, your grace."

I spent another hour with the people who were getting things organized for the raid. Many of the things and people we needed were located north of here, on the way to Constantinople. We would be able to pick them up on our way to Mongolia.

I was told that some sixty-five Big People had collected in the courtyard. I went down to talk to them.

"Sisters!" I said to them in Polish, the only language, besides the simplified Polish Pigeon, that they could understand, "The Mongols are planning to attack Europe again! I think that if we raided them first, and killed most of their horses, we might be able to stop, or at least delay their next invasion. To do that, we have to go to Mongolia, and we don't know the way there. Some men have said that they can guide us, but I don't know if they can be trusted. I need you to tell me if each of these men will serve us well, or if they will betray us. If you find one that you feel is a good man, he can be your brother, your partner. But if you reject him, we will dispense with him. Do you understand?"

They all nodded 'yes', just as their ancestor Anna had always done. In fact, they all remembered being Anna. They had the same ancestral memories that my bodyguards had.

"Very well. I know that I can put my faith in you."

Terry and her sisters got there just before Ahmed and his men arrived.

"Gentlemen," I said in Aramaic to the guides, "You will observe the beings here that look like very excellent horses. They are not horses. They are people, people who are members of our army, and paid as much as you will be, if you are accepted. And if they accept you, they will soon be as members of your own family. They will be your sisters, and you will learn to think of them as such."

The Big People entered into the mass of men, looking each of them over carefully. Ahmed was quickly accepted by one of them, and led to the side. This soon happened forty more times. But in the end, there were twenty men who had not been selected.

I turned to Terry, who was standing at my side.

"That's one hell of a rejection rate! Are all of those men truly evil?"

"Most of them are, your grace. But those two over there, who are holding themselves apart, have done some very wrong things, yet in their hearts they are not truly bad men. There is hope for them, yet."

"Bring the two of them over here."

When this had been done, I said to them, "You two have done some very wicked things! Yet there is still some hope for you. Get out of here and find some honest work. But if you commit another crime, know that you are being watched! You will be punished!"

That wasn't true, but it seemed to have the desired effect.

They looked at each other and left, quickly, without saying a word.

I turned to Ahmed.

"What's the story with these men?"

"My lord, I do not know!" Then he bowed his head and said, "My lord, I have not been completely honest with you. I told you at noon that I had sixty men, and this was completely true at the time. But when I went to them and told them what our job would be, a third of them refused to go! Things are moving in Mongolia now. The Mongols are probably preparing for yet another war. As individuals, or in small groups, these people can be reasoned with, but when gathered into armies, they will often slaughter anyone they come across, just to keep them from reporting that an army of Mongols has passed in such and such a direction!"

He took a deep breath, and then continued, "But I had promised you sixty men, and I knew of another, smaller group, who were also looking for work, although I did not know them well. I suggested that they join us, and they were willing."

I said, "So all of the men who were accepted by the Big People have worked for you for years? And all of these others were hired an hour ago?"

"It is true, your grace."

I found that I believed this man.

I said to my bodyguards in Polish, "Ladies, I want these rejects escorted to the palace prison. We'll sort this out later."

Then, in Aramaic, I said to those who had been rejected by the Big People, "Something is very wrong here. I'm placing you in detention until we can resolve this matter. My bodyguards here will escort you. If you are innocent, you will be well paid for your time, and you will be well fed in any event."

Ahmed said, "These pretty little girls are your bodyguards? Surely, your grace, this is madness!"

"Appearances can be deceiving," I said.

The girls went to the rejects, put their hands on the men's upper arms, and started to lead them away. Then one man, apparently the leader of the group, shook himself free. He shouted something to the other men, drew his sword, and swung it at Terry.

This was the wrong thing to do!

Faster than a human eye could follow, she stepped inside of his swing, drew her knife, and slashed his throat from ear to ear!

His men saw their leader's sword out and swinging, and quickly drew their own swords. The battle involved seventeen adult men, armed with swords, against eight naked and apparently adolescent girls, armed only with small knives.

It wasn't a fight, it was a massacre. I didn't even bother going for my own sword. I knew that I'd never get it out in time.

Beautiful, naked girls are not usually perceived of as a threat to a man, and there is no instinctive reaction to keep them back. My bodyguards took full advantage of this. They got in close, and they killed.

My deadly ladies went for the throat whenever possible, because there was always the chance that their victim was wearing armor beneath his clothes, and armor could ruin a good knife.

Before the first man's body hit the ground, all seventeen of the others had their throats slashed, with every artery squirting bright red.

None of my bodyguards were injured, but all were splashed with blood.

"As I said, Ahmed, appearances can be deceiving."

"Indeed, your grace," he replied quietly as he stared at the still twitching bodies. "Be assured that never will I try to trick you."

I switched to Polish and said, "Terry, have housekeeping notified about the mess out here. Leave me two guards, but the rest of you should go and wash up. You ladies did a very nice job, incidentally."

As most of my bloody bodyguards left, I handed Ahmed a bag of coins. Still staring open-mouthed at the dead bodies on the paving stones, it was a minute before he noticed the money, and accepted the bag.

I said, "This is an advance on your salary. This afternoon, make arrangements for whatever horses, clothing, arms, armor, and other property that you may have. Sell them or store them, it is up to you. See that all of your debts are paid before this evening. Take your men to a public bath house tonight. Get your hair cut short, and get shaved. It may be a while before you can get clean again. And in the morning, leave whatever lodgings you are using. Come back here with your men at dawn. Someone will meet you and take you to a place where you and your men will be equipped with the finest clothing, arms and armor that you have ever seen. You, and the six men of your choice, will get golden armor, incidentally, the same as mine. Your Big People will all get new saddles, but not bridles. They don't need them. Spurs and whips are not permitted. Tomorrow night, we'll find room for you in the palace."

"I shall do these things, your grace."

"Good," I said. "We need your help, but there is much that you and your men will have to learn quickly. Our Big People cannot speak, but they are very intelligent, and they understand Polish. It is a difficult language to learn, but we have a very simplified version called Pigeon, which will let you communicate with Polish speaking people, and most of my army, as well as with your Big People. It is possible to learn it in a few weeks. Many of our weapons will be new to you. We will do our best to train you in their use while we head north, although in fact, you have not been hired to fight, but rather to guide us. One of my battalions is from Central Africa, and all of them speak Aramaic. You will be assigned to that battalion, and they will assign a man to you and to each of your men, to act as an instructor."

"This would seem to be a very wise program, your grace."

"I hope so. Well, I will see you later. For now, we both have much to do."

I went back to my office to see how things were going. Two blood splattered nude girls walked behind me, and eighteen bodies were lying dead on the ground behind us.

From the Secret Journal of Su Song, Part Two

The compound we were assigned was once a military post surrounded by small farms. The brick outer walls enclose an area of about two acres with barracks, offices, stables, repair shops, and warehouses. The stables were cavernous buildings ideal for holding our new mechanisms and the adjoining repair shops were perfect for our craftsmen.

At first, our footsteps echoed in the empty rooms, but they were soon filled with the sounds of workmen and women.

The compound has turned into a virtual city in a very short time. In addition to my original five assistants and two secretaries, we have added metal smiths, blacksmiths, and artists of several types, five more secretaries, an archivist, wood workers, and shop managers. Most brought families as this will be a long project.

Most of the staff live in apartments on the grounds and we now have food stores, clothing stores, two restaurants, a school, and, of course, a tea house because even dedicated scientists need a place for quiet cup of tea or sake away from the eyes and voices of the wives we love so dearly.

I assigned each of my assistants one of the major artifacts and gave him a team of artists and a secretary. For the first week, they just sketched, measured and examined each of the artifacts as much as possible without major disassembly. As they completed their tasks, they were rotated to other artifacts, so that each was examined and documented by at least two teams. During that first week, I demanded and got visits from warriors who had seen, or claimed to have seen the artifacts in operation. It turned out that we were completely wrong in our assessment of some items and had to start over with them.

The chief of the artillery noyan that had recovered the water mechanism was very uncomfortable at first. The Mongols had few ranks and honorifics. Everyone below the khan and above a common soldier was *chief*, whether you were the commander of a thousand man noyan or a million man army, you were *chief*, until you were khan. Honorifics were not needed for vassal people any more than they were for dogs. *Pig* was a polite way to address a subject person, and he was not certain how to address a vassal people who obviously had such power and favor from the khan.

In spite of his expensive Chinese clothes, Chief Gan was obviously a Mongol. His skin was lighter than Chinese and if his round eyes didn't give him away, his mild odor would. I broke the ice by bowing, not too deeply, and opening the conversation. "Chief Gan, do you mind if my assistant translates your words as we talk? Several of our people speak only Chinese, but what you have to say is very important to them."

"I don't mind."

"I have been told that you were the one who brought back the biggest and most impressive artifacts to the khan. It must have been a journey such as few men have seen. Please tell us how you did it."

"It was a great adventure. This stuff was on the damndest boat you can imagine. We took it out with two trebuchet shots, and it was only one that we got much off of because we had to burn most of them stop 'em and the Poles tried to burn any boat they abandoned.

"Near the end of the battle, we saw a boat beached on our side of the river. We dropped the two rocks on it and then charged hard before they could burn it. We lost four hundred men getting across the beach, but once we got on board, it was pretty easy to kill the crew. We knew the khan always rewarded men who brought back new weapons, so we immediately began to salvage what we could.

"We were able to chop most of the works out of the hull and load them onto our artillery wagons. That big thing there lay across three wagons and needed over a dozen horses to pull it. Once we were out of Poland, we had the engineers build some big wagons like our grandparents used to move their yurts, only much bigger, and then it took us over four months to get it home."

"Your adventure was an epic one and I have personally heard the khan praise your accomplishments. However, we are ignorant scholars please explain to us what made these boats worth the effort. What was so special about the?'"

"For that, you must know something about the battle. I was in charge of over a thousand Chinese engineers and two hundred cavalry. We didn't have cannon because this was supposed to be a fast raid and there was no time to drag cannon across the steppes. If we had had our cannon, these boats might not have been so dangerous.

"We did, however, bring the metal parts needed to build trebuchets. My men had been cutting logs and loading them onto wagons in the week before the battle, so when we reached the river we were able to assemble several good machines over the period of a few days.

"We reached a wide river, perhaps a *li* across, but before the bridging crews could get anything up, we saw boats approaching, about as big as a standard river cargo boat. It took a little while to realize that they were being moved by that paddle wheel over there. We figured that they had men operating the wheels from inside, like they row Korean battle boats from inside, but they were damned fast and damned big.

"They were also bigger and better armed than the Korean boats. The Korean boats had low metal roofs with blades sticking out the top to keep you from boarding and a fire thrower in the bow. Some had small cannons or crossbow platforms. We killed them pretty easy by just putting a lot of men on top of them and chopping a way in.

29

"These were a lot different. They were bigger and looked like a floating fort. They had six *bu* high walls covered with metal and battle towers at each corner, and they didn't use crossbows.

"The first time I saw one from the bank, they opened up with those small cannons you have over there. One shot killed my chief engineer, wounded the assistant standing behind him, and broke a horse's leg. The damned things shot almost as fast as a bow.

"I got my men off the bank and down behind a hill but then we started hearing strange sounds, something like a clap mixed with a bellows sound. I never heard anything like it before and grenades started dropping on us.

"I thought that they were tossing grenades with small trebuchets, but when I peeked over the top, I saw men dropping grenades into tubes."

He walked over next to a five foot high tube and rested his hand on the rim.

"We kept this one off the boat we captured and there's another one in one of the wagons. They would light the fuse on a grenade, drop it into the tube here, then stomp their foot and the tube would make that weird sound and toss a grenade the size of your head about ten times as far as a man could, and they could fire as fast as a bow.

"When one for the bridging crews decided to ignore the boats and bridge the river anyway, when we found out that they had fire throwers on the front of the boats. We weren't able to salvage the one off of our boat, but I see that you have a smaller one sticking out of that war wagon.

"They aren't much better than our own fire throwers except that they seem to shoot a lot farther and ours were thousands of *li* away.

"About the middle of the second day, we got orders to cross the river. Ogedei must have thought that no matter how good those little cannon were, they had to run out of ammo sometime, and we had armies of auxiliaries that we didn't want to feed on the way home. In fact the boats were a probably what made him attack. There must have been fifty on this river and any country that can afford to build that many must be very, very wealthy.

"We could easily have turned south and taken Hungary, but Poland was obviously much richer and, as I said, we had a lot of surplus auxiliaries to use up.

"I don't think it turned out like he planned. Every time we charged over the banks, the boats showed up, and they had another weapon. The men called it the Demon's Breath. Every boat had a tower at each corner and those towers began slinging metal balls faster than you could count."

Chief Gan paused to look around the floor. "There. These things are mixed up." He picked up a large leather bag off the floor. "These are what they fired. They're metal balls about the size of a china man's nuts. We dug these out of one of the riverbanks and cleaned 'em up. They came out of that wheel thing on the wagon."

He dropped the leather bag next to a one *bu* wheel sitting on its side in a wagon. "This thing sat the other way up in a tower. It spun like crazy and threw these balls like a magic sling. They came like hail stones and there was no way past them.

"I think Ogedei just didn't believe how bad they were. I heard that we lost over three hundred thousand auxiliaries and twenty thousand real troops before we learned how to kill the boats.

"After a couple of days, they started running out of ammo and we learned to kill them with our trebuchets. Mostly we burned them with bags of flaming oil, but this one we killed with two stone balls.

"It was in some kind of trouble and was up against a river bank. We smashed it up and then managed to get on board before they were able to burn it. It was the only unburned one we captured.

"Even then, we didn't have much time. The Poles always came back to burn captured boats and we couldn't stand up against a boat with a working flame thrower and Demon's Breath.

"We had five hundred men with axes alive after we boarded. The engineers pointed out what they wanted, and we chopped it loose with our battle axes as fast as we could. The men were told to chop things out without hurting them, and they did their best. As fast as they chopped things loose, riders roped them and dragged the stuff over the bank, sometimes thirty or forty horses pulled at the same time.

"Sometimes we had to make fast choices. There were four towers where the demons breath was mounted, so we chopped one down and took it with us. There were two identical mechanisms attached to the paddle wheel, one on each side. We could have gotten by with only one, but I didn't want to damage the paddle wheel by hacking one side off."

He motioned us to follow him as he walked over to the large machines that were attached to the paddle wheel. "These were all that were attached to the paddles. You should lay them out straight. The paddle wheel was at the back and there was a machine on each side of the boat attached to a crank on the paddle. There wasn't any place for rowers and we didn't kill anyone that looked like a rower. These things were also attached to big tea kettles inside the hold."

"Tea kettles?"

"I don't know what else to call them. They were big round barrels lying on their sides. There was water running out of them and there was fire under them, so 'tea kettle' is the best description I know.

"They were pretty badly smashed by the second rock we threw and too big to get out, so we didn't bring one back."

"Were there tubes running to other things on the ship?"

"There were tubes and wires running all over the boat, but we didn't have time to find out where they went. We were still dragging stuff over the riverbank when another boat showed up and started burning the one we were on."

Two days later, we started disassembling the little cannons.

Several teams are now dissecting those artifacts which we have in duplicate. Of course, the major interest of the khan is in the small fast firing cannons. The procedure is a complex one. We have already made external drawings and detailed as much as we can about the internal works. Now two teams are disassembling a cannon and reproducing it the same time.

The artists continue to make accurate drawings of each piece as it removed from the mechanism, then two wood carvers duplicate the part in wood. The wood model is then turned over to metal smiths who cast a duplicate metal part.

Once the part is polished and hardened, we attempt to replace the original part with our reproduction, and usually fail. The tolerances on the weapons parts are very tight. As it is impractical to have more than one craftsman simultaneously, I have had gaslights installed in the workrooms so that two or three shifts of craftsmen can work around the clock.

Even with skilled craftsmen, and sometimes because of them, things go wrong. The glider project was one of the biggest problems in the early part of the investigation. We had been totally unable to get the engine to run. We knew from eye witnesses that the machine attached to the propeller was some sort of engine and we knew from the smell of what we identified as a fuel tank, that it consumed some sort of petroleum project. Our chemists and alchemists tried for weeks without success to produce a fuel and a procedure to get it to function.

I decided to divide the project into two parts. One team could continue to work with the engine and a second team would begin the duplication of the glider itself. If the damned thing could really fly, we might find some other way to power it.

We gave the project to a team of military kit builders. These men claimed to have built man carrying observation kites for the Jin Empire. As I do not remember anyone but the Koreans having fielded such kites, I had my doubts about their veracity, but their skills with lightweight wood and fabric were immediately obvious.

I told them to duplicate the glider exactly and then left them to work, forgetting that they were not scientists. A few weeks later, they sent word that they were ready to show me their new *kite*. It looked about like the Polish kite. It was about the same size and it had the same wires and moveable panels in the same place, but it had a huge bird's beak on the front, scalloped trailing edges on the wings, a horizontal seat for the pilot to lie in, and the damned thing had skids on the bottom instead of wheels.

I called the team leader over and asked him why it didn't look like the Polish kite. With exasperation, he explained, "Why that thing would never work right. The seat had the pilot sitting upright. How would he see the ground? And what good would wheels do you on a kite. It takes off straight up and lands straight down. And it was ugly! Any proper kite should look bird like if you want it to fly like a bird. We did our best to correct their mistakes, but I still doubt that this thing will ever fly right.

"You certainly have made improvements. We'll have to show this to everybody." I turned to my assistant, "Please tell all of the other team leaders that we are having meeting in this room, immediately. Have them drop whatever they're doing and run, not walk, to this room."

When most of the managers were in attendance, I stood smiling between the Polish kite and the new one. I gestured at the new kite. "This is the product of almost a month of hard work by the kite team. They have made a considerable number of improvements to the Polish design. As a result, they have set back the kite project by at least a month." I dropped the smile and addressed the leader of the kite team, "If the khan ever finds out what you cost us, you will each be about one *chi* shorter by the end of that day. I think that the better punishment would be the removal of your ears, since you seem to have no use for them. You will each lose one month's pay and there will be additional punishment to be decided by tomorrow.

"Let this be a lesson for every team. There will be a time, soon, when we will need all of your knowledge and creativity to use what we are learning here, but your job now is to reproduce as faithfully as possible all that you see. This is a factory, not your home workshop. You follow orders and if you have any ideas, you get them approved before you do anything."

The next day, each member of the team received one lash, delivered publicly in front of the workshop. The team leader received an additional lash for impertinence. The punishment was mild to point of almost symbolic but it made the point.

It is almost time again for my monthly progress report to the khan, and I fear that he will not be satisfied with the results this month.

"For God and Poland! We go to War!"

Some things just don't work out the way you'd hoped.

Four radios were working non-stop, with messages going to every city we had taken within hundreds of miles. The necessary troops and equipment were being found and either being sent to Jerusalem, or to defined points along the railroad going north from here.

There was only one big hole in our equipment. We didn't have any winter clothing in the entire Middle East! There was plenty of it in our warehouses in Poland, but none had been sent to Africa or the Middle East. It just hadn't been needed in the south.

Perhaps we could steal what we needed from the Mongols. Perhaps, a supply column could get to us from Poland. Both possibilities were a bit iffy. As it was, we were heading into a Russian winter without heavy boots, long underwear, and overcoats.

Napoleon had tried that once, and it hadn't worked out too well for him. He'd lost about four hundred thousand people.

Sir Piotr said that he would try to get a supply column to us, although we might have to swing west a bit to meet up with them. That would cost time, but it was better than having fifty thousand men freeze to death, with our mission unaccomplished.

I contacted Sir Stefan, the commander of the African Corps, and told him that I was temporarily assigning Ahmed and his people to the African Corps battalion. I asked him to assign a good platoon under a knight banner to act as one on one instructor for the guides, to teach them Pigeon, and teach them army ways. They were to be at the palace courtyard at dawn to get the guides equipped.

That night I told my harem that I wouldn't be able to take them with me. They each had their choice of staying in Jerusalem, or of going back to my palace at Okoitz.

Their main concern was that they each had insisted on giving me a proper sendoff. I would do my best, but I think that I'm getting too old for this sort of thing.

Late the following day, it looked as though things were coming together. We would be able to leave on schedule.

I invited Sir Vladimir and Sir Wladyclaw to have a last, civilized dinner with me at my quarters in the palace. During the meal, I told all present that Sir Vladimir was taking command of Jerusalem, and the entire Southern Expeditionary Force. I gave him my chambers in the palace, and offered him the use of my harem, during my absence, except of course, the two pregnant girls who would have the choice of traveling to my castle in Poland to give birth.

"After all, there is no point in letting them go to waste," I said.

The girls looked surprised, but made no objection to this plan. Instead, they looked Sir Vladimir over, appraisingly.

Sir Vladimir took a considerable time before he accepted my offer. He usually stayed true is wife back in Poland, but she was there, he was here, and she was getting long in the tooth, anyway. Rank has its privileges, after all.

The next morning, at dawn, my not so small army of almost five battalions was ready, with the supply wagons already on the railroad tracks. Counting food, ammunition, camping equipment, artillery, and engineering equipment, it came out to some six tons per man. Multiply that by the over fifty thousand men we had along, and you were talking about a lot of stuff. This was in addition to the personal weapons, clothing, armor, and equipment that each man carried on his Big Person.

Twelve tons was about the upper limit for one of our pneumatic tired carts, and once we got off the track, it would take two Big People to pull one at a decent speed. For use on the tracks, the carts were fitted with bolt-on, oversized, flanged steel rims that raised the rubber tires a bit above the tracks. When we left the track in Lesser Armenia, the rims would be taken off and discarded. Or at least we would discard them. Somebody else was supposed to collect them up later.

The road north was double tracked, as were most of our main lines. This normally let carts be pulled in both directions without excessive amounts of scheduling being required. It also simplified construction, since it permitted materials to be delivered continuously, while empty rail carts could easily return for more. Then again, it took twice as much track, and twice as much labor to prepare the roadbed, so we only used the system on lines that we thought would get heavy usage.

For this mission, I had demanded and had gotten both tracks, with all other traffic being stopped until we went by.

Big People pulled army carts down the two tracks, without needing a human driver riding aboard. Mounted men rode on the bridle trails on either side. Flankers, point men, and a rear guard rode farther out.

Standing orders were that if any cart broke down, it would be shoved off of the track, with some men to repair it, and then they had to try to catch up later, once they got it fixed. The last company in the column included engineers equipped to make any repairs a cart could need, or to salvage useful parts if the cart was totaled.

My column was over three dozen miles long, and we would be picking up more men and supplies as we went down north. It stretched from the city gates of Jerusalem almost to the Mediterranean Sea. This put me at the tail end of the column. Once we got off the railroad, and into possibly hostile territory, my personal party would move up to the center, where a commander belongs. I promised myself that this time, I'd do things properly. No more silly heroics for me!

The physical arrangement of my troops was a bit haphazard in the beginning. We were in protected territory, and not everybody had joined us yet, so it really didn't matter, yet. Tonight, I would have to come up with a sensible order of march.

I had three carts for myself, my eight bodyguards, and my seven household troops, who did the work around my camp. I also had seven messengers attached to me, although I wasn't sure why. They'd been with me since I'd left Timbuktu, and I guess that they'd become a tradition. They still wore the red dyed ostrich plumes on their helmets, too. They'd have a hard time replacing them in Mongolia!

My bodyguards preferred to ride with me or one of the household troops, riding pillion, behind the man. I had a double saddle on Silver, which permitted Terry to ride side-saddle in front of me. Shauna was usually riding behind, often standing up on Silver's rump, just looking around, keeping an eye on things, even when we were at a full gallop!

I also had my own radio rig, with two independent radios, and three operators for them. The men doubled as buglers, for short-range communications. These radios were built in an enclosed cart that was pulled by a single Big Person, with plenty of room for the batteries and sleeping spaces for two of the operators. They were expected to work around the clock, with one of them always on duty. A generator connected to the rear axle kept the batteries charged, although there was also a manual charger for use when we were stopped for any length of time. The cart had my flag, the white eagle on a red background of the Christian Army, flying above it from the antenna, to let people know where I probably was.

My column had well over a gross of these radio carts in operation, maintaining communications along the huge mass of men, Big People, and equipment. Every company, and every unit bigger than a company, had one just like mine, but with their own unit flags flying above them.

There was no possibility of giving orders directly to something three gross miles long. Right after we said the Army Oath, I just picked a radio's microphone and shouted, "Brothers! Sisters! For God and Poland! We go to war! Advance!"

Bugles blared immediately down the entire line, and the whole column started moving, almost at once!

36

Soon, we were moving at seventy miles in one of our double length hours, a speed that our Big People could maintain all day. This let us move at over three gross miles a day, an unheard of speed in the 13th century. That was while we were on a railroad track, of course. Over rough terrain, and especially in the mountains, our speed would be greatly reduced.

Still, it would be much faster than the two dozen miles a day that we had managed on our way from Timbuktu to the Mediterranean Sea coast. Of course, then we had only camels, horses, and mules. And over half of the people with us were non-combatants. There were women, children, and a few old people, many of whom had to walk.

After moving for an hour, riders came to us on each side of the track with big bags tied to both sides of their saddles. The bags were filled with cans of food. They gave each man two cans, labeled *breakfast* and *lunch*, with no further descriptions on the cans.

I'd complained about that, insisting that our suppliers give an accurate description on the label of what exactly was contained within, and a picture of the main animal products as well, for the benefit of the illiterate.

I imagine that this re-labeling was being done, but the Quartermaster Corps had apparently decided to use up the old stuff first. It was sensible in its own way, I suppose, but it meant that we'd be eating *mystery stew* for the duration of the campaign!

I took my two cans without comment, but my bodyguards insisted on, and got, six cans each. Those little girls have fantastically high metabolisms. They really needed that much food.

In front of the rider, the oversized saddle bows on our army saddles were waist-high and a span thick. They mostly contained extra ammunition, but they also contained a first aid kit, a personal hygiene kit for the warrior, another one for his Big Person, a map case with a compass and a telescope, a canteen, and eating utensils, including a can opener.

Opening a can and eating its contents was not difficult at all. At a full gallop, the ride on a Big Person is surprisingly smooth, if more than a bit windy.

The food really wasn't all that bad, being rich and meaty. It was just what an active man needed, and there was plenty of it, but I feel a lot better when I know what I'm eating.

When I'd finished with breakfast, I put the empty can back into my saddle bag. Army regulations required that all trash be collected at the end of the day and buried, because otherwise, we would be leaving an easily read trail of where we had been.

I rode up to the radio cart and banged on the side. When an operator opened a window and stuck his head out, I told him to thank whoever had decided to deliver our breakfast to us, but to put out a column wide message saying that as of tomorrow morning, every man was expected to put at least a day's supply of food into his saddle bags before we started the day's run.

While I was still there, I told the operator to get a message to Ahmed, telling him that tomorrow we would be leaving the railroad track west of the City of Osmaniye, and would proceed from there around the east shore of the Black Sea, and then north into the Russias. I wanted him to think about our route, but not to report to me tonight. Rather, he should study his Pigeon.

Early tomorrow morning, before dawn, he should go to the head of the column with his men and their instructors, and when we got to Osmaniye, he should point the way to the advance guard.

Also, I mentioned to him that the Polish often ate pigs, and that if this offended any of his people, they should insist on being fed from cans bearing the Star of David. These contained kosher food prepared for our Jewish troops, who had similar dietary restrictions to those of the Arabs.

Actually, I doubted if any Jews at all were with us on this expedition. I believe that they all had wanted to stay in Jerusalem, their ancient homeland. They were strongly attached to the Holy Land, and I had no doubt but what they were willing to die to the last man defending it.

Since the usual army company had some six Jewish men per gross in it, the food containers contained about twelve cans per gross of kosher food. Many gentiles liked kosher food too, after all.

My general orders for this mission had us spending all of the time, from sunrise to sunset, traveling at the best speed we could make. Since we were very near the equinox, that meant half of the day.

We'd be eating cold canned food the whole trip, unless some people felt like heating their dinner around the camp fire. I just hoped that they had brains enough to open the can before they did that!

Every man here was a warrior. We had no cooks, clerks, or other dead weight with us. And certainly no camp followers. We were out trying to save Europe from another brutal Mongol invasion, and that required a few sacrifices. So what if the food got boring, things became uncomfortable, or our clothes got dirty?

On the other hand, there were a few advantages to the new system. No one had to stand night guard duty. We had a lot of Big People with us, and Big People don't sleep. They could put out a tremendous amount of energy during the day, but then they had to spend the entire night eating, to recuperate.

Their favorite food was fresh, green grass, but if necessary, they could eat anything with carbon in it. They could chew up whole trees, if need be, although they preferred fruit trees to pines. Well, they didn't like high sulfur coal, but coke was okay.

They would scatter into the surrounding areas during the night, and they were fully alert. Their senses were superior to those of any ordinary human. Their sense of smell was better than any bloodhound. Their hearing was outstanding. They could see far into the infrared, and the dead of night was as bright as high noon to them. They never got lost, and their sense of direction was flawless, as far as we could tell.

And, they were very good fighters. Riding Silver, I was once attacked by a gang of over a dozen thugs. She killed them all before I could do more than draw my sword!

If there was any threat, they would let the rest of us know about it in no uncertain way!

There were a few casualties during the day. Not many, and none were caused by enemy action. But with fifty thousand men on the move, and twice that number of Big People, accidents happen, and humans sometimes get sick, although Big People and bodyguards don't.

With humans, our practice was to put the man on top of a cart, or sometimes inside of a radio cart, with a medic attending him, and to take the injured man along. His partner, a Big Person, normally ran along side, anxiously.

Injuries among the Big People were rare, but they too happened. Here, because of their size, we had to leave them behind, in the company of a man, usually her partner, and another Big Person. Big People healed quickly, even faster than I did, after receiving my Uncle Tom's magic cures. Even with a broken leg, a Big Person could move along, slowly, in the manner of a dog with an injured foot. Her escorts were to stay with her until they could rejoin the rest of the column, or they could make it home, whichever the three of them decided was best.

There were many switches leading to side tracks on the railroad heading north, each manned by a lance of our Christian Army warriors. We were going through the Crusader States, some of them still intact since the First Crusade that started in 1096, and some which we had recently re-conquered, and made army property.

They all had painted wooden signs saying things like *Ascalon, Two Miles*. As the day passed, they said *Jaffa*, then *Arsuf*, and *Caesarea*. Acre went by, along with Sidon, Tripoli, Raud, and Tortosa. The names seemed to have magic in them.

We passed Masyaf, which had been an Assassin castle before they encountered the Christian Army.

39

The Assassins had hollowed out whole empires by carefully studying the men who ran them. The incompetent were left alone, but anyone who did his job well was selected for death.

One of their junior men, well-trained in the art of murder, was selected for each job. Before he left, they got him stoned out of his mind on Hashish. The words *hashish* and *assassin* have the same linguistic root. Then, he was taken to a large and lovely chamber that was stocked with the most beautiful young women that the Assassin leadership could obtain, often by kidnapping them and then torturing them into obedience.

The kid, who had lived a celibate life until then, was told that he was being given a taste of the heaven that was awaiting him, if he succeeded in his mission. A slightly lesser fate awaited him if he failed, but had done his best. Indoctrinated and drugged, he believed them.

And after the mission, whether he had killed his man or not, he committed suicide, in order to obtain his eternal prize.

It had taken us two days to smash the place, and we had killed every adult man there. Some people just needed killing!

The women and children were spared, of course. We weren't Mongols, after all.

Sahyun went by an hour before sunset.

For me, these were all magical names, and magical places, but I'd never visited them. There just hadn't been time. Someday, much later, I hoped to have a chance to look them over. This was assuming that I survived the current mission, of course.

At sunset, the column stopped. The length of track we took up had grown another ten miles during the day, and almost all of the new carts had been put in front. A few, catching up with the rest of us, were added to the rear. But I was still just ahead of the rear guard, as we camped well south of the City of Antioch.

The carts were left on the track. The Big People towing them released themselves, and went out looking for food, over two hundred pounds of it per Big Person per night. Those Big People being ridden were unsaddled, although they too could release their saddles. There was a leather strap between their front legs that pulled a large pin out of the cinch strap. Then the ridden Big People also went out foraging, and guarding the camp. The men set up a sixty mile long camp on both sides of the track.

Setting up camp only took a few minutes, and most of that was spent finding firewood. We weren't cooking anything, but people still like to sit around a fire and talk for a bit before going to bed.

The army used green, oiled cotton, six-man dome tents, with floors, zippers, and window screens. They were tall enough to stand in, they set up quickly, and they were a good design.

40

I, however, had picked up an Arabian tent when I was in Timbuktu. It was quite large, made of royal blue silk, and had a lot of real gold embroidery on it. Call it vanity if you want to, but I liked it, so I brought it along.

I also had a large camp table, plenty of camp stools, and a few other amenities, like wall-to-wall carpeting, a liquor cabinet, and a large, recently acquired air mattress. I told myself that this tent let me conduct meetings, and to be a proper host to visiting dignitaries, but mostly, I just like to be comfortable.

I'd also brought along a sufficient supply of brandy and cigars. I'd promised my men that I'd be eating the same food that they would, and I did, but rank has a few privileges!

I had a lance of men whose job was to do the camp work, as well as a lance of messengers who usually were able to help out. Personally, I had other things to do.

After another can of mystery stew, labeled *dinner*, I was working under a kerosene lamp, figuring out our order of march. Outside, some of my bodyguards were singing and some of the others were taking turns dancing, being cheered on my warriors. I continued working. Rank also has its responsibilities.

Ahmed walked in, having been permitted to do this by the three bodyguards on duty.

"My lord, forgive me for disobeying you by coming to you tonight, but there are matters that must be discussed immediately!"

"Very well," I said, laying down my felt tip pen. "Sit down and tell me about it."

I didn't offer him a drink of brandy. Ahmed struck me as a person who took his religion seriously. I did offer him a cigar, which he declined.

He sat awkwardly on a three-legged camp stool. Sitting on a stool just wasn't an Arabian thing to do.

"My lord, I must tell you that I believe your proposed route to Mongolia is ill-advised. The usual route would have taken us east out of Jerusalem. We then would have gone north along the Jordan River."

I said, "But that would have been impossible for us. For one thing, we have not yet conquered the land along that route. It is heavily populated, and we would have had to fight our way the whole trip north. Then again, many of the men and supplies we needed were located along this railroad we've just built along the Mediterranean coast. It would have taken us days longer to wait for them to all get to Jerusalem. And there is the fact of the railroad itself, which again saved us a lot of time."

"But, your grace, by going through the mountains of Lesser Armenia, we will lose much time. This is a rarely traveled route. Neither I nor any of my men have ever taken it. Well, the father of one of my men went through here once, and he described the route to his son, but that is not the same thing as actually having traveled through it one's self."

"I see. Well then, there's nothing for it but to hire some more guides," I said. "Don't look so frightened. You are not being dismissed. But as soon as we get to Antioch tomorrow, I want you to take a lance of your better men, and another lance of your instructors, and, if you can find one, someone who has been in the town before. I'll write you a note to take to one of the radio operators, instructing them to send out a message to everyone with us, requesting a guide to the city. Ride into town, and try to find us someone who knows the route that we must take. Offer to pay him well. But be quick about it. It should only take us a few hours to get our order of march squared away, near Osmaniye, and I don't want to lose any time. Also, have the man who has heard of this route lead a party of our advanced guards and engineers up the trail immediately."

"Very well, your grace. It shall be done as you say."

Ahmed got gratefully off of the unfamiliar stool, bowed, and left my tent. I got back to my paperwork.

It was very late at night before I had the radio operators send out the marching orders to the entire column. I began to think that maybe I should have brought some staff people along.

Thinking about it, the radio operators were a literate bunch. The next time that I have to do something like this, I will draft two of them to help me. I wished I'd thought of that earlier.

I was getting ready to turn in when Terry and Shauna came in.

Terry said, "Your grace, was there anything else that you wanted?"

"Well, yes, thinking about it. Some sex would be very nice." Rank has other privileges, too.

"We were hoping that you would say that," Shauna said.

My bodyguards' body temperature was higher than that of an ordinary human. It gave the expression *bed warmer* a whole new meaning. This might be very useful, going through a Russian winter without an overcoat!

A Prince Among Men

Francine's Diary

It has been a very peaceful year since Lord Conrad, my true love, my master, and my soul mate was lost at sea. Now the bastard is sending some more of his whores home for me to baby-sit. At least we all get along. When you have all been screwed by the same man, in more ways than one, you have something in common. I have heard that there is a woman in Cracow that my husband has not bedded, but if so, she must be over sixty, under sixteen, or grossly ugly.

The meeting of the executive council went well today, considering that the hetman is back in business. King Henryk has gotten used to being his own man again and is starting to make firmer decisions – and he is firm in bed for a man his age.

Henryk has been under Conrad's thumb virtually since his coronation. Now Henryk and the crown prince are showing their impatience. Conrad claims that his fortune is modest compared to the crown, but as long as he is Hetman of the Christian Army, he commands more wealth than Midas. His fleet is a hundred times the size of the Polish fleet; he effectively controls all of the railroads and most of the factories, and the crown is increasingly jealous.

Sir Piotr will continue to be a problem. He has an unfortunate amount of influence among the officers paired with unwavering loyalty to my bastard of a husband.

On Campaign with Conrad

The next morning, I discovered that my boots had been polished, my weapons had been attended to, and my clothes had been cleaned. It seems that my lovely bodyguards, who didn't have to sleep any more than the Big People did, and had decided to make themselves useful. My messengers, the radio operators, and the camp workers had gotten similar services.

"Thank you, ladies," I said. "But, if you have time tomorrow night, try to do something for my senior officers as well. It is important for morale that they look decent."

I gave Silver a decent currying down. This is something that every warrior always does himself, every morning, no matter what his rank is. She is your partner, after all.

At mid-morning, we got the word that the head of the column had reached the cut off point near Osmaniye and things started slowing down.

I rode on ahead, to see how the re-sorting was going on.

The army had rented a large, recently harvested wheat field for the operation. Yesterday, our engineers had added a pair of switch tracks to the railroad, and our carts were being pulled into the field. As they went in, they were being sorted into some two hundred separate lines. Ammunition of various sorts were in some lines, food in others, and other things each in their own lines. Things had been well planned, and were going smoothly.

With the steel rims that let the carts run on the railroads still on their wheels, they were making a mess out of the field. Or perhaps, they were just giving it an early, free plowing.

Once they were in line, crews of men were jacking the carts up, removing the rims, and then setting the carts down on their pneumatic, off-road rubber tires. And repairing a few flats.

Someone was supposed to come by later and collect up the steel rims. We wouldn't need them for the rest of this mission. We'd be going far beyond where the Tracks of Civilization ran.

In the distance, I could hear the engineers, backed up by twice their numbers of mounted infantry. They were improving the road ahead with shovels, star drills, and dynamite. When they were through, the carts would be able to go through without hindrance.

Dynamite is easy enough to make, once you know the formula. Nitroglycerine is first made by treating refined animal fat with concentrated nitric acid and concentrated sulfuric acid, in a five-to-six ratio. It is then added to wood powder, compressed into sticks, and dried. The less wood powder you use, the stronger it becomes, but also the more dangerous.

As I watched the cart sorting operation, one of my captains rode up to me.

"Sir, there is a Prince David here who wants to speak to you. He says that he is the son of the King of Lesser Armenia."

"Then by all means, bring him to me, captain. Will I need a translator?"

"No sir. He speaks excellent Polish!"

The man who the captain brought was well dressed in a conservative fashion, rather short, and in his mid-thirties. He had dark hair, he was physically fit, and he had the bearing of a warrior. He had six armed and armored men with him, but he motioned for them to stay back. I returned the courtesy by sending my standard-bearer, both of my bodyguards, and my three runners away.

"Welcome," I said. "I am told that you are Prince David, the son of Hethum, the Most Christian King of Lesser Armenia."

"This is true, my Lord Conrad," he said in perfect Polish.

"I hope that you don't mind meeting like this, on horseback, but my tents are packed in carts, many miles behind us. I am surprised that you speak excellent Polish, and that you have the bearing of a true warrior."

"You wouldn't be, your grace, if you knew my story. After your victory against the Mongols, over twenty years ago, my father thought it would be best if one of his sons went to Poland to see the manner with which you accomplished this great deed. Being the youngest of three brothers, I was the one he sent. After studying for a year in Cracow, I determined to join your army. My companions here were sent with me to Poland. We each ended up joining a different branch of your army, and we wrote to each other often. We each enlisted and served the usual twelve years. I left with the rank of captain."

"I assume that as a nobleman, you joined the Wolves," I said.

"My companion, Sir Jan did, your grace. I could have, but as a young man, I was more attracted to the Eagles. I wanted to fly! I applied there, and was accepted."

"Few noblemen are intelligent and learned enough to pass the entrance examinations for that elite group, and their physical fitness requirements are very high."

"I come from an old and honorable blood line, your grace."

"And doubtless a very competent one. I am impressed. But what can I do for you, Prince David? Or do you prefer to be called captain?"

"In truth, I am prouder of being a captain in your army than I am of being a prince, which is a mere accident of birth. And I am prouder yet of having been a qualified pilot. Leaving the skies, in obedience to my father's wishes, was the hardest thing that I've ever done. As to your first question, my father has bid me to ask you why you seem to think that you can take an army through his kingdom without so much as asking for his permission."

"Your father is right to ask this of me. There are two reasons. The first is that only three days ago, I learned that the Mongols were planning to attack Europe again. I have quickly gathered up this force to see what can be done about slowing them down, somewhat."

"Yes, your grace. We have received information about a new Mongol offensive, although we have not been informed as to who will be the victims of this new war. And what was your second reason?"

"My second reason was that although your father, and your people, are Christians, you are in fact subordinate to the great khan! As soon as the Mongols came anywhere near this part of the world, your father immediately sent his submission to Genghis Khan! This makes you my enemy, and it is not customary to ask permission to enter an opponent's lands! I am not happy about having a Christian kingdom for an enemy!"

"All of what you say is true, your grace. I make no apologies for my father's actions. But consider that Lesser Armenia does not have any great mass of fighting men available to it. We have neither Poland's weapons nor its wealth. If my father had not done what he did, the Mongol Horde would have killed our people and burned our cities, as it did to those of so many other nations. We now must pay a yearly tribute to the Mongols, but my people are still alive."

"I can understand that," I said. "But now, the Christian Army is here. We could equip and train your men, if you would join with us. We could provide your men with Big People. We could even provide you with a squadron of our newest aircraft. I think that you would be impressed by them. The landing gear is retractable, they are well armed with machine guns, and they are made entirely of metal, you know."

"No, I didn't know that, your grace. I don't even know what some of the things that you mention are! Considerable progress has apparently been made since I was forced to leave your army. Then, the aircraft were made of wood that had been covered with painted cloth. I helped build many of them. They were not armed at all! I would love to see one of these new planes! I will convey your very tempting offer to my father. But for now, I must tell you that it is impossible for you to take your forces, with all of these carts, through our kingdom."

"You are refusing us permission to go through your lands? I am in a hurry, sir, and rebuffing me is not a safe thing to do!"

"It is not a question of refusing you, your grace! I meant that it is physically impossible for you to get these carts through! About a hundred miles north of here, there was a major bridge that collapsed during last winter's heavy rains. Paying our tribute to the Mongols has kept this kingdom impoverished! We have not been able to afford to re-build it. There is a place that can be forded by horsemen at this time of year, but your carts could never make it!"

"I see. Well then, in that case, besides the repairs we are making to your road, we'll be building your father a new bridge as well."

"The last bridge was two years in the building. It had a span of over a hundred yards!"

"Then if that's all, the next one will be built in about a day!"

"This is something that I would have to see!"

"You are welcome to watch, Captain David. You can even lend a hand, if you want."

"I might do just that, your grace."

"Good. I invite you and your men to join me at my camp, tonight. We have a few spare tents in our carts. The food will be cold, but there is plenty of it. I have a very good brandy along that we liberated from a city in Africa that we called Shangri-La. You might like it, as well as some of my own twelve-year-old whiskey."

"I've heard stories about your excellent whiskey, your grace. I look forward to trying it."

The prince re-joined his men, while I sent one of my runners out to let the komander of engineers know that a bridge would be needed tomorrow. Another runner went to tell the people who were putting the column into order that my personal carts were to be put not in the middle, the way I'd originally set it up, but near the front. I'd be after the advance guard of Wolves, the six companies of engineers and twelve companies of their pick, shovel, and axe men from the mounted infantry, and after two of our breach-loading artillery pieces, one large and one small, that were needed in case we ran into something that needed blowing away.

This rearrangement was so that Prince David could be close to the bridge that we'd be building tomorrow. We needed to impress him and his people.

Of course each company would have its own carts of food, ammunition, and camping equipment traveling near it. The advance guard of Wolves would carry a three-day supply of stuff on their Big People, and be replaced every few days by another group brought up from the rear.

The engineers had a lot of equipment with them, but still, I would only be a few miles from the head of the column. Only a few minutes when riding a Big Person.

I sent another runner to scrounge up seven Big People, with saddles, for Prince David and his men. We'd had more than that number of warriors sick or injured so far, but Big People were far more durable than the men riding them. On normal horses, our guests would never be able to keep up with the rest of us.

I rode ahead to watch the road repairs in progress. The trail went generally north, up a rugged, medium-sized mountain river valley. Some sections were fairly flat, while others needed work, if we were to get the carts through.

The land about us was fertile, irrigated, and intensively farmed, with many small villages scattered through it. Very few people were to be seen, however. They had apparently gone into hiding when they saw us coming. We meant them no harm, but there was no way to tell them that.

Maybe they would figure it out for themselves, when they saw that we'd done them no damage, and left them with a decent road behind us.

The more technical work, such as surveying, mapping, drilling, and blasting, was done by the engineers themselves, with some help from the mounted infantry, sledge hammering on the star drills. Sometimes, as many as six men were beating on a single star drill, while a single engineer kept turning it, and keeping it going in straight.

Inserting the dynamite, tamping it down, and setting the fuses were jobs that the engineers kept for themselves.

The real grunt work, removing trees, shoveling dirt, and using pick axes where needed, was being done by the mounted infantry, who were farmers, essentially. Their Big People were helping out where they could, dragging rocks, hauling dirt, and often eating the trees that were in the way.

The surveyors and map makers worked just behind the advance guard of Wolves, who were led by a few guides. They dropped off supervisors as needed for such repairs as were required.

The drillers, blasters, and pick and shovel men followed in order.

All three groups rode ahead on Big People until an engineering supervisor stopped the ones in front, and put them to work on some new job. When they finished it, they rode forward until they were stopped again.

My eyeball estimate was that they would make better that a gross miles of improved roadway a day. It occurred to me that someday, we might end up putting a railroad through here.

I was making my way back when I came across Prince David, with four of his men, riding Big People.

He said, "My lord, you can have no idea how good it is to be riding a Big Person again!"

"I can relate. Not too long ago, I too was deprived of their services. It was definitely and most emphatically not good. I'll tell you the story tonight... By the way, captain, looks like you're short a couple of subordinates."

"Companions, sir, not subordinates. They're taking our horses back, relaying your offer to my father, and, with any luck, impressing him with the Big People and your weaponry. Sir Wladyclaw detailed a lance of Wolves to... accompany them."

Bonus for you, Wladyclaw, I thought. Captain David may be a future ally, but as of right now, his kingdom was a Mongol khanate by proxy. *Doveryai, no proveryai,* "trust, but verify," as our Russian comrades used to say.

"Your men here are remarkably efficient and energetic."

"Well, the Construction Corps' motto is, *Opus Operis Perfectus.* It means, more or less, *finished without flaw.* They're also 'on one, off two.' After today, red and orange companies, will rest up. Yellow and green were on yesterday, and blue and purple will be on tomorrow."

"I wish it was possible to show him one of the aircraft. He's never seen one. Sometimes, when I talk about flying, I'm not sure if he really believes me."

"Perhaps, something can be arranged. One of our types of airplanes operates from some of our ships at sea. I'll find out if we have any seaplanes near here, and if we can get a radio to your father, we can coordinate a demonstration."

"Your grace, that might be just what he needs to change his loyalties."

"One can always hope!"

I found a radio cart and commandeered it. My first messages were to the frigates and battleships we had on the Mediterranean, to see if they had any seaplanes in range of us. I soon found that we had a frigate that was close enough by to give us a two plane demonstration tomorrow afternoon.

Then I contacted Sir Wladyclaw, and told him to send a company of Wolves, under a captain who was a good diplomat, to visit King Hethum. He was to take two radio carts with him, two cannons, and at least one of Prince David's companions, as a guide and translator. Their mission was to create a favorable impression, and to show off our air power and artillery.

Then I had a message sent to King Henryk, telling him about the opportunity we had to take a Christian kingdom currently subservient to the Mongols, and bring it in on our side. Properly speaking, diplomacy was Henryk's job, not mine.

It took us three long army hours to get the column sorted out, but by mid afternoon we were on the move again. We were only doing half the speed that we had done on the railroad track, but that was still much faster than the road ahead of us could be improved.

Later, I'd talk to our komander of engineers about the possibility of using more of our warriors as laborers. The Wolves weren't of much use when there was work to be done, but the African Corps were useful warriors, willing and able to do just about anything.

A general rule in the Christian Army was that you just did the best you can, and pressed on regardless.

A half an hour before sunset, I once again ran into Prince David.

I said, "I've made arrangements to send a company of Wolves to your father, with some artillery and some radios. I can arrange a two plane demonstration tomorrow afternoon, as well."

"Yes, your grace. Two of my companions have already left with a company of your people. I only wish that I could inspect the aircraft myself, but I thought it best to remain here with your army."

"I'm afraid that you wouldn't be able to inspect those planes close up in any event. Seaplanes don't have wheels. They can only land on the water, and they need the steam catapult on a warship to take off."

"Ah, I see, your grace. I'd hoped that these would be of the sort that you talked about earlier."

"Sorry, but all of our land-based planes have been sent to Poland, in preparation for the upcoming Mongol invasion."

"Yes. A pity, that. Especially since my own country is contributing to the Mongol side of that invasion."

"How so? I thought that you were only giving tribute, money, to the Mongols."

"Lesser Armenia ran out of gold and silver many years ago, your grace. Our Mongol masters are a greedy bunch. But we breed some very good horses, and they have been demanding them from us for some years now."

"Indeed, my prince. And just how severe are their demands on you?"

"Not five days ago, we were forced to send twelve thousand fine horses north on this very road, your grace."

"This is a truly onerous taxation! Let us hope that your noble father decides to join with the European Christian Federation, and to make an end of this extortion!"

"One can only hope, your grace."

"Yes. Well, don't forget my invitation to come to my camp, this evening. Cold food, but good drink and fine entertainment will be awaiting you."

"Entertainment, your grace?"

"It happens that I have some of the finest dancing girls in the world, who normally refuse to wear clothing. I'll see you at sunset. Your Big People will know the way."

I went and found another radio cart, and called Sir Wladyclaw.

That night, Prince David was indeed amazed at the dancing that my bodyguards were capable of. Those little girls could do things that would put an Olympic gymnast doing floor exercises to shame.

The evening was in full swing when Ahmed and his party showed up.

I said, "Well, Ahmed, I had expected to see you in the early afternoon. What happened?"

"I have failed in my mission, your grace. I was not able to find a single guide willing to lead us to the east shore of the Black Sea. They all feared the Mongol Horde, and they would not go against the wishes of the king, Hethum, who they say is subservient to the Mongols."

"Indeed. Prince David, is there anything that you can do to help us with this?"

He talked a bit with the two companions that he still had with him, and then he said, "I believe we can, your grace. My friends here know the route well, since we came on that road on our way back from Poland. They would be happy to guide you as far as the Sea of Grass. One of them was once a member of your Wolves, incidentally, and the other was a qualified navigator on one of your first steam ships. He says that with the surveying instruments that your engineers have, and knowing the exact time from your radios, he can pinpoint our exact location, on any clear day at noon."

"Well then, that's another problem solved! Ahmed, thank you for doing your best. Get to know our new guides, as best you can. But for now, there are two of my bodyguards who have not yet danced for us!"

One of my bodyguards, Rebecca, was favorably inclined toward the prince. My impression was that the two of them had a very good time later that night.

I don't think that such favors were offered to Ahmed.

Disaster in the Mountains

Road improvements took up most of the next morning, with a lot more blasting, shoveling, and pick axe work being required than on the day before. Since the African Corps was now helping out, work was proceeding almost as fast as it had been going.

From what our captain of Wolves reported, King Hethum was very favorably impressed with our warriors, our weapons, and most especially our Big People.

The grand finale of the performance was the appearance of two seaplanes from the frigate *Marauder*. Her pilots strafed some sheep slated for the fall slaughter, then dropped some napalm on a harvested field. Napalm is just a two-to-one mixture of gasoline and soap. This forms a gel that sticks nicely and burns merrily to whatever it hits.

The spectators were impressed with the demonstration.

The pilots had enough fuel left to fly low over my column to give Prince David a look at their planes. While he talked to them on the radio, they did a victory roll, and then they flew their planes back to their ship. The prince later spent over an hour, talking on the radio to his father in Armenian. He told me that the king was very pleased with the Christian Army.

The company of Wolves, with a lance of mounted infantry, and three lances of artillery, stayed at King Hethum's capital, and set up a training camp for his men.

About a week later, King Henryk told me that King Hethum was ready to renounce his allegiance to the Mongols, and to join the Christian Federation. For the price of some arms, armor, and Big People, all of which we had plenty of, we turned an entire kingdom from an enemy into a willing ally, with not a single Christian warrior lost!

I wish that all of our battles could be won that cheaply.

The valley that our column was climbing up narrowed greatly, and became a steep-sided canyon. There was a small stream running in it, but it was obvious that during the wet season, this road would be impassable. Putting a railroad through here would require putting a major storm sewer underneath it.

Then again, there might be a good possibility of generating some hydro-electric power. Unfortunately, just now there wasn't time to explore the idea. Still, a man must think of things.

It took a lot of blasting to get the winding, rocky trail to the point that we could get our carts up it. Even then, some sections took three Big People, and a few men, to get the carts up that steep slope.

It was late in the afternoon before we won our way to the top of a rocky plateau. But only three miles after that, we came to the fallen bridge that we had been warned about.

Our komander of engineers, Sir Eikmann, was there before I was.

He said, "This bridge wasn't washed out by a flood. It was a wooden bridge that just rotted away.

"If you keep it very dry all of the time, or if you keep it wet, without much air getting to it, wood will last damn nearly for ever. Those wooden water pipes you used at Three Walls, almost forty years ago, are still in good shape, you know. I was one of the crew who checked them out.

"A wooden bridge needs either a good coat of paint every other year, or it needs a roof built over it to keep the rain water off of it. This one never got either one of those things, and it's gone."

I said, "You might have learned that from a book I wrote some years ago."

"Yes, sir. Thinking about it, I did. I'm too used to explaining things to these kids. Sorry about that. However, your grace, our job of replacing the bridge won't be all that hard. The masonry abutments here are still in decent shape, and we can use them again. It will be a good, permanent job, if you can talk the local king into giving the ironwork a coat of red lead paint every few years. We'll have the new bridge up by this time tomorrow, if we work all night on it."

I said, "I'll hold you to that time schedule. We're in a hurry. About maintenance, if nothing else, we'll send King Hethum some paint, brushes, and instructions."

"Thank you, sir. I hate to see our work wasted. One last thing, if I may. You invented this bridging system, I understand. You've called it a *Bailey* bridge. Now, a bailey is the land between the inner and outer walls of an old-style castle. What does that have to do with a bridge?"

"Well, first off, I didn't invent it. I'd heard about it, and it was invented by a man named Bailey, or maybe by a company of that name. I just adapted it to our standards, and made it all fit properly into our standard containers."

"I see. Thank you, sir. It's a fine system, no matter who invented it."

"True."

The Bailey bridge was a system of prefabricated structural members that permitted a wide variety of bridges to be assembled on site without needing much in the way of heavy equipment, cranes, or special engineering. Furthermore, it let a bridge be assembled from one side of the river only, which let you go where you had not gone before.

53

There were two basic types of members. One was a side rail, six yards long and a yard and a half high. Eighteen of these fit snuggly into one of our standard carts or containers. They could be bolted end to end, or one above another, or side to side, as the particular length and load required. A small book in every cart contained charts and diagrams for dozens of possible truss bridges. It was simple cookbook engineering to assemble one.

The other member was a floor board, three yards wide and a yard and a half long. They came thirty-six to the container. There were also some light weight stringers to connect the side rails on particularly tall bridges, and of course, lots of nuts, bolts, and washers, all carefully galvanized. If we'd been building a railroad, we would have had rails that bolted to the floorboards, but we weren't, so we didn't.

The components were very carefully made. Rolled steel channel iron and I-beams were precision cut in jigs; the parts were assembled in other jigs, and welded together with Metallic-Inert Gas (MIG) welders. That's sort of like an arc welder that uses a continuous wire rather than a straight stick, while a flow of inert gas, carbon dioxide, kept the metallic arc from oxidizing.

Our welding rigs took three men to operate one. One man to control the wire feed and the gas, another to take care of the electrical generator, and a third to do the actual welding. Our industrial controls weren't up to those of the late [20]th century, yet. I'd have to work on that, if I ever got back.

Following a trip to heat treating, the assemblies were shot peened, with thousands of ball bearings dropped on them from thirty yards overhead. This puts the surface of the metal under compression, and increases the strength of the thing by a factor of three. Metal failure usually starts with tiny surface cracks growing larger under tension. With the surface under compression, those cracks don't occur.

Following this, they were put into a drilling jig, and all of the bolt holes were precision drilled, to fit exactly with everything else.

After that, they were pickled in an acid bath, galvanized by deep dipping them into a tank of molten zinc, and finally dipped into two sequential tanks of paint. They didn't rust easily.

It wasn't a cheap process, but it gave us a strong, lightweight bridge that could be put together in a hurry.

Only two tools were required for assembly, besides wrenches, crowbars, and jacks. One was a roller that was four yards wide. It had a ratchet mechanism built into it that permitted it to be turned slowly. The other was a much smaller roller that supported the bridge from the other side while it was being built.

The bridge went up fast. It was assembled on one side of the gap and then rolled over to the other side. The wagons had wheels mounted on the beds to facilitate rolling out the parts. When you dropped all the sides down, the wagons formed a wheeled ramp. The framework of the bridge was light enough to be tipped up, rolled up, and dropped to the other side. In World War II, army engineers did the deed under heavy enemy fire and often had to patch the roadway or add a second level to the bridge to compensate for the holes the Germans made. Fortunately all of our troops and carts were light enough to cross the standard bridge.

We didn't cross right away. I wanted a big ceremony to impress the troops and our hosts and needed to get the order of March right before we started, so that we wouldn't be held up once we crossed.

I sent four scouts across with instructions to scout the next fifty miles and report back in the morning. My three carts, personal troops, and messengers were near the front of the column. However, this time a company of Wolves and artillery pieces went first. The engineers that were not needed on the bridge went right after me.

There wasn't much I could do about the rest of the column. Most of them were passing time in a ninety-mile long narrow valley. Rearranging them would be difficult in that terrain, so I left them alone. By chance, most of the front of the column was made up of the regular Christian Army. The Christian Knights, new recruits, and African Corps were mostly near the rear of the column.

Then it started to rain. Torrential rain. Buckets and barrels of rain. Miserable, cold, windy, down-the-front-of-your-shirt and soaking-your-boots rain.

Of course, the Christian Army could move in any weather. We could march a hundred miles through a hurricane and then attack a fortress in the middle of a blizzard. But, the fact that you can do something doesn't mean that you should. The men had settled down to wait for the bridge to be finished. It would take a few hours for everyone to re-pack, mount up, and move off.

I had a miles-long column of men, horses, Big People, and carts strewn out over miles of boulders, rocks, bare riverbeds, with water now sheeting down on them. If we moved, there would be injuries. Horses and men would break their legs, and even the Big People might have trouble with their footing on wet rocks. In normal battle conditions, a Christian Army can be on the move in less than an hour, but these were far from normal conditions.

So I seethed. I sent word down the column to dig in, get comfortable, and get the hell off of the valley floor. The rain, so far, looked as if it was going to bring a foot or two of water to the old river bed. Even a single foot of fast-running water is enough to sweep a man off his feet – and kill him if he doesn't get help.

After a few hours, I realized that I had made a terrible mistake. The rain wasn't letting up. It was getting worse, and the entire run off from the hills was running down to my army. For the men in that narrow valley, this could be worse than the biblical flood.

I sent word for the column to decamp now! The men in the first ten miles from the summit were to move forward as much as possible. There was a good chance that they could reach safety. That meant crowding the summit area, but it was safest for them. The men in the next ten miles were to head for the high ground. "Tell them to get as high on the walls as they can and dig in hard. They are going to get very wet. No one should be a hero to save a cart or equipment." The message for the rest of the column was, "Advance to the rear with all possible dispatch!" In other words, "Run like hell!"

I wanted to ride down the column to help, but my mind kept reminding me that it was stupid to compound a mistake by getting myself killed. The men under my command were smart and resourceful. They would cope as well as anyone could without my help.

Troops and carts began to crowd the summit area. I ordered that everything that didn't breathe was to be cleared out to make room for troops. The extra bridging elements, the equipment carts, my tent, my cigars, and even my whiskey disappeared over the edge. As more troops and carts showed up, we began sending them across the untested bridge in the rain. It was a dangerous last resort. I told them to make as much room as they could on the other side without getting themselves killed.

Down valley, things were getting bad. Five miles down the valley, the water was two feet high, rushing and rising. Ten miles down it was over four feet deep and people farther from the summit than that were too busy surviving to report to any jackass in headquarters.

It rained for two more days. In that time, twenty thousand troops with a random selection of carts and equipment had straggled up to the summit and were scattered over the hills on both sides of the bridge. The reports downstream were bad.

It became so crowded on our side of the bridge that I crossed to the other side myself on the second day. I found a clear place to pitch a standard tent, my nice blue silk one being at the bottom of the ravine, and waited for the radio messages to come. All I could do was to wait. There was no point in giving orders to men who knew their situation better than I could.

When the rain stopped, the staff conference was grim. I asked the quartermaster, Sir Ivanov, how badly we were hurt.

"The fatalities were rather light, considering the situation. The Big People managed to get most of the men to safety. They abandoned the train, mounted everyone on their backs and headed down the valley. Almost everyone mounted on a Big Person lived. Among the regular army, the fatality rate was about ten percent from riders falling off the Big People, hitting rocks, or not finding their mounts. About twice that many have broken bones, contusions, and concussions. About fifty Big Persons suffered broken bones, but they will all survive. Several groups emptied out carts and used them for boats. One Big Person could save several humans that way and some of the men actually poled themselves through the rapids.

"Of course, the auxiliaries are pretty well gone. The Christian knights were at the back of the pack and should have done well, but they were on horseback and weighed down with that silly armor they wear. Most didn't make it, and the rest have decided that God has left you. They and all of their men have decided to take God's advice and get the hell back to where the loot is easier.

"Most of the ex slaves also have left. When they saw the knights going, they decided that their newly won freedom would be best enjoyed if they were alive.

"It will take days, perhaps weeks, to gather up all of the supplies and get an inventory. Much has been lost, but nothing that cannot eventually be resupplied," Sir Ivanov finished.

"Then", I said, "it's not all bad news. The people who left were undisciplined and mostly unsuitable for the long road ahead. We are left with the professional core of the army and enough supplies to get by until we get re-supplied. I am sorry about the men that died, but we do not control the weather. We can only cope with it."

We stayed just long enough to make certain that the recovery efforts were underway and to move most of the surviving carts to the bridgehead. Of course, there was an additional day for funerals. We are the Christian Army and we care for our dead.

Then we moved out. There wasn't as much organization as we were used to. I kept my tent up near the bridge and watched the units straggle over. My aid and a few helpers sat at a desk and made a list of personnel as they passed by. The scouts had chosen a pasture about 20 miles past the summit and had marked out a campsite.

The parade went on for about three army hours before the next disaster hit. Several engineers were down under the bridge abutments watching for problems.

In hindsight, we should have been staggering loads over the bridge better, but everyone was wiped out from the flood, and they were just thinking about getting into camp, so they tended to bunch up at the bottleneck.

The bridge was loaded with men, Big People, and a few artillery pieces when one of the engineers blew a horn and came running out from under the bridge. He was waving for the traffic to stop and he seemed very adamant about it. He conferred with his companions and then ran over to me while they ran onto the bridge. Traffic was stopped and the engineers were running by assuring everyone – and making certain that no one was moving.

When the young engineer got over to our table he blurted out, "Knight Bachelor Danuta, sir. That bridge is going down! The rain washed out the foundations from the inside. We're going to get everyone off, carefully, and the see what we can to do buttress it."

"How the hell can this happen?" I said. "The damned bridge stood for hundred years and you inspected it before we started."

He was clearly not in the mood to have a discussion. "You saw the shape that bridge was in. What makes you think the foundations were good? And how the hell do you think we could examine the foundation on the far side before we had a bridge to get to the far side? And what makes you think that the damage would be visible from the outside... Sir."

I would have busted the little jackass for insubordination, or cut his throat, except that he was right and I was letting my bad mood keep him from attending to the people on the bridge that needed him worse. I waved him off with a surly sneer.

The engineers were carefully moving people off of the bridge, one at a time. Everyone headed toward the closest end, so the ones on the far side had to turn around to make their escape. It was slow work and the bridge was creaking ominously with each movement.

Eventually everyone cleared the bridge and Danuta started to rappel under the foundations. Two of his companions and couple of grunts played out the rope while he dropped down and started to swing under the bridge. It was almost the last thing he ever did. He was, fortunately, on an outward swing when the abutment gave way and the bridge joined all of the spare bridge parts at the bottom of the ravine.

We walked slowly over to the edge. No one said a word as we looked down at the mass of twisted steel far below us. I remember that I was still looking down when I said, "We're going to need a staff meeting. Call the department heads and barons together."

The meeting started out as dismal one. I had asked for department heads and barons, but most of them brought an aide or two. We put two tents together and opened up the sides to get enough room for everyone. Since we were a little short on camp chairs, most people ended up sitting on the ground.

Before we started the meeting, each of the commanders had met with one of my aides and the quartermaster, Captain Ivanov, to work on an inventory of people and supplies under his command. I noticed that my staff and the quartermaster had both saved their clipboards.

It was almost two hours before the quartermaster was ready to open the meeting. "Your grace, we have lost much, but the situation is better than I had hoped. We started out with well over sixty thousand men, counting the knights and auxiliaries who attached themselves to this force. Over forty thousand regular Christian Army men, including all of the Wolves, crossed the bridge before it collapsed. None of the auxiliaries or volunteer knights made it. Only the Big People carrying partners or pulling carts got across, but we still have more Big People than soldiers.

"We didn't do as well with the supplies and equipment. Baron Kowalski sent the artillery through as fast as he could instead of keeping them together, but he still only saved about a hundred pieces. We don't have an accurate counting of the shells, but we are not flush with ammo.

"In fact, we are now short of everything. We were hauling about thirty thousand carts of supplies, but only about six thousand made it over the bridge, and most of the specialty carts for engineering supplies, medical personal, radio carts and so on were lost. We did get about twenty-five radio carts across.

"Most of the lances got their personal cart through, because they were riding on it, so we have enough tents and sleeping bags to look like an army.

"That means we have about a quarter of our small arms ammo and about a month's supply of food. If it takes more than a month to get where we're going, we'll arrive with empty bellies, and we won't get home without raiding or hunting. We have enough ammo for a battle or two, as long as they aren't too long or too bloody."

I signaled the end of his presentation by rising to speak. "Gentlemen, as bad as this is, it leaves us in good shape to complete our mission. All of the Wolves are with us, and every other man is a mounted cavalryman worth ten of any soldiers that we meet. Those who were left behind will not be missed. We're leaner, faster, and more deadly then we were yesterday. As for weapons, we may someday be short of bullets, but swords never need to be reloaded.

"As many of you know, this is not a mission to demolish Mongolia. As much as we would all like to see the last Mongol cease to share our air, this is a raid.

"We know that the Mongols plan to attack our homeland in less than three months. Our mission is to delay or stop that attack by denying the Mongols the means to go to war, and we can still do that.

59

"We are going to backtrack the path that they use to get to our homelands and destroy any bases or villages that would give them support, and if we run across an invasion army, we'll bloody it good.

"We will decimate their resources this time, and destroy Mongolia the next.

"We will proceed to the new encampment. Tomorrow, you will each receive your marching orders."

We broke camp at the bridgehead and headed inland. Before we left, I called in my radioman. "Prince David said that there was a place where the Big People could ford the river below. Have him show the Big People where it is. Send a message for all Big People, except those who are wounded or carrying wounded, to ford the river and join us at the new camp. They should not bring their riders as the mission that I have in mind will not require riders and we are too short on supplies to feed more men." I briefly considered having the men rig cargo panniers on the Big People to bring us more supplies but then I realized that we could not afford to either lose Big People on the crossing, or waste the time to collect supplies and load the panniers.

As it was, we wasted two days at the new camp. The first Big People showed up by morning. I gathered the first half gross and told them that their job was to gather six gross of their companions spread out between our latitude and the tree line to the north. They were to space themselves out about a half-mile apart and then sweep to the east. The purpose of the sweep was to kill every horse they could find. At first, there was an unusual quiet. They didn't move when I finished the orders. Then I noticed that the Big Person nearest me was looking at my bodyguard instead of me.

"What the hell is going on?"

"Lord, they cannot speak to me either. However, I think that they are uncomfortable with your orders. They will do as you command, but they are not natural killers and this much carnage will make them uncomfortable. They will kill to protect humans and they were willing to kill the battle horses going to the Mongol army, but I think that they also know that killing all of the farmer's horses will cause good people to die. One of the side effects of being able to detect evil is an abhorrence to kill the good people, even indirectly."

I was pissed. I am not used to defending my orders, particularly to my engineered servants. "Big People. Ladies. These horses are not people, good or evil. They are livestock. Each one you kill will mean one less Mongol can kill the good people you work with. I will, however, make one modification in my orders. If the animal is yoked to a plow or a farmer's wagon, you can let it live." The Big Person in front of me nodded and turned to move out. All of the Big People moved with her. They would pass the orders to the other Big People, and I would continue to wonder how they talked among themselves.

60

Moving up the River

The column moved out the next day. We were moving north, into the remnants of the Cuman Khanate. The land was flat, easy traveling, and mostly empty. The Cumans were nomadic warriors and, to my eyes, hard to tell from the Mongols. They had been beaten senseless by Mongols a few years back, and integrated into the Golden Horde. Now the rulers were scattered and large parts of the steppes in the khanate were empty.

We weren't looking for trouble, but we were moving so fast that they often didn't have time to get their encampments out of our way. When we ran into them, the advance guard tried to kill their horses and move out without a battle. It didn't often work out that way. They had become Mongol clones. They were warriors who could move out without baggage and travel fifty miles a day. They went on campaign with nothing but a sheepskin cloak, composite bows, arrows, and a feed sack for their horse, and came back with everything they could carry. Each warrior was required to carry two bows, one long-range and one short-range, and sixty arrows. He typically carried twenty standard arrows, twenty armor-piercing arrows and twenty fire arrows in his quiver.

Composite bows don't match machine guns for firepower, but they are no joke. We lost a few mounted infantrymen and even some of our Big People were wounded by lucky long-distance bow shots. We also began to pick up a distant following of very angry little men with composite bows. They were a damned annoyance. Our machine guns and field pieces weren't much good against a single rider on the horizon and I didn't want to risk casualties and lose time by chasing them around. When they got too close, an infantryman with a scoped rifle would encourage a little distance while I settled for moving forward and setting more guards at night.

We were moving north-east at about a gross miles a day. The Big People could move a lot faster, but we were burdened with our supplies and a small but increasing number of wounded. As we approached the Volga, we ran into larger settlements and even some small towns. If they didn't bother us, we left them alone. This was a raid, not a campaign of conquest.

The riverbanks themselves were too populated to travel though as fast as I wanted, so began to run north on a path about ten miles east of the Volga. One incident almost made me decide to stop for a few days. One afternoon, a trooper rode hard back into the column. He pulled up next to me and held out a rifle. It wasn't one of ours. "Your grace, You'll want to look at this. It isn't one of ours. This thing killed one of our Big People and its friend killed one of our troopers."

I turned the rifle over in my hands and looked down the barrel. The damned thing was rifled! It was a muzzle loader with a steel barrel and bronze working parts. It even worked with a percussion cap.

There was a clever ram rod attached to the barrel. For centuries, muzzle loaders carried their ram rods in a small tube attached to the barrel. This one had an attached slider that looked like a skinny saxophone slider. The ram rod was actually two rods attached at one end. When you pulled it out, one rod stayed captive in the tube. You then swiveled it around to put the other rod down the barrel. When you were done, the whole thing slid back down and clipped to the side. It probably saved several seconds on each reload because the user didn't have to fiddle around with getting the ram rod back into its holder. There was even a nice grip where the rods were joined to help you ram better.

I noticed that the trooper had a leather ammunition bag over his shoulder, and that turned out to be even more worrying. The damned thing was filled with ammunition tubes. They were tubes of paper with powder at one end and a ball with wadding at the other. You only needed to bite the end off and ram the whole paper tube and ball into one end of the tube to load up a measured power charge and wadded ball in seconds. In my time-line that wasn't invented until the 19th century.

These people had access to technology far in advance of what should be out here and it was not made in our domains. There were several Chinese symbols stamped on the butt of the gun. I handed it back to the trooper and said, "Find someone in the column that can read these and send him up to me."

About an hour later, Sir Grzegorz rode up with the rifle in hand. "Sire, you wanted to know what these symbols mean."

On this expedition, Sir Grzegorz commanded the wolves, the Christian Army's komand of old-style nobility. As an old style count, he was technically my peer in spite of his lower army rank, so I suppose I should be grateful that Sir Grzegorz and the rest of the Wolves preferred the army style of address. It kept the hierarchy of command clear and remined everyone that I'm the boss, but I still found dealing with him a little uncomfortable. I sighed, rubbed the back of my neck, and grimaced at the dust and grime it left on my hand.

"I'm a little surprised to see you. I expected one of the guides we picked up."

"The guides speak a little chink, but they don't read it. Fortunately, not all nobility spends its days beating serfs and raising turnips. My family has been dealing with traders from the silk road for several generations. I don't speak the language, but I can recognize some of the common symbols in Chink and Mongol."

"Can you read these?"

"Most of them, sir. The first four characters say *Great Khan Armory Lanzhou*, so if I'd have to guess, I'd say it's some kind of trade mark. The last two read something like *Builder of the Universe*. By the way, the *great khan* part is in Mongol, not Chinese."

This rifle was a load of bad news that just kept coming. This meant that the Mongols had completed their conquest of the Song Dynasty, even after the drubbing we gave them in Poland. The Mongols had gunpowder grenades and some primitive cannon even before they attacked us, but they shouldn't have come up with this rifle for about three hundred more years. This thing showed that they had learned at least something from meeting us. Shit, shit, and even more shit.

"Staff meeting, 0500," I said to no one in particular. One of the nice things about being in charge is when I said something, things just happened.

"Mongol riflemen," I sighed. This was going to an interesting excursion. About that time, I decided that we needed a little more privacy. I sent out a squad of fifty mounted Wolves to circle around behind the Cumans who were trailing us. Theoretically, we could have taken their horses and left them stranded on the steppes, but in reality few of them were likely to surrender and this was not a war where we could take prisoners. They were to trap anyone behind us between themselves and the rear guard and eliminate the danger. I gave specific instructions that we needed at least one prisoner who had one of these guns. If they ran into someone carrying a rifle, they were to do their best to capture him and his ammunition.

The staff meeting was not a comfortable one as my big tent, all of our conference furniture, and my cigars were at the bottom of a gorge. I called in the head of our scouts, the quartermaster, Baron Kowalski, Sir Wladyclaw, my adjutant, and our civilian guides. We sat on blankets with cans of cold food in front of us, and wished that the cigars had not been discarded.

The quartermaster started the discussion. "Gentlemen, we have about six weeks of canned food left. We have over a million small arms rounds, and you all know the artillery situation. We have made better inventory while we rode and I can now tell you that we have exactly one hundred and thirty-eight field pieces, and each of them had a hundred rounds stored in the carriage. Unfortunately, most of the shell carts were lost, so that's about our total supply of shells. I would not suggest a pitched artillery battle.

"Our biggest problem will be with clothing and personal supplies. Each trooper has only the clothes from his personal kit, and cold weather is coming. You may have noticed that it has already gotten cooler than when we started. In a few weeks it will be a lot colder and we are going to be on the steppes, with high winds, no cover, and no coats."

I said, "A lot of the men brought blankets to augment their sleeping bags. We should encourage them to make ponchos. It's a Spanish form of coat. You take the blanket, cut a hole in the center just big enough for your head to fit through and then wear it like a cape. A rope around the waist will keep it closed if you're riding."

"Sir, we are even short of rope."

The head of scouts was next. "My lord, we have sent scouts out fifty miles in every direction. Except for some small settlements on the riverbanks, the last hundred miles we covered is empty of people, and it is no different ahead. We run into an occasional Cuman or Mongol yurt surrounded by horses, but this place is almost eerily empty. I have heard that the Mongols killed eighty or ninety percent of the people they conquered in some areas. This must be one of those areas."

Ahmed, our Arab guide, was anxious to talk. "Your grace, gentlemen, I know that you plan to avoid battle on this raid, but, if you can change your plans a little, I may have a solution for your immediate problems. In the middle of this wilderness, there is one great bazaar.

"We are fifty miles from the Volga. Two or three hundred miles north of here, the new city of Sarai sits across this very river. It was established about fifteen years ago by Subedi, one of the sons of the great khan, as the administrative center of Golden Hordes and it sits where it does to prosper on trade. Many rich caravans travel from China. They meet boats that travel the river all the way from the Rus' territories to Constantinople. The merchants there have everything you need. Of course, the administration there, being Mongol, may not welcome your shopping trip but, if the merchants cannot supply coats, dead Mongols will oblige. The rest of the country may be empty, but I hear that there are over two hundred thousand inhabitants in Sarai."

My mind drifted back to the cold and miserable ride we had that day. The dress of the day had been full armor for several days. Even the average Mongol could hit a man at 350 yards and there are reports that exceptional archers pushed to almost 400 yards; that's over a quarter of a mile. This place looked rather empty, but no one wanted to give an easy target to any passing Mongol.

It was not a comfortable way to ride. You have your undershirt or long johns, then heavy cotton padding, a vest of lightweight chain mail, and then the armor plates over that. Standard Christian Army armor consisted of a breastplate, backplate, greaves for the legs, and vambraces to protect the upper arms. Cavalry added arm greaves, a thigh plate, and chain mail gloves. By medieval standards, our armor was remarkable. The plate and chain together would stop even an armor-piercing arrow or musket ball, and it took a close up shot to get through anyplace else. Of course, there was always the chance of a lucky shot through the face plate or in a joint. The armories had gotten the weight down to less than forty pounds, and it was stainless. Of course, even the best armor clinks, creaks, and occasionally chafes.

However, the usual problem with armor is that the damned stuff is too hot. Because of the padding, it was sometimes deadly in the tropics. Today was different. I could feel the wind chilling my face and hands. Cold little knives seemed to reach through the cracks and prick my exposed skin, and this was only late fall. Soon, it would be really cold.

I came out of my reverie to see that everyone was waiting for a response from me. "Ahmed, you are right. As far as I can see, we have only one course of action. We are going shopping.

"Gentlemen, any thoughts of how we do our shopping?"

The head of scouts spoke up. "Sir, we should be watching the river. If Ahmed is right, we need to know what's going in to the city. We don't want to advertise our presence, but we could dress up as locals, take a few Mongol horses, and camp high on the banks. A couple of days of observation should tell us a lot about the city."

"That's a good idea, but it may take you a full day just to get the fleas out of whatever Mongol clothing you liberate. These are the filthiest people in history and we don't need their parasites or their diseases."

Baron Kowalski spoke up, "Your grace, I would suggest that we bypass this city." Seeing my surprised look, he continued, "Sooner or later they are going to know we are out here. However, if we march westward and bypass the city, we may convince them that we are on the way somewhere else and reluctant to attach a fortified city. We camp up river just long enough to lull them a little and then attack from the north."

"Baron, that's close enough to the truth to work." In actual fact, I didn't relish attacking a fortified city with less than fifty thousand men and a few field pieces.

"Tell the scouts to try to question anyone they find, who doesn't shoot too fast, about the location of the city. We'll need to plot a course."

That night was a cold but one of my guards zippered her sleeping bag to mine to make a double. There are some advantages to having a nubile and mostly naked young lady as your bodyguard. Her slightly higher body temperature was also welcome. As a rule, I considered it immoral to have sex with something that was, technically, non-human, but it had been a long day and I desperately needed relief before I could sleep.

Four days of empty steppes later, I was almost nodding off atop Silver. One great advantage of a Big Person is that you don't need reigns. A gentle tap of your knees will suffice, or you can just explain where you want to go and nod off. The only thing keeping me alert was that the backplate of my armor was digging into my lower back every time I tried to lean back in the saddle. Good thing, it doesn't help morale to see the boss asleep at his desk.

I became aware of someone riding hard behind me. When I turned in the saddle, my first thought was "How the hell did Mongols get Big People?" Then I realized that the men in the sheepskins must be from the squad sent out to watch the river. Behind each of them, a rag doll of a man bounced around much more than anyone should on a Big Person.

I told Silver to slow down and waited for them to catch up. They were soon riding along side of us. "Trooper, I would address you by your rank, but you forgot to put your insignia on your sheepskin. Where did you get your baggage?"

"Sir Kiminovsk, your grace, knight of the scouts. We got them on the river, and you'll never believe where they come from."

I looked over the men they had brought and suddenly realized that the red and white jackets they wore could actually be a version of my company uniform, if it was cut sloppy, the sleeves truncated, the buttons moved, and a lot of dirt and grime added. I looked at the nearest one and asked, "Who are you?"

He answered in clear Polish, "I'm Sir Willard, merchant cap'n of the Commercial Corps, commandin' the river boat *Wanderwind*, and couple more. That there is my navigator. Who are you?"

This man was my employee! On a Mongol river! I leaned forward, "I'm your boss."

He looked doubtful. "Don't make much sense t'argue with any man who has an army with 'em, but last I heard, Sir Boris was sittin' on his ass in Kiev, spendin' the money we merchants send 'em."

Kiminovsk glared at him and hissed, "Not Novacek, you idiot. This is Hetman Conrad, and I'll thank you to show some respect!"

"Hetman Conrad! Couldn't be. He's dead 'bout a year since. What's he doin' out here?"

I waved the trooper off. "As you can see, I am breathing very well for a dead man. Now I want to know what you are doing trading on a Mongol river!" My patience was running thin and my hand was tensing on my sword hilt.

"Sorry 'bout that *dead* thing, sir. But we been on the road, or river, fer months and, of course, Novacek don't let us bring a radio, or much of anythin' else out of Christian Army territory. We didn't know you was back. We don't hear nothin' out here." He reached over to Kiminovsk and touched his armor padding. "We been tradin' fer the silk you cover yer paddin' with. The Chinee brung it overland to Sarai. We buy from 'em and then float it down to the Black Sea to meet our ships. It's a long trip because we start in the Rus' territories and go down river to Sarai. That way we don't have to row on either leg. It's the same way the Northman got to Constantinople in the old days. We gonna be here long? These men of yers have got three boats of ours parked on the bank."

My scowl relaxed a little, "It depends upon what you mean by *long*. You've wandered into the middle of a war zone and you will be here until we are finished questioning you. At least you will be here long after dinner and maybe for a few more days."

I saw from the shadows that it was getting late in the afternoon. "We will be stopping early tonight. There will a staff meeting during dinner. Our guests are invited."

Since the blackboard had also gone down the gorge, we were sitting cross-legged around a spot of bare dirt where Willard could draw as he talked. Most of us were still munching on our canned dinners. Willard started by drawing a long line in the dirt, and then a half circle beside it. "The city sits mostly on the east side of the river. The Volga is a huge river and it's hard to control traffic, so they picked a spot where there's an island in the middle of the river. There's a fort on the island with about twenty cannon and a musket team, so they can control traffic.

"The old part is protected pretty well with a timber palisade, a dry moat with stakes on the bottom and cannon emplacements. It's about five miles long and stretches about the same from the river. However, the city must have gotten a lot bigger a lot faster than the Mongols thought it would. It must have a hundred fifty, two hundred thousand people now and half of the city is outside the walls.

"They're building a new set of stone walls around the whole thing, but it's going slow and they don't seem to be much worried about it. It's just foundations in most places.

"The piers are on the city side of the river, and there are a lot of warehouses behind them. It's like any port city, the bars, brothels, and Inns are just behind the warehouses, mixed in with the tariff houses and some traders offices. The main government offices are right in the center of town. They're the only stone buildings in town. Rich people and government officials fill up the rest of the inner city.

"Most of the rest of the inner city is divided into guild sections. There are areas for rug merchants, coppersmiths, leather works, silk merchants, and so on."

He drew another bigger circle around the first. "Between the inner wall and the city edge, Genoa, Vienna, Egypt, China, Korea and a few others each have section of their own. Some of them have low walls around them."

Willard scratched a line through both circles opposite the river. "The overland trade route enters through a caravan gate on this side. That's also where most of the Mongol guards are housed."

Sir Wladyclaw asked, "How many Mongols?"

"At least thirty or thirty-five thousand cavalry, probably more, and there's a bunch of Chinese troops that do most of the police work. There weren't that many cavalry the last time we were here, but a bunch of new troops showed up in the past few months. There are huge stables near the barracks and a bigger herd of horses outside the city. Oh, and there's a yurt village along the trade route, but I don't know if that has more soldiers or just Mongol families who don't like cities. There are cannon on the inner walls. Large-bore brass muzzle loaders. I've seen both solid and canister shot stacked near them. I haven't seen anything resembling a mobile field piece, but then they don't let outsiders get near the armory. The small fort on the island has about twenty large cannon facing the west bank and only about five big ones facing toward the city side. I guess that they want to make certain that no one skirts customs by bypassing the city, so they concentrated the guns that way.

"Most of the cavalry still prefer their bows when they're on horseback. We see them practicing a lot over by the barracks. The range is as good as a musket and the rate of fire is ten times as fast. However, every soldier and policeman has a musket and a single shot pistol for emergencies. In a crisis, they can station citizens on the walls with rifled muskets and do some real damage."

As he spoke, I realized that he was quoting from some report that he had already written, probably for Novacek's spy agency. His bumpkin speech had totally disappeared.

"The moat is dry now, but the Chinese engineers have installed flood gates where the moat meets the river. They can flood the moat, and there is a system to drop the bridges into the moat by pulling a few chains. The thing is too big for a horse to jump and once the bottom is mud, it would be very hard to cross."

When he paused, I said, "Your report is very complete. I assume that you have this written down somewhere, perhaps for later transmission to Novacek."

He shook his head, "No, sir, a smart man doesn't write down anything about Mongol fortifications while he is still on a Mongol river, but I have thought about it."

"Sir Willard, I am still having a hard time getting my mind around this whole concept of trading in a Mongol town. Why aren't you dead?"

Willard stroked his beard for a second. "Well, it's been twenty years since any Mongol met a Christian Army soldier. Maybe they forgot we're at war.

"You have to remember that when these people aren't busy cutting off heads, they're heavy into trade. They have been since the first great khan figured out that it was more profitable to get the peasants to farm instead of killing them off and grazing horses on their land.

"Of course, they're still psychopaths. When the Khwarazmian guy refused a trade mission from the great khan, and then killed his representatives, they went berserk and totally wiped out the Khwarezm civilization. I hear that the blood made the river run red for days.

"Sarai was established by Obedei and Subedi after you kicked them out of Poland. The two brothers are old school, but even they're learning. They're pissed because the great khan doesn't share much of the wealth he gets in China. The only income these guys have is tribute from the Russian states and a couple of Balkan cities and what they make from the trade going though Sarai. Of course, now that the khan has the Silk Road open all the way from China to Constantinople, business is pretty good."

My ears were buzzing and I could feel my blood pressure rising. "What the hell do you mean? You're saying these Mongols are peaceful merchants. These are the bastards that killed half of Russia and tens of thousands of Poles! I don't want to hear any crap about how peaceful they are!

"And how the hell are they getting tribute from anyone in Russia, we kicked their asses when they attacked?"

Willard was quieted but not cowed. "Yes, we kicked their asses in Poland, but we were too busy cleaning up to chase them all the way back to Mongolia. They had already taken Tver, Moscow, and several other Russian principalities and they still pay tribute. Since that time they've consolidated their gains in the Caucasus and convinced several more Russian cities to sign up as vassals. They sent representatives to places like Novgorod with a simple ultimatum – 'Either pay us and we will protect you from the Christian Armies or fight us and we'll kill you now.'"

I couldn't listen to any more crap. "Why the hell would anyone need to be protected from us? We don't attack our neighbors! And, our allies are the richest, best-fed people on Earth!"

Willard just sat quietly.

"Well," I asked, "What the hell is going on."

"Our citizens are the luckiest people on Earth, but the Mongols pointed out that the old Polish nobility doesn't seem to be doing as well. When we move in, the old estates decline in value and Polish products dominate the market. We put up a couple of snowflake forts to 'protect our friends,' we sell cheap goods, we accept anyone as a recruit, and everyone is better off except the men who used to run things.

"The Russian boyars like running things. They'd rather have power and money than foreign troops and hot water. All the Mongols ask is to send a lot of money, do the census, and accept their rather remote authority. A lot of cites joined up.

"I think the common way of describing the Christian Army was that it was like sleeping with a pet lion. It makes you feel safe and warm, but you have to hope that it doesn't need a snack in the middle of the night."

It took awhile to digest what I was hearing. My staff recognized my mood and sat quietly. The decisions that I finally made were obvious and unavoidable. "Gentlemen, the situation is worse than we could have imagined. If the Mongols are getting help from Christian traitors, they are more dangerous than we knew. Now we will remove this city of traitors by burning the bastards to the ground. When we leave, this must be a plain empty of all but ashes. There will be no place to for the traitors to pay tribute or give allegiance."

Then I laid out my plan. Wars, they say, are won by those who get there firstest with the mostest. I had spent thirty years in this place making certain that I had the mostest. Now I was spoiled, and we were short of men, short of ammo, and short of time. I could still smash that city. Even with their cannon and muskets and fortified walls. We could still kill fifty Mongols to one Christian trooper – and I couldn't afford the losses. This was going to be a long, dirty campaign.

"Sir Kowalski, we will start by implementing your plan, with a few additions. Sir Grzegorz, select a lance of wolves and polish them up until they shine. I want them to gleam when they ride with flags flying, but the first two flags in the front will be white. He's going visiting. Willard, what languages does he need for a message to the khan?"

"Mongol is best, my lord, just to be courteous, but they have Russian and Polish interpreters and part of the population speaks Mandarin Chinese."

"Include a couple of interpreters to help him with the Mongol language. We'll depend on his trader background to keep him breathing."

We go Shopping

At daybreak, we broke camp and headed north. I instructed all of the men to look very busy and make a lot of noise, but to move as slowly as possible. I planned to camp on the banks of the Volga, less than thirty miles north of the city. I hoped that the Mongols following us would see nothing unusual in a European army making so little progress. We were, after all, the only modern army they had ever seen and they were used to outrunning and outmaneuvering every army they met.

Sir Wladyclaw had assigned Sir Gorski as the tribute bearer. He broke off early and headed for the city, unit and truce flags flying, Mongol speaking trooper in tow. I found out that we still had about four hundred pounds of gold coins with us for payroll and emergencies, so Kowalski was carrying about thirty pounds of gold coins as a present for the khans. I figured it didn't matter how much gold we sent, as we were going to get in back in a day or two anyway.

His troopers had rigged up a very special wagon for the gold. They emptied out on of the supply wagons and then scrounged some fancy velvet cloth, gold braid, and a couple of gold candlesticks that one of the troopers had in his bags. The chest of gold was placed in the back of the wagon on that beautiful velvet cloth, surrounded by braid and flags. It was enough to take the observers mind away from the fact that, behind the chest, the cloth actually ran on a raised floor all the way to the front of the wagon.

Under that false floor sat a very heavy machine gun and a lot of ammo. Pull the cloth, pull the pin holding the gun carriage retracted, and wagon became a 13th century super tank. Of course, Willard had assured us that these peace-loving bastards would respect the parlay flags, but a little insurance never hurt.

The mission turned out to only partially successful. A Mongol squad rode out from the city to meet him within sight of the walls, and didn't kill him. However, they understandably weren't going to let armed foreign nationals into the city under any circumstances. His interpreter told the squad leader they had a present for the local khan, but they would not be able to leave it with anyone but a high official.

That became a problem that took a few hours to solve. In the 13th century, people didn't carry a driver's license. Without seeing a throne room or some other evidence, it was hard to know who to give the gold to. Eventually someone showed up with enough fancy dress and enough retainers to convince Kowalski that he really was the assistant to the khan. A man claiming to be the local military commander was with him.

At that point, Gorski and his crew all made serious attempts at groveling and bowing. He explained through the interpreter that his commander knew he was making a serious error riding through Mongols lands without permission, but gave a convincing story of insurrection and betrayal in Poland that demanded that we go home the fastest possible way.

Then he pulled back the purple cloth and opened the chest of gold. He explained that this was a token of our respect and hinted that we would be willing to send more back from Poland once we reached there.

I doubt that the Mongols believed a word of his story, but they took the chest of gold and let them leave unmolested. We failed to get an inside look at the city, but perhaps we spread a little confusion and doubt about our intentions.

The rest of the troops moved out to our next campground. I had instructed the officers to have a lot of visible problems today. Wagons should appear to break down; horses would need a lot of rest; the midday meal would require a dismount while the men searched for fuel to heat their cans with.

I wanted to convince the Mongols that we were moving as fast as we could, but being an incompetent Christian army, our best pace was not too good. The Mongol warrior would carry raw meat under his saddle and pull out strips to eat with one hand while in full gallop. They should find the spectacle of soldiers hunting for dry horse dung to heat their canned meals hilarious.

Of course, the problem was getting the best trained and most motivated army in the world to act like bunglers. It is amazingly hard for competent men to act like idiots and still look natural.

Myself, I tried hard to look as if I was dozing in the saddle, but I was thinking about how we were going to eliminate the city. Normally, I would just reduce the island fort with artillery, and then cross to the island with a few thousand troops covered by machine gun fire from the banks. Once on the island, we would occupy the remains of the fort, install our own artillery on the city facing side and reduce the city defenses from there. Machine guns on the island bank nearest the city and air support would prevent any counter attacks on us until we had softened up the city enough to send the troops in to mop up. No problem.

Modern army meets medieval army. Score: modern army, thousands of kills; medieval army, zero. Works every time.

Unfortunately, we were short of artillery shells and artillery period, and way out of range for air support. We had enough machine gun ammo for a couple of battles, but no re-supply. We were also short of boats in a region devoid of boats, trees, and anything else that floats. Just getting across a two kilometer wide river with any equipment was a major problem.

So, we were going to Mongol it.

I had Willard's river pilot riding along side me. We had reached the banks of the Volga far enough north of the city to keep suspicions down. The Mongols had built their city on the best crossing within a few hundred miles, but the pilot had mentioned a particularly treacherous section where the river was filled with sand banks and low marshy islands. It was hell for boats, but might give our Big People enough intermittent traction to keep them from floating too far downriver when they crossed.

The "bad" section of the river was about two miles long and hard to miss. As planned, two of the artillery carts broke down there and had to be upended for repairs. We moved most of the shells to other carts, but we "had to leave" the two artillery pieces and some shells behind while we moved on. Of course, we set also left enough troops to guard our equipment and set up a couple of machine guns to discourage curious tourists.

By strange coincidence, they just happened to break down near a rare stand of trees. As we left, the troopers were cutting down some trees to improve their camp while they waited.

The main body of the army moved north another forty miles and camped on the riverbank. We had made less than a hundred miles that day. The officers and I met for about two hours and went over the plans for the morning, but we sent the troops to bed early. Armies are forever forgetting that one of the most important elements in a battle is a well rested army.

It's a good thing that the nights are long this time of year because the bugles sounded an hour and a half before first light.

Before we moved, I addressed the troops. I know that Caesar did it by shouting loudly, but I stood on a radio wagon and used an amplified microphone. "For thirty years, the Mongols have murdered their way across the world. In Baghdad and Samarkand and a hundred other places, they put the entire populations to the sword. They murdered men, women and children indiscriminately. They have murdered and depopulated entire nations. Tomorrow, you will have the chance to change a lot of bad Mongols into good Mongols. How will you do this? It is a matter of grass. Any Mongol riding on the grass is a bad Mongol. Any Mongol sleeping under the grass is a good Mongol. Tomorrow you will make many good Mongols."

When the cheering died down, we moved out thirty-five thousand men and Big People by moonlight. Few armies aside from Patton's or Caesar's could have moved so fast.

The men left behind began moving the equipment into a defensive ring with their backs to the river. By dawn, they would have machine gun emplacements and be behind low walls made out of whatever they could scrounge: brush, trees, dirt, sod, whatever was there. There wouldn't be much point in reducing the city if we lost all of our equipment while we were gone.

74

We were no longer a fifty-mile long train, but even formed up two hundred fifty men across, our formation was almost mile wide and nearly two miles long. We were going to need a little elbow room for a fast ride.

How fast? The Mongol Post and the Pony Express using relays of fresh horses both averaged about ten miles an hour. A good quarter horse can hit forty-five miles-an-hour during a race, but only for a few minutes. As far as any conventional wisdom went, the Mongols knew that we were at least a day away – and on the wrong side of the river.

Even in the moonlight, Big People could make forty miles an hour on the tundra – if your kidneys could stand it. We reached the river crossing in just over an hour but it was a nightmare ride in the dark. My armor clinked and jangled and pinched everywhere. My back was killing me, my scrotum was on fire, and there was no way to judge distance or time and I thought it would never end.

When we got close the crossing point, the troops we had left behind lit torches to mark the end points of the crossing and that yellow light was the first thing we had really seen for an hour. We didn't stop. The Big People knew what to do. They plunged into the river and swam hard. The sand bars and small islands gave some purchase, but it was a rough crossing.

It took about an hour to form up on the eastern bank. We waited only about fifteen minutes to give the last crossers time to catch their breath, and then we moved out for the city, still moving about forty miles an hour – and my butt hurt even worse than my back.

Somewhere in the darkness ahead of us were the two artillery pieces that we had left behind. As soon as it was dark, the troops had roped the trees they cut to the artillery carts for extra buoyancy and began to manhandle them across the river. Sandbars and islands do NOT help a raft so it took hours to get to the eastern bank. Then they moved out for the city in the moonlight. They couldn't move as fast as we were, but they had enough head start to get there before we did.

It was first light when we stopped just out of sight of the city. Miles behind us here were probably a few dozen Mongol lookouts trying desperately to warn the city. I wanted to smash straight in, but we needed to rest and walk the kinks out before we went into battle. The field pieces were already there and the troopers with them had scouted out good firing positions during the night. The Mongols were famous for moving fast and appearing from nowhere. Before full daybreak, they would see how that worked from the other side.

I quickly conferred with the knight that I had sent ahead with the cannons. "Lord," he reported. "It looks about as we expected. There is only a moat and a timber palisade on this side. Seems they weren't too concerned about an attack from the east, and once we take out the gate, it will be down permanently. The moat's also too small to stop a Big Person. We can jump it once the wall's down."

I clapped him on the shoulder, "A lot of lives today depend upon you opening that gate for us. Once you open it, work both ways opening up as many gaps as you can. How fast can you be in position?"

"The cannons are already out there. We put them in position last night, sighted them in on the gate, and disguised them as mounds of hay. Give us a one-minute head start and we'll have the gate down as you go by."

"Go now". I mounted and moved to the head of the column. I took that one minute to verify that we were in formation twenty abreast, with my personal lance in the first rank, raised my golden sword and shouted, "For God and Poland, to defend our homeland, and to improve a lot of murdering Mongols, charge!"

They knew we were here now. Thirty five thousand horses at full gallop made a lot of noise as we burst over the last little hillock between us and the city, and the cannon that fired as we passed made a lovely pair of door bells. As we charged, the cannon behind us continued to fire at a steady pace. I hadn't been flattering the artilleryman. This campaign depended on those two cannon. The Mongols themselves had learned in the early days that pure cavalry was a lousy siege tool. Several Russian cities survived their raids by just staying behind the walls and refusing to come out to play. Calvary is fast, hard-hitting, and dangerous, but makes a lousy can opener.

We made that last mile in about three minutes. As we approached the gate, we had to swing the formation to follow the road. A little town of wooden buildings had grown up along the road outside the wall. We swept past sleepy early risers who stared at us but were too surprised to shoot at us or who were armed only with the honeydew buckets they were emptying. Behind me I heard sporadic fire from the Sten guns as the troopers picked off armed men or men who looked as if they might want to be armed. The village would be cleared by men nearer the end of the column.

As I looked down the road, I could see the wooden gate in ruins. The boys had done their job and were now whittling down sections of the wall on both sides.

76

As I passed the gate, some little bastard shot me with one of their muzzle loaders. It hurt like hell, but he had only about ten seconds to gloat before a knight beheaded him. I led my lance aside to let the Wolves do their job. The first lance behind us turned left at the gate and began to clear the defenders from the inside of the wall. Behind them the second lance carried heavy grenades to open more of the wall. The third and fourth lances did the same on the right.

The rest of the troops headed for the barracks. We wanted the Mongols dead before they had a chance to mount up. For several minutes we were choked up at the gate, passing four or five at a time, but as more holes opened up, lance leaders spread the column out and troops began to pour into the city. As I watched the troops go by, I glanced down at my breastplate. The ball had penetrated the armor but didn't have enough left to get through my chain mail. I was going to have one damned big bruise and it felt like something was broken. I was going to have a hard time swinging a sword with that arm. When I saw that the insertion was going well, I headed for the barracks. I wanted to be where the most Mongols were. The battle plan pretty much ended after we got into the city. This was a smash and bash, kill the bastards raid. The lances had their orders, most to go to the barracks, others to assault the city center and so on, but we didn't know enough about the city to make a clear plan. It really came down to, find 'em, bash 'em, kill 'em

Sir Gorski had peeled off as we charged and headed east with the last four thousand men. Their job was to sweep the yurts and pastures on the road clear any threat of a counter attack, and then join us in the city.

It worked as well any battle plan does.

At the barracks, the mounted infantry had dismounted and was firing into the barracks. Dead Mongol guards littered the doorways and courtyards, but there was return fire from muskets and bows. Fortunately, the Mongols were nice enough to build wooden barracks. I claimed executive privilege to deliver the first incendiary on Silver's back. My arm hurt like hell when I threw the bomb, and I damned near missed but I was followed by a long line of knights with burning presents. Within minutes, we had twenty barracks buildings blazing.

When the fires were going good, I headed back to the gate. I never did really enjoy butchery, even when it was necessary, and this was not a prisoner taking day.

Back at the gate, the troops were still coming through. Other than our men and dead Mongols, this side of the city was deserted. I could hear steady fire as the Wolves continued to sweep the inner walls. Apparently, none of the Mongol cannon got off a shot. Sporadic gunfire echoed all around me.

I decided it was time to visit city hall. Perhaps I could register my complaints about their treatment of Poles with the proper authorities. I had to sheath my sword and take up my Sten gun. My arm was just too sore to swing a sword. A couple of times, I had to remind troops that we did *not* kill traders, blacksmiths, and shop keepers but they were generally pretty well-behaved. The administration building was one of the few stone buildings in town. We couldn't burn it and we needed at least a few of the inhabitants alive. I was too late to join in the assault. The first troopers on the scene had just burst through the doors and captured or killed everyone before they realized they were under serious attack.

They had gathered the captives on the street in front of the building. While I was looking them over, troopers brought in several prosperous and important looking prisoners. We weren't looking for prisoners, but the richer Mongols would be questioned. One particularly large fellow was dressed in rich furs and still wore a gold embossed breastplate. The troopers said that this was Batu, one of the head guys. They said they had jumped him as he left his bedroom and still had a damned hard time. To his credit, he was bleeding from several wounds and still had to be both bound and restrained. He didn't go easy.

We found a large room with a city map on the wall, set up a temporary headquarters, and sent messengers out to tell the officers where we were. Our lightning raid had conquered the city in a matter of minutes, but it would take hours to clear out the remnants of resistance.

As reports came in, we identified the foreign enclaves and sent troopers out to guard the ones that were staying neutral and close out the ones that were resisting. Here, we would take prisoners, and rape was not allowed. We probably missed a few and would have to apologize to a few foreign powers later – if we ever got back to Europe.

It was more important to send excess troops to the docks to protect the warehouses and organize fire fighting where necessary. This looked like a battle, but it started as a shopping trip and we needed the contents of those warehouses. The troops were given orders that no one was to enter the warehouse and that no one would be allowed to leave with any merchandise. Boats were also forbidden to leave.

By ten, we were able to hold our first staff meeting. As I sat at the desk, a combat medic stripped my armor and began a painful examination. The first report was from the commander of the Wolves. "It took us over two hours sweep the walls. Most of the wall standers were Chinese troops who were impressed by the Mongols. As we agreed before, we let any Chinaman who dropped his weapons leave the battlefield. They didn't want to be here, and we didn't want to waste ammunition. By the time we had cleared the first mile, the other positions were deserted. One position was commanded by a real hardass who managed to get his piece turned around and got off one shot in our direction. He took out a nice civilian house before he croaked.

"We control the entire perimeter of the city; our men man all the gates."

"How about the barracks?"

"Komander Jazinski, your grace, representing Baron Krol. The baron was unable to come in person.

"The battle is still in progress. Most of the Mongols were still asleep when we hit them and we fired most of the buildings. At first it was a turkey shoot. We finished them off as the fled the buildings and most of them were too smoke addled to get off a shot, but there were about a hundred barracks buildings and we couldn't get to all of them before they woke up. We now control the perimeter but a few thousand have broken out of the buildings and set up a perimeter of their own.

"They learned that they couldn't pierce our armor and developed some new tactics. From inside the buildings or on the roofs, they aim for the face or joints on our troops. When they are out of arrows, they change to their muzzle loaders. They saw that a shot to the head with a large-caliber ball will kill a man even if his armor is intact, so they concentrate on head shots. We've lost about fifty killed and two hundred wounded so far and we will have to charge them before dark or lose them. We will lose more men when we do."

I signaled to the komander of artillery. "We don't have our artillery, but there is a lot of Mongol ordinance on the walls, and most of your men used muzzle loaders before we got the new cannons. Get everyone you can find, impress civilians if you have too, and get some of the Mongol cannon pointed at those barracks. Most of even loaded already. A hundred rounds of cannon fire could soften them up nicely and make the clearance project easier. Go now! We'll have to finish the briefing without you. Sir Jazinski will give you your targets.

"Before you leave, Sir Jazinski, in your opinion, does Sir Krol need reinforcements?"

"No, your grace. He has a dozen companies with him and the casualties have been light. There is no more room in either the frontline or reserves to use more men effectively."

"Who knows what's happening on the streets?"

A Knight glanced around for a moment and then stood. "Lord, I think I can address that as well as anyone.

"The streets are as calm as could be expected with a battle going on. These people are aware of what happens to losers in Mongol wars. Those that aren't cowering in their homes or running over the tundra are packed into churches or mosques, praying and waiting for death. My men are avoiding contact with civilians where possible because of their terrible panic. I suggest that we give them several hours to calm down before we begin house to house.

"A few of the Chinese police put up a resistance, but as soon as they realized that they could surrender, they all went home or over the hills, except for the few that we held on too for to give us directions

"Early on, Sir Ryszard's command found an area of rich homes surrounding two rather modest palaces flying personal flags. The baron, as commander on site, determined that it was best to engage immediately, so they split into ten-man groups and stormed the houses, with larger groups assaulting the palaces. They killed about sixty Mongols, but even when it was Sten gun to sword, these boys are tough. They report fifteen wounded and ten dead. There were also a number of civilian casualties as it was hard to tell combatants from non-combatants.

"The area is secure. You have Batu as a prisoner and the man purported to be his brother lies dead in bed. A good Mongol now.

"The baron could not break away from his command to report here personally, as he is still engaged in combat. Unfortunately, it was not obvious that the region to the east of the palaces was devoted to residences for the permanent garrison and civil servants. Unfortunately, these people had sufficient warning to act.

"Most of their fighting men exited the palisade and rode east, probably planning to get reinforcements and counter attack. The others formed a battle group in one of the compounds. While the baron prefers direct action, he is mindful of your order to limit our casualties, so he has surrounded the compound with riflemen and is whittling away them away rather than doing a frontal assault. Time consuming, but effective."

I interrupted, "I appreciate the baron's concern with casualties, as no man's life should be wasted, warrior or not, but perhaps he could speed up the battle by burning the bastards out or bringing over some of the Mongol cannon to hit the compound."

"The baron is aware of those possibilities, but the Mongols are sheltering their families behind them. Burning or blasting would kill more women and children than enemy warriors."

"So what? They're Mongols."

"My lord, they are also children and women. To kill them needlessly would be against the Warrior Oath that you yourself wrote. It is neither kind nor fatherly to kill children."

I could feel my temper rising again. This day was not going well. I planned to spend a good part of it joyously swinging my sword at the worst bastards in the world. Instead, the only fight I had was with a gate guard and my arm hurt too much to swing a sword. I was stuck here listening to the people who had the real fun – and now my army didn't want to kill Mongols!

Sir Ryszard was one of few of the old nobility who actually believed in chivalry. His rank entitled him to command a battalion but he had accepted the leadership of a single komand in order to join the fight against the Mongols. He was a man who stayed faithful to his wife, his god, and his country no matter where he was. He was a competent warrior, a natural leader, and a man who made my teeth ache.

My jaws were so clenched that I had a hard time speaking, "You will tell the baron that he has three hours to reduce that compound or, by the God Above, I will burn and bombard it to rubble, no matter who is in it, and if we end up having a few less breeding age Mongols in the world, I will personally have a hard time finding tears for them."

He was scuttling out the door as I asked, "Has anyone heard from Sir Gorski?"

I spent another twenty minutes listening to reports and sending out orders, before my patience ran out. The medic had bandaged my broken ribs and taped extra padding over the one foot wide bruise on my chest.

This battle was not going to pass me by, but I wasn't sure where to go. The only good fighting was at the barracks, but someone needed to look over the dock area and see what the island fort was doing. The docks won out.

When the medic finished bandaging me, I had him help me back into my armor. It hurt like hell where it pressed on my right side and chest, but it was the price of command, so I rested my right arm on the back of my shield, and led my lance out to the docks.

A few people scurried from place to place, probably checking on family members or businesses, and small groups of our warriors were on the move. I saw a few Mongol and Chinese corpses, but there were fewer bodies no the street than usual in a battle zone, probably because of a speed of our attack didn't give the enemy time to spread out. In one store front, our surgeons were tending wounded soldiers.

I always found that odd about battles. In every battle that I have been in, there were hot spots and cold spots. I could be battling overwhelming odds in a fight to the death, so weary I was ready to lay down and die, and two hundred yards away, things would be so quiet a knight could enjoy a little wine and cheese. I could hear the fighting at the barracks, but here it was a stroll around town.

There were soldiers at the waterfront, and they weren't ours – or Mongols. In front of a couple of warehouses, men in crimson uniforms stood with crossbows, pikes, and a few muskets. They were Italian guardsmen working for the merchants. As we went by, a knight banner yelled out to them, "Get off the street, you idiots, there's a war going on!"

At the waterfront, one of my komanders had four of his six companies of mounted infantry dug on the beach in facing the river front. He kept two of his companies mounted and placed well out on the flanks, almost out of sight, in case the fort commander tried to bypass the beach.

The komander smiled when he saw me at his side, and handed me his field glasses. "Your grace, I think that you are just in time. After all of these hours, it looks like the morons in the fort are trying to find out what all the gunfire is about."

Sure enough, three boats were setting out from the fort. Each seemed to hold ten fighting men, the standard Mongol squad. "Have you any orders, your grace, on how to handle this?"

I shook my head. "You seem to be doing well, but I might suggest the Lost Legion tactic. The only thing scarier than seeing your buddies get blown to hell, is to never know what happened – to have them just disappear. Your men are so well dug in that the fort may not have seen them yet. You might pull back your men from the beach as soon as you can tell where they are going to land and then take them out of sight of the fort."

"A devilish idea, lord, if you will pardon me a moment." He dismounted and went toward the beach and I decided to pull my lance back out of sight as well. I stayed to watch thirty surprised Mongols meet their maker after they passed by our hidden warriors. Yes, we shot them in the back after they passed our positions, but as the western hero said, "Of course, I shot him in the back. His back was to me."

Then I left final instructions for the komander, "This will be your responsibility. If they do not send any more men over by evening, billet your men in one these warehouses and leave only watch on the beach. The men will fight better with sleep and we could have real fighting tomorrow. You know where the headquarters is. Send a messenger there if they come in force."

The word from the barracks was that everything was going slowly, but progressing, so I rode to Sir Ryszard's position. He was still wasting time taking pot shots at Mongols hunched behind the walls in a large courtyard, so I called him over for a conference. "Baron, I realize that you don't want to kill innocent people, but I need these men dead and I have an idea that will satisfy both of us. As I see it, most of the men are in that courtyard and on the rooftops of the building behind it. We assume that the women and children are in those connected buildings at the back of the courtyard.

"Now, you will bring over some cannon – I don't care where you get them - look on the palisade walls – and blow some holes in this side of that courtyard wall. Make an obvious escape route for anyone desperate enough to take it.

"Then, go about a block up wind of these buildings and start the biggest fires you can. The Mongols will see, smell, and hear the fire coming. When it gets too close, they will panic and try to escape. The opening you make will be the only obvious exit for warriors and civilians. Kill those armed or armored as they come through and capture the women and children."

We both knew that it wasn't going to work that cleanly, but it gave him an excuse to carry out the attack without being *immoral* and gave me a way to get him moving without humiliating him.

The rest of the battle was routine. The troops on the island never attempted to relieve the city. We eventually bombarded the fort with all of the Mongol cannon and ball we could salvage and reduced it to rubble, without expending a single item of our modern ammunition. We did loose some buildings and suffered a few casualties when they returned fire, but, eventually, we won the duel. When the final troops tried to leave the fort, we changed to grapeshot and continued firing. They were so demoralized that our invasion of the island a few days later was only a cleanup operation.

Sir Gorski showed up a few hours before dark, driving an angry mob of armed Mongols in front of him. He was damn near forcing the Mongols to flank us with a counter attack. Fortunately, the baron was able to send a Big Person ahead to warn us. By the time the Mongols got the gate, they were in crossfire from warriors firing from the homes that lined the road near the gate. Not one got through.

The baron did report that it would have been harder, but most of the Mongol horses and a few of their guards had died in a vicious wild animal attack several nights before.

Street patrols and house-to-house searches over the next two days led to small skirmishes, but the city was effectively ours the first day. As the fighting diminished, more troops were sent to the warehouse area with orders to billet there and maintain a tight blockade.

By the time night fell, my bodyguards had cleaned Batu's bedroom and set up my quarters in the former khan's palace. The bastard had converted to Islam, so there weren't any cigars or booze around and the servants, even the pretty maids, had all run away. I spent my victory night in a soft but cold bed comforted only by a little wine found in the Italian quarter and the warm bodies of my bodyguards snuggling on each side. Victory deserved more.

The next day, we got down to real work. The city was calm enough to allow a staff meeting. We met in the same town hall meeting room as the day before. The military part was quick and simple, but we needed to start working on the next part of our mission.

My original intent was to just sweep the grasslands, killing every horse we could find, since a Mongol without a horse was just a smelly little man with a bow and some arrows.

What we had learned during the trip caused me to rethink that decision. The Mongols were decades ahead of where they should be technologically, even considering that they had seen our equipment in Poland and the manufactory of the rifle we found indicated that they had conquered a large part of China and maybe even the Song dynasty. If so, they had plenty of resources and spare horses.

That meant that killing their horses and burning a few supply depots wasn't going to be enough to discourage them. We needed to make a big statement that it was dumb to screw with the Christian Army. After all, the Christian Army was basically a pacifistic organization, and the best way to get peace was to kick the crap out of your enemies.

We were going to have to go Mongolia, and since Mongol armies often moved in the winter, we had to go now.

The next day, I sent out an invitation to all of the trading houses to send representatives to at meeting a noon in the town hall. I might have saved my breath, most of them were already there bitching, complaining, moaning and demanding loudly. By the time we let them into the meeting hall, I had two large iron rings mounted about two meters high on one wall, with handcuffs hanging through the rings and whips hanging on the wall next to them.

I began the meeting as diplomatically as possible by shouting, "Shut the hell up! This meeting is not an open forum and there will be no question and answer period.

"I have no patience for traitors who trade with the Mongols and my first impulse is to lock you all up in your warehouses and set them on fire. Unfortunately, that would cause a certain amount of unpleasant talk back in Poland, so I am going to do business with you instead.

"By nightfall tonight, you will present my quartermaster with complete inventories of all of your trade goods and supplies. Tomorrow, he and his representatives will inspect the merchandise in every warehouse and store in this city. They will verify the accuracy of the inventories.

"As we have no time for lawsuits, courts, explanations, or recriminations, the penalties for lying to or misleading our representatives will be as follows: Any warehouseman guilty of lying to us will be cuffed to those rings you see on the wall to your left and be given twenty lashes. The merchant who employees him will be cuffed next to him for twenty lashes and the hidden merchandise will be confiscated without payment.

"Over the next two days, we will decide what supplies we will purchase from you. If anything you have is of value to us, we will pay full value plus a seventy-five percent inconvenience fee.

"The payment will be in zinc chits on the accounts of the Christian Army and will be redeemable for immediate cash at full value at any of our outposts."

There was an uproar at the mention of *chits*. "Gentlemen, gentlemen, I know you would prefer gold, but a chit on the Christian Army is as good as gold anywhere in the world, and you are being paid well for the inconvenience of visiting one of our offices. Of course, if you prefer, we can just burn everything here as contraband found in a Mongol town, but I think this is better.

"I suggest that you hope we like your merchandise. Anything that we do not purchase and which is deemed to have value to the Mongols will be burned without recompense.

"As I said, there are no questions. You have about seven hours to produce your inventories and bring them to this room.

"I suggest you hurry. Dismissed."

I should tell you how much I regretted having to ride roughshod over the merchants, but I'd be lying. We needed stuff in a hurry, and I didn't need arguments, and sometimes it feels good to just cut through the crap and get people to do what you want.

We spent the afternoon discussing what we needed. Eventually, we listed the absolute minimum that we had to have and decided we would scan the inventories for opportunities.

Fifty five thousand warm coats (one per man plus spares)

Ninety thousand pairs of gloves (two pair per man)

Ninety thousand pairs of warm socks. Christian Army boots are waterproof and strong but lightly insulated for a Mongolian winter

At least four thousand tons of food. (Four pounds per man for forty-five days)

Axes, shovels and other hand tools for the engineers

All of the explosives that the Mongol garrison had. (Black powder was weak stuff and useless for our guns, but it made decent blasting powder for the engineers and was useful in grenades.)

Cooking pots for forty-five thousand men. We would be out of canned food in less than three weeks and then we have to cook. In fact, we would be cooking from the start and saving the canned goods for later.

Several thousand board feet of lumber for the engineers. We wouldn't see a tree for a while and they needed something to build with.

Wagons for most of the food, all of the powder, all of the cooking pots and whatever else we were taking.

Fuel for cooking.

The great grass sea was short on fuel and we didn't have time to scrounge for enough dried animal droppings to fix dinner.

The wagons were going to be a problem. We were going to need several thousand and every one was going to be a boat anchor slowing us down. Unburdened, the Big People are fast. Mongolia was about thirty-five hundred miles east of us. Silver and I could be there in less than two weeks, and be dead in fourteen days since we'd only have my sword, a rifle, and a day's worth of food left. If the first fifty Mongols we met didn't kill me, I'd starve on the way home.

So, we had to go packing a lot of gear.

We were already down to a hundred miles a day because no matter how good your engine is, there are no roads around here and the wagons can take only so much jostling. A radio cart dragged over rough ground at thirty miles an hour is soon a cartload of broken tubes.

This was a major caravan route and there were thousands of wagons in town, all of them 12th century wagons designed to move about one mile an hour. Half of them didn't even have pivoting front axles.

I had no idea how we would use them, and decided it was stupid to speculate without all the facts, so I called in Sir Eikmann, a komander of engineers. "In a few days, we are going to leave here with at least four thousand tons more food than we have now and probably two thousand tons of engineering supplies, clothes, cook pots, ammo, and miscellaneous stuff. By tomorrow, I need you to tell me how to do it.

"I suggest that you send your best men out immediately to canvas all of the available wagons. Figure out what you can modify to keep up with us and let me know tomorrow morning, no, tomorrow noon how you're going to pull it off."

In the old days, I would have pulled out a drawing board and done it myself, but that's what staff is for, and I had trained a good one.

By morning, the inventories were in. In addition to the quartermaster, only myself, the two counts, the heads of artillery and engineers, and their assistants were present. The rest of the officers were still busy with cleanup skirmishes, and the thousand details of bivouacking and feeding their men and handling police duties.

We had well over a hundred pages of inventory in front of us, and I had forgotten to specify that they had to be in Polish, so many of the merchants had prepared the lists in Italian, Dutch, or Byzantine Greek, and one bastard turned in a list in Chinese. I was tempted to pillory the bastard just for being a smartass, but I settled for sending a messenger to find the merchant and make him come in NOW for translation.

The rest of the lists we divided up by language and started going through them. As we went through the assistants translated the descriptions into Polish and made margin notes.

One of Sir Eikmann's assistants made the first find. "Merchant out of Novgorod, has twenty-four thousand fur coats, mostly bear, in stock. In transit to a company in Constantinople.

We soon realized that there was no list of Mongol military supplies. I had forgotten that there were no living Mongol officers. I sent one of my assistants out to find at least a company of men to search the city for Mongol material. It was a big place for a medieval city, and three hundred men wouldn't be enough to cover it in one day. We also sent out a command for all personnel to be on the lookout for military stores and to report any found to my office.

The traditional personal looting would have to wait for later. The men didn't have space for much booty anyway.

Food wouldn't be so easy. When we left the railroad, we stepped back into the 13th century. Without 747s and steamships, food was pretty much a local matter and I didn't expect to find a lot of it in the warehouses. Eight hundred years earlier, Romans in Italy fed on rice and wheat from Egypt and the Romans in York fried in olive oil from Lebanon, but they had better roads, fewer bandits, fewer borders, and much better wagons.

I had no compunction about raiding the city stores and stripping every farm in the area. It was certainly less trouble than the Mongols brought with them. However, it was time-consuming to go from farm to farm packing up barnloads of food, and I was short on time.

87

Fortunately, rice was still considered a luxury food in Europe, worth importing from North Africa, so there were two shiploads of it on storage. That gave us about a thousand tons of rice, and there were plenty of spices to go on it. Nutmeg, pepper, cinnamon, cloves, and salt were all luxury goods worth shipping. I noticed dried fruit, nuts, and other items on the inventories. We might get most of what we needed.

We ate while we worked when the staff brought in platters of roasted mystery meat, bread, and beer. The canned goods would have to be kept for the trip. By noon, all of the lists were translated and we were through a hundred pages of inventory. We'd found most of the supplies we would need. We had found another ten thousand coats, enough blankets to make another ten or fifteen thousand ponchos, twenty tons of lumber, two thousand axes, five thousand shovels, and almost two thousand saws. We were still desperately short of food and clothes, but it was enough to survive on.

There were a thousand other things we'd like to have, everything from tent canvas to rope to cooking pots, but that could be left to the Sir Eikmann's engineers and the Quartermaster Corps to pick out.

During lunch, we discussed strategy. We decided that anyone that we did not find a coat for would be issued two extra wool blankets and sewing supplies. The men could turn than into simple ponchos in a few minutes and then improve them with sleeves, buttons, and hoods during their down time. The spare wool from cutting the blankets down could be used for mittens or boot padding.

Sir Wladyclaw suggested that we find local talent to sew for the men. I agreed it was a good idea, but since the population was pretty much in hiding, I didn't have much faith in the plan.

After lunch, we sent all of the assistants away. The quartermaster staff would set up a central office where they and the other staff could examine the thirty pages of inventory that we skipped, and where they could receive reports from the field.

Then we got down to the most important problem: how to move all the supplies. By this time, I know that I could handle almost anything. If we ran out of artillery, I'd build trebuchet out of tree logs and fire boulders at the enemy. No ammo, we'd build crossbows and puncture the enemy to death. We could handle almost anything, but the nearest place to get a pneumatic tire was a thousand miles west, and you can't build a good shock absorber out of a tree trunk. We needed to move at least a hundred tons of stuff three thousand miles in thirty days.

Sir Wladyclaw, Captain Ivanov, and I looked expectantly at Sir Eikmann. He shuffled papers for a few moments. "We don't have a final answer yet. We're good, but we've had less than a day to work on it. First, we may have a partial solution." Looking at me, he asked, "Lord, may I ask what is the *real* capacity of our carts is? Oh, I know that the manual says that they can handle twelve tons each, but I also know that every cart carries two complete spare wheels with tires underneath and that there's two sets of spare harnesses in every cart."

"What does that have to do with anything?"

"I know that you personally designed the basic army cart and I've seen your other designs. You, lord, believe in reliability, strength, simplicity, and spare tires.

"That tells me there's a big safety margin in the design. I believe we can safely load the carts to at least fourteen tons and maybe a little more."

He was a smart little bastard, and I hate having other people analyze me, especially if they're right. "There is a safety margin. I had them tested up to fifteen tons, but the carts tend to waddle and vibrate when they get over twelve tons, and they stress the track too much in rail mode."

He had the good manners, or enough regard for his own safety, not to wear a knowing smile. "That's about what I suspected. That's our first resource. We have about six thousand standard carts with us. They were all loaded close to capacity when we set out, but we have been eating, drinking, and shooting for about three weeks. So, we've burned off part of the weight. With an extra two tons per wagon and filling in all of the space we've emptied, that will give us about fifteen thousand tons of capacity.

"After that, we have to look at local resources and the news is not as good there.

"Over by the north palisade, there is about a square mile of wagons. This is major caravan terminus with thousands of wagons and over a hundred repair businesses. Unfortunately most of them are totally useless for us.

"Your grace, you specified that we will be doing over a hundred miles a day, so we need wagons that can handle eight miles an hour over unprepared grasslands. That's about four times the speed that most of these wagons were designed for.

"The most common are European wagons and they are totally useless. It's just like the crap we had in Poland twenty years ago. They don't even have steerable front axles. They just use oxen to drag them around corners. All of the bearings are wood on wood splashed with lots of grease. When they do have suspension, it's chains. We'd be better off carrying stuff on our backs.

"The second type might be useable. There are over a thousand two-wheeled wagons around. The locals and the merchants both use them for smaller loads. The wheels are larger than the four-wheeled wagons and they're built stronger. They derive from farm wagons so they're crude and heavy ox carts and some don't have any suspension at all. Some have solid wooden wheels, but if we band them with iron, they'd probably hold up. Given a little time, we could reinforce the boxes, add tops, and make them useable. Problem is that they only hold about two or three tons and they're going to ride rough. You don't want to put the family china in one.

"I did see a couple of Byzantine wagons parked out there, and the boys are out looking for more. They are almost identical to the Roman wagons from a thousand years ago and a real find. They're closed boxes with steerable front axles and a leather suspension. The axles and running gear are wood, but there are iron bearings on all the moving parts. I would estimate that they hold over five tons of cargo. I don't know if they can handle the speed without some modifications, but they're our best bet. It's strange that a thousand-year old Roman design is the most modern thing around.

"We also saw a few hundred Chinese wagons. They seem to be similar in quality to the Byzantine design, but we haven't had time to evaluate them yet."

My patience was growing thin, "Sir Eikmann, time is the one thing we don't have. You keep talking about modifying hundreds of wagons. That could take weeks and if we aren't on the road in a few days, the road will end in our graves."

He didn't back down, "Your grace, if we can't feed the troops, it will be a grave full of starving men, and I do have a plan to do the modifications quickly."

He was, of course, right again. Over the next few months, Sir Eikmann and I would save each others lives more than once and I would promote and reward him generously - but you can understand why I would never like him. He went on confidently, "I've got several teams of grunts out counting and listing wagons. We're limiting ourselves to the types in the main yards, because we don't have time to go from house to house looking for wagons.

"I've already got, as of an hour ago, five teams of engineers working over farm wagons and five working on Byzantine models. They are being helped by the owners of the ten repair shops we paid generously to help us.

"If we find enough of the Chinese models or any other promising types, we'll start doing the same for them.

"I'm certain that by the end of the day we will have complete plans for at least the farm models and soon after the modifications on the Byzantines.

"Then, tomorrow, we find every wagon repairman in this caravan town and get them down to the wagon yards. We demonstrate the modifications and offer them triple the usual pay rate for each wagon they modify and deliver. We'll pay them with that good Mongol gold we liberated and provide every shop with all of the extra craftsmen we can find in the Christian Army. Our boys are pretty handy bunch.

"There are over a hundred wagon repair shops in this town. With the incentive pay, the help, a simple upgrade plan, and clear instructions we could get as many as five hundred to a thousand carts ready every day.

"We could be ready to go in a week."

Silently, I calculated Murphy's Time Factor into that week and decided it the week would be at least ten days long, but it was the best plan we had.

"I'll have an order prepared for the purser instructing him that you have unlimited use of any captured gold and a general order giving you the authority to co-opt any soldier not engaged in combat or scavenging for the quartermaster.

"Now, gentlemen, I think that we have made a good start. I will be available whenever you need me, and I expect to be kept informed of your progress, but now I have a long trip to prepare for.

"Unless there are other items we need to discuss, this meeting is adjourned."

There were difficult to decisions that only I could make, and I lot of them I didn't like.

We had several hundred Chinese prisoners. They weren't a big problem. Most of them didn't want to work for the Mongols and refused to fight as soon as they found out they could surrender. The ones not smart enough to hide out or run for the hills were housed in a couple of surviving barracks and lightly guarded.

We were burdened with twenty-two Mongol officers that had been captured before they had a chance to fight to the death, and my inexperienced troops had allowed over two hundred Mongol fighters to surrender – against my orders.

The officers were no problem. No one felt sorry for enemy officers. This afternoon I would declare them guilty of war crimes and have them executed. The Mongol soldiers were a problem. Ordering an army like the Christian Army to carry out mass executions could hurt morale. Even Hitler had learned that the hard way. The Wehrmacht carried out his orders to execute every Jew they found for only a few months before morale dropped precipitously and they refused to do more executions. Noble soldiers see a difference between killing in combat and killing civilians and I had built a noble Christian army.

I decided to recruit the Chinese soldiers to carry out the executions of the Mongol soldiers because they would probably enjoy doing it as much as I would enjoy ordering it. After all, morality applies only to people and these were Mongols.

Before I returned to my temporary palace, I penned an order for all foreign merchants and all warehouse owners, or their representatives, to present themselves two hours after dawn each morning at the city hall for orders and questions.

I also sent out orders: all komanders were to identify Mandarin-speaking troops and send them to the city hall tomorrow morning for translation duties; detailed my adjutant for find whatever passed for a real estate agent in this town; and, find out what a fully equipped wagon repair shop was worth. The last item was a personal note to Captain Ivanov reminding him to fill at least one of the wagons with wine for our staff meetings and rugs for the executive tent. I also needed a new tent and one or two wagons for it. If one couldn't be found ready-made, we would have to scrounge material for it.

I ate what my men ate, went were they went, recited the oath every morning, and curried my own Big Person, but in this world a leader had to keep up appearances. My tent also functioned as a meeting hall and a sleeping quarters for my bodyguards. I also needed something to sleep on.

Of course, I didn't go straight home. There's no replacement for eyes on the environment. I visited one of the shops working on the farm wagons, gave personal greetings to some of the troopers, and stopped by to watch the cannon firing at the island forts. Then, I went home to a nice warm bed and a pair of warmer bodyguards.

My first job in the morning was to find our guides. We could hire professional merchant guides easily, and we would get a few, but they were business men who might bolt at the first sign of trouble.

I decided to recruit some of the Chinese troops who might want to go home. As our Chinese-speaking troopers straggled in, they were sent to the barracks to interview Chinese troops who claimed they knew the way and either spoke Polish or seemed smart enough to learn it.

Once a candidate pool was selected, they would be put though the usual procedures. We were short of Big People and I didn't trust the Chinese in battle anyway, so they would be mounted on Big People who were pulling carts and had no current partners. If selected and passed by a Big Person, they would be uniformed, mounted, given the oath, taught how to care for their partners, and be sent to school.

Until we left, they would spend ten hours a day learning pigeon. A guide isn't much good unless he can say, "Go past the river," "Turn Left," and "Look out for that damned big avalanche!"

Sir Eikmann was as good as his word. Before noon, he had gathered all the wagon repairmen in the parking yard and shown them the conversion he wanted made on the two-wheeled wagons. He specified a heavy iron tire and iron crossbars be added to each wheel. Seen from the side, each wheel ended up looking like a tic-tac-toe pattern inside an iron circle.

Since most of the utility wagons had slat sides instead of boxes, he lined the box with two layers of canvas and made a quick and simple cover to weatherproof it. There was lots of canvas available. The first three hundred conversions would even have iron sleeves in place of wood bearings in the wheels since his staff had found that many sleeve sets in storage.

The first conversions rolled over to the warehouses before the end of the day. They had to compete for loading space with our regular carts that were already being re-loaded.

The city was awakened that morning by Sir Ivanov's men blasting a hole in the palisade near the docks. When they filled in the moat at that spot, our returning carts were able to enter the city right at the warehouse district, drive straight to the warehouses, load up, make a left turn, and proceed straight out the East Gate to our campgrounds.

I watched the loading for a while until I realized that planning and overseeing the loading was a matter for a hundred officers to manage, and they didn't need my help.

They also didn't need me at the merchants meeting where my staff laid out the instructions for cashing our vouchers, and arranged individual meetings to go over inventory lists, and agree on prices. We agreed to some pretty good prices.

It looked as if we actually might make our one week deadline.

I had made my decision about Sarai even before we attacked the city. I had a flyer printed up and on the morning of the seventh day, it was introduced at the merchants meeting.

"Gentlemen, the Christian Army will leave this city during the daylight hours tomorrow. Unfortunately, this city has great political and strategic importance to the Mongols. This is where the Russian princes and all other vassal states come to pay their taxes, do obeisance, and get their patents to rule validated. It is a great symbol of their power.

"It also holds a population of tens of thousands of Mongols, and their subjects, which makes it a dangerous place to have behind us.

"In this situation, the Mongols have consistently followed a simple plan: massacre the population and burn the city to the ground.

"We are not Mongols, so the population will not be slaughtered. However, we cannot allow this city to continue to exist.

"Therefore, today we will distribute the flyers that my aide is passing out to you now. In four languages, it reads:

The Christian Army will leave this city tomorrow and that the city will be burned when we leave.

All citizens are warned to leave as soon as possible. They can take anything with them except muskets and bows and may go anywhere they want, but they must leave.

"We will not torch the foreign compounds, the docks, or your warehouses but neither will we be able to assist with fire fighting, I suggest that you spend the next twenty four-hours preparing fire breaks, filling barrels with water, getting your boats loaded and underway, moving your merchandise out of the city, or doing whatever else you can to prepare for a fire storm.

"On a personal note, I remind you that merchandise can be replaced and wealth is only temporary, but your families are forever. I suggest you look to your families first."

The meeting immediately split into two halves. Half the men ran for the door to warn their people and the other half jumped up screaming that I couldn't do it. I left my aide to quiet them down.

Of course I could do it. I didn't bother to explain that the only reason we weren't torching their property directly was that King Henryk wouldn't like all the complaints from European governments. I would just as soon put all the Mongol-trading, treacherous bastards into their warehouses and then burn them down.

There were a few other details to handle. Before we left, I met with Eikmann and Ivanov again.

"Gentlemen, you've done an excellent job getting us ready to go. Now before the general panic paralyzes the streets I have one last job for you. I had my aide estimate the fair value of a wagon repair shop on the second day we were here.

"I want your men, Sir Eikmann, to contact all of the shops that helped you and pay them double the value for their businesses in Mongol gold.

"As much as we want to impress upon people that helping or working with Mongols is dangerous, we also need to prove that we stick by our friends.

"Sir Ivanov, please do the same for any local businesses that have volunteered, and I emphasize *volunteered*, helped, or sold us supplies. You don't have to do anything with the foreign merchants or businesses because they have been paid well in army scrip, but the Christian Army rewards its friends."

Of course, part of the reason for my generosity was that we had more damned gold then we could carry. Sarai was where the Russian princes paid their annual tributes and we found several tons of gold in the vaults. Most national treasuries had less gold than we did.

I had already shipped over a ton of gold down the Volga with Sir Willard in the *Wanderwind* and still had more than I wanted to drag to Mongolia. Normally I would take every ounce with me because it was easier to drag one ounce of gold than the months of food that it could purchase for a warrior, but there weren't many stores between here and Mongolia.

Meantime, Gorski and Krol were firming up their plans to burn the city. It required a lot of planning. Miss's O'Leary's cow got lucky. It's hard to burn a city. Sarai was about twenty square miles of buildings, walls, and roads, and we weren't going to be able to burn it all. I needed to burn enough to make certain that no one wanted to rebuilt here and that took planning.

The two barons had divided the town and were planning the routes their troopers would take to fire the place. Sir Ryszard was in charge of warning the population. If he didn't like killing Mongols, he could take the job of getting them to leave. I know he would fail. No matter how much we warned them, some would refuse to leave out of disbelief, stubbornness, or just plain stupidity. I considered it a practical demonstration of Darwinism that wouldn't affect my sleep at all.

The day of our departure, I was sitting on Silver's back in the town square, flanked by Gorski and Krol. The bulk of our forces and all of our wagons were fifty miles away in our new camp on the grasslands.

I leaned down for a torch, lit the two red and gold flares that would signal the fire starters to commence their runs, and then tossed my torch through the open door of the city hall. As we galloped for the city gates, Sir Krol called out from my left side, "Lord, isn't this a strange way to burn a city? Don't we usually just burst in with guns blazing and swords flashing and toss torches as we go?

I yelled back, "Yes, but we don't usually go shopping first."

From the Secret Journal of Su Song, Part Three

It has been eight months since we began dissecting the artifacts and the time for our report to the khan has come and gone without a visit from our leader. He has been on his annual campaign against my old masters, the Song Dynasty, south of here. The reports are that the campaign has been a frustrating one.

The Song Empire is an advanced county with a large population. They fight with fire lances and have thousands of well-trained crossbowmen for every battle. After generations of fighting invaders, their cities are well walled and they do not act as foolishly as the Europeans who would leave the safety of their cities to meet my masters' people out on the open plain. When attacked, they retreat to their fortresses and shower the invaders with gun powder grenades and use trebuchets to lob gunpowder bombs and pots of boiling oil. The larger cities fire scrap metal and rock balls from cannon placed on the walls.

The khan may someday conquer them, but the campaign will take decades rather than months, and I suspect that he will have to wait until the loses in the European campaign are replaced. His people have never been as numerous as his enemies and there were too many deaths to ignore in Poland. Our progress in his absence has been good on many fronts. I suspect that the most powerful things we have learned are from the war kite and the tracked wagons, but the khan will be most interested in the guns. He is still a warrior at heart and horses, women, dogs, and weapons are his loves.

It has been close. We realized within a few weeks that the Polish guns would be of little use to the mounted Mongol army. The damned things needed an alcohol lamp burning constantly. Even if we made them small enough for horseback, the lamp would be a problem and the ammunition would be prohibitively expensive to make.

The first ten copies we made were useless because they leaked like fish nets. It took our most skilled craftsmen weeks to make each mechanism with enough precision to fire repeatedly. Learning to make the ammunition took several chemists, several expert brass workers, two fireworks technicians, and too much time. Now that we knew how to make them, each bullet still takes much longer to make than even an armor piercing arrow.

I am certain that the Poles have cheaper manufacturing methods that make the guns practical, but for now, they are not good enough to make the khan happy.

I am proud of the fact that we have done as well as we have. Imagine if a Polish craftsman had found one of our bows lost in battle. He would have in his hands the most powerful weapon in the world, but he would also have a problem. He could see that one layer was made of sinew, but he couldn't know that wild antelope sinew was much stronger than sinew from farm animals, until he spent years experimenting. He would have the same problem with the glue. He could see it was animal glue, but how would he know that only fish based glue would be strong enough for battle use, and if he did, how would he learn to make the glue?

There are at least fifty steps in making one of our bows, and even if you know them, it takes over a year and a half to construct and age a proper bow. It would be years before the Poles could make a decent one.

We had copied their work in less than a year and then found out that it was not good enough for us. We needed to do more than tell the khan that the Polish guns would be limited in their usefulness to him.

We did come up with an answer. The imminent threat of losing face, literally, while it is still attached to your head, is an effective motivation but, even so, it was a close thing and we only firmed up the design weeks before the meeting.

Someone on the staff had the inspiration to turn the simplest weapon on the battlefield into the most effective, using what we had learned from the Polish weapons. The most advanced personal weapons on the battlefield were the Mongol bows, but the most kills were made with crossbows.

The horsemen are the shock troops, but the backbone of an army is the crossbowman. While the bow takes years to master, a crossbowman can be trained in few months, and crossbows are relatively cheap. The problem with the crossbow is that its range is limited to the power one man can pull and it can only fire until the bowman's arm wears out.

Tan Li, one of our casting experts who worked with cannon, came up with the solution. Before joining us, he had been working on hand cannons. Every army had a few, but they were almost useless. They fired about once a minute and were so inaccurate that you weren't certain which army you were going to hit.

However, he loved his useless noisemakers and in his mind, he kept overlaying his visions of hand cannon with visions of the Polish guns. First, he realized that if we used something like the Polish bullet, packaged ammunition, it might be fired as fast as a crossbow. If you made it a little smaller and lighter than the Polish gun, it could be fired from the shoulder like a crossbow. You could even use something like the crossbow stock and trigger mechanism.

As for accuracy, we had already learned that the twists in the Polish barrels spun the bullets and made them more accurate.

When he brought the idea to me, I assigned an army of technicians to work with him, night and day. The reality was much more difficult than his vision. The basic design was sketched up in a day, and redrawn day after day until we had something that looked like it would work. We settled on a barrel that would be about three *chi* long and which would set on a crossbow frame. We already knew how to make cannon barrels and producing some long skinny ones with spinning grooves was a lot easier than getting a gas tight seal on a complex sliding bolt.

The main problem was ignition. Even the first model loaded easily. The powder and ball were packed in a rice paper tube. When the tube hit the bottom of the barrel, it broke, exposing the gunpowder for lighting.

The first model had a lighting hole in the top. The gunner just struck a match on a rough place on the barrel and touched it to hole to fire the gun. It worked the first time, but there were problems. Matches have been around for a long time, but the reliability has never been good. Worse yet, when they did work, the gunner often ended up with burnt fingers from the flash of the touch hole. The standard match was too short, and if you made it longer, the flex in the wood made it even less reliable.

Our next try used match cord from a cannon. We built up a funnel around the touch hole to guide a hot cotton cord. Instead of clipping the cord onto a stick and guiding it to the touch hole manually, the cord was clipped into the mouth of a small, curved metal dragon. We used a crossbow mechanism to tilt the dragon and lower the cord into the hole.

It worked great, sort of. Unfortunately, the touch hole was on top of the gun, right on the sight line of the gunner, and the flash and the thick smoke blowing out of the touch hole was enough to blind a man. If we rotated the touch hole to the side, we weren't able to get a smooth action on the dragon head and the cord tended to drop away from the hole.

Our third try was better. We went back to the Polish gun for inspiration. They were using a fuse that they lit with a lamp. Our fireworks expert reproduced a similar fast burning fuse, but made it thicker and much stiffer. It was a little stick about as long as a thumb, skinny on one end and fatter at the end you held. We glued one to each ammunition package.

We then turned the barrel on its side and added a small trough to the bottom side of the funnel to steady a fuse. To fire the gun you ripped the fuse off the paper package, rammed the package into the barrel, and stuck the fuse into the touch hole. Then you shouldered the weapon and fired with the match cord.

It worked well. Using the fuse sticking out of the side, the touch hole could be much smaller than the cord, so we dramatically reduced smoke and flash and got a considerable boost in power. We could get four shots a minute with a little practice and the rifled barrel was accurate to over two *li*, three times the range of the standard crossbow.

I actually had hope that we might live past the khan's visit.

Even when not on campaign, he traveled constantly, moving with the seasons from palace to palace with a large retinue of advisors, guards, and servants. We prepared an opulent audience room well in advance of his visit. As soon as he was seated and the honorifics said we presented him with two brand new Polish-style guns replete with engraved brass plates and decorative gold bands. On one side, the engraved plate showed a hunting scene featuring him on his great horse, and on the other, his traditional nomadic tent surrounded by images of conquered peoples.

As he fondled his new toy, I said "That is a fine weapon, and we can provide them for all of your bodyguards, but, as you know, they are useless on horseback because of the alcohol lamp, which may be why the Poles only used them for defense.

"In six months, we can provide weapons for all of your bodyguards, and if we use every trained steel artisan in your domains, we could produce about five hundred weapons in the next year."

He looked unhappy enough to make my neck twinge for fear of being detached. Fortunately, if the topic was interesting, he was willing to listen to longer explanations.

"The Polish guns have to be made by creating forged steel blocks and then filing and lapping each block into an intricate, gas-tight part. It's even harder than producing one of our recurve bows, and, as you know, it takes well over a year to produce each bow. We only have hundreds of thousands of them because we have thousands of craftsmen able to make them.

"However, we have learned enough from Polish guns to craft a new type of gun that we can make in sufficient quantities to be useful on your next campaign."

I think the phrase *new gun* cheered him up. He was interested enough to ask, "And what does this new weapon look like?"

I motioned to the assistants kneeling near the khan. The each lifted a long narrow wooded box and shuffled forward on their knees. Each box was polished walnut with brass hinges and decorated with semi-precious stones and lacquered paintings.

When the khan opened them, he found a gleaming bronze gun in one box and a polished steel one in the other. Each box also held a small bandolier of bullets and a cleaning kit. As with the Polish replicas, each gun was decorated with hunting and battle scenes on gleaming engraved brass plates and resplendent with gold trim everywhere we could find an excuse for it. He was fascinated by them. He turned them over and over in his hands, raised them to his shoulder, pointed them at people in the room, pretended to fire them, and examined them again.

"How well do they work?"

"They will fire about four or five times a minute, and can kill at three or four times the range of a crossbow. We have a demonstration range set up outside where we can show you how they work."

The rest of the day went perfectly. The demonstration area was deliberately set up about two *li* from our central building to show off our new rail car system. We had built a one *li* circle of track out to the range and back and built a rail car to look as much as possible like the royal coach, same size, similar decorations, gold plate all over to simulate the gold fixtures on the real coach. It was, of course, a little wider and we added a platform to the rear of the car where bodyguards could stand. We added a glass front window and made the door windows much larger so that the khan could see how fast he was moving.

The khan loved it. Virtually every existing form of transportation except river boats is painful and uncomfortable. The best coaches sway and bounce along the roads, horses require a well-padded or well-hardened butt, and even palanquins sway with the steps of the carriers. This time two jet black horses pulled him to the range in a few minutes with all the comfort of a flying carpet.

Behind him, a single horse pulled each of the eighteen-man cars holding his retinue.

At the range, we had man-sized targets set up about sixty *bu* from a firing table. The khan watched while we did volley fire with our ten muskets. Five would fire and then load while the other five fired. We did about eight volleys in a minute and the targets fell over with satisfying regularity. We did very well considering that guards held naked swords over the heads of anyone handling a weapon in the presence of the khan.

After a few minutes, he wanted to try out all of his new guns. He already had experience with his Polish gun, so he wanted to try the new ones. The gunners loaded his two new guns and then placed their ten guns loaded on the table in front of him. He fired about twenty rounds at targets placed so close together that he had to hit something. Then he called over his military advisors and they all blazed away. The gunners kept a steady supply of loaded guns ready, but both the khan and one of his advisors insisted on learning how to load their own guns – once.

They stopped for food and wine, examined the guns in detail and then did some more target practice. I was beginning to fear that we would run out of powder when he called a halt. He was still grinning but even a Mongol can stand only so much smoke and noise.

On the loop back, he had me ride in his rail car while he quizzed me on costs and production schedules. As we left the car, he congratulated me on the smooth ride. I thanked him profusely for the compliment and then mentioned that these cars were the secret that let the Poles always have reinforcements and supplies everywhere we attacked.

Back at the compound, he looked over the battle kite were making, inquired about the Devil's Breath which we had not had much success with and marveled at the tiny model steam engines. We didn't yet have satisfactory full-sized engines ready, but he loved the little lamp driven toys we build for research. We presented him and several of his advisors with the toys.

Before he left, he insisted on several more rides around the track. We removed the staff cars from the track so his coach could run free. He and his advisors laughed it up on the padded seats, leaned out the windows to feel the wind, drank wine just to see it not spill and acted like kids. Then they had more horses hitched up to see how fast they could make it go. At one point, he had his coach removed and put an open staff car back on the track so they could feel the wind while they rode around and around.

He left happy.

Across the Sea of Grass

The first week out of Sarai was an easy one. We camped about fifty miles east of the city on the first night. That was far enough to outpace any refugees from the city and kept us from listening to recriminations, complaints, and demands for help.

By the time I lead my column into camp, the tents were set up and the cook fires burning. My new tent was near the center of the encampment and my new bed already warmed by my bodyguards.

Captain Ivanov had been sending supply columns into the grasslands for the last five days we were in Sarai. As the advance scouts confirmed our belief that there weren't any mounted Mongols left in the vicinity, he became bolder at sending out advance parties.

As the older wagons were loaded with food and fuel, they were grouped with a lance or two and sent out to set up base camps ninety to a hundred miles apart. The old wagons couldn't stand the speed our column marched at, but with a five-day head start and running fifteen hours a day, they were able to keep up for a while.

It was three thousand five hundred more miles to Karakorum, and I wanted to be there in forty days. It looked like the first thousand miles was going to be an easy ten-day ride.

As I leaned back in my saddle, I was feeling confident. My army might look a little odd with most of them carrying or wearing bear skin coats and the rest wearing hooded wool coats that looked like they belonged in a manger scene, but morale was high and eating was good.

The shopping trip was a success and we had enough supplies, barely, to get us to our destination. I even had a new tent and a barrel of wine for staff meetings and quiet evenings.

We had lost only a little over two hundred killed and about seven hundred wounded at Sarai, and we disposed of around thirty thousand Mongol troops. That's a kill ratio of fifty-to-one. At that rate, we could stand up to a Mongol force of two million men.

Of course, not everything was perfect. Hitler's army had killed over fifty Russians for every German soldier who fell, and we all know how well that worked out.

There was also a distinct chill in the air. I thought it was the middle of October, but it could have been either the beginning or end of the month. I knew the date, but it was wrong. The world was still using the Julian calendar and I knew enough history to know that it was off by about ten days from the real year now, but I didn't remember if the calendar ran fast or slow.

My conversations with Sir Piotr had been frustrating. I had left the Holy Land over-supplied for a quick horse killing raid and ended up critically short of ammo, weapons, artillery, and supplies for a raid that has now turned more serious. It still wasn't an invasion, but we would probably be in at least one pitched battle.

We were just over one thousand miles from Crakow. In the 20th century, I could hop in my car before breakfast and sleep that night in my own bed in Poland. In the 13th century, I might as well have been on another planet. We were weeks away from reinforcements and months away from heavy equipment supplies.

Sir Piotr was sympathetic when we spoke on the radio.

"Your grace, the only fast enough to get to you is an aircraft, but our standard fighter has a range of only three hundred miles and can't carry anything heavier than the pilot's lunch.

"You may remember that Novacek and I both recommended that development of multi-engine, metal aircraft be initiated, and you firmly insisted that it was a bad idea."

"And I still feel the same way. Those aircraft need high-octane fuel and a lot of spare parts. Until we have depots around the world, they are going be of limited use. It's better to put our resources into better railroads and harbors for now."

"You are almost fortunate, Lord Conrad, that in your absence we felt that we had to use our own best judgment as to what programs to continue. Thanks to your efforts and those of Sir Boris, the Christian Army does not have to be selective about what programs it funds. There are three prototypes of a new twin-engine cargo aircraft sitting in a hangar in Warsaw.

"It has not completed testing and only the prototypes are available, but it does have a normal range of fifteen hundred miles and can be flown almost twice that far if the cargo is replaced with spare fuel tanks.

"I say *almost* lucky because you are already at the extreme range of the aircraft. From where you are now, we could possibly provide you with a ride home or deliver a few hundred pounds of cargo, but in a few days, even that will be impossible.

"If we had begun sooner, there might be enough planes available to create a supply chain, but the best I can do now is to suggest that with Herculean effort we could begin to turn out a steady supply of the planes in less than two months."

It had come to the point where I was no longer surprised that Sir Piotr was thinking ahead of me. Perhaps I was getting too old for the game of Save the World. "The new planes were a good idea, but they won't help me. I fully plan that in thirty days we will be in combat or on our way home, but I'll keep it in mind in case need something both vital and light weight, such as radio parts or medical supplies."

"You are probably right, your grace, but I will put a team on the problem of getting some supplies and air cover out to you. Maybe they can find a way to stage out supplies with three or four planes, or find alternate routes, or something to get help to you."

I had the feeling that I was not only on my own, but going to stay that way.

Betrayal. Dirty, Rotten Betrayal

Francine's Diary

It was a busy day at court today. Both the Italian and the Dutch ambassadors were seen in open court. The Italian ambassador was particularly livid, "MY BROTHER'S WIFE! The bastards raped my sister-in-law! She'll probably spend the rest of her life in a convent! If they couldn't tell she wasn't Mongol from her looks and her language, the lack of SMELL should have told them. If it weren't for your Christian Army, this would be war, and there will be repercussions in spite of them."

He went on for a while about treaties being meaningless and rights of passage being revoked and so on, and the Greek ambassador was just as angry, "One hundred thousand guilders! They burned one hundred thousand gilders of merchandise and three warehouses. We lost a half-dozen men fighting the fires. Who is going to pay for this?"

The king raised a weary hand and said, "There will be reparations. The Christian army will repay you the entire cost of the damage, and provide pensions for the families of them who died. Isn't that right, Sir Piotr?"

Sir Piotr had stood with head down during the entire audience and still did not look up, "As Your Majesty commands, we obey."

King Henryk waited until the ambassadors left before he continued rather angrily, "By the way, Sir Piotr, where the hell is Sarai and what is Conrad doing there? I don't seem to remember authorizing any new expeditions. Last I remember, I ordered him to invade the Holy Land three years ago and he responded by disappearing for a year, and then showing up to the battle late with a bunch of black Africans dressed in Christian Army uniforms."

"As you know, my liege, he has information that the Mongols are about to launch a new attack on us. He decided that it would be best to delay them as much as possible."

"We are very aware of the rumors on a new attack. Half of the army is back in Poland and moving to the borders. However, we are not particularly concerned. We are surrounded by Conrad's snowflake forts, armed with machine guns, and protected by an air force. If the Mongols come again, we would slaughter them."

Sir Piotr finally looked up. "Duke Conrad believes that they will not come the same way they did before. Mongols learn fast and adapt other people's technology for war. Even if they cannot conquer the forts or hold the cities, they can still kill millions of citizens.

"The way to stop it, he believes, is to head off, or at least delay, the invasion by taking the fight to the Mongols.

"Sarai is, or was, a major administrative center on the Volga River about a thousand miles south of Moscow and Tver. It is now a major center of ashes."

The king was not mollified, "I repeat, I do not remember authorizing such an expedition. Your lord already has the Holy See angry with us from his refusal to lead the Crusades and refusing orders to deal with a heathen pack of heretics. Now he has half of Europe after our blood.

"I want him back here as soon as possible. You will radio him our royal order that he is abort this mission and to return to this court as soon as possible."

Piotr's head was bowed again, "As Your Majesty commands, we obey."

On Campaign with Conrad

Things went well for the first ten days. Captain Ivanov's plans were good. On seven of those days, the army arrived at the camp grounds at dusk to find fires lit, latrines dug and campsites staked out. Twice it required that we travel a few hours into the darkness when our progress was slow and on day nine, we had to radio the supply column to move back to a new position when it was obvious that we had no hope of meeting them.

Meals were different, as we were hoarding the canned goods and using perishables first. We had only combat staff with us, so it was necessary to expand the quartermaster corps with troopers who were also cooks. Fortunately, any group of men this size has a mass of hidden talents. Morning meals were fresh bread, baked overnight by the newly appointed kitchen staff, and cheese or dried fruit. If our enemies were having any problem finding us, the smell of baking bread was certainly giving us away. Before we moved out, the cooks would pass out more bread, dried meat and fruit. Lunch was taken in the saddle. Of course, the fruit would give out in a few days, but it was good while we had it. The cooks tried to provide a little more variety at night. We had a lot of flour, but no time to bake raised bread at night. One of our Jewish troopers showed the kitchen staff how to make unleavened bread in about thirty minutes. It was dry and tasteless, but was good for scooping up oatmeal or rice from a bowl. The grocery shopping at Sarai had gone better than I expected.

We had constant problems with the new wagons, and on some stretches we simply had to slow down to keep the radio carts from shaking themselves to death. Each night, the cook fires were partly fed with the bodies of no longer needed old style wagons, so I expected that problem to burn it self out in another week.

106

Of course, we couldn't burn all of the empty wagons. Some of them had to be converted into fuel wagons or as the troops called them "shit wagons". There wasn't a lot of cooking fuel where we were, so whenever we came to a stand of trees the Big People would chew them into handy logs and load them into the fuel wagons. When there weren't trees, dried bovine end product was gathered during the day and shoveled into the shit wagons. We were moving pretty fast, so we weren't very successful poop pickers in the early days, but we learned to send workers ahead of the column and find moments to shovel.

This was definitely not the way I had planned this trip. I pictured fourteen non stop hours in the saddle, traveling light, eating on horseback, and dashing to Mongolia. We were still moving faster than most armies could in this century, but it was beginning to feel like a camping trip. I hoped that as we consumed the old style supplies and lightened up, we could begin to move the way I planned.

We were traveling parallel to a branch of the Silk Road and about thirty miles north of it. The road itself was useless for us since traveling it would stretch us out to a fifty mile long column dodging one mile an hour camel caravans. I also didn't want the hassle of going through the small towns and villages that serviced the road, so I settled for having the road scouted periodically for Mongol troops and food supplies. Neither appeared on the road.

In fact, we were traveling through an eerie emptiness. There should have been people on these steppes, but the farmsteads we passed were empty and there were no horsemen shadowing us, no figures watching from the horizon. Occasionally we passed small herds of dead horses, their skulls crushed and their bodies rotting. Whenever we saw them, it obviously disturbed the Big People and they refused to pass close to them. I suppose we would feel the same way seeing dead gorillas or Neanderthals. It's just too close to home. There was a lot of peaceful time in the saddle to think ahead and plan, but after a week of deep thought, the plan was still just, "Find Mongols", "Kill Mongols", "Go Home before you die". Simple but elegant.

Then things began to change. Over a period of two weeks, I was betrayed by one of my own men and then by God himself.

If I ever find the man who did it, I will give him a short trial and then kill him slowly with my own hands! He will curse his mother for giving birth to him! Screw the rules of civilized punishment. The bastard deserves all the pain I can give him. To this day, I dream of his neck between my hands.

On the tenth night, I was sitting next to a campfire roasting a bread stick. The cooks had passed out lumps of bread dough, bundles of small sticks, and something that looked like sour cream. You wrapped the dough around the stick in a lump about the size of a hot dog and roasted it over the campfire. When you pulled the stick out, it left a hole for the sour cream or whatever else that tasty stuff was.

The stars were bright and life was good when I was told that a coded message had arrived from Sir Piotr. It was in my personal code that only I and Piotr could use. By the time I decoded it, I was livid. I was recalled! King Henryk was calling me back to Poland to explain my actions in Sarai and my general unwillingness to follow his orders. The list of transgressions was a long one, including refusing to attack the Holy Land when ordered, misappropriating Crown funds, and insulting the Pope. My orders were to turn back immediately and they were signed by Count Piotr, Hetman of the Christian Army. My most loyal friend had sold me out for a promotion to count and stolen my army.

My reply was short, obscene, and used the word bastard more than once. I paced the tent angrily, barely resisting the urge to smash everything around me.

The reply came back from COUNT Piotr much too rapidly. As I decoded it, my anger peaked and then subsided. As I remember it, the message read:

My liege lord and old friend. You have my greatest respect and all of the loyalty that my oath allows. However, you personally required that I swear to my king with all the force of my faith in God. I have no choice but to follow the orders of the king here in Warsaw. I cannot provide any help or support if you do not do the same.

I especially urge you not to corrupt the personnel that are still loyal to you. We both know that the Eagles and some other personnel, such as the young man you selected for special promotion a few years ago, would put their moral souls and their ability to breath in severe jeopardy to help you.

You must not put them in danger. Return as soon as possible.

I have convinced our sovereign not to transmit your orders or your demotion in the clear, as any appearance of disloyalty would be damaging to Poland. I have further imposed a radio blackout on traffic to or from your command to reduce the chance of confusing orders being received.

Your loyal friend, Count Piotr

It was clumsy, but he was reassuring me as much as he could without risking a treason charge. Nothing in the letter was incriminating to him even if the letter was decoded, but it was clear between friends.

He couldn't support me openly without chancing execution, but he could work behind the scenes. He had just told me who was still loyal to me and given me a hint as to who had access to our private code. A few years ago, I had chosen a few young men to be trained as my possible replacement. One of them, Krzysztof Osiol, was now a komander in the Eagles. He was our most promising candidate and I had made certain that he had experience with several branches of the army and acquaintances in all of them. My bet was that he now had access to my private code.

But I had still been betrayed. The first message referred to events that happened in Sarai only two weeks before. In this century, it should have taken months, not days, to get a message to Poland. The only fast communication within a thousand miles was our radios. One of my own operators had to have taken a bribe to send a message from the merchants to their representatives in Poland. If I ever find out who he is, I will end his miserable life.

His mention of radio blackout was depressing. It reminded me that my position here was not my normal one. I never worried much about rank and orders because of my firm belief that men will follow a good leader and abandon a bad one no matter what his rank.

So far, I had been proven right repeatedly. As a loyal vassal to men of higher rank, I had changed a nation, built armies and industries almost changed a world and my rank was never the highest among the players. Hell, I even conquered North Africa with an army I built and led personally starting with the rank of *slave*, with no help from kingship or kinship.

Now I was in the middle of the steppes leading almost forty thousand strangers, and a few hundred personally known vassals into battle. I had sent most of my African army home and now led men I didn't know personally. Now Piotr was implying that if my army knew I had been recalled, they would mutiny; that they would not follow me into battle willingly.

Despite a copious amount of wine, I slept fitfully that night and awoke unrested, but I knew what I had to do. I splashed my face with cold water and called for my adjutant. "I have an important announcement this morning. In one hour, I want every radio wagon listing to my broadcast from here. Tell them to rig speakers outside the wagons so that every man can hear me."

It took almost two hours to set up, but eventually I stood at a mike before my tent and before the thousands of men who could personally see me I addressed the troops. "I have news from Poland. The nobles there have decided that our mission is a failure and that we must return home now. I have orders to turn coward and retreat immediately.

I will not follow those orders. I am going to kill Mongols and you are invited to join me.

It is each man's decision. If you stand facing the sun this morning, Poland is over your left shoulder. In that direction lays home, safety, and failure. If you go that way, you may be able to make it to the Volga River and follow it down to Polish domains, or you may be able to fight your way across the Ukraine to reach the Polish border.

In front of you is a different world. In front of you is the chance to make certain that your wives are never raped by Mongols, that your children are never enslaved and your homes never burned. In front of you is the richest and most evil empire in the world. Those who conquer it will gain glory from God and immense wealth.

I will march forward. I choose glory, and fame and family. I will fight for Poland, for my family and for my God. Those of you who feel the same will follow."

When we resumed the march, all but a hundred men followed me. The ones who stayed behind were left with two carts of food, the ammo in their saddlebags and whatever booty they had personally taken. They looked like a lonely and scared little group. I never found out if the rotten little cowards made it home, and never cared.

The Second Betrayal

I don't expect my God to answer me. I've raised armies in His name, prayed every day for years, vanquished His enemies and honored His name, but I'm also an engineer. I also believe in the laws of nature and understand that "God helps them that helps themselves" and "Prayer works, as long as you keep working your ass off while you pray." are the real laws of prayer.

Unlike my bumpkin friends, I don't think God hands out favors to his friends and smooths the road ahead for the faithful

But you'd think I'd get a break once in a while.

Things went well for over two weeks. It became obvious that we were not going to make my thirty-day goal for the trip, but we weren't going to miss by too much, and in a sudden plan like this, plus or minus fifty percent was right on target.

Despite Ivanov's best efforts the old equipment picked up in Sarai couldn't handle the pace we tried to set and after the first week, a couple of hours a day were being lost in cooking and repairing. There were also the usual streams and rivers and rough ground slowing us down even on the steppes. Since the weather was holding, I decided it was best to reach Mongolia with a well fed and rested army and I slacked off from a hundred ten miles a day to about seventy-five miles a day as a goal. I figured that as the old equipment dropped off and we leaned down to canned goods and modern wagons, we could make up a lot of the time lost in a final dash for the goal.

Then it rained. Ever wonder why the steppes are treeless grassland? Because it doesn't rain enough to support trees. There's no damned water on the steppes. It snows enough in winter to feed the groundwater and streams and grow some grass, but it rarely rains. As long as we got where we were going before the snows, we didn't have a lot of weather worries.

Except this year, it rained; buckets and barrels and cats and dogs, it rained. I tried to keep going the first day, rain or not, but by the time we camped, I knew we were there until the rain stopped. One of the problems with armor is that the padding under it soaks up water and holds it next to your skin. When the wind blew, we were in danger of hypothermia, in addition to being miserable, dog tired and damp.

Each of the columns found the highest and driest ground around and pitched camp. In the morning, it was obvious that we were stuck for awhile, so I had each camp set up dry R&R areas by stretching canvas between rows of wagons using whatever they had for tent poles. It gave us dry places to cook and areas for the men to congregate for cards and lies and just to avoid tent fever.

111

It rained for seven days and seven nights. I felt like Noah without an ark At least I was in good company. I remembered Napoleon and Hitler both being destroyed by the Russian winter, the Mongol invasion of Japan twice thwarted by the Great Wind, and the Spanish Armada driven to sea by a storm. If this killed me, as least I was in good company.

We were screwed by nature, our second betrayal, and the one that hurt the worst.

From the Memoirs of Duke Osiol

It was a dark time for the Christian Army and for the country that it served. At the time, I was Komander Osiol of the Christian Army, assigned to central command.

We had experienced years of prosperity and success, but jealousies and power were pulling the army apart. We had been led ably by Lord Conrad for many years, but now the king was becoming jealous of Conrad's power and influence and was casting a greedy eye on the wealth of the army. The final straw came when Conrad casually ordered the building a massive rail road over the Suez. When the king realized that the budget for that project alone was several times the annual income of the crown, he decided that the army was too wealthy to leave alone.

Conrad's closest ally and friend has always been his wife, but she now said in private that she was tired of his whoring ways and wanted a man who at least remembered where his home was. I think she was mainly lonely and tired.

In truth, Lord Conrad brought on many of his own troubles. He disappeared for over a year and the fact that he re-appeared at the head of a conquering army did nothing to endear him to his wife, as he immediately set off on another adventure without even setting foot on Polish soil.

Fortunately, Lord Conrad still had some friends. Among them was the new Hetman Duke Piotr, a man of his word and therefore loyal to King Henryk, but also loyal to his old friend. Piotr managed to help by setting up an emergency *research* committee and then refusing to have any knowledge of what it was doing.

Our first meeting was productive, but less than momentous.

First meeting of the Emergency Contingency Planning Commission

I opened the meeting with introductions. "Gentlemen, I think that I am known to all of you. I am Komander Krzysztof Osiol and I am chairing this committee at the request of Hetman Piotr. Most of you know each other, but in dealing with a matter this serious, it is important that we are all comfortable with each other. So, would each of you introduce yourself to the committee?"

The first man to my left was perhaps forty-five, fit, and short-haired. He rested his arm on a clipboard that probably never left his side. "I am Captain Aleksander, head of production at the military aircraft factory. My main job at this time is designing the production methods for the new two engine metal aircraft. I worked side by side with Lord Conrad designing the first aircraft engines."

The next man was ten years older and considerably wider. His shirt sleeves were rolled up, revealing muscles that belied his girth. "I am Baron Gwidon, representing the Military Naval Yards. I worked on the first concrete ships with Lord Conrad and now I oversee the yards in Gdansk."

The man next to him was fifteen years younger. The effect of his trim mustache and neatly cut hair was partly spoiled by his almost rumpled clothing. "I am Captain Gustav, and I am in charge of long-range aircraft research for the Christian Army. You all know that most of the research I have overseen for the past few years has been done without the involvement of Lord Conrad. However, I am his loyal liege man and feel that we are doing work that will benefit him in the future."

Baron Aleksander said he was representing Count Vladimir, commander of the mounted infantry. "The count would prefer to be here himself, but Lord Conrad has need of his services in the Holy land. He asked me to keep you informed of the needs of MI units."

Kolomel Jakub looked like a clerk. There is a "clerk look" shared by every clerk from the Sumerian grain counter to the teller at a Cracow bank. He was thin, slightly stoop-shouldered and despite his warrior's muscles, quieter than the rest. "I would be representing Hetman Piotr, if the count were aware of this committee's work. He has not asked that I file regular reports."

Komander Edmund was head of weapons research. He was muscular man of about sixty. He had a reputation for a creative and brilliant mind, but he had the look of a man who really enjoyed swinging a sword. "I have been working for Lord Conrad for nearly forty years and if it were not treasonous to say so, I would say he is still my boss."

The next two were obviously a pair. "I am Captain Feliks and the man to my left is Captain Fryderyk. We represent the Quartermaster Corps. There is an unsubstantiated rumor that one of our best men may be a long way away and need of resupply. We're here to help."

The last man really didn't need to introduce himself. He was Count Grzegorz's right hand man in the Wolves. He was a man proud of his nobility. His hair and beard were immaculate and he was shaved blue where the beard didn't cover. His uniform was expensively cut and his boots were polished to a bright shine. There was a rumor that he could fall into an outhouse and emerge with his creases still intact. "I'm Baron Boleslaw. You all know who I am. You know that I have fought beside Lord Conrad for many years. I'm here to represent Sir Grzegorz. He is, unfortunately, unable to attend himself and has asked me to come in his stead."

When the meeting got back around to me, I started with "For the record, let us record that the purpose of this committee is to form and test contingency plans for various emergencies, including, but not limited to: foreign invasions, natural disasters, stranded personnel, and the support of long-range missions."

At that point, I was interrupted by a frantic finger wagging from Baron Boleslaw. "Are you serious about keeping minutes for this meeting? I had the distinct impression that the topics to be discussed here might be of a delicate nature and not fit for general consumption."

"I assure you, baron, that nothing untoward will be done by this committee. We have been tasked with carrying out research and pilot programs that will benefit the entire Christian Army. As we are operating entirely on funds provided by the army and are using no crown funds we will not need individual authorization for any of our projects.

"If any of our projects provide unforeseen benefits to members of the army, we will cheerfully accept credit.

"As we are carrying out our mission with scrupulous honesty, we will keep careful records and forward them to Hetman Piotr as requested. I believe that the hetman has requested that we forward all project notes with our annual budget request."

I turned to my secretary "Anna, we are going off the record for a minute to discuss matters not pertinent to this meeting. Please note that and close the minutes until we resume.

"Gentlemen, we all know what is going on. We all have a valued leader and friend in trouble. Of course, we can't support treason, but nothing yet stops us from rescuing troopers in trouble, so our projects may have some unspecified goals.

"To make certain that we are never accused of treason or subversion, we will be the most open and honest committee in existence, with only two exceptions. We will discuss our friends in the East only theoretically as possible cases, and any slippage of the tongue that implies otherwise will be edited out of the record by Anna as irrelevant to our work.

"I have been chosen by the hetman to chair this committee because I have personally worked and sometimes drank and wenched with all of you. Most of you are the old guard, the ones who watched Lord Conrad build this army and this nation, and I can assure each of you as to the loyalties of the man sitting next to you.

"It won't be all smooth sailing. I can't guarantee what will happen if, through our efforts, Lord Conrad returns with another million Mongol heads and a snooty attitude, so, if I have misjudged the loyalty of any of you, this is the time to speak up. When I re-open the meeting, things will start to get serious."

There was an awkward moment while everyone looked around the table, then Sir Boleslaw spoke up. "You can hem and haw all day, but you're not going to find anyone at this table who'll betray Lord Conrad. However, before you re-start the record, there is something we have to discuss that we can't hide later.

"How much time do we have? When Lord Conrad left Jerusalem, he assured my lord that he would be in Mongolia less than thirty days from now. If that's our time limit, there isn't much we can do."

Baron Gwidon leaned forward. "I've been working with Lord Conrad for fifteen years. He's a great engineer and a good leader, but he often refers to a great philosopher named Murphy, who seems to rule his life.

"If our lord says thirty days, we probably have sixty, and that's only if nothing serious goes wrong. There's even a good chance that he will still be on the road ninety days from now, so I wouldn't rule out projects in that time frame.

"Sir Boleslaw is right, there isn't much we can do to help if Lord Conrad makes his initial schedule, but if he does, we have lost little by planning for the chance that he will take longer."

I stepped in, "To summarize, then, we seem to agree that we will try to get supplies and help to Lord Conrad in less than sixty days, but we will pursue anything practical that can probably be done in ninety days.

"Now, Anna, we go back on the record.

"Captain Gustav. As our first theoretical scenario consists on supplying a distant army cut off from the normal supply routes, it would seem that your work on the new two engine transport aircraft might be our best starting point."

Gustav shuffled papers in front of him. "Unfortunately, we are postulating an extreme case here, and the planes as they exist now would be of limited use. We are postulating an army that is over twelve hundred miles from base now and moving away at about a hundred miles a day.

"The maximum range with a normal cargo load is only fifteen hundred miles, enough for a one way trip. By replacing the cargo with fuel tanks, and dumping the empties at the far point, we can double the range, but we wouldn't have the capacity to deliver anything useful and all we could do would be to offer evacuation to a few officers or wounded men.

"As it is not the way of the Christian Army for officers to desert their commands, this ability is of no use to us.

"My staff has looked at the possibility of having the planes set up fuel depots for themselves. It is possible, but tedious and expensive. The concept would be that the planes would fly their normal radius, seven hundred fifty miles, with a cargo of fuel tanks several times, until there was enough fuel out there to set up the next stage.

116

"Unfortunately, the math looks bad. To reach out three thousand miles with seven thousand pounds of cargo and return home requires twelve round trips at extreme range. Eleven of those trips just deliver fuel to be used on the next leg or on the way home. Add another thousand miles and you need over sixteen round trips for each cargo delivered.

"However, in recognition of the importance of this commission and its mission, work has begun on a number of interesting solutions. The three aircraft we have finished are being relocated to a new base on the Black Sea, courtesy of our grateful friends in the Byzantine Empire. All ships in the area have been instructed to offload their supplies of aircraft fuel for the use of the land based aircraft, and more is on the way by fast steamship. That will cut almost a thousand miles off of our travel distance, when... *if* this scenario ever becomes reality.

"We already had three new airplanes under construction. By devoting all available personnel and supplies to them, we can finish all three in about ten days. They will join their sisters in the Black Sea airport as soon as they are ready to fly.

"As we are working with hours here, the first missions to establish forward fuel dumps are expected to take place in less than a week.

"By temporarily suspending certain other projects, we can lay the keels for ten more aircraft as soon as the new plans are available. It is planned that those next ten aircraft will be tri-motors, scaled up about thirty percent from the current models. We have teams working in the wind tunnels and doing the math to verify that we will get extra range and cargo.

"We are also looking at every damned fool idea our staff has come up with, and a couple look promising. One of our younger engineers has suggested that we strap solid fuel rockets under the wings of the aircraft to assist with takeoff. They would burn for about a minute and then drop off. We have already tried to increase lift off capacity by hooking up two fighters to help pull the cargo plane into the air. It works, but is too clumsy for regular use and, of course, there are no fighters in the forward bases.

"Another group of technicians is running tests to determine the best altitude and speed for maximum range.

"These steps will not by themselves solve our current problems, but they are the most productive things we can do now. They also address King Henryk's concern about the coming Mongol invasion. If we can patrol a thousand miles out from our borders it will be impossible to catch us unawares.

"On a final note, I received a message about two hours ago. A group of who worked on the first all metal fighter models are aware of our current problem and they want to propose another solution. According to the message, the idea came from an offhand remark that Lord Conrad made while working on the engine for the fighter. As the idea is *very original* they have asked to present it in its entirety at our next meeting."

There was additional discussion about what supplies and equipment might help the "theoretical" stranded army, but the air force had offered the only firm plans, and we agreed to meet again in three days to hear the rest of their proposals.

It was actually less than a week before the committee was able to meet again. This time it was a breakfast meeting held in conference room big enough for twice the dozen people present. As they filled their plates at the usual drinks and donuts table, the members tried to ignore the two oversized rifle crates near the foot of the table. Curiosity and surprise were not expressions allowed to military men.

I draped my fancy coat over the back of my chair, to signal that this would be an informal working meeting. The relaxation in the room was audible. "I know that we normally work over food at these morning meetings, but today we are going to see some things that require undivided attention from all of us. I suggest that today only, you chug your food down like hungry beggars while the minutes are being read, get some wine in front of you, and then we'll start real business. This may be a long day."

The minutes of the prior meeting were read over the sounds of munching and crunching and then conversation was carefully limited to hunting, wenching, and few feeble jokes between bites. The stewards came in a quarter-hour later to clear the table, pour the watered wine, and refill the sideboard with snacks, cold water, and weak wine before disappearing.

When they were all relaxed and certain that the room was secure, I began the real meeting. "Gentlemen, we have an extraordinary proposal brought to us by Captains Aleksander and Gustav. I believe that Captain Aleksander if going to take the lead this morning."

In the absence of junior staff, Alexander was already applying a crow bar one of the boxes while Gustav hung a large paper pad on an easel at the foot of the table and flipped up the first page. "The idea we are going to discuss was actually brought to our attention by groups that approached both me and Sir Alexander separately a few days ago. When you see it, you will understand why the first reaction from both of us was to reject the idea out of hand.

"However, we learned that the idea actually came from Lord Conrad. It was something he said to a technician when he was touring our first aircraft engine plant that suggested it. He saw the tech playing with a toy he was making for his son. We have one of the toys with us. In fact, let me show you what sparked the conversation."

From the crate, Aleksander produced a lamp and set it on the table. The shade was a large bulbous silk shape with a small hole in the top. The light source was a wax candle sitting in a wire basket below the shade. Alexander produced a lighter, lit the oil and stood back while Gustav continued. "Some of you may have seen these before. They're rare here in Poland, but I hear that they are common in China and thousands have been imported into Constantinople."

On the table, the lamp began to stir. It shook a little, rattled a little, and then rose off the table and gently bumped into the ceiling. "Cute, isn't it? Well, obviously we aren't going to re-supply Lord Conrad with silk balloons and candles, but our lord was in a talkative mood when he saw this toy and he informed the tech that it was possible to make huge rigid balloons that held hydrogen or even helium inside in bags and which would fly the sky like ocean liners. He called them *rigidibles*.

"The tech tells me that as soon as he said that, Lord Conrad's face stopped smiling and he hurriedly added, 'Of course, we'll never need to build anything like that because we have ocean liners and we're going to have huge airplanes pretty soon.'

"As you all know, our leader does have that stubborn streak. Once he says something, he rarely backs down and he firmly refused to talk on the subject any more.

"However, the tech, Captain Lawson, turned out to be also a hot air balloonist. You all remember that before we had airplanes, hot air balloons with varnished cotton canopies and wicker crew baskets were used for military observation. We closed the unit down when we got our first powered aircraft and forgot about them.

"Like most of you, I thought it was a dead field. However, it seems it's fun and clubs have formed to continue flying them. The reason Lawson was working on that particular toy was that he was member of one of those clubs, and he had even tried at one time to add a pedal powered propeller to a slightly elongated balloon. It was a miserable failure, but when Lord Conrad proposed a rigid skeleton, hydrogen, and an engine, Lawson was set on fire, along with a lot of his club members.

119

"Lawson is an engineer of the best, and worst, type. You've all met men like him. If weren't for the intervention of his captain, he would have died an old virgin because, aside from his balloon club, he'd rather spend his time puttering with models and drawing diagrams instead of learning how to get laid. The man had to be physically hauled out of his lab to get to his marriage ceremony.

"It was lucky for us. With your permission, I will have him join us to show what he came up with. He is known to me personally to be completely loyal to Lord Conrad and the Christian Army. However, until you all know him and are satisfied with his loyalty, I suggest that we keep the conversation theoretical. He only knows that we are interested in long distance transportation and has not been briefed on our immediate needs.

"Captain Gustav, if you would show in our young captain."

Lawson must have been surprised when a captain came out to escort him, but he didn't know that he was the only outsider ever allowed in the meeting. He was tall, thin man who looked like he needed a good meal and some sunshine. His clothes were a little short everywhere and he moved a little awkwardly as if his body didn't fit well either, but intelligence and confidence showed in his eyes. He may be embarrassed at the dance, but here he felt confident.

Captain Gustav resumed his seat as Captain Aleksander showed Lawson to the easel at foot of the table. "Captain, feel free to drop the dress coat and get comfortable. I've shown them your toy, told them about your meeting with Lord Conrad, and opened the first crate for you."

Lawson pointed at the toy now resting at the other end of the table. "Looks just like a kid's toy doesn't it? It's hard to believe that it can lead to a massive ship with an almost unlimited range.

"I know that you are used to people proposing impractical projects. I've heard about flying boats, six engine bombers and steam-powered rolling fortresses that either can't really be built or would be so expensive only a fool would build one.

"This project is neither. The math has been worked out, the models tested, and the money counted. These ships would be cheap, easy to build, and have a range that would span the world. Let me show you what it would look like."

The model that he took from the box looked like a cloth-covered signal rocket about two yards long and fatter than the average rocket. It was painted bright red with a Polish eagle blazoned on the rudder and fins. It took a moment after it was placed on the table to realize that the small two-inch high structure running from nose to tail along the bottom was, in fact, a gondola big enough for men to stand and work in. Then the perspective clicked in, and disbelief came with it. Komander Osiol spoke for all of them. "My God, man! This thing is bigger than a battleship. It would take years to build and our entire annual budget to fill it with gas. We're wasting our time."

Lawson shook his head, "Give me just a moment to explain. It's a lot easier and cheaper than it looks at first. It *is* big, literally bigger than a battleship. In full size, this model would be over six gross feet long, but remember that it's hollow and lightweight and hydrogen is about the cheapest gas there is.

"The cloth envelope in the middle is just tacked down with mild adhesive. If someone on each side of the table will peel back the covering, we can look inside and I'll show you how it's built."

With the center section of cloth removed, the members peered inside at the struts and bags and a few tiny crew members included to help the visual perspective. After a few moments, he resumed the description. "Some air bags have been removed so that you can see the structure. When it's flying, the entire space above that catwalk is filled with gas bags. The bags are cigar-shaped, tall and skinny and coated with a flame retardant. That way they don't all explode if one gets punctured.

"The real secret, though, is the shape. The reason that it's shaped like a bullet is that it only takes one element to build the sides and another to build the catwalks. Every section of the side is one sixteenth of a circle and is identical to every other section. You can have teams assembling the sections on the hangar floor and then just drop them in place in the rigidible and rivet them in. The speed of construction is limited only by how many teams you have room for.

"The horizontal sections are the same. Every element is the same triangular box beam. Make them anywhere, weld or rivet them in, and put planks down for flooring. It goes together easier than a Christmas toy.

"Of course, there is some custom work. The thing needs fins for steering, a pointed bow, engine mounts, a gondola, but all the parts are lightweight by necessity and simpler than what we build now for our bigger aircraft. Building one of these would be a big job, but no more complicated that the tri-motor we're now working on.

"The important thing to see is if we build this thing, we shrink the world dramatically. The entire world. Since it doesn't need engine power to stay aloft, the range is measured in thousands of miles instead of hundreds. On engine power alone, this thing could fly non-stop to Brazylport in four days or to the center of the Mongolian steppes in less than two.

"One thing that helps the range is that this is more an airship than and airplane. We know from our aircraft pilots that there are high level winds flowing west to east at over gross miles per hour and our ships have mapped trade winds in the other direction. This thing flies like an airplane up to about ninety miles an hour and uses any wind that you can find from five hundred to fifteen thousand feet to travel like glider."

Someone asked, "Aside from the winds and hype, what it the real range and speed of this thing running on its own power?"

"If the first one is built as planned, with existing bomber engines, it may reach only about eighty miles an hour in calm weather. We can't tell you range exactly. It can easily carry enough fuel for a ten thousand mile trip, but I'm not certain that would leave enough cargo capacity, so let's say six thousand miles range on the first one.

"The real limit on range is the hydrogen supply. There will be some steady leakage, no matter how well we build the bags and we're pretty certain that we'll have to both drop ballast and valve hydrogen into the air to adjust the altitude. You can see on the model that there are those blue tanks along the center ridge. That's the spare hydrogen supply. My best honest guess is that we can still guarantee that ten thousand mile range without a problem, but we can't be accurate until we try it."

Osiol interrupted with a grunt and a gesture toward Captain Aleksander, "This all sounds too good to be true. Have you given any more thought as to why Lord Conrad didn't want to build these supposedly marvelous machines?"

"Yes, sir. Remember he said that someday we'd have huge airplanes. Right now, our aircraft are severely limited but they constantly improve and eventually, they'll be five times as large as they are now and there will be airfields and gas all over the world. It will take thirty or forty years, but then the rigidibles will lose most of their advantages. As marvelous as they will be, they will always be more vulnerable to weather and slower than the best aircraft. I think Lord Conrad foresaw this and didn't want to put resources into a field that would die someday.

"Of course, he never realized that his life and Poland's future could depend on having something like this in a lot less than thirty years."

When I looked around the table, I saw uncomfortable faces. "Gentlemen, Captain Lawson's loyalties are well-known to me personally, and I am comfortable recommending that we address specific issues with the captain." When there was no dissent, I continued. "Captain, we are facing a specific problem that we need to discuss. While I, and I am certain, others at this table are very impressed with your model, I am not convinced yet that it will help us."

I saw that Lawson visibly made a decision. He stood taller, his shoulders back and his voice deepened. "Komander, gentlemen, I assume that the most secret and delicate mission that you have in mind is the re-supply and rescue of our Lord Conrad. If it isn't, then I've got a lot of useless charts on that stand."

"Captain! How the hell do you know about this? Who talked?"

"Who talked? No one talked. Everyone knows. Last month you could have made good money at the local Pink Dragon by guessing the exact date that he would attack Sarai. There were also pools on how long the battle would take, the number of casualties, and whether he would turn back or continue on to Mongolia.

"If you weren't betting, your staff was."

He looked around the table until he saw the embarrassed smile Captain Feliks's face. Feliks shrugged, "I made fifty pence on the pool for the day but Captain Fryderyk made a weeks pay by winning the casualty count pool."

Lawson continued, "The entire army knew when Lord Conrad went on campaign against the Mongols, and radio silence wasn't imposed until very recently. Everyone knew about his victory in Sarai, and since radio waves are embarrassingly public and clerks embarrassingly chatty, most knew when he was abandoned by the King and the new Hetman.

"Lord Conrad has many friends, particularly in the Wolves and the Eagles. He is no longer known personally to most of the army personnel, but among the Wolves, many have fought side by side with him or are the sons and bothers of those who did. The Eagles have also remained fiercely loyal."

He looked around for a moment unsure that he had not said too much, and then hurried on, "There have been a lot of late night bull sessions. Young officers have spent endless hours over charts and drawings, trying to find a way to help. Nothing untoward of course, as these are honorable men, not given to mutiny or oath breaking, but we have your answer and I have it laid out on that flip chart."

There were doubtful looks around the table, including mine, but I decided, "Alright, I guess we should look at your charts. Proceed, captain."

Lawson hurried to the back of the room and nervously flipped a page forward. "As you can see from this time-line, the first rigidible could fly out of the navy yards in just under sixty days."

There was an explosion from Baron Gwidon's seat. "Son, I hate to laugh in a meeting like this, but I run the shipyards and we couldn't lay the keel on this thing in sixty days."

"Normally, sir, I would totally agree with you, but there are some factors here that you are unaware of.

"Normally it would take over sixty days just to decide how long a keel to lay, but the engineering has already been done. The rigidible is a favorite topic among engineering students and aeronautical dreamers everywhere. Every detail has been thought out and argued about endlessly in labs and bars and officer's dorms around the country. Thousands of man hours have gone into the five hundred pages of technical specifications and plans that I brought with me. That model is so accurate because there are many man years of planning in it.

"Not only do we know the length and design of the keel, the tools and fixtures to build it already exist in the Cracow Aluminum Works.

"This chart shows the first ribs being put in place in less than a week. I know that sounds silly, but the fact is that two molds for the rib sections already exist. If Captain Feliks checks his order book, he'll find that he approved an order for *aluminum roof ribs* for the new royal exhibit hall, which coincidently looks just like the top half of a rigidible. The first ones can be delivered to the navy yards in less than a week."

His eyes lit up and he babbled like a true believer, but he seemed to know what he was talking about. I didn't know whether to have him arrested or give him a medal. Baron Gwidon was asking, "Why our shipyards? Shouldn't this be an air force project?"

"No, sir. We don't have a facility big enough. You have four adjacent dry docks that can be roofed over with canvas to make quick and simple construction sheds for rigidibles. Two of them are empty now, one will be empty in less than a week and the fourth contains a hull that could be floated out and anchored to make room."

"And I suppose that I have already given orders to use the docks."

"Of course not. However some of your junior officers have prepared the necessary movement orders to empty the two occupied docks and possible work schedules for your signature."

It went on for a couple of hours. The kid had all the answers.

"Where are we going to get that much cover material?"

A page of the flip chart contained figures on current stores of aluminum, copper, and duralumin and estimates on production times for additional stocks. "Now that all the new planes are aluminum covered, we have thousands of square meters of unneeded airplane cloth and dope – and idle facilities that can make more."

"How do you plan to get that much work done in sixty days?"

Another flip chart page contained man hour estimates and sample work schedules that covered seven days a week. "When you work around the clock seven days a week, the sixty days turns into two hundred normal work days, well over six months of normal work time."

"Where the hell are we going to get that many men?"

"We just recalled them from the frontiers. We've got thousands of soldiers recalled from the frontiers who need some kind of garrison duty to keep them busy. It doesn't take a lot of training to assemble this."

Eventually, the charts and schedules and the captain's enthusiasm won the day. By evening, the first orders had been signed. Captain Aleksander had been put on temporary duty at the ship yards to add his aircraft expertise to the building crew, and the adventure had begun.

My last comment to Captain Aleksander was, "We never suspected that there were such active unofficial groups among the young officers. I am still somewhat torn between giving you all medals and promotions, and having the shipyards build galleys so that we can bust you all down the rank of galley slaves. It has been an interesting day."

One of the most interesting things was that Lawson turned to Alexander as they left and said, "Too bad we didn't have time to talk about the other project."

It was only two weeks after our momentous rigidible decision that the committee met again. The reports were encouraging. Aleksander and Quidon had identified over twenty junior officers who had engineering experience and had worked on the rigidible design over the years. They were spotted throughout the project as advisors and managers. In some cases they were given temporary rank to fit their new responsibilities. There were an additional thirty juniors familiar enough with the project to seed work crews and staff offices.

The keel of the first ship was down and the first shipment of rib sections had arrived on site. Design modifications were being made on the fly. This was going to be a minimal build. In place of small individual cabins, the crew would have an open deck with aluminum and cloth camp beds clamped to deck and hammocks for passengers. Toilets would be holes in the floor and bathing facilities would be buckets of water. The officers would live no better. Instruments would be pirated from existing aircraft and bolted in.

The original design called for two gross cigar shaped gas bags with complex plumbing for re-filling and dumping hydrogen all controlled from the bridge. That had been simplified to ninety fatter bags manually operated by the crew. The engineers would have preferred highly modified engines designed for low-speed and high power, but had adapted the nacelle design to accommodate four existing bomber engines on each rigidible.

Despite the last-minute changes, the basic design was working and, so far, Murphy was taking a vacation. We were confident enough to begin discussing what supplies should be ferried out first. We were somewhat hampered by the fact that Lord Conrad could not ask for what he wanted. The airwaves were still public and his codes were known to more than us. Captain Feliks took the lead for the quartermasters. "We have decided that the first requirement of an army is food. Hungry soldiers get sick and die. Of course, we can't send our standard rations in the first few shipments. Canned food is over sixty percent water and Lord Conrad's problem right now is that he has too much water, so we have ordered a hundred and fifty tons of rice and flour. Cooked rice is about seventy five percent water, so a hundred tons of dry rice will make four hundred tons of cooked rice, and a man can survive on as little as two pounds of cooked rice per day and live well on three pounds. Wheat does not have as good a ratio of dry-to-cooked weight, but in a gruel or porridge it comes close.

"As we get closer to launch, we hope to identify other lightweight, high calorie foods to ship. It's taking some time because the priorities are somewhat different from normal expedition planning. On the ground, space is primary and weight secondary, so we look for dense products to ship. In the air ship our primary concern is weight, so we need to reevaluate potential foods."

All throughout the meeting, we had been wondering about the six-foot long crate that they brought. The last crate launched massive program and I wondered, no, *dreaded*, what this one would do.

Then the rest of the meeting was concluded, it was Lawson and Alexander's turn. Lawson was now a regular member of the committee, but he still tended to talk hurriedly as if no one would listen.

This time they uncrated a six-foot long wing. It was a white wing with two tiny motors, one on each side, and a spindly looking elevator sticking out the front. I was about to ask what the hell it was, but Captain Lawson never needed any encouragement to talk.

"This is a project that we didn't have time to talk about at the last meeting. Unlike the rigidible that we're building, this one carries less cargo and is therefore less pertinent to our current situation. It's about the same gross weight as the other ships, but it has other strengths.

"This is a fast courier ship with unlimited range and high speed. This ship could fly from Cracow to Cracow, around the world, without refueling and averaging well over gross miles an hour.

126

"We didn't press it in the last meeting, because we weren't certain what role it could play in the very near future. During the last two weeks, we figured out how it might save Lord Conrad's butt, I'm mean, how it might have a significant effect on an effort to rescue and supply a possible future distant force, and we figured our how to make one with the material and manpower the air force has on hand."

Baron Quidon was our savior, or tried to be. "The last time we let you talk, you got us into a mulimillion pence project, used up all the aluminum in Europe, got a commitment for two thousand workers, and possibly got us all charged with treason.

"I don't think you can do that again."

I don't know if Lawson was supremely confident, or just unaware of reality. "You forgot that we didn't use up all the cloth, hydrogen, or wood, and a lot of air force workers are still available, and this is a great machine. As a soldier, you'll love it, and we don't need any more money."

Quidon shook his head, "I know I'm going to regret this, but why will I love it?"

"Well, you notice it's a different shape. The regular rigidible is a cigar shape and this is a flying wing." I guess the kid liked repeating the obvious. "But the real difference is inside. You'll notice that the center third of the wing is a slightly different color than the outer thirds. That's because only the outer thirds contain hydrogen, and they hold only enough to almost, but not quite float the ship.

"We decided to call this a compound airship because part of the lift is provided by gas burners in the center section. The center section is, in effect, a hot air balloon very much like the toys we demonstrated at the last meeting.

"Remember that the ultimate range limitation on the pure hydrogen rigidible was the need to frequently valve off and then replenish the hydrogen. In this one, you never need to valve off hydrogen. If you want to go down, you turn the burners down and light the fires to go up. Since the ship is near neutral buoyancy anyway, it doesn't take much fuel to lift it and the liquid fuel is a lot easier to carry than spare hydrogen is.

"It's not immortal, but its range is several times that of a hydrogen only ship."

Komander Evan jumped in. "So, you can stay up a long time. So what? You still have to carry fuel to drive this thing. What's the advantage?"

Lawson was almost gleeful. "That's the other thing. You don't need fuel to drive it. The lift does it. Those two little engines on the wing are just for maneuvering. Some of you have flown gliders or read about them or had friends that flew them. One of the tricks of getting speed out of your glider is catch a thermal and get up high. Then you nose down, glide forward, and trade your height for speed.

127

"That's what this does, but it makes its own thermals going up or going down. On the way up, the wing shape lets you angle the ship forward to move horizontally. When you reach the top, you cut the heat and do the same glider trick on the way down. It might make you seasick, but it'll move you farther and faster than anything else on earth."

I still wasn't convinced. "As usual, you've done a great job and made fantasy almost believable, but I still fail to see any urgency to build this. Perhaps when we have more time…"

But he wasn't done. "Please, just another thirty seconds. Let's all imagine that somewhere out there forty thousand brave Christian Army warriors are facing, let's say, a hundred and fifty or two hundred thousand Chinese infantrymen and mounted Mongol warriors.

"Now picture yourself being one of those infantrymen or Mongols and you look up in the sky. Something is dropping out of the sky. It's big, but so high that you really can't tell how big. It's the biggest and fastest thing you've ever seen. You shoot at it, but it's way out of range. Then as it levels out above you, twenty pairs of machine guns open up and tear up the surrounding ground. You're dead and everyone near you is dead.

"That's what this machine does. That rigidible keeps you alive and this kills your enemies. Anywhere in the world. We'll call it *Equalizer*."

There was less discussion this time. If Lawson said that they had the manpower and materials, we were inclined to believe him. If he said that he would deliver it on Saturday, I might have believed him.

We built it.

Wisdom from Conrad

Have you ever noticed that we thank God for good things, but we curse "the gods" when things go wrong. Catholic or not, I was tempted to start the cursing.

It rained for seven days and seven nights, and then just kept on raining. Not the buckets and barrels of the first seven days, just enough mist and drizzle and showers to keep everything damp, cold, and miserable. This was the second time that rain had brought disaster to this mission. One more time, and I would change my name to *Noah* Stargard.

Even the Big People weren't able to move more than ten miles an hour in this muck, and wagons sank in axle deep when they were moved. It was far less fluid than pure mud would have been, but you still couldn't put any real pressure on it.

The cold was getting worse. By the calendar, we were now in November and even though the medieval calendar was flawed, it was obviously close to winter. We had made another eight hundred miles before the rain started so we were now almost two thousand miles from Cracow, and well beyond the range of rescue or arrest.

The scouts were still reporting an almost eerie emptiness on the Steppe. There were a few Mongol yurts but no herds of animals, no moving bands of men. We had drifted away from the Silk Road, but a reconnaissance showed that traffic was stopped there too.

Of course, we weren't running parallel to the real Silk Road. The traditional route ran far south of us. It started near modern Beijing, skirted the northern edge of the Gobi Desert, crossed the Middle East south of the Caspian Sea and ended in Constantinople or Alexandria, but for about a hundred years the Mongols insisted that the caravans follow a route from Sarai through Karakorum, so we were a lot of miles north of cities, supplies, and good roads.

The men played cards, polished weapons and armor, dreamed about, bragged about, and lied about women, but mostly they tried to find a dry place to stretch out. We were camped on the highest spot in sight but there just wasn't enough high ground for a city of forty thousand men. We had done our best to ditch around the camps, but the damned sod was three feet thick. You couldn't get a shovel through it.

Someone got the bright idea of cutting the sod and using it to build low walls around the tents to deflect the water. Of course, we didn't carry sod cutters with us, so they used what shovels we had and the two thousand saws the quartermaster had insisted in bringing from Sarai.

129

A few of the men used their swords to cut sod. My first reaction was absolute rage that someone would defile a sword that way, but then I realized that the sword was just a tool to keep you alive and if keeping you dry kept you healthy, cut with my blessing. We'll sharpen them again before we go.

Me, I sat in my tent and planned. I'm not the worrying type. I plan ahead and in fact plan a lot for every contingency that I can see, but I don't "worry". This time there had been little time for planning. I knew when I heard the Mongols were coming that they had to be delayed so I reacted the most rational way possible. I got all the men and weapons together that I could lay my hands on and went to harass the enemy.

It's possible that plan was accomplished when I sent the Big People out to kill the Mongol horses. My reasoning was that a Mongol without a horse was just a nasty little man who needed a bath. We hadn't heard back from the Big People, but we hadn't seen any herds of horses in weeks. I might have been able to turn back then, but I was convinced that there was a Mongol invasion force forming somewhere and we needed to bloody it before it got to Poland. It felt good to wipe out the garrison at Sarai, but forty thousand Mongols was a damned small outfit for an invasion, and I was convinced that there was another force forming in Mongolia or already on the trail.

My plan was to find that Mongol army, hit them hard before winter set in, and high tail it back to Poland before the worst of winter stopped us. It was more than the horse raid plan I started out with, but if it succeeded the Mongol threat would be gone for many years.

Unfortunately, we were having problems finding any sign of a Mongol army or even any sign of living Mongol horse herds, and I did get fired.

As a result of being re-called, I had promised the men with me untold riches and glory. If we couldn't find a Mongol army, the only way to fulfill that promise was to empty the treasuries at the Mongolian capital at Karakorum, and we were rather short of artillery, ammo, mines, men and everything else needed to storm a fortress city with high stone walls.

I needed a plan. I couldn't very well assemble the army and announce, "We've had a nice little walk our here, but now it's time to amble back home." Neither would I ever return to Poland. I had spent a lifetime making the Christian Army and Poland the most powerful force in Europe, made a county preacher into a pope, cherished a wife for many years, and made a minor king into one of the most powerful monarchs in Christendom and my reward was betrayal by virtually everyone I had helped.

I was recalled to *explain myself.* If I returned, the only possible explanations would require a lot of blood be spilled, some of it royal and some of it holy. My anger was only dampened because I was bored with my life anyway and had enough gold with me to form an empire anywhere I went. The army and the Mongols were my real problems.

So, I sat cross-legged on the carpet and thought and drank liberated wine and stared out at the rain for three days. Occasionally one of my bodyguards would offer a back rub or sex or bring me a meal. I accepted the back rubs and meals, but passed on the sex.

I still hadn't decided what to do when the answer dropped out of the sky, literally. We were buzzed by an airplane. Almost two thousand miles into a barren steppe, an airplane buzzed us. I ran outside and looked up to see twin-engine aircraft about the size of a DC3 circling overhead. The brilliant and beautiful crest of Poland gleamed on its bright aluminum tail. Obviously Sir Piotr had once again gone against my orders and this time built the twin-engine cargo plane I didn't want. When he wasn't busy betraying me, he was a handy man to have around.

After several passes, the pilots apparently identified my tent and circled tightly over it. One of the pilots leaned out of his window and dropped a canister with a long green ribbon streaming behind it. I was still putting on my armor when a trooper brought it to me.

Inside, a message read, "Will land on high hill three miles west of your location." I told the trooper, "Get a squad together. Full armor. We've got visitors." Silver was waiting for me when I left the tent. She must have also seen the plane. As I swung up in the saddle, I felt a twinge of guilt because I hadn't curried or brushed her for three days. I had never before missed my morning rituals.

We headed west and a squad formed up around us as we approached the camp perimeter. It was slow going. Silver picked the driest, highest, firmest paths but her powerful legs still often sunk inches into the ground. It took us over an hour to reach to the relatively high and dry hill the plane was on.

Even close up, the plane still looked eerily like a DC3 until I noticed that it had huge puffy rolligon tires on it. The pilots were sitting lazily in the open cargo door but they both jumped to attention when we topped the hill. They were like twins. Both were less than six feet tall and wiry rather than muscular. Their chiseled faces and easy lithe movement showed that they were in as good a shape as any warriors. Their brown leather jackets and the gloves in their epaulets would have looked natural in World War II, except for the one inch orange crest on the leather helmets.

They saluted as I dismounted and one handed me an official envelope in royal colors, sealed with wax and tied with an official ribbon. "Lieutenant Goetz, sir! This message is the official reason that we have made this trip, and with all possible respect, I suggest that you do not open it."

"You might want to explain that, lieutenant. I am in the habit of reading my mail."

"Sirs Piotr and Krzysztof are sticklers for oaths and rules, sir. So, the official purpose of our trip is to deliver that message from Sir Piotr, and we can swear a holy oath to anyone without offending powers, secular or holy, as to the truth of that. The real message is still in the plane.

"And, with respect, I have recommended that you discard the official message because it is both unpleasant and irrelevant. I am privy to its contents and I know that Sir Piotr has been instructed to order, again, your immediate return now under threat of courts-martial. Your rank is to be revoked if you are not in Cracow in thirty days, your lands are subject to confiscation in that case, your titles are in jeopardy, and the pope has threatened excommunication if you do not apologize publicly for your disrespect to the papacy.

"As none of this is relevant to the Christian Army, you neither need to read nor respond to it. Sir Krzysztof recommends that you spare yourself the aggravation of communicating with fools.

"I apologize, sir, if I have spoken out-of-place. The real reason for the trip is in a locker. Have I your leave to fetch it?"

Well. I guess I didn't need to read it after all. The kid probably had a point. I often told my staff, "If you feel an irrational need to talk sense to a fool, spend your time teaching a frog to sing or a horse to fly instead. It will have the same results and at least the frog won't talk back."

"Lieutenant, you have my leave, but I am anxious to inspect your craft, and I would ask your permission to board."

It was a thoroughly modern plane. It was aluminum ribbed inside, all metal outside. "Aluminum and copper alloy," the lieutenant pointed out, "poured and then cured at room temperature for six days to strengthen it and then covered with a thin layer of pure aluminum to stop corrosion." In America, we called that *duralumin* and I was surprised the metallurgists came up with it without my help. I would have to send a message back that the addition of a small percentage of manganese would strengthen it even more.

There was a passenger door ahead of the wing and a large cargo door that swung up from behind the wing. Most of the floor was taken up with two rectangular tanks running the length of each side. We were sitting on those tanks because there was room for little else in the plane. Goetz tapped the tank he was sitting on.

"The tanks will be staying here. They were fitted for this trip because we are way out beyond our normal range. They're empty now and we'll drop them to save weight. Even with the tanks out, it'll be a little close getting back."

"Speaking of that, how the hell did you get here? We're three thousand miles from your base. Even with these tanks, you couldn't possibly make it that far."

"It was an adventure, but we didn't come from Poland. A navy flotilla prepared a rough landing field at a place called Anapa on the Black Sea. They offloaded fuel for us. There were three of us, all with extra fuel tanks, that flew down to the base in easy stages. That left us just over two thousand miles for the last leg.

"From the Black Sea we headed inland about a thousand miles. We found your trail and followed it until we found a nice flat pasture to land in. Then I refilled from their spare tanks and came on to find you.

"The other two planes are still sitting in that pasture with a couple of lances of warriors, waiting to refuel us for the trip back, if we make it."

"That was a hell of a trip to deliver a message that you didn't want me to read," I said.

"There wasn't much room left over for cargo, but the real message is still in the locker, along with a couple of boxes of cigars and some fine whiskey Sir Krzysztof threw in at the last minute."

He leaned back and flipped open a locker bolted to the floor. He first handed me a heavy set of saddlebags. "This is from Sir Krzysztof: your cigars and whisky." Then he retrieved a rather large leather blueprint case. "This case contains plans for your re-supply mission and a new code book. This you will want to read."

I opened the map case and glanced at the first page and then back at the pilot, "You are serious that they are going to build this?"

"Not just serious, sir, and not just planning. That ship and its three sisters are a third done already. I'm under orders from Captain Aleksander and Baron Gwidon to get your feedback on the best use of the ships."

Outside, the squad had already dismounted and broken out rations. We joined them and the co-pilot on the ground while I perused the other drawings.

Goetz pointed out, "Those aren't the actual engineering plans, of course. There are five hundred pages of those, but these should give you a good sense of what we're doing and let us get your feedback."

Between munches, I scanned the ten pages of drawings. The first five were cutaway drawings of a standard looking dirigible, but the last three were pictures of a flying wing with ridiculously small engines. "Lieutenant Goetz, I'm not clear on what this is, but I'm pretty sure that we don't have the technology to keep a flying wing in the air."

"I'm not sure what a 'flying wing' is supposed to be, but the *White Dragon* is a rigidible and it should at least get up in the air. After that, it might have problems.

"The official description is a *compound rigidible gliding gun ship*, but the workers just call it the *Sea Sicker*. It flies, or will fly, with a combination of hydrogen and hot air. It has enough hydrogen to maintain neutral buoyancy but the idea is that you open the gas burners and, as it rises, it glides forward then the crew cuts the burners and it slides forward again on the way down, trading height for speed. It ought to be a wild ride, but I'm not certain that even the builders really think it'll work."

I suddenly realized that I had the scale very wrong. This thing was going to be as big as the dirigibles! "I've got a hundred more questions, but we should get this back to camp before dark." I called over the lance's leader, "Leave half your men here to guard the plane and tell them to give the copilot any help he needs to ready. As soon as we get to camp, I'll send another lance out with supplies for a few days. Oh, and someone needs to give the pilot a lift back to camp."

As we left, I looked back to see the Big People were eating their lunch by clearing grass and vegetation from a runway behind the plane. No one gave them orders to do so. Someday, I'm going to figure out how they know what to do.

By the time we reached camp, night was falling. I left word that there would be a staff meeting for Sirs Wladyclaw, Eikman, and Ivanov at two the next morning, and retired to my tent. I still had to remind myself that two on the new clock was ten AM on my old clock.

I decided that since I had to waste time eating, I might as well use the chance to finish my talk with Lieutenant Goetz. We laid two of the drawings out in front of us as we sat on the floor eating bowls of rice and cooked vegetables. It was obvious that Goestz's enthusiasm came from more than duty. He loved the airships, and never gave a simple answer.

"What's the cargo capacity on one of these ships?"

"It depends a little on how it's manned and how long the mission is. Gross lift is about five hundred and fifty thousand pounds. The structure is about two hundred and fifty thousand pounds. The weight of the crew, fuel, food and water, and ballast varies, but for most missions it won't be over thirty thousand pounds. That leaves a theoretical capacity of around two hundred thousand pounds. After you figure in Murphy's Factor for unseen contingencies, you might get a hundred fifty thousand pounds fo useful cargo. Figure seventy-five tons on most trips, or a little less to be safe."

"How fast do they cruise?"

"These first four may be a little underpowered. They've diverted sixteen engines from the bomber program for these four ships. We figure seventy-five or eighty miles an hour in calm air. But you gotta remember these are ships, not airplanes so they're sensitive to wind speed. Some Eagles claim they've encountered high-speed trade winds at about nine thousand feet, going from west to east. If they're right, they could get here from Gdansk in a day. If not, then three days each way. In fact, the wind resistance of a rigidible is so high I doubt they will ever get much over a gross mile an hour in calm weather.

"The *White Dragon* is another matter. No one has any idea how fast it'll go. The builders say that they are stressing it for a hundred eighty miles an hour, but not many people believe their calculations."

I pulled out the *White Dragon* plan and Goetz leaned over to point out features. "It looks a little different that this drawing now. The first test flight did not go all that well. They built a ten foot wide model and rigged it up with a timer that would cycle the heater on and off.

"It made one hell of a leap up and glided down according to plan, but on the top of the second cycle it flipped over. I guess that's what you meant about keeping a flying wing in the air. Since this drawing was made, they've shifted a lot of the weight lower in the fuselage to give it a lower center of gravity and they're debating whether to add a tail boom.

"If you look at the control cabin, you'll see how fanatic they are. You see how there are only three main controls? The cables from the two ailerons, the gas valves, and the control cables for the top vents, all come into the rear of the main cockpit. Eight men could fly this thing if they had to.

"And, look at this little thing below the cockpit. That's a small gas engine running an air pump. The entire cockpit is sealed and pressurized. This thing is designed to get to thirty thousand feet and the constant change in pressure as it went up and down would drive the crew crazy if they didn't stabilize it."

Later, as I reclined under the stars with a cigar in one and a glass of whiskey in the other, I reviewed the day in my mind. In truth, I had found the conversations unsettling. I had almost come to peace with the betrayals by my wife, my liege lord, and half the people who owed their lives and prosperity to me. I had decided to move on from Poland and never return, but this conversation was upsetting.

Without me, Poland would have ceased to exist in another hundred years. In my own time-line, there were centuries where an independent Poland was missing. I had done my best to raise them out of the mire of medieval ignorance. With my guidance and knowledge, they built river boats, steam engines, and guns. I had introduced paper, printing, and indoor plumbing. The entire Christian Army was my invention.

And now they didn't need me. I had always passed on my knowledge to others and I had formed and worked with engineering teams for years, but I was always the real leader; the spark of invention. Now they didn't need me. Even the last drawing, which Goetz and I had not discussed, showed how far my pupils had come. They needed a larger plane than the DC3 type that they had, and the designer had not wanted to wait for new engines to be designed and tested and a new airframe tested, so he just scaled up the exiting twin-engine plane by fifty percent and added a third engine. Need more power, just add one more engine just like the ones already in production. It worked for Junkers and Ford. Whoever the designer was, he came up with it without any advice from me.

The dirigible projects were well thought out and well planned. I was certain they would work and the only input I might have is to tell the aluminum foundry that adding a little magnesium and zinc could improve the strength of the duralumin.

My students, my *children*, had grown up and were surpassing their parent. In truth, what more could a parent wish for than that his children would grow up, be successful, and surpass even the parent in competence and success? Indeed, what more, except maybe a little more damned gratitude!

I was going to save their sorry butts one more time. One last time I would go into battle and relieve them forever of the Mongol threat, and then I'm out of here. The ungrateful bastards will never hear from me again.

The staff meeting was a large one, but at least we didn't need to sit on the ground. I had the quartermaster set up a canopy well away from the camp with folding chairs and two large folding tables that we liberated from Sarai. Lieutenant Goetz sat on my right. I opened the meeting as if everyone already knew what we were going to do.

"We came out here to kill Mongols. We got a nice batch of them in Sarai, but a lot of them are left. Like you, I thought we would have run into their main force by now, but I have no intention of speculating on why they are absent.

"However, we are less than a thousand miles from their heartland with a trained force of almost forty thousand warriors and well over forty thousand Big People. Our men are fired up about the glory and considerable wealth that would come from ending the Mongol terror for good.

"We can do that by destroying Karakorum. That won't end all Mongols everywhere, and we cannot expect to attack the Chinese Mongols. They now control single cities with populations as large as our county and manufacturing resources that are antiquated, but massive. If threatened, they could field several million man armies, but there is little love lost between the various Mongol families, and it is unlikely that the Chinese Mongols would spend a lot of time avenging their poor cousins. They might even see it too their advantage if their troublesome cousins ceased to exist on their flanks, and frankly, if the Mongols and Chinese want to keep killing each other, it's none of our business.

"Karakorum is an old and well defended city. From what we have learned on this campaign, we believe that it has high stone walls and other good defenses. Up until yesterday, I was uncertain of how we would take it.

"We have the best trained and best armed warriors in the world, but as Captain Ivanov will tell you, we are painfully short of artillery and siege equipment. The solution to that problem has come to us. The man to my right is Lieutenant Goetz. He flew here in one of our new long-range aircraft to show us the plans you see before you."

Of course, Goetz and the plans were just there to raise morale and impress the troops.

"These are drawings of new air ships that we are told will be in operation within six to eight weeks. If plans go well, we should start receiving about two deliveries a week of about seventy-five tons of supplies.

"Among those supplies, I plan to request a large number of artillery shells and the biggest damned artillery piece they can fly in one of these. This time, we'll stand back and blast the walls down the old fashioned way. We'll stand off, kill most of them with high explosive, incendiary, and gas artillery shells and then mop up the rest.

"Obviously, this will take time to arrange, so we will be spending winter out here and attacking as soon as the weather clears.

"Some things we have to do are obvious. Captain Ivanov, you will spend the day prioritizing the supplies that you need shipped in. While we have a pressing need for ammunition, it works best when fired by a healthy and well fed warrior and that's your field.

"Sir Wladyclaw and Kolomel Eikman will work with the guides to determine the best place to hole up. We need a place that is isolated, lightly populated, or, even better, deserted so we don't have to fight with current residents and near our line to Karakorum.

"We could stay right here on the steppes, but it's short of water and there will be a damned cold wind blowing through here next month.

"Lieutenant Goetz needs to get back in the air no later than tomorrow morning so Ivanov's crew will need their lists ready by the end of the day.

137

"That's the obvious. What am I missing, gentlemen?"

Of course, the main reason for the *isolated* location is as long as we are more than walking distance from civilization, we won't have any desertions. You simply cannot desert on a Big Person. As soon as she realizes what you are doing, she will turn around and dump you in front of your commanding officer. Big People are smart and loyal.

By the next morning, the pilot was on his way back to his plane, and we were well on our way to making decisions. The guides had pointed out that we were probably less than fifty files from the river Ortz. It was directly on our line of march and eventually flowed down to the Cuman Sultanate.

We were in the middle of nowhere, but the sultanate's borders were only about three hundred miles south, beyond a low mountain range. I decided that we would march east-northeast until we met the river and then follow it to within a hundred miles of the sultanate. We would make camp there for the winter.

We didn't know if the Mongols had taken the sultanate, but my guess was that gold and greed were a powerful combination. Once we were established, Captain Ivanov would send a crew dressed as civilians into the south to buy a herd of cattle and whatever other supplies were available. Even if there were Mongol overlords, my bet was that the cattle and wheat merchants needed cash and wouldn't care who had it.

Our most annoying discussion was about what to do with the river residents. Any river was going to have towns, villages, settlements, and farms along it. I saw no problem but Sir Wladyclaw asked, "If we travel down the river, we are going to run into a lot of civilians. What are we going to do about them?"

"Oh, I don't know… Since they're Mongols, how about killing them all?"

"Your grace, we have discussed this many times. The Christian Army is not a barbarian horde and, thanks in large part to your influence, we don't kill women, children, even unarmed men. The villages and farms will be mostly women and children and will include a lot of slaves and tradesmen who have never warred on anyone.

"We can't massacre the civilian population, can't herd them along with us, and can't afford to leave garrisons behind to control them. We're going to leave a lot of spies behind us."

I could barely control my anger. Why couldn't I have troops as loyal as Caesar's? When Vercingetorix sent his women and children out to the Roman lines, Caesar's men turned them away to starve in the no man's land between the lines. I was cursed with an army that didn't even want to stop a Mongol woman from breeding more enemies.

When I had my breathing under control I told them, "With that in mind, these are the rules of engagement. When we reach the river, we will travel south, but we will detour inland to avoid any villages or cities by at least two miles. Likewise, we will give any farmsteads at least a bowshot's room.

"We won't pick a fight with anyone except armed troops and garrisons. If however, we see a garrison, we will destroy it, and anyone who fires on us will be left for the buzzards. Farmer or fireman, you fire on us and you die.

"As for leaving spies behind us, good. If any Mongol force attacks on these open plains, our superior range and machine guns should make easy work of them, and there will be fewer to face at Karakorum.

"Does anyone see any problems with these marching orders? Good. The meeting is closed. Everyone get back to work. The rain has stopped. Tomorrow we march."

We could have used another day or so to dry out the grass, but I was in no mood to sit around. I am not used to having my orders questioned.

The movement to the winter camp went better than I expected. The steppe was drying and we could move fast again. We no longer used the empty carts for firewood as we might now need them.

We found the river two days into our journey and began following it south. Despite relatively heavy traffic on the river, the banks were sparsely populated. We put lances on both banks to stop any traffic that might be carrying food or other supplies we would need, such as tent canvas. Most boats pulled over when hailed by an armed lance, and most of the rest headed for the bank when a few heavy caliber rounds landed near them. We only had to sink one or two.

We paid the private owners with a little of the gold we liberated from Sarai and left script with captains of government or corporate owned cargos. Carriers of Monogl tribute and supplies were given their lives in exchange for their cargos. I would have preferred to charge them with aiding and abetting the enemy, but we didn't have time to assemble firing squads.

We picked up enough food and supplies to fill all of our carts to overflowing and I debated putting prize teams on the larger ships to carry the supplies downriver for us, but I decided that we didn't have the men or expertise to pull that off.

As planned, we gave the civilian population a wide berth. Occasionally, a farmer would take a shot at a scout before he realized there was an army behind him, but generally they left us as alone as we did them.

We didn't find any cities and we gave the towns and villages a wide berth. One larger town was brave enough to send out emissaries to ask for peace. We thanked them, and then paid well for their extra grain stores and some wagons to carry it.

Something about that meeting bothered me. Three old men came out to meet us. They were obviously peasants, but I couldn't tell if they were Mongols or Turks. They were scared stiff. When they delivered the wagons of grain and meat that we purchased, they were very surprised to get paid. They seemed to think that we were going to kill them and take the goods. I particularly remember one small girl who, for some stupid reason, rode out with her father. She had the most beautiful brown eyes, but when she saw me she screamed in terror and couldn't be comforted. Her father apologized through the interpreter but said she couldn't help it because she had heard that Christians killed everyone, everywhere they went.

I blamed the papal troops that scourged the Holy Land for the rumors, but decided that we needed to do some better PR work.

We were only moving about two dozen miles a day because we were dragging a lot of medieval carts with us, but there was no hurry as we had almost three months before we could attack Karakorum.

We still reached the borderlands of the steppe in about three weeks. I stopped short of the foothills and their trees because I decided that with our firepower advantage, a clear field of fire was more important than any shelter that the trees would provide. We picked a flat area near the river and set up the camp about a thousand yards from the bank.

Well, a thousand yards on one side of the camp and fifteen miles on the other. The camp was huge. We had about the same number of men as Caesar had in Gaul. His nightly camps were twenty miles in circumference and the ditches and palisades were sometimes visible to low flying planes as late as the twentieth century.

Ours was a little smaller, but I decided to follow his example of a round palisade with a major gate at the four compass points. It wouldn't give a definable corner or side for enemies to concentrate on. Caesar surrounded every camp with a palisade, dirt hill, and a moat. He had timber. I didn't. However, we had plenty of the world's oldest building materials: dirt and sod. This land hadn't been farmed in recorded history so the sod was almost three feet thick.

I called Wladyclaw and Eikman together in my tent. I explained what needed to be done, "Sir Eikman, your men will have to take the lead on this project, but every man in this army is available to you as workmen. Requisition as many as you need from anywhere – and that includes the Wolves.

"We need a sod wall at least eight feet tall and five foot wide around the entire perimeter. Use the current camp size for your template, but make it circular and keep the walls at least gross yards out from the nearest tent. Your men can get the material by cutting the sod away from the outside edge of the wall. We've got about two thousand saws and, in a pinch, swords and axes will cut the stuff.

"When you get the right height, you should have ditch about a two or three-foot deep and twenty feet wide where you removed the sod. Dig out the center of that hole to about six-foot deep and use the fill to build a rampart around the outside.

"When the perimeter is safe, you can start working on machine gun emplacements. You'll have to make them the same way. The only thing to work with here is mud and grass. Put up enough gun platforms and ramps from the interior to defend every wall section. Of course, we won't have enough machine guns or artillery to populate every platform, but place some at regular intervals around the wall and keep enough in reserve to fill in where needed if we are attacked.

"It's your job, Grzegorz, to handle the grumbles from the Wolves. I know that some of your men are a total pain in the ass when it comes to grunt work. This time, everyone has to do their part. However, you can select fifteen lances of your most pain in the ass aristocrats and send them out on scouting parties while the work is done. Pair each squad with one of Ahmed's translators and tell them we want a complete map of everything within thirty miles of us. It's better to have them gone than have the men see them slacking off or arguing about joining in real labor.

"Oh, and tell the squads going south that they should go as far as the foothills and keep an eye out for any bogs."

Despite the size of the job, the fortifications would only keep the army busy for a few days and then I would have to come up with more tasks. Nothing is more dangerous to an army than boredom.

Letter home from Captain William Orbitz

January 12, 1264
Dearest

I may not be home for several more weeks, but with military secrecy the way it is, I may be reading this to you myself.

I am still getting used to working with a mixed crew. It was decided that the common crewmen should come from the Tall Ships. This thing is more of a ship than a plane and it needs crew used to handling a nine-hundred foot long craft. Our pilots are knights from the air force but they answer to a first officer who is from a cargo ship. The radio operator who got your job is also from the air force, but the rest of the crew is pure navy.

We anticipate some problems convincing the pilots that they will fly the way the first officer orders rather than by the seat of their pants. The pilots have never flown on a craft so big that they had their commanding officer sitting behind them.

The ship will be almost empty for the first flight. In addition to the regular crew, we'll have twenty technicians with their tools and spare parts, hydrogen tanks, tanks of sulfuric acid and crates of iron filings. Baring unforeseen trouble, it was decided to make the shakedown cruise the first operational cruise. We'll fly to a seaport (I don't know which yet), pick up cargo and head out into the wilds on our first real trip.

You know it took three days to fill the balloons the first time, with technicians hanging everywhere looking for leaks and tightening up connections. You would have loved the controlled chaos. There must have been two hundred workers here at one time, testing control cables, running the engines, erecting partitions in the crew quarters. It reminded me of an ant heap that had been stirred with a stick.

You've seen the flight deck or course. It still looks roomy even with the five flight officers and all the equipment in it. I finally convinced the engineers that we were NOT going to literally stand watch for twelve hours a day and they welded tall stools at most of the stations, then the pilots had another argument about seat belts. They finally convinced the engineers that even though they weren't going to do loop the loop, a firm seat is important even in a swaying boat.

The crew quarters are about the same as you saw them three weeks ago. A few partitions, some light weight tables bolted to the deck, some posts for hammocks, and no galley. It was decided that the first ship would go with cold sandwiches and canned food. The galley, if you can call it that, consists of a gas-powered samovar for hot tea and a couple of trays of hot water that you can heat cans of food in.

I have the only private cabin, a spacious eight foot cubical with a bolted down bed, a bolted down table, two chairs and a sink – with a water bottle over it and a bucket under it. Not luxury, but it does give me a place to write this letter.

You asked how they were going to handle "personal functions" and it was handled with engineering efficiency. There are three closets in the crew quarters and two in the rear cargo hold with little red lights in them. The navigator has a switch on his panel that turns on the lights when we are over populated territory - if he remembers.

Welcome to the Christian Army Economy Outback Cruise Line. No frills, no food, no warmth and if we get too damned high, no air. I love pioneering. Hey, they gave everybody nice new warm leather jackets, leather helmets, and wool scarves. How could anyone complain?

The kidding stops and the gasping starts when you get to the cargo bay. You've seen it before it was enclosed or floored, but now that it's finished, the scale is enormous.

You now step down from the crew quarters to the cargo deck that is slung under the envelope. Now you really see that it is a two dozen foot wide, and eight gross foot long cavern. Since it hangs beneath the ship, the entire space is clear of obstructions. Overhead you can see the structural rings but the four cargo cranes are lost in the darkness. During the day, light comes from the windows and even suffuses through the thin fabric on the sides. There is a two foot wide duralumin grid on each side and one in the center. The rest is floored with wood. The grids are partly structural and partly to provide places for the cargo hold downs.

You can't see the ballast and hydrogen tanks anymore and that makes it look even bigger.

I have to close now. We're leaving in a few hours and I'm needed on the flight deck.

January 16, 1264

We're here. In fact we're here and ready to leave. We've learned a lot and survived the schooling, always a good combination.

Our first learning experience was the launch. The creaking and crashing of lines letting loose was exciting and we majestically rose slowly into the air until a wind gust shoved us sideways and we hit the dock with our cargo bay. This thing is almost totally uncontrollable at low-speed and low altitude. I intend to name it *Zephyr* because you can only control it in a light breeze. We are going to need a ground control system at the docks. Perhaps several donkey engines pulling cables to control it until it is away.

When we got a few hundred feet up, everything changed. This ship loves the sky. The engine noise is a low, steady, pleasant growl in the background and you fly with the air instead of fighting it like an airplane.

We headed out to sea on our first leg. In part, we didn't want to shock the entire city of Gdansk and in part we didn't want to danger groundlings if we crashed. In spite of a thirty mile an hour headwind, we were able to keep up a good speed down the coast.

The orders were to "maintain a low profile". How do you maintain a low profile in a ship the size of a battleship flying through the sky? Do you only fly at night and hope that no one notices the stars going out? We decided to hide very high in the sky.

The grey canopy is rather close to sky color and I figured if we stayed high up, the perspective would hide our size and we would even benefit from any clouds under us. We dropped ballast and went all the way up to sixteen thousand feet. Boy that was cold.

The construction crews were still installing the hooks and hold downs on the cargo grid and had to work in padded gloves. Valve and meter techs were wiping the frost off of their instruments, and the only happy people were the mechanics stationed in each engine nacelle. They were warm.

Once we passed the borders of Poland, I bled off hydrogen and brought us down to a more comfortable six thousand feet. We still avoided major population centers until we reached our port on the Black Sea.

The only problem was that bag sixteen developed a slow leak. The crew evacuated the gas, dismounted the old bag and had a new one ready to go into place before we reached the base.

The facilities were new, built by Byzantine engineers at our expense and on land donated by the Empire. You'll be impressed when you see them. When we kicked the crap out of the Mongols and the Muslims, we saved their ass and restored some lands to them. They are now firm friends of the Army, if not of Poland itself.

The landing field is in a sheltered valley near Anapa on the coast. They poured huge concrete pads with one foot iron rings and winches imbedded in them to control the hold down chains. They built it right next to large lake where we can refill our ballast tanks. In the last two months, the army construction crew installed a rail spur from the coast and put up some rough warehouses.

The landing was an anticlimax. Less than thirty hours after we left, we bled off hydrogen and dropped slowly into the landing field. Before we were even winched down, the ground crew had attached hoses and water pumps from the lake to top up our ballast The floor of the cargo hold is heavily reinforced and we wanted to be held down firmly during our loading.

We dropped half of the sulfuric acid and iron filings to refill the hydrogen tanks later. It took a full day to load fifty tons of rice and ten tones of crates. That was our second learning experience. The cargo cranes were rigged to load and unload cargo through the deck, like a ship except they were being lifted through the deck instead of dropped.

However, that required hovering the rigidible in one spot and at one altitude while cargo offloaded or uploaded. Rigidibles do not hover, they float.

Raising cargo through a hole in the deck was a pipe dream or something you might do once in a total emergency. Cargo loading is something done while you are firmly tied down and done through the side cargo doors.

Unfortunately, the side cargo doors were too small and the ramps too weak for fast loading. That will have to be redesigned before our next trip.

Lesson number three was evident as soon as we lifted. It really looks bad to be in a three gross yard long ship that is slanting down at the front by, say, thirty degrees. There had been confusion because of the time constraints and the restricted access and the cargo handlers had stored all the boxes near the rear of the craft and stacked the rice near the front. It looked good enough for a sailing ship, but rice is heavy and now so was the bow.

We could have dropped ballast and restored balance, but I swallowed my pride and had the shipped winched back down to the ground. It took several hours to shift the cargo around to balance the load better.

The rest of the trip was uneventful except that the rear port side engine began to knock badly about twelve hours out from Anapa. We had made the assumption that since this thing flew, it needed engines like a plane, fast and light. We were wrong. Engine weight is not a problem with this beast, but the engines have to run for days without maintenance. When I return, I am going to recommend that the engines on the unfinished ships be replaced with marine engines.

Since the engines are in their own standing room sized pods, we took the engine offline and the mechanics were able to start the repair in flight. They had the engine stripped down and the crankshaft shimmed almost before we reached Lord Conrad's camp.

Conrad's Diary Continues

Staying three or four months on the tundra is different than overnight camping. I had to build a temporary city, and there weren't a lot of bricks and mortar around.

One purpose of the project was to fight camp fever, that morbid bored attitude that saps the will of even the best army, but it had to be done anyway. The Steppes were going to get cold and damp and miserable and a cotton tent, waterproof or not, was not the place to live through the winter. There were some wooded areas near enough to be used, but they were too small to provide housing materials for forty thousand men, so I settled on the same material that we used for the ramparts, sod. If it could house thousands of American settlers, it could house the Army. The wood would be only used for ridge poles and sills.

Each company theoretically had two hundred and fifty-two men so we made that our standard housing unit. Each housing unit would have buildings arranged around a square. Three sides of the square would each have six soddies for the warriors and two for the knights. In the center would be a soddie for the knights banner facing one reserved for the captain.

The fourth side would be the large dining/recreation hall and two latrines would be in the corners, far enough away for sanitation and odor control. The engineering company experimented with several designs and settled on a dozen foot wide, three dozen foot long soddie tall enough to allow the erection of two standard tents inside. The roofs sagged or collapsed on the first three they built, but they eventually came up with a solid design that could be built with three ridge poles, two sills on top the side walls, a sill for the top of the door and a lot of sod.

Windows were placed at the top of both walls, just under the sill for fresh air, light, and smoke evacuation and a door cut in the long side. The units were paired less than five feet apart with the doors facing each other. The entryways were a little claustrophobic, but we hoped that they would shield each other from the wind and share what heat escaped, and the close spacing of the houses left a lot of open space compared the usual camp layout. We would need over three thousand of the houses.

The captains got the same house but it had only their tent in it, leaving ample space for a waiting or conference room. Each unit needed a long narrow latrine made the same way, but only two yards wide and an eating/cooking/social hall big enough to seat over a hundred men at a time. Fortunately, our standard baggage included a lot of folding chairs, not enough, but a lot.

The roof was the tricky part. Even poor farmers tried to buy enough cut lumber and tar paper for a roof. If you were poorer than that just lumber would do. No lumber? Put a canvas over the rafters, stack bushes and small limbs over that, and then a thin layer of sod. No canvas? Put lots of bushes and limbs and maybe some woven grass mats over the rafters and then a thin layer of sod. That kind of roof guaranteed two things, it would admit bugs, rats, spiders, and various nasties and was one hundred percent guaranteed to leak.

We probably had enough canvas on hand to roof the big halls and the latrines, the rest of the houses would show why we erected tents inside them. Unfortunately, my personal tent was too large to fit inside a sod structure, so I settled for three walls to buffer the wind and a canvas roof.

It turned out that boredom was not as big a problem as I feared. About half the food we had left was canned, but the rest needed to be cooked four times a day, and people needed to clean up afterward and handle the garbage. For the first month, we had teams of sod cutters going out every day making bricks for building and repair. Then the water teams had to bring water from the river to every dining hall. After the first rain, most squads sent men out to the small forest areas to gather more bushes and foliage for their roofs. By the time we had all the construction done, there were no more forest areas around, but there were still bushes and branches left over. Some troopers wove grass mats for doors and window coverings.

Exercise took part of each day and while we were too short of ammo for target practice, we had sword, hand to hand, and bayonet practice. Then there were organized sports, disorganized contests, card games, practical jokes, equipment maintenance and constant improvements to the palisade. For the first few weeks, we had the shit brigade out every day. Since the main fuel on the steppes was dried animal dung, unfortunate troopers with shovels and a wagon scanned a larger area each day for dung.

The only thing we didn't have was gambling. It was forbidden on pain of the worst punishments that would leave a man combat capable – when he healed. I have no moral objection to gambling and damned little sympathy for someone dumb enough to gamble his poke away, but I couldn't risk breaking camp with an army where half the men were broke and carrying grudges against the half who had their money.

We did get one major break. I had read somewhere that in the 19th century, the major commercial fuel in Russia was peat. It was even used for power generation for part of the 20th century. The crew I had sent to scout downriver had paid off. In an area where the river had once run, they found a small peat bog. Maybe enough fuel for one winter.

We dropped the shit wagons and organized crews to cut peat every day. It gave us enough fuel to cook with, heat the soddies, and boil our water.

147

We needed a lot of hot water to keep the men healthy. One of the major fictions in modern history is the story that Napoleon was defeated by the Russian winter. It makes a grand story and caused a lot of dramatic art work, but it just isn't true. The weather didn't turn really cold until he had crossed the borders out of the country. For most of his retreat, the weather was clear and about fifty degrees Fahrenheit. His men died of disease, not the cold. Some died of hunger, thousands surrendered to avoid starvation, but two hundred thousand died from disease. Typhus was the biggest killer, a disease from which clean healthy men rarely die.

We had enough food and vitamin supplements for a few months, chemicals to sterilize water, lime for the latrines, and exercised the men regularly, but we had to keep them clean. I built several large bath houses near the river and, since sod house walls tend to run when steamed, we used some of our precious wood supply to make saunas. The men were required to strip to the skin, scrub down, and wash their clothes not less than once every five days. Tubs of hot water and toweling were available sixteen hours a day.

I brought forty thousand healthy men into this camp and intended to take the same number out.

The time passed rapidly. About six weeks after we arrived, the group I sent south returned with a large herd of cattle and a week behind them there was a smaller herd of sheep. They had gotten as far as the edge of the Cuman Sultanate when they found estates with herds for sale. The owners were probably nominally subjects of the Mongols, but the conversation was limited to hand gestures, grunts, and head shaking and did not lend itself to irrelevant political talk. Gold, as usual, was the real ruler.

Fortunately the Christian Army contained a large number of former farm boys who could butcher crudely but adequately.

After the first few weeks, we knew we were being watched. The Big People patrolled a twenty-mile wide area while they fed at night, and with their sense of smell, they could find a Mongol a mile away, even if he recently had his annual bath. On a regular basis, they brought in the bodies of spies either crushed or wiggling in the morning. We set up posts ten miles up and down the river to monitor boat traffic. We continued to purchase or commandeer a few useful cargoes whose owners had apparently not believed the rumors that we were here, and I am certain that many of the riverboat men reported to the Mongols.

For reasons of their own, the Mongols made no serious attempt to attack us. Either they were not certain of our intentions, or lacked local manpower, or were just waiting to set up a trap, but we did not even suffer from serious sniping all winter.

The ten weeks before the dirigible arrived passed rapidly.

I was in a staff meeting when I heard engine noises and commotion outside. Sylvia ran in from her post yelling, "Master, Master, there is a monster in the sky!" Apparently she hadn't been at any of the staff meetings about the dirigibles. It circled overhead twice, keeping several thousand feet up, wisely out of rifle range and then dropped a canister near enough to make me jump. The message was "Meet us at the river. Bring strong, heavy men." You could hear the engines rev up as it headed east.

It took a lot of shouting to convince thousands of medieval men that the thing was not a monster, and when that failed, that it was our monster. The barons and knights had their hands full keeping the panic down. Even the ones who had been briefed on the dirigibles hadn't realized how big they were until that moment. Twentieth century men facing a flying saucer would have been calmer.

The captain loitered over the river until I put on my golden armor and joined a thousand men at the riverside. I knew I wouldn't need to armor for fighting, but I wanted the captain to see where the boss was.

I sat on Silver for about twenty minutes as the captain lined up his ship over with the river and dropped large rubber hoses over a hundred feet down. He waited until the breeze was blowing toward our side of the river and started up his water pumps. The ship slowly sank as he filled the ballast tanks and floated down toward the bank. At about thirty feet, the crew dropped a dozen ropes from the cargo doors and gestured for men to grab on. It would have been easier to get them to grab live rattlesnakes, but discipline finally got enough to grab ropes to drag the ship further onto the bank as it sank.

Once he was settled, the water pumps sped up to fill the ballast tanks. I realized that he was making certain that his big gas-filled balloon didn't get knocked around while it was beached. These people were learning a lot faster than I expected. The most common accident that killed the early zeppelins was gusts of wind that dragged them around on the ground but this captain had good feeling for his ship and a sense of how to run it.

I waited until I saw men leaving the control house and then rode over to meet the officers debarking at the front loading ramp. The captain stood in the doorway, waiting for me. He must have known that I would want the tour. As I approached the ramp, he saluted and called out, "Captain Obitz, commanding the *Zephyr*, your grace. We bring you presents, and a great new toy!"

I shouted back, "That was a hell of a landing, captain!"

"I hope I never have to do it again!"

By that time, I was standing beside him, "Maybe next time we can drop straight down on the bank and have your men drag the hoses to the river. It's easier than waiting for the right breeze. We can land without taking on ballast, but I have to dump a lot gas to do it.

149

"We've been up there over an hour watching your camp. It was easy to follow your trail in the grass, but we didn't expect a mud city. We weren't even certain it was you until we saw your tent and then got low enough to see some of the flags."

I was looking over his shoulder at the biggest enclosed space I had seen since I left the twentieth century. It was filled with cargo. "What did you bring me on the first trip?"

"Mostly Food. Captain Feliks was in charge of the cargo. His philosophy is that there's no point in giving a man a gun if he's too cold or too hungry to use it, so I've got fifty tons of rice, wheat, and dried fruit, twenty thousand pairs of socks, twenty-five thousand pairs of underwear, five thousand shirts, and a lot of toilet paper. Maybe next time I'll be able to bring some military stuff."

"Feliks was right, that is military stuff, but I'll send back another list of what we need. We've done better with local food than we expected. How long was your flight?"

"About thirty hours. We flew out of the new base in Anapa. Komander Osiol is having your supplies shipped there, so we won't be going back to Gdansk on every mission."

Captain Ivanov already had a crew unloading the supplies, so the airship captain and I got out of the way by taking a tour of the ship. I was impressed by the Spartan layout. This thing was optimized for cargo.

The captain explained that the ground was not a good place for a *rigidible* and expressed a desire to get back in the air as soon as possible. I had a table set up for us to work at and sent for food for everyone, including both crews. He told us what he needed for landing spot, and we agreed to prepare the best we could, and have designated teams of men to help on the next trip. The crews had the ship unloaded in four hours and we sat down to a good meal of fresh bread and beef. Captain Ivanov handed over a list of critically needed supplies and then hurried off to supervise the storage of the new supplies.

The last thing offloaded was a tank of acid and a large box of iron filings. It would provide enough emergency hydrogen to lift off in an emergency.

The captain explained that he was going back to Gdansk on this trip for a post fight evaluation, but that we should see one of his sister ships in less than ten days. Then he jumped back on board grinning like a kid with a new bicycle and rose into the air.

The navy was a good as their word. A second airship showed up in nine days and in the ten weeks we waited out the winter, the four ships delivered eighty tons of supplies four times a week.

The war was saved.

The only casualty was the R3 *Vagabond*. During our last week in camp, she was driven to the ground by a severe winter storm on her return trip and significantly damaged. On her last trip here, R1 *Zephyr* took a lance of infantry aboard to drop at the crash site for protection and labor. Every 'rigidible' built in my time-line had disintegrated if it hit the ground at more than ten miles an hour, so I assumed that the crew would gather up the pieces and ship them back to Poland.

I learned later that these engineers had built well and the Vagabond had been salvaged. Her crew stripped the canvas cover from the bent frame, replaced enough gas bags to get the wreckage aloft, repaired two of the engine mounts, and flew the skeleton back to Gdansk in a painfully slow ten-day long trip. The medal shops must have worked overtime to reward them.

We only needed about one load a week to maintain our food supplies. We had plenty of beef and mutton and you only needed to add a hunk of bread and a few vegetables to have a balanced diet. Fresh bread was particularly popular so the smell of baking bread permeated the camp night and day. One load a week brought in carrots, potatoes, pickles and onions and sometimes more flour. The rest went to war.

I did a lot of planning during the boring winter evenings. I doubted that the Mongols would be the pushovers that the Moslem armies had been. They were more experienced, motivated and from what we saw at Sarai, they had almost modern weapons. This time we would be going up against an organized force that had long-range rifles and cannon.

We had done well riding into Sarai like avenging angels on horseback, but odds were almost one to one and most of our success was due to our men's Sten guns, twelve shot rifles and superior armor.

We weren't optimized in our tactics. All of our Wolves had Sten guns, but I still had problems convincing them that charging the enemy with a sword cut their killing range down from fifty yards to two. Pretty, but not good idea unless you were out of bullets.

In fact, up close in a sword against Sten gun battle, some of the Mongols had done serious damage to some Wolves. It was time to rethink our tactics. If we were going up against serious numbers of disciplined soldiers, we were going to have to make better use of what we had.

I decided that the coming battles would have to be fought stand off. Despite our success in Sarai, it was foolish to expect my forty thousand men to go toe to toe swinging swords and shooting machine pistols at a Mongol army thirty or forty times their size.

Occasionally I pictured a cartoon that I had seen in the twentieth century. It showed five British Soldiers standing across from five American colonials. A referee between them was saying, "O.K., the Americans have won the coin toss and they choose that all the British soldiers will wear bright red uniforms and stand in straight lines while they will wear camouflage colors and hide behind rocks and trees. Play War!"

I decided we would use the German tactics from World War II. Every German squad was essentially a group of machine gun tenders. They carried a heavy machine gun that was moved, loaded, aimed and maintained by four of the squad members. The other seven carried spare ammo and used their rifles to protect the machine gun. Forget what you saw in the movies, the machine guns did ninety percent of the killing and until they ran of ammo, food, and shoes, the Germans killed Russians at a fifty to one ratio. We had done that against medieval armies, but the Germans did it against a modern foe. They lost, but not by much.

Against Karakorum itself, our artillery was better than the Mongols, so we would stand back, punch the walls down, and level the city from a distance. Hopefully we could sucker them into sallying out and meeting us in the field, where killing them would be easier than house to house fighting. Eventually, it would come down to man on man, hand to hand fighting, but by that time I wanted the odds in our favor.

The first order of business was machine guns. By then, most of our armament factories were well automated. We could turn out rifles and machine guns by the thousands. Money was also no problem. In addition to the vast wealth of the Christian Army, I had sent back enough gold from Sarai to equip an army several times our size. A single cargo run brought in an additional fifteen hundred medium machine guns, still just light enough to be carried on horseback and fired from a tripod. The carpenters used parts from the now useless medieval wagons to build mobile gun platforms, essentially two wheeled wagons mounting one or two machine guns with thick wooden walls and carrying a lot of ammo under the floor. If necessary, they could be fired on the move.

Two more cargos were filled with ammunition.

Artillery was my next concern. We had salvaged about a hundred field pieces after the bridge collapse, but we were short on ammo and the pieces we had might be too lightweight to punch through the stone walls of Karakorum. Even with the carriages, the dirigibles were able to deliver another fifty field pieces in a single trip and have capacity left over for ammo. Since they were light and cheap, I ordered enough Sten guns and ammo to equip most of the Mobile Infantry with Stens as backups to their rifles.

We ordered anti-personnel shrapnel rounds, incendiaries for the city, and lots of old fashioned simple high-explosive rounds. Osiol came up with it all. I don't know if he stripped the defenses of Poland, robbed the armories of the navy or if we just had more manufacturing capacity than I realized, and I never asked.

Sir Eikman and Ivanov had their own long lists of radio parts, soap, tools and gadgets, but the only other thing I needed was a Great Turkish Bombard. When the Ottomans finally conquered Constantinople, they used a specially build gun to knock down walls that had stood for over a thousand years. It was about twenty feet long and threw a two foot diameter rock ball over a mile. The sound of its firing could be heard ten miles away.

Of course, I didn't literally need the Bombard. It used stone balls and took four hours to reload, but I need something smaller and more powerful that was guaranteed to bring down the walls of Karakorum.

I sent a coded message to Komander Osiol describing what I needed. On the next airship visit, I got a package from him. It contained drawings of a five-inch naval gun, another project that I hadn't authorized, and a note, "Your grace I have one of these on a naval ship near the Anapa base It was added after the ship was constructed, so the base and gun can be unbolted relatively easily. It throws a fifty-five pound explosive shell over sixteen miles and it should knock down anything up to and including the Gates of Hell.

"If we remove it from its mount, it will fit through the rear cargo door of a rigidible. The Rigidible Corps assures me that at fifteen thousand pounds for the gun and three thousand more for the mount it is well within their capacity to lift and even leaves room for ammunition on the same trip.

"The commander of the *Zephyr* suggests, however, that we make it the last thing we deliver to you. While this thing is relatively easy for a rigidible to carry, you don't want to drag twenty thousand pounds of stubborn metal over the steppes.

"His suggestion is that he deliver the base to your camp and as much ammo as you want to haul with you. Then when you reach your destination and set up the base, he can deliver the gun directly to your battle site.

"Captain Obitz has already received permission to fly air support during your campaign. He has had an extra radio and generator, and several telescopes mounted on the *Zephyr* for spotting. He's recruited two cartographers and a couple of artists to map for you. He will arrive in the area of Karakorum at about the same time you do and will remain in your command as long as his supplies hold out."

153

As soon as the machine guns arrived, I began to drill the Mounted Infantry in dragoon tactics, riding into battle, but dismounting to fight. The Wolves would continue to be shock troops that fought from horseback with the Stens. Getting them off their horses would be nearly impossible when I was still having trouble convincing them to keep their swords sheathed unless they were out of ammo.

We set up a training ground outside of the compound. It needed to be large because we were training lances to ride hard to just outside bow range and then dismount. They formed up with the machine gun in the center manned by a gunner, a loader, and an ammo fetcher. The four other men in the lance took positions, two on each side, to protect the machine gun. The Big People then retreated out of range as they weren't needed until the next move and made big targets.

We drilled them until they could dismount, set up the gun, and get the first rounds off in less than thirty seconds. Then we practiced swiveling alternate gun groups to the rear in case of an attack from that direction. The complex move was re-aiming the wings to defend from flanking attack. They had to change position to keep from shooting each other when they fired left or right. When we were done, an entire wing could pick up their guns, swivel to the side, reposition, and resume firing in less than half a minute.

By the Ides of March, we were ready for war.

Su Song's Fourth Entry

I have now spent ten years on the Polish project. A fifth of my life has passed on this project, and it is time again to evaluate my progress.

The great khan is dead. His successor Ogedei has passed on, and the Emperor Mongke rules in his place.

Looking back on the last ten years, it has been worth devoting much of my life to the project.

All three of our leaders have been pleased with our progress in firearms. Genghis Khan was elated when the guns we produced gave him total superiority on the battlefield. For years, no army of the Koreans or the Song could stand against him in the field.

However, we continued to improve the weapons. Five years after we introduced the fused firearm, one of our chemistry teams developed a new ignition system. It consisted of a paper strip with caps of mercury fulminate embedded about an inch apart. In place of the match cord and dipping dragons head, there was an enclosed cylinder holding a roll of caps and a hammer operated by the trigger. In place of the fuse hole and fuse, there was a small bent tube that ended right under where the hammer hit the cap. To fire the loaded weapon, you pulled the next cap over the tube mouth and pulled the trigger. It operated much faster than the fuse system, worked in any weather, and you didn't need to keep a lighted cord around.

Unfortunately, it was not, in itself, enough to assure victory over the Song and Korean empires. No matter how badly the khan's beat their armies in the field, both countries were old and rich and their cities were well walled and defended. When they were attacked, they took their citizens inside the walls and waited us out. The khans could devastate the countryside, but could not conquer it.

We used what we had learned from the Polish guns to improve the cannons. The grooves that improved the aim of the hand cannons worked as well with siege cannon and we began to produce some of our cannon with the rifling. When their aim improved, it was more likely that they would be able to hit the city walls repeatedly in the same area and knock them down.

With the help of the replicas of the Polish hand cannon to clear the walls, the new cannon to punch through the walls, and bigger gunpowder bombs slung by trebuchets to keep the defenders from repairing the breech some Song cities began to fall, including my home town of Hue.

Fortunately, I was able to convince Odegi that Hue held men of my acquaintance who could help with our work, so most of the population was spared.

The team working on the Polish kite was never able to get the engine to run for more than a few minutes, and within a few months it was obvious that we did not have the materials or skills to reproduce the engine. The tolerances were closer than those on the guns or the other engines and even some of the materials were strange to us.

However, the reports of them flying over the battlefield for hours and appearing over camps many *li* from the front was appealing. No commander had ever had such intelligence. Battle kites were well developed by the Koreans, but they were limited to the areas that could be seen from a tether and needed a stiff breeze to work. The Polish devices were obviously not kites, but flyers.

We built several flyers and launched them like kites or dropped them off hillsides. It took months to sort out that the shape of the wing had to be curved just as the Polish flyers were and how the movements of the flaps controlled the flight.

Our first models were hopelessly heavy, and it took months to find materials light and strong enough for flight. We ended up with pine and bamboo parts covered with a painted silk. Our first successful flyer was model number twenty two. It glided for twenty minutes and did not kill its pilot.

Working with wing shapes and balance, we were finally able to produce a flyer that could stay aloft for an hour – if you launched it off a high hill into a strong wind. It was still a glider.

As with the guns, we needed to use our own expertise to adapt the Polish devices. We couldn't reliably reproduce the Polish engine, but metal and wood were not the only things that flew. We turned our glider into a flyer by adding a solid fuel rocket. Instead of throwing powder balls into the air, it threw a flyer. The families of the first few pilots are still receiving their pensions.

Eventually our powder experts developed two types of rockets. One is still fast burning and is used to launch the flyer. It's mounted in a fixed tube under the tail. The other type of rocket was harder to develop, but eventually we produced a slow burning powder that gave a gentler push for up to a minute. The pilot had a carousel of ten to twenty slow rockets in the space where the Polish flyer had its engine. The pilot would rotate the next rocket to a position under his feet and fire it as needed.

With a full carousel and a little luck a skillful pilot could make a flight of several hours – and it was amazingly simple compared to the complex Polish engine.

The guns and the flyers changed the face of warfare. A surprise attack or ambush was virtually impossible against a force of flyers, and our new guns dominated the battlefield everywhere.

For all of that, most of the Song Empire still holds out. In any case, compared to the other changes the Poles caused, the battlefield successes were almost trivial.

As I expected, the rail cars changed the face of our county. We laid the first short tracks to feed materials for the new capitol from the quarries to the nearest canals. Our second phase put down track between all of the major cities and the new capitol. Genghis was delighted when he saw that the price of materials for his new capitol was cut in half by the better transportation. Ogedei was the khan when the tolls began to roll in from the rail systems. They cost less than one percent of what a canal would and dropped costs almost as fast. Of course, they belonged to the government and the government charged for their use. The empire began to make more money off of the rail system and the increased business taxes than it did from conquest.

Emperor Mongke ruled when we rolled out the first steam engines and changed the world again.

It was surprisingly difficult to produce the steam engines. At first they seemed very simple. Once you had diagrammed the working parts, an apprentice could see the principals in a few minutes. A few pistons and valves reminiscent of a bilge pump or fire extinguisher, a fancy set of valves and some steam and anyone could understand it.

When we produced our first working models for Genghis' initial visit to our facility, we certainly had no idea how many years it would take to go from the models to practical engines.

The first models leaked. They leaked so much steam that there wasn't enough left over for real work. When we got the joints tight, the bearings wore out and the pistons overheated and the push arms bent. In one early model, the engineer did not understand the use of the spinning balls on top of the Polish engine and without a safety valve the engine ended the career and the life of the engineer and his assistants.

The water heated slowly and the heat was hard to regulate. The fuel was burning inefficiently, so we called a baker and a potter. Actually, we enlisted families that had been making bakery and pottery ovens for generations. At first they were reluctant to share their secrets, but a discussion of the importance of this to the empire and to the probability of their families breathing the next day convinced them to help us.

They taught us about flue sizes, air paths, stoking techniques, firebox sizes, venting and controlling the flames. We transferred their knowledge of brick and ceramic ovens to copper and iron construction.

Eventually we developed models that worked for large stationary jobs like pumping water, grinding grain, and running hammer mills. I began to understand how the Poles could afford their guns. A grinding machine powered by steam could reduce weeks of hand lapping down to days or hours. We have only begun to roll out the engines and the cost of manufacturing many things has already started to drop.

We were still stymied when it came to mobile power. The Poles had used the engines to power their boats and I wanted to power the rail cars with them, but they still had problems. To move even a medium sized boat, we needed to heat four or five hundred gallons of water. That wasn't a problem in a factory or a mine where the engine would run twenty four hours a day, but with a kettle that big, you would have to start the fires on Sunday to move your boat on Tuesday morning. It just wasn't practical.

Eventually someone realized that we had never seen a Polish steam kettle, and realized that must be the missing piece. We talked again to everyone that had seen one of the "kettles". It wasn't easy to get them back again and their memories had faded in the intervening years, but we learned that the first descriptions had been inadequate. The boilers had not been barrels with open flames below them, but had been integrated boilers with a fire and an enclosed water tank inside.

One of my engineers insisted that there had not been enough water. "If there were thousands of gallons of water in a big tank and it leaked out when the trebuchet hit it, the decks would have been two chi deep in water. They would have stormed a boat knee deep in water. Something else is going on.'" He spent three days sitting on a mat, staring at an engine, and drinking too much rice wine. I don't know if he came up with the same solution that the Poles did, but he solved our problem. It was another "Why didn't we see that before?" moment.

He moved the water supply to an external tank, then, instead of single large tank in the boiler, he created long thin tanks that ran the length of the boiler. They were about four inches thick, two feet high and ran the entire length of the boiler. They were placed about six inches apart. Water was sprayed into one end of each tank and steam came out the other end within minutes. We were only heating as much water as we needed at one time and we had a lot of surface area to heat it with. It took a few months of experimentation to get the size and spacing optimal, and we eventually added a long tube down the middle of each tank to distribute incoming water better. It still took almost an half an hour to get useable pressure, but we had mobile steam engines.

We were frustrated in only one minor area. When I suggested to the khan's advisors that a rail way built along the Silk Road route would cut shipping times across the road from months to a few weeks, his response was, "Of course. And that is why we will never allow it to be built. You are aware that all of China is covered with well built paved roads laid down by wise rulers over a thousand year history, but you may have missed the fact that those roads were of incalculable help in moving our armies into battle with the Jin and now with the Song.

We are never going to move armies toward Europe and the Poles as long as there are any other enemies to subdue and certainly not in your lifetime or mine. We trade with them at the end of the Silk Road, the Emperor accepts delegates from their Pope and kings, and we learn from them, but they are a dangerous enemy and we have no intention of providing them with a railway or even a roadbed to move their armies on. Never!"

Interlude in Uncle Tom's Control Room

I hit the control button again.

"What the hell is going on? This says that the Mongols were never going to attack Poland again."

Uncle Tom shrugged, "That's right. It was just bad intelligence such as often happens in wars. Several of Novacek's spies reported the same thirty thousand man relief column going to Sarai on their annual rotation. The same one Conrad has already destroyed.

"There was confusion that led the staff to assume that they were different columns and much bigger than they really were. You combine that with a few ambiguous references to a ninety-day time-line and someone suddenly sees a massive invasion, but Poland was never in danger."

My frustration was evident. "That means that this whole campaign is a waste. He could turn back now, or could have turned back at Sarai, or could just have relaxed in his palace in Jerusalem and it wouldn't have made any difference. Shouldn't someone tell him?"

"I don't think so. He was getting bored and, frankly, boring to monitor. What fights he had were so easy they looked like a bad cowboy movie and every day was mind-numbingly the same. A few meetings, food, cigars, whiskey, watching more naked girls dance like the naked girls did last night, sex with another girl who looked like the one last night, and a lot of snoring.

"It wasn't that he wasn't bored with naked dancing-girls; he just didn't know what else to do without television. For God's sake, the man was so bored he spent a year drawing pictures of his new home.

"I had to do something or we'd both die of boredom.

"This way, he has an adventure, we have something interesting to monitor, and if he succeeds a railroad will be built on the Silk Road and stimulate both regions into tremendous progress."

I leaned forward, "But what if he gets killed on this useless campaign?"

"Then we can start monitoring someone else.

"Besides, he knows. He has to know. How stupid would he have to be when he has been in Mongolian territory for months and hasn't seen so much as a squad of soldiers since Sarai? If there was a million man Mongol army out there, he'd be dead by now, and he knows it. Hell, he built that camp like a fort because he knows that the Mongols favorite time for war is winter. When not a single Mongol showed up all winter, it was obvious that there was no one out there."

"Then why is he still there?"

"Hatred. Blood lust. I'm certain that he still sees himself as a paragon of virtue, but he has become very casual about human life. A lot more people died during his Africa trip than he admits too, and his attitude has changed. Once killing bothered him, but now he can execute a thousand prisoners or a hundred *evil* men and still enjoy his lunch.

"His hatred of the Mongols has grown over the years. You saw how he was genuinely angry when his generals objected to wiping out the Mongol civilians. I think he is planning genocide and is only restrained by the necessity of convincing his army to do it."

I leaned forward and pushed the Resume button.

The Trip to Karakorum Begins

It took several days to get ready to move. Commissary had to pack their pots and pans, the wagons – thousands of them – had to be inventoried and reloaded. Everything got polished, repaired, sharpened, and packed. Two days before breakout, crews began to remove two large sections of our outer wall. The day before breakout the tents were removed from the soddies, cleaned, and packed away. The men would sleep under the stars that night and move out fast in the morning. The same day, the now useless medieval wagons and every scrap of paper and garbage was piled into a trash mountain that burned all night. Anything we weren't taking was burned.

The R4 *Wanderlust* landed in the early morning and took the tanks of spare acid and iron filings aboard. We hadn't needed them yet, but there was no reason to leave them behind. I had requested that *Wanderlust* fly observation for us until *Zephyr* arrived or until they ran low on hydrogen.

The next morning, a few minutes after our morning rituals, *Wanderlust* rose majestically into the air, leveled off at about four thousand feet, and led forty thousand men up the river.

The plan was simple. We were obviously under some observation unless the Mongols had lost all of their wits, and stealth was not a requirement. So, using *Wanderlust* to avoid traps, we would travel north up the river until we got to the northern branch of the Silk Road, then turn right and go to Karakorum, looking for a fight all the way. Within a few days, we would be in the foothills of the Altai Mountains, and the road was the best route through to the capitol.

Once we left the river, we should make the gross mile days that I expected on the last trip. Now we were lean, well equipped and should make the nine hundred miles to Karakorum in ten days.

It was fast. We traveled better than ten miles an hour in open country, ate lunch in the saddle, and stopped only for a few short rest breaks every day. We had saved the canned food for the trip and it was nice to taste mystery stew again.

Several times, we overran small groups of Mongol soldiers who had probably been told to shadow us from the front. When they couldn't match our pace, they fell back into rifle range. We took neither prisoners nor casualties for three days.

About noon of the second day, we reached the road. As before, we paralleled the road to avoid traffic. There wasn't much to avoid, the word was out that we were coming, and this time we moved within sight of the road.

The marching orders were simple: keep moving! By the second day, we were leaving the steppes and closing in on the Altai mountains. This area was populated much more heavily than the steppes. There was a major town about every hundred miles, villages about every twenty miles, and a lot of small settlements. We flowed through it all without stopping.

I knew that if there was going to be trouble, it would be in the foothills of the Altai. It was the first place the Mongols could hope to set up an ambush. Sure enough, in the afternoon of the third day, I received a radio call from the *Wanderlust*.

"Lord Conrad, you have friends preparing a welcoming party for you. They seem very anxious to make your acquaintance. About twenty miles ahead, you have hostiles on hidden ridges both sides of the road. We count eighty cannon with heavy supporting infantry. I would estimate two thousand hostiles, half cannon tenders and half infantry. Looks like they've been waiting for awhile."

"Thank you, *Wanderlust*. Do you see any alternate routes? I hate to stop for a party."

"No, lord. They obviously picked this spot because it's the first bottleneck on the road. You'll pass a good-sized village a few miles ahead of you and then follow a river eastward. The river will broaden out to a lake for a few miles and then narrow as you start into a valley. At that point, there are foothills on both sides of the route. Cannon are dug in just over the crest of the hills. The troops are camped between the foothills and the mountainside. You can identify the hills by the Chinese-style pagoda high on the right side.

"You might be able to get Big People around the back by skirting the mountainside, but they'd be single file sitting ducks. I should also warn you that the cannon are well dug in. They're ready for a slug fest."

"Thanks, we'll take care if it."

I wished that I did know how to *take care of it*. I was feeling the normal anger we all get when our enemies stubbornly fail to fulfill our expectations for their stupidity.

Since they hadn't even made a probing attack all winter, I had assumed that the mission to kill their horses had been a success. I believed that, being short on horses to support an attack, they would hold up in their walled cities and wait for battle. Unfortunately, someone seems to have read the story about the Persians and three hundred stubborn Greeks.

I guessed that whatever mobile forces they had left were now in a reserve column ready to reinforce the ambush on whatever pass we took through the mountains. If we took a different pass, we'd probably run into a similar force whose job would be to hold us there until the reinforcements arrived.

It was a good plan. Too damned good. If we had stumbled into it, it could have seriously wounded us. Even knowing about it, we were going to have a hard time getting through. We had plenty of artillery shells now and we outranged the Mongol cannons, but *Wanderlust* told us that their cannon were well dug in. That means we would need almost direct hits on most of them to put them out of commission. That could take days, during which their reinforcements would arrive.

Our only chance for an easy passage was to move much faster than they expected. I called over one of my messengers. "Send a message out to the scouts. There is a valley about twenty miles ahead. They'll see some hills with a pagoda on the right side. There are Mongols beyond those hills. They are to make a lot noise going through the valley and back but are not to find the Mongols. We want to convince them we're too stupid to see them. Then report back to me as soon as we camp."

I called over Sir Wladyclaw and asked, "How many night fighters do we have along?"

"Three companies. They aren't operating as night fighters now, but they have been trained for it."

"Tell them to get well rested as soon as we camp. They may be getting up very early tomorrow morning."

We stopped in full daylight and camped by the lake about five miles short of the ambush pass. I hoped it was late enough in the day to seem natural to the spies watching from the mountainside ahead. The staff conference started almost immediately.

It was crowded with fifteen people around the two tables. Most of the barons, all of the counts, and two komanders made a group almost too big to work with. The cooks, realizing that this was a working meeting with no time or space for plates and manners, set up a sideboard with fresh bread and chunks of meat, vegetables, and onions that could be skewered one-handed. I told the two scouts that I was conferring with to get some food and opened the meeting.

"Most of you know that we stopped early because there is a Mongol ambush ahead. The *Wanderlust* tells us that the enemy has dug in about eighty cannon on both sides of a valley ahead. Of course, we could blast them out with our artillery or the Wolves could go up and kill them all, but an artillery duel would be long and expensive and even the Wolves would be foolish to charge up a hill with forty cannons and hundreds of rifles waiting at the top.

"Armor or not, it would be foolish to crest a hill in front of a cannon firing grape-shot.

"I'm certain that they have sent for reinforcements. We can, of course, kick the ass of any army that comes at us, but we want to avoid a nasty firefight in a narrow pass. We know that close up, they can still hurt us so we should clean up this mess before they get friends.

"I have a plan for an attack that should solve the problem, but it requires several steps, careful timing and lots of cooperation. I expect you all to work out the details before we retire.

"The moon will set just after midnight tonight, leaving us a lot of dark to work with and Baron Krol is leading three companies of trained night fighters. That gives us about seven hundred men to sneak up two hills in the middle of the night.

"The scouts over there at the sideboard report that the hills hiding the ambush are barely able to qualify as *hills*. They have a rather gentle slope: perhaps three hundred feet high and less than a half mile long on both sides of the valley. We know from *Wanderlust* that the cannon are spotted along the crests of the hills and the camps are further back near the mountainsides.

"So, here's the plan. After moon sets, the night fighters and four other companies of Wolves ride out as quietly as possible to as near to the ambush as they can get without being heard. That should leave them about two miles out.

"The night fighters will wait until an hour before first light and then sneak up the hills and take out the sentries as quietly as possible. When the sentries are neutralized they will take out any soldiers sleeping near the cannon. That'll require rifles and Sten guns and it'll wake up everyone.

"When Baron Kowalski's men hear the gunfire, they'll start lobbing star shells over both enemy camps, and the Wolves will charge both hills. If you're two miles away, they should crest the hills in less than four minutes. With the cannon neutralized, it should be a cake walk. Their job is to sweep the camps near the mountains. It's a smash and bash. Fly through without stopping, shoot everything in sight, and then pull back to the infantry line.

"When the sun rises, we can finish off any survivors."

The staff did come up with some improvements. The infantry commanders suggested that when the fighting started, three of their lances should take machine guns up each hill and set them up at the ridge to cover any retreat and add long-range firepower. The Wolves could sweep through the camp and back toward the ridge and be supported by the machine guns.

Then someone mentioned that having your own machine guns firing from behind you might place a severe burden on the widows and orphans fund, so the plan was revised to place the machine guns between the cannon emplacements and the Mongol camp and not use them unless the Wolves were in serious trouble or after the Wolves exited the camp.

165

Baron Kowalski pointed out lobbing star shells that far out would be inaccurate unless we moved the artillery up closer to the ambush site, so we decided to use illumination flares instead.

The night fighters pointed out that neutralizing the sentries on both hills was absolutely essential before either force infiltrated the cannon field. If either force jumped the gun it could sabotage the other, do they worked out a series of signals using lighters.

The session went on for almost two hours, but an operation like this often took days to plan, so it still felt rushed. If anyone thinks that we were overplanning, that we didn't need to think so hard when we had the best guns, fastest mounts, and all of the machine guns, they should look up the Battle of Isandlwana where a Zulu army wiped out a modern British force using only spears against rifles. The Gods of War favor those with the mostest and the bestest, but only if they don't act the stupidest.

Word had already been sent down to the troops to sleep soon. Even four hours of sleep can make the difference between a battle won and lost. The knights began waking their men an hour after midnight. A small scouting party had left half an hour before to mark the place where the Wolves would wait while they still had moonlight.

I was up before my bodyguards called me. I had not been sleeping well anyway. I am one of those lucky people who dream in full color and 3D and my dreams are endlessly entertaining. I spend every night slashing my enemies to death, rolling in fabulous wealth and bedding every woman I ever dreamed of. However, lately I sometimes found that when I slashed my dreamland enemy or touched my dreamy date, they would suddenly look up at me with big brown eyes and begin to scream in terror and then cry inconsolably.

I buckled on my armor and was leaving my tent when Sir Grzegorz approached me. "Going for a moonlight walk, your grace?"

"You could not have forgotten that we have a battle, kolomel."

"Indeed, I remember it. In fact I am leading the right hand column of Wolves and Baron Krol is leading the left hand column. Which of us do you expect to be incompetent? Or do you plan the lead the charge up the middle?"

"Do I need to remind you, kolomel, that I am in command of this army and I lead them?"

"You are my commander and greatly respected. However, with all due respect, a general does not need to lead every patrol. You have competent officers and, again with respect, I suggest that you might let them do their jobs. In any case, that bright golden armor of yours might not be the best thing to wear during a sneak attack."

That's when I noticed that his armor was covered with a black poncho. I fumed anyway. First, they make dirigibles and airplanes and machine guns I didn't order, win wars I didn't start, and now they wanted to fight without me! But he had a point. My getting killed on a minor raid would end this campaign and my presence at the head of the troops would undermine the other commanders.

"Alright, I'll take my personal troops and accompany you as far as the waiting area. We'll wait there as a ready reserve. I'm sure as hell not going to sit in my tent waiting to hear if we won a battle!"

Shortly after moonset, the entire group moved out as quietly as possible. It was very dark and slow. With the moon gone, we moved by starlight. It would have been impossible without the superior vision of the Big People. We never saw the advance party waiting crouched in the darkness, but the Big People let us know when it was time to stop. In a world without machines, noise carries a long way, so we stopped well over two miles from the ambush site. I didn't even see the night fighters dismount and walk into the night, led by two Big People with better vision. There was a rustle, the sound of padded hooves for a few seconds and then silence — and darkness. In the darkness, time is eternal. The only light was the stars overhead and the only measure of time was their slow movement across the sky. The silence stretched on forever. Like everyone else, I dozed in my saddle and waited, resisting an overwhelming urge to strike a light and look at my clock. I must have slept for an hour because I looked up to see the slightest hint of false dawn in the Eastern sky. It was the ideal time to strike and still we heard nothing.

Suddenly, there was the sound of Sten guns. Bright flares arced up from both hilltops. Moments later, the first illumination flares jumped up from the valley floor. The battle was on. Beside me, two companies of Wolves galloped off to battle. They would crest the hills in less than four minutes and be in battle in less than five, while I had to steady Silver and sit and wait. I waited until I could hear that the battle was much more intense on the right side hill before I told Silver to charge. Screw the feelings of the other commanders. I was the boss and I wasn't going to miss this.

The flares were giving us enough light to charge up the hill at full gallop. When we went over the top I saw that the Wolves had penetrated to the main camp and were in heavy fighting. Between me and the edge of the cannon emplacements, there were a few individual fights going on, but they didn't need help. The Mounted Infantry had set up their machine guns, one on each flank and at the center, but they couldn't use them because the Wolves were still mixed in with the Mongols.

As we galloped past the machine guns, I could see that Sir Grzegorz was going sword to sword with a Mongol standing on the ground. That's when I realized that I was holding my own sword, and quickly changed to my Sten. I blasted two Mongol troops on the way to Sir Grzegorz and shouted at him, "The machine guns are in place! It's time to go! Get out and let them work!"

"Bullshit! We've got 'em on the run!"

"Get the hell out and let the machine guns run them into their graves!"

For a minute, I thought he was going to refuse the order, but he gave me a disgusted look and signaled *follow me* and led his men back. Two Big People picked up their fallen riders by their belts and carried them back in their mouths. One Big Person was down and probably dead and her rider was picked up by another trooper. As we passed the machine gun line, they opened up on the remaining Mongols.

The bullets tore through every standing tent, smashed the supply wagons, and dimpled every inch of the campgrounds. Big People delivered more ammo twice. As Sir Grzegorz and I watched the battle from our saddles, we had a few minutes to talk. He told me, "The commander was better than most. He had a second line of lookouts around the camp. By the time we charged, he already had his men in a skirmish line. We lucked out because they fired too soon and we were still out of range. By the time they reloaded, we were in among them. A few of them got off second shots, and those damned guns are dangerous close up. Lost a few men…"

I told him, "When the machine guns have killed everything moving, take your men in a finish them off." I turned to leave, and then turned back again, "I know that you are an honorable and brave warrior, but this is not a game. There are no extra points for nobility and the rewards for doing things the hard way are written on tombstones. If we are going to win this campaign, we must all remember that." Then I rode over to the other side of the valley without saying what was really on my mind, what I really wanted to say, "You disobey my orders one more damned time and I'll bust you to dishwasher!" I held my temper instead.

On the other hill, things had gone closer to plan. The Mongols were more careless there, and the Wolves were able to make an easy pass through the camp, killing anyone in sight and keeping them busy while the machine guns were set up.

As soon as the guns were set up, Krol split his men into two columns and rode back at full speed through the firing line. They hadn't lost a single man in the charge and had only two Big People wounded. He left one column to reinforce the machine gun line and sent the other column back into the cannon emplacements to help the night fighters.

I never saw any of his men draw a blade that night. He was more in tune with the future that either myself or Sir Grzegorz.

Overall, we had done amazingly well, but not because of my brilliant planning. Apparently the Mongol commander was convinced that his trap was still undetected and he had ordered that no campfires be lit for fear of giving himself away. Our night fighters crept into a totally dark camp where even the guards were having a hard time staying awake. If the camp had been normally lit, they would have had a real fight, but, as it was, half of the Chinese died before they even knew they were under attack.

There were about a thousand Chinese foot soldiers and engineers manning the cannon and most of them had the good grace to die quickly and easily. Hand-to-hand was not their field, and the best they could do was to wound a few of the night fighters.

There were also over a thousand Mongol troops in the two camps. We killed about half of them before the other half got to their horses and escaped down the canyon or just stumbled away hidden by the darkness.

They were alert fighters, and as the Wolves quickly learned, their rifles could penetrate our armor close up. We even lost two Wolves to sword thrusts through the joints in their armor. We lost about fifteen killed and more than twenty seriously wounded.

When full morning broke, we spent a few hours destroying the Mongol weapons and disabling the cannon. For a big heavy piece of metal, a muzzle-loading cannon is amazingly easy to destroy. The vent hole where the power is ignited enlarges over time, causing the cannon to lose power. To counter this, the vents are removable and replaceable. If you blast or pry the vent out and then enlarge the vent hole with a chisel, the gun will never fire right again.

I had planned to ambush the relief column when they came down the canyon, but the escaping Mongols would certainly have blown that chance for me. When the rest of the column caught up with us a few hours after dawn we moved out down the pass.

I rode near my radio cart and asked the operator to contact *Wanderlust*. It turned out that she was over the other end of the pass and in visual range of the Mongol relief column. They reported that the Mongols were moving back toward the Mongolian plateau. They must have found out that the ambush failed and decided wait for a better time for battle. It made sense. To cover all of the possible routes that we could have taken, they would have had to split their forces. Once the ambush failed, the best strategy would be to avoid battle until they could consolidate their forces.

I suspected that our vacation was nearly over. The loss of most of their horses, assuming that we had successfully killed them, would explain the eerie calm over the winter, but the months of winter would also give them time to replenish their stocks by importing horses from China. It would take months to import and train them, but they had months while we sat hunkered down in sod huts. Thinking back, I realized that allowing for draft animals for the cannon, the Mongols only had about the same number of horses in the camp as there were soldiers. Since the Mongol warriors normally took four of five horses with them on campaign, they may not be up to full strength yet.

Soon, we would find out if I was right, but for now we had at least fifty miles of clear road ahead.

From the Secret Journal of Su Song, Part 5

We are now at the twenty year mark on our project, and we continue to change the world.

Progress has hastened since our Emperor established partial dominance over the Song Dynasty border lands. Even though the Song still hold their positions there and live in their palaces, they answer to Mongol overlords for every important decision and send half of their tax revenue to my masters. The additional income has paid for a new capital city, huge new palaces for the Emperors relatives and thousands of miles of railways hosting hundreds of the new mobile steam engines.

My own reward has been considerable. I now live in a small palace surrounded by a hundred acres of fruit trees and gardens, and my wife now spends her time directing dozens of servants and household workers. She insisted that I take a second wife and chose a particularly attractive young woman of noble Chinese birth to, "Keep me relaxed and able to concentrate on my work."

The empire has grown richer and the fast communications provided by the railways have enabled the Emperor to have much firmer control over his dominions. In an emergency, no major point in the empire is now more than five days away from the capitol.

Once the peasants and even the regional governors would say, "As the sun is high in the heavens, so the Emperor is far away," but now the Emperor's mail box and his troops are next door.

As a bonus we learned who the Polish genius was. The Emperor of Song had trade relations with Europeans who brought with them a book of knowledge purported to be written by a Polish genius. Except for the fact that he is of very advanced age, we do not have his real name or description. We know that he uses the grandiose pseudonym that translates *Conrad, Protector of the Heavens* or *Conrad, Guardian of the Stars*. Of course, the name could designate either an individual or a group of engineers and scholars.

The book is divided into thirty-five topics, each shorter than the usual textbook. Some of the passages are arcane because they were originally written in Polish then translated to Latin or Greek by church scholars and finally translated into Mandarin by Chinese merchants who traded with the Romans and Italians. It is sometimes difficult to know if some terms apply to new concepts or are simply garbled because the translator did not know the term in the new language.

It took awhile before we realized that the math was garbled. Some of the terms were in base twelve, which means that *Conrad* either was polydactyl and counted on his fingers, or just had a wicked sense of humor.

The quality of the chapters varies widely. There is nothing on pharmacology or math and very little on alchemy. The book on bridge building is interesting, but smaller than the one I wrote before joining imperial service and it is missing basic fundamentals. You could not build a good stone bridge with it.

There are several chapters related to invisible *lightning* power. Each chapter seems simple, but it will take years before we understand it enough to use it. On the other hand, the chapters on steam power, production tools, steel production, and optics have saved us years of research. We cut fuel consumption and startup time dramatically in new steam engines by adopting the tube boiler shown in the book, and the section on steel production will allow us to triple the production of high quality steel within a few years.

Our independent efforts have also born more fruit. The stationary steam engines have cut the cost of machining dramatically and allowed us to build more of the Polish rifles and shells. Every city now mounts at least a few of them on its walls. Hand crafting the ammunition is still expensive, but with the stamping process and hydraulic press shown in Conrad's book, ammunition should soon be cheap enough to make it a common weapon.

As the weapons we have are sufficient to dominate all of our enemies, there has not been great incentive to improve them, but one of my teams has produced a practical breech-loading rifle for the troops.

He did it by cutting the barrel into two pieces. The shooter uses a lever that runs along the right side of the barrel to pull back a short breech section, just long enough for a charge of powder and a bullet, and swivel it up. He pulls the lever back slightly to release the breech from the main part of the barrel, pushes down to swing it up, drops the charge into it, pushes up on the handle to lower the breech. When breech is aligned, he moves the lever forward and down into a strong clip to clamp the joint tight.

Sometimes there is a very slight leakage, but the gun will fire ten rounds a minute through a rifled barrel, and it is cheap enough to give one to every soldier.

In truth, my lord Kublai has lost some of his drive for conquest as a result of our progress. He now controls the richest and most powerful nation in the known world and has real wealth beyond imagining. He still plans to consolidate his conquest of the Song Empire, still battles with the Koreans, and occasionally sends small raiding parties south and west, but the returns from such ventures are small compared to the taxes he now collects. He battles now only for honor and glory, not for profit.

As we learn more about Europe from the Song traders, he has also lost some of his concern about the Polish army. We now know that the entire population of Poland would fit into one of our larger cities and leave room for the population of a small town to visit. They may be wealthy and powerful, but there are just too few of them to be a serious threat. He is content to leave the Kipchak Khanate, the Golden Horde, as a sufficient buffer between us.

The War on the Tundra

I was wrong about the fifty miles of clear road. We weren't even clear of the mountain pass before the harassing attacks started. Less than two hours later, we were moving at a good dozen miles an hour through the pass when gunfire sounded ahead of us.

We were moving with a pair of forward flankers on the left and right and two pairs of scouts straight ahead of us when the Mongols managed to hit the left flankers and both pairs of center scouts at about the same time. Two dozen Mongols appeared out of camouflaged holes in the ground, firing rifles and arrows at close range. Two warriors died instantly from rifle shots, one was mortally wounded by a hail storm of arrows, and no one was unscathed. All but one of the Mongols died during the battle and the Big People ran down the one escapee and finished him off.

I had never even considered the possibility of such a sneak attack by Mongols. Hell, they were light cavalry and supposed to ride into battle. We changed the order of march and replaced the pairs of scouts with lances of scouts and pressed ahead. Speed was still our best protection.

An hour before nightfall, we were past the low mountains and out onto the Mongolian steppes. The men were exhausted, but I drove them to build a simple palisade before we bedded down. We ditched around the entire camp and built a four foot sod wall around the twenty mile perimeter before settling down for the night. War was really here now.

Two days later I received an early morning call from the captain of *Wanderlust*.

"We've been watching a sizeable enemy camp for about two days. They moved out this morning and are headed in your direction with about twenty, twenty five thousand men. The way you're closing, you could run into them well before nightfall.

"The formation is odd. They've got about ten thousand men in a group out front, but the main force is trailing a few miles behind. Maybe they'll be moving out to flank you."

I had read about this often repeated Mongol tactic. "*Wanderlust*, the Mongols are famous for rope-a-dope tactics. They engage a larger force head on and then pretend to retreat. They lead the enemies on until his horses are tired, and then they switch to fresh horses, join their reserves and wheel around to attack. They beat European armies again and again with that tactic.

"Watch for any signs that they are going to try that with us."

"Yes, your grace. Now that you mention it, we can see that the main force is leading a large number of spare horses.

"Hold it. Hold it. Damn! I'm looking down at an airplane, and it isn't one of ours."

174

"Are you certain of that, *Wanderlust*?"

"I'm the only Christian Army thing flying within a thousand miles. I'm at sixteen thousand feet and I'm looking down at a bright red airplane at maybe six thousand feet. Hold it... I've got my spyglass now. It's not an airplane. There's no engine or prop. It must be just a damned good glider.

"Wait a minute. Correction. It is powered! The damned thing just lit off a rocket engine. Shit! It's a damned rocket plane, and it's coming up in our direction!

"Emergency dump all ballast!! Open all hydrogen fill valves! Full ahead! Bow elevators full up. Rig for altitude. Let's get out of here."

The last think I heard before he remembered to key the mike off was the sound of alarms going off in the airship cabin.

The radio was silent for several minutes. When the captain came back to the mike, he was almost laughing with relief.

"We're out of danger. We grabbed our masks and bounced up to about thirty thousand feet before the plane dropped off. The damned thing climbed straight to about fifteen thousand and the pilot lit off another rocket booster, but he never got close. He fired an explosive rocket when he peaked out, but it made nice fireworks about a thousand feet below us."

I asked for a description of the strange plane. "It was a high wing monoplane, fabric covered and designed with very large glider-type wings. I would guess that the rocket engines are strictly for emergency boost. The thing was too slow and clumsy to reach much over twenty thousand feet.

"They had to know that we were here. We're so high up that we're damned near invisible from the ground. Also, I don't think the thing is normally armed. It carried a rocket in a tube attached to the side of the fuselage that looked like a slapped up job.

"My guess is that they had reports about us and they tried to kluge up a reconnaissance glider to take us out. As long as we maintain altitude, it isn't a big danger for us.

"However, while the thing is obviously too small to hold a radio, it could over fly you and then drop a message on its headquarters, so don't assume that the enemy is unaware of your location."

There was another long silence.

"My first mate just told me that they have succeeded in taking us out of action for awhile. We had to dump all of our ballast for the emergency climb. By the time we dump enough hydrogen to get down to a normal altitude, we'll be too low on gas to stay here. We're going to have to return to base now or risk being stranded on the tundra.

"Captain Helman should have the *Zephyr* here late tomorrow, but I'm afraid you're blind until then. Good luck, lord."

175

Good luck? I thought things were bad enough when the Mongols came up with rifled muskets. Now they had aircraft. I wondered what else they had cooked up. In a year or so, would they be bombing Poland with nuclear bombs made from cast bronze and rice paper?

Secretly, I was happy. My doubts were gone. This proved that we had to take them out now, before they became a bigger threat. I knew now that the expedition was the right decision.

I decided to postpone the battle until morning.

We camped for the night in a mountain valley, surrounded on three sides by mountain walls and by a palisade on the fourth side. I stationed troopers on the mountainsides to watch for intruders and sent out nighty-night squads on the open side. Normally the Big People provided all of the watchdog duty we needed, but in combat zones, I often sent out some of them with night riders. The riders would nap in the saddle or on the ground near where the Big People were grazing and if the Big People detected any incursion bigger than they could handle, they would nudge the troopers awake to provide firepower where needed. Traditionally, the teams would announce themselves to intruders with the phrase *nighty-night* before they fired. The sounds of short bursts of firepower in the night were actually soothing to those of us in camp.

I decided to move the staff meeting outside into the fresh spring air. We met even before the camp was established, but night had come early and was just cold enough to require cloaks as we sat around the fire on logs and boxes munching our dinners and drinking fresh brewed beer. I was enjoying the beer, the fire, and the cool breeze that tickled the exposed skin under my fur cloak, but not the companionship. The boss gets respect, get listened to, and gets obedience, but the boss never gets to hear the latest jokes and if he wants to hear the latest gossip, he has to hire spies. It is the greatest price of leadership.

As the eating slowed down and the drinking sped up, I announced, "Gentlemen, our scouts tell us that we are only a gross miles from the Mongol capitol. Tomorrow we will have a delightful battle with the Mongols and tomorrow night we will camp under the walls of Karakorum.

"The Mongols are going to execute a strategy that has worked well for them against the European knights in the past. They will seem to attack viciously and then retreat. In battle after battle, they got the knights to chase them until their horses were exhausted, their battle order in disarray, and the knights themselves tired. Then the Mongols would meet up with their reserve forces, jump onto fresh horses and counterattack the exhausted Christians. It worked in battle after battle.

"It also worked fast. As you who have been cavalry in the days of standard horses, you know that when you load a horse with two or three gross pounds of knight, armor, saddle, and weapons and then run it at full trot, the horse tires quickly. Within a few miles, they are useless in fighting the Mongol counterattack.

"Of course, we won't have those problems tomorrow. Our Big People can run any Mongol horse to death and have enough energy left to dance on its grave all night. Sir Grzegorz, it will be your men's job tomorrow to hide that fact. Your Wolves will have the key role tomorrow.

"Your Wolves could easily defeat any Mongol force that faces you man to man, or perhaps horse to Big Person, but then we would only get the diversionary force. The main Mongol force will scatter if they think they are losing, and we don't want to be chasing them all over Mongolia engaging in small firefights, so tomorrow we will bait them into chasing us.

"This meeting will be a short one, but you each face a long evening because your orders for tomorrow require careful coordination and once the attack starts, we will be moving too fast for radio carts to keep up and even too fast for message runners. Tomorrow depends upon everyone knowing his job and doing it on time without orders.

"The order of march tomorrow will be a little different than usual. We'll move as one unified body spread out across the landscape. The Wolves under Sir Grzegorz will lead the way. All of the Wolves need to travel together spread across the front of the column. As I said, they are the key to our success.

"Sir Wladyclaw, your mounted infantry will follow the Wolves. Place all little space between them and the Wolves. Intersperse enough mobile infantry between the machine gun carriers to provide support and cover when the battle starts. I would suggest about ten men to support each gun.

"Reserve about a fifth of your men to guard the baggage train, artillery and wagon mounted guns. They're going to get left behind if the battle goes as planned and we don't want them left without defense.

"Baron Kowalski, you'll take command of your artillery and all the wagon mounted guns. Sir Wladyclaw will leave you a contingent of mounted infantry. When the Mongol chase starts, your job will be to guard our baggage train. Don't try to keep up. Circle the wagons, set up a strong defensive perimeter and then use your best judgment to decide when, or if, to move forward to join the rest of us.

"If the Mongols act as they usually do, there will be a frontal attack early in the day. The Wolves will take them on. Sir Grzegorz, try not to kill all of them, as we want them to think that their plan is working. You must impress on your men that this part is play acting, very important play acting. The Mongols will break off and seem to retreat. The Wolves will lead the chase. Keep close enough to them to discourage their artillery but carefully do NOT catch up to them. If you catch them before they rejoin their main group, we'll be chasing Mongols for weeks. Scream, yell, shoot guns, and look as if you are hell bent on battle, but no not catch them.

"Sir Wladyclaw, your men will follow. They must not intermingle with the Wolves because they have a different job to do. Stay close enough at first to look as if you are trying to keep up, but immediately begin to drift back until there at least three gross yards between your men and the Wolves. Try to look tired, in case the Mongols are watching.

"If the Mongols are true to form, they will link up with their main force, jump on fresh horses and counter attack. At that moment, two things have to happen simultaneously. The Wolves must put up a token resistance and then retreat. Behind them, Sir Wladyclaw's men will dismount, assemble their machine guns and set up a fire line over as wide an area as they can cover.

"The Wolves will lead the Mongols right back to you. As soon as the Wolves pass the fire line, the machine guns can open up on the Mongols. Take lots of bullets. You'll have a lot of targets. Everyone will pull up behind the fire line and wait for the machine guns to do their work. When they are done, we counterattack. The Wolves will sweep right, half the mounted infantry will sweep left, and I will lead the rest of the infantry up the center.

"The two flanking columns have the most important job. They need to move fast, surround the remaining Mongols and kill them before they can scatter.

"When the battle is over, I want to move on quickly to Karakorum before they have time to react. It is a hard gross miles ride, but if the battle goes well we can do it tomorrow.

"Now you gentlemen have a hard night ahead of you. This entire operation must be coordinated without radio wagons or runners or even signal flares. Every officer must know his part perfectly before he beds down tonight.

"Drill them in the moves. The Wolves fight the Mongols initially while the Mounted Infantry holds back. Everyone chases the Mongols, but the Wolves take the lead while the machine gun carriers hold back enough to give themselves time to set up a firing line. The Wolves try to look surprised then the main force attacks them and pretends to retreat. No one fires a weapon until the Wolves are safely behind the fire line.

"Sir Grzegorz, you have the hardest job tonight. The Wolves will lead the attack because they are our elite force and they have earned the honor, but they are not good at holding back and have had no practice even pretending to retreat. You must convince them that this is a clever and honorable trick. Stress the humor in the situation, talk about the look on the Mongol faces when they run into the machine guns, but convince them any way you can to follow the orders."

Sir Grzegorz managed to look mildly insulted, "The Wolves will follow orders, my lord. They know neither cowardice nor rebellion. They will do as they are ordered."

I nodded in his direction, "I do not doubt their honor in any way." In fact, it was their *honor* that worried me. I looked around the fire, "The plan seems simple. Does anyone have a question?"

Sir Wladyclaw spoke up, "Sir, we are going to do this without signals, but would it be possible for one of the Wolves to carry something like a signal rocket to tell us when they wheel about?"

"I considered that, but we don't want the Mongols to know anything is different than a normal charge and retreat. A rocket might spook them."

"Perhaps a blunderbuss, then. We captured a couple of large bore muskets months ago and the men used them for amusement during the winter. The barrels are a big as a small fist and you can load anything into 'em. I think the original owners fired rocks and scrap metal. The point is that they make a load booming sound when you fire 'em. The sound carries about half a mile and no soldier would confuse it with a modern rifle sound. The Wolves could fire off a couple of them when they see the real Mongol force."

I considered it for moment. "If you think it will help, give two of them to the Wolves, but remember how noisy a charge is. Forty thousand charging horses with forty thousand clanking knights and screaming Mongols could drown out the God's last trumpet."

"Good point, sir. I'll load them with lots of smoky powder and ashes. If they are fired upward, they should make a big cloud to go with the big bang, and as you point out, we will keep a sharp eye on the Wolves anyway."

We went around the fire one last time as each man summarized his duties for the following day, and they left to conference with their officers. Me, I went into my tent for a drink and a cigars and some companionship. The brisk spring air might be bracing for a few minutes, but the warm flesh of a female companion is forever delightful. It forever amazes me that people who watch the same boring television show every day or play bridge every day for years can wonder how, after all of these years, I still like to end the day watching a naked girl dance.

My work, after all, was done. I had formulated a beautiful plan. Unfortunately, in the back of my mind, I kept thinking about Custer charging the Indians because he was afraid they'd get away.

We broke camp slowly the next day, making certain that each unit took its proper place in the line of march. I wore my brightest golden armor and rode at the head of the column with a retinue of shining companions. I insisted that Sir Grzegorz, likewise dress brilliantly and be surrounded by gleaming, banner carrying companions. We were bait and needed to be seen.

It took an hour for the entire army to start moving and two more boring hours passed as we ambled down the road. The army stretched out of sight to left and right and stretched back miles behind me. I felt like I was leading an army of ants on a food quest. Frankly, boredom was a real problem. My armor itched and my right foot was going to sleep. I tried watching Terry's butt for awhile as her figure was always delightful, but even that couldn't keep my attention. I was keyed up for killing and still having a hard time keeping awake.

Thank God, someone finally tried to kill us.

They appeared in the distance as a line of black dots and became a line of men trotting in our direction. For a diversion, they looked like a pretty big force. Their line was only a few men deep, but it stretched almost as far across the horizon as we did, and they made a lot of noise. They screamed a lot and who knew that Mongols blew on horns when they charged. About a hundred yards out, they drew their bows and launched a flight of arrows. I raised my shield above my head and Silver's and ignored the volley. Twenty yards later, they fired their guns and bullets clanged off our armor, still too far away to penetrate. Fifty yards closer and we could smell the filthy bastards.

I raised my sword above my head and led the charge. I knew the damned thing was useless these days, but it looked good. It also felt good to skewer the first Mongol I met before changing over to the Sten gun. He was an officer who could afford actual chain mail and a real sword and he looked very surprised when my sword cut through him. I switched to the sten, flipped the selector to single fire and used the gun like a pistol at close range. It was hard to find a target. Around me Mongol and Christian were firing and flailing at each other in close quarters and the ground was becoming littered with bodies, mostly Mongol. Then after only a few minutes, a gong sounded from behind the Mongol lines and they broke off in seeming disarray.

We followed, leaving our dead and wounded behind, knowing that the wave a few minutes behind us would care for them, and assist any surviving Mongols in finding their God.

We could have caught them easily, but we kept a deliberately ragged line scattered out behind them. I noticed that some of the Wolves even hammed it up, bouncing around in their saddles or pretending to whip their Big People as if they were going all out.

It was fun, for the first half hour, but it got old eventually. I knew that the Mongols historically had done the fake retreat for any time from less than an hour to up to two or three days. I figured that they wouldn't be able to keep it up long here because after a couple of hours we'd be in Karakorum. They had to turn soon.

Then red flares began dropping beyond the Mongol line. They were coming down from too high to be rocket launched, and they kept coming down every fifteen seconds or so. The only thing that could be that high was the Zephyr. She must have returned but I had to figure out what she was signaling. Red flares were for danger and a lot of them meant a lot of danger. Suddenly I was certain what she was saying. The Mongols were not going to counterattack! The Zephyr saw something else coming, something bad, but how do you turn around eight thousand galloping men when most are out of earshot and some even out of visual range? Medieval warfare is a bitch.

I slowed down and grabbed a bugler. "Sound retreat! Now! Ride down the line and get everyone to sound retreat!" I caught the eye of one of the men carrying a blunderbuss and gestured for him to fire it. I must have looked stupid, holding my hands up in the air and pantomiming pulling a trigger, but everyone would look stupider dead.

I stopped Silver and over the next few minutes, most of the line started moving rearward. The second blunderbuss was fired and I joined the retreat when I saw that I had the attention of most of the men near me on the line. It wasn't fast enough.

As I turned to lead the fake retreat, the Mongol line ahead suddenly split into neat columns that ran through the spaces between their camouflaged cannon and our fake retreat turned into a deadly real one as they opened up with grape shot and explosive shells.

In a truly modern army, it wouldn't have been as big a disaster. The Mongols had fired all their cannons at once so we had over a minute before they could fire again, plenty of time to cover the distance to the cannon and kill the cannoneers, but I had eight thousand men galloping the wrong way and no way to turn them again.

We'd have to spend that precious minute getting out of range. My mind was racing. Big People can sprint maybe forty miles an hour or more. One minute at forty miles an hour was about two thirds of a mile, call it thirty five hundred feet, over a thousand yards, maybe fifteen hundred. Oh, Hell. Might as well slow down. Grape shot is only effective out to three or four hundred yards.

I guess Mongols also knew that grape shot was limited and they took time to switch all their cannon to explosive shells. The second volley came slow, was all shells, and was not as intense as I expected.

What I didn't know at the time was that Sir Grzegorz and Baron Ryszard didn't suffer from my over thinking syndrome. They immediately noticed that the mounted Mongols had overrun their own lines and were in no position to defend the cannons. Not knowing that they couldn't turn an army that fast, they led their lances straight at the Mongol line and were racing up and down behind the row of cannons gleefully shooting cannoneers. Other lances had done the same, and on both ends of the line, the commanders realized that they were in position to flank the cannon line also attacked.

After a few minutes, the Wolves remembered that they were, after all, supposed to LOSE and joined the general retreat that I was leading, stopping only to pick up their comrades who had fallen to the cannon fire.

It was not a good day. I never led a retreat before, and I didn't like it.

Our forces straggled back past the machine gun line that the Mobile Infantry had set up. It wasn't quite the noble scene I had pictured. Instead of a wave of disciplined troops galloping by the machine guns with Mongols hooping and hollering behind them, the units came by in a ragged line, some carrying their wounded, and the Wolves followed last and later.

For the moment, there wasn't a Mongol in sight.

Ten minutes later, there still wasn't a Mongol in site or sound of us. That's when I saw the rocket burn a few thousand feet above us. It went on and on, slowly pushing that damned spy plane back to the Mongol headquarters. The Bastards knew exactly where we were and they weren't coming to play with the machine guns!

But I knew where they were. We were just being diverted from their main goal. I sent a messenger to Sir Grzegorz "Forget the flanking move. Get your men back to the baggage train immediately. Make all haste. They are probably under heavy attack."

I personally found Sir Wladyclaw. "The Mongols aren't coming in force. Pack up half the machine guns and prepare to move out to cover the baggage train. They may make another diversionary attack, so place the other half of the guns in a wedge to cover both forward flanks and keep enough troops inside the wedge to provide cover for the wounded and kill any Mongols that get through the first line. Send half your troops back to the baggage train. If the Mongols don't attack in the next hour, pack up and move west to cover our backs."

Of course, it didn't work like that. In an army our size, some of the men were almost a mile away and without radios. It took half an army hour just to pull them back into a tighter formation. We sent a cohesive force back to the baggage train, but it left us disorganized looking as the men scrambled around to get into new positions.

Thank God, the Mongols helped at last. Seeing that we were splitting our forces, the Mongol commander decided this was the time to counterattack. We had just finished pulling in the machine guns to the tighter formation when Cynthia banged on my helmet and pointed to the horizon. A few minutes later, we all began to feel the deep vibrations in the ground that had alerted Cynthia. The sound of thousands of horses reached us when the Mongols were still too far away to see as anything but a blurry dark line on the horizon. It seemed to take forever for them to reach of and we couldn't do a thing about it.

From a two mile wide front, we had shrunk to a triangle less than a quarter mile on a side, packed with too many targets. Our real strength lay in the gun emplacements and we had to draw them in a close as possible before we fired. I lowered my shield in front of my two bodyguards, sheathed my sword and waited. There was very little movement among our troops as they waited for the Mongols. At two hundred yards, the Mongols fired a volley from their guns. I heard bullets pinging off armor, but only a few lucky shots found flesh instead of metal. Then they began to fire armor piercing arrows in a high trajectory. Like everyone else, I moved my shield above my head. On the ground, the gun crews hunched down under their shields. Most arrows pinged on armor, but there were too many thunks as arrows found flesh, mostly on Big People whose mailed rumps were too large a target.

The warriors waited until the Mongols were close enough to smell and then opened up. We had a machine gun nest every fifty yards and four or five riflemen stationed between each nest to pick off individual targets. It was like cutting grass. There was nothing for the men inside, including me, to do except keep our heads down and pass ammo and barrels up to the front line. When we did look up, all we saw was greasy little men in leather armor fall off of horses or fall with their horses. They turned back as soon as the guns opened up, but the men had let them get very close, so they were in range for a long time.

The firing was continuous. I had remembered from World War II reports that the only two things that stopped a good machine gun from firing were a lack of ammo and overheating barrels, so every one of our guns shipped with three quick change barrels and we brought lots of bullets. It was a gunner's dream party.

When they got out of range, Sir Wladyclaw called "Cease Fire" and the mounted troops swept out in two columns to finish the job. Well, not exactly "swept". The Big People tended to be fussy about stepping on dead horses and there were a lot of dead horses out there. Even Silver did a prancing gait while we moved through the field of dead enemies. I decided to ride with the right hand column because I was just tired of not killing anything.

We could do double their speed and within minutes we were coming up on the stragglers. The machine guns had spooked them so bad that most of them never even looked back. The men took out their pistols and began to pick off riders from the back as they came up on them. We pressed them so hard that there was no time for the Mongols to stop or rally, but some of them were good enough to turn in the saddle and send arrows back at us. Christian troops that got too close found out that Mongol arrows were, in fact, armor piercing at close range and capable of going through exposed chain mail like it was paper.

Still, our loses were small and we were leaving a path of Mongol bodies behind us. I decided it was time to bring this battle to an end. I raised my sword, useless now as a weapon, but a bright golden beacon for the troops to follow and urged Silver to speed up. As the troops followed I passed the Mongol leaders and we began to turn them like a stampede. It's easy to pick out the Mongol leaders. Most commoners only have leather armor or leather with metal plates sewed to it. Only the leaders can afford chain mail, metal helmets, or plate armor. A big fellow in full plate smiled at me and pointed his rifle in my direction. Then we opened up again with the Sten guns and he was nearly unhorsed by his own troops trying to get away from us.

The Mongol column came to a halt with the Mongols crowded together too close to dismount or even fire their weapons effectively.

There were probably two thousand of them alive when they stopped and fifteen minutes later there were none. I shot the big guy myself.

I rode back to join the troops we left behind while the Mobile Infantry checked for wounded Mongols and helped them end their suffering. The warriors would be busy for hours doing cleanup work. A later count showed we had killed almost ten thousand Mongols in that one battle. That meant that there were twenty thousand recurve bows and five to ten thousand rifles and muskets out there. Each bow took a year to make and the rifles were probably hand manufactured, taking months for each one. There were a few thousand man years of weapons and equipment out there that could come back to kill us if we let the Mongols recover them. So, the men would work their way back to camp smashing bows, collecting rifles, and cutting purses off the Mongols. For this work, they men were allowed to pool the purses and share the contents with everyone who fought in this part of the battle. It made them diligent in their searches.

By the time I returned to the battle line, the ranking officer, Komander Nalchick, had everything well organized. I passed by the main battle site to see crews doing the same cleanup work there as was being done out on the tundra.

The gun crews and their supporting rifle men were now dug in behind individual dirt and grass barriers surrounding a square camp big enough to protect the wounded and provide working space. Inside the makeshift camp, the largest area was given to the medical corps treating the wounded. There were separate triages set up for wounded troopers in one area and wounded Big People in another.

There were a lot of wounded. The grape shot and explosive shells had been effective. We hadn't taken this kind of casualties since the Mongol invasion. Over three hundred troopers lay dead and double that were seriously wounded. Five hundred Big People were wounded but most were walking wounded as was hard for an arrow of rifle bullet to penetrate something the size of a Rhino. Unfortunately, it was "most" not all. In one field the Big People were silently praying over the twenty of their comrades killed by explosive shells and lucky shots.

I found Nalchick sitting on the ground eating lunch surrounded by his officers. Around them the rest of his command had been ordered to dismount, rest, refresh and recharge their energy. He was smart enough to know that tired troopers made lousy fighters so everyone not on duty was ordered to rest.

As I approached, I heard him order several lances to dig temporary latrines just outside the perimeter. I dismounted and squatted near him, "You seem to have everything under control here."

"I'll feel better when Sir Wladyclaw rejoins with his force. My main problem is that I've got almost eight hundred wounded and dead troopers and hundreds of limping Big People that I can't abandon and can't move. We didn't bring a single wagon with us and there are no trees we can make stretchers or travois from. We've got about two days of supplies and we're stuck here.

If we're going to be here more than a day, I need to get crews out butchering horses. It'll make the Big People uncomfortable but they'll help to keep their troopers fed."

I stood up to stretch my cramped muscles, "As soon as my men eat and stretch, I'll take them back to where we left the wagons. It should be less than ten, fifteen miles west. You stay put and we'll try to rejoin you here. Today if they haven't had any trouble. Tomorrow at the worst."

185

I still had not seen the main Mongol force and had no idea where the bulk of my army was. I started the day with over forty thousand men in a well supplied, cohesive force and ended up with the army scattered in four places and hundreds of casualties that tied us down. They Mongols were probably attacking our supply train as I rode back. If they succeeded, this campaign was over, and the ranking officer in the supply train was Captain Ivanov, a steady, unimaginative officer who had never led a battle charge. If anyone ever writes a book on how to lose a war, this will be one of the chapters.

It was easy to find where we left the baggage train. Eighty thousand thundering hooves leave a clear path on the tundra. A couple of times we saw small groups of Mongol horsemen moving east, but they weren't looking for a fight and we ignored each other.

As we approached the camp, we began to see Mongol ponies grazing aimlessly. Most were still saddled and I saw one in the distance that carried a dead rider.

One of my knights rode up beside me, "It must have been a Hell of a battle if they didn't even have time to recover their ponies – or their dead." As he moved out to his point position, he added, "I wonder how we did."

When we finally topped a little rise and could see the camp, it looked like a small town with wooden walls. We could see the full width of it, but it stretched back past the horizon. The outer walls seemed to be two wagons wide, surrounding a clear area with several more rows of wagons stretching out of sight.

Whatever happened here hadn't been over for long. Smoke was still rising from inside the camp and from spots around the horizon, and I could see a dead trooper still slumped over his gun. As we approached, two wagons moved aside to let us through the wall. Inside most of the troopers were sprawled out on wagon tops or blankets, with the blank look of total exhaustion on their faces. They barely moved their heads to watch us as we rode by. As we approached the center of the camp, more and more of the exhausted troopers dragged themselves through work details, moving the dead, tending to the wounded, throwing dirt on burning wagons, eating with hands like lead weights, all moving painfully slow, and eyes to the ground.

Captain Ivanov was no exception. He was at the center of the formation, sitting on a wooden ammo crate, leaning forward, hands on his knees. He was breathing slowly, his chest moving in an out like a runner recovering from a race, staring at the ground and only raising his head to give orders to the men who came up to him.

He made a motion to stand up when he saw us approaching. I immediately jumped to the ground and told him, "At ease, Captain Ivanov. You've obviously had a harder day than me." Looking over my shoulder I said, "Someone bring the Captain a drink. A real one."

He was quiet for a moment then, "Well, your grace, it wasn't too bad. I'm afraid that we have expended a lot of your ammunition, and the water wagons are empty. It will be a dry dinner tonight, and we lost about fifty wagons of supplies. I haven't had a chance to inventory the lost wagons yet…"

"Captain! I appreciate your dedication to our supplies, but I need to know how the battle went. What happened here?"

"As I said, Sire, it wasn't too bad. We moved out this morning in a defensive layout and maintained it all day. We had all the mobile machine guns in the outer layer, interspersed with durables like rice and flour wagons. Baron Kowalski arranged his artillery in the second layer. He wasn't happy out spreading his command out like that, but he kept a good order. All the tender breakables were in the center of the formation.

When you left us to chase the Mongols, we just pulled the formation tighter, released the Big People, backed some artillery wagons into the gaps on the outer wall, and waited. We had plenty of time. The Mongols didn't attack for maybe a half an hour. Oh, during that time, the men piled dirt up under the wagon and in the gaps. It's amazing how fast eight thousand men can dig when their lives depend on it.

You know, Mongols are pretty stupid."

That had certainly not been my experience that day. I wanted to ask something like "What??" but I just waited for him to go on.

"I learned in Sarai that Mongol families and craftsmen often follow their armies. Their wagons are driven by men too old or boys to young for battle or women or slaves. They must have thought that we did the same. They certainly came over those hills like they didn't have a care in the world.

I must say, your grace, that your supply decision on bullets was a very sound one. After food and boots, they are the most important thing. I'm glad you ordered a lot of them. We used a lot of them today.

Anyway, instead of the few thousand old men and boys that the Mongols expected, we had four thousand drivers, radio operators, medics, and other personnel all trained troopers and all with your excellent ten shot rifles. Of course we also had the four thousand troops that Baron Ryszard brought with him. They were very helpful. Everyone who didn't have a machine gun or artillery station was either lying on top of or behind a perimeter wagon.

As I said, Sire, they were very stupid. They hit us from three sides at once. You know that you ordered more than one hundred wagon mounted machine guns? They pretty much wiped out the first wave before the riflemen got off a shot. The second wave was right behind them and things got a little dicey then. There were just so damned many of them that they got close in a couple of places. Not hand to hand, but damned near. We took some loses.

The third wave was different. They took their time coming. They concentrated on the south wall and started by pushing wooden barriers in front of them. They were about as tall as man, a little wider than that and had wheels on them. Three or four Mongols would push them forward while one of them fired a swivel gun through a slot."

"A swivel gun? One of ours?"

"No Sire, not one of ours, but a damned good copy. Looked like one of ours. The mechanism was a little different, but it was obviously a copy, same caliber and just as nasty. They concentrated on the machine gunners and it was damned hard to hit 'em back through those little slots.

While they was hitting our gunners, other Mongols moved up small siege towers. They were only twenty or thirty tall, but they gave the Mongols enough height to shoot down at the troopers lying on top of the wagons with swivel guns and small cannons. Zephyr warned us they were uncovering a lot of equipment from camouflaged valley, but we never expected siege towers in the middle of nowhere.

While they kept us pinned down, the rest of them attacked again, all from the north. That time it did get down to hand to hand. They got past the first line of wagons Baron Ryszard got his men there to repulse them. He rallied several lances with Sten guns and pushed 'em back."

That was when I noticed that there was blood mixed in with the grime and dirt on his tunic. I suspect he was minimizing his own part in the battle.

"Baron Kowalski was really the hero that time. His men concentrated all of the field pieces on the siege towers and mobile bunkers. By the time the troopers killed all of the Mongols in the compound, the towers were gone. We re-manned the machine guns and cut most of them down as they retreated."

"Things got quite for a long time. The Mongol commander was directing the battle from a platform on top a hill in that direction. Kowalski wanted to take him out with a five pounder, but Baron Ryszard asked him not to. He said that if we killed the commander, the Mongols would go away, and it was a lot easier to convert Mongols to righteousness when they brought themselves to the ceremony.

It was quiet so long that I would have thought they left if that commander hadn't been still standing on his platform.

Then a big bag of flaming oil landed right in the middle of the camp and its five bothers followed a few minutes later. Whatever they used, it burned like the fires of Hell and stuck to everything like Greek Fire. That's where the water went, and a lot of the blankets and other stuff.

I figured they weren't using cannon because they didn't know how tough we were and they wanted to capture the supplies, not destroy them, but I can't figure out why they brought trebuchets. Where the Hell were their cannon when they decided they weren't going to capture us and decided to destroy anything?"

"Actually, Captain the cannon were shooting as us. I guess they figured they weren't going to need them here."

"Oh, well, they lucked out. They could lob into the camp on a high arc, but the trebuchets were in a little valley and we couldn't get a good angle on them with the artillery. They were too close to drop shells on.

The three of us, Ryszard , Kowalski and I had a little conference. I know, your grace, that you told us to only fight standing off from the enemy, and we always respect your orders, but sometimes you just have to out and kill your enemies face to face.

Zephyr told us the main body of Mongols was in one formation north of us. It took us almost half an hour to prepare the sortie, but Baron Ryszard led all of his men out of camp at about the same time the second volley of fireballs came in. Same time, Kowalski's men took out the Mongol commander with a volley of five pounders. There's a big hole in the ground up there where his platform used to be.

Baron Ryszard was barely out of sight when the Baron Grzegorz showed up with the relief column. We didn't need him here, so he took most of his men and followed Baron Ryszard .

I haven't heard from either one of them since, but it's getting dark soon, so they should be on their way back.

Guess we should get some campfires going."

An hour later, in the increasing darkness, Barons Ryszard and Grzegorz led their tired troops back into camp. Captain Ivanovs' men had campfires going and food cooking by then. The sound of bubbling stew and the smell of baking bread raised everyone's spirits. The wounded troops had been moved to a treatment area, the dead to a temporary morgue area, and the fires were still being fought. Captain Ivanov himself was busily accounting for the supplies that had been lost. They had fought a battle, killed thousands of Mongols, and fixed dinner. There are no words for them.

Starting with his investment ceremony the next day, Captain Ivanov was now Baron Ivanov, with a rank of Kolomel.

Kolomel Ivanov had been right. We were lucky that the Mongols acted stupidly. If the Mongol commander had waited for his equipment to be ready instead of being overconfident and hurried, he might have done serious damage. As it was, his first wave was slaughtered on the way in and the second wave so close that both groups blocked each other. The first wave couldn't retreat and the confused second wave stumbled over the dead bodies of the first.

By the time he had his equipment ready for a real attack, half of his men were dead. Baron Ryszard's men found the engineers around the trebuchets virtually undefended. They were still mopping up engineers, guards, and ground troops and burning equipment when Baron Grzegorz rode by in search of Mongols.

There weren't any. With half of their number dead and the commanders gone, the Mongols had split into small groups dispersing into the countryside. Any one group was an easy kill, but Grzegorz would have had to split forces a hundred ways to chase them. Unwilling to set his men up for ambushes, he settled for helping Ryszard destroy the Mongol camp and equipment.

We didn't make it to Karakorum that day. The next morning, we sent out wagons and escorts to bring the wounded from the stranded Mobile Infantry camp and reunite the army.

We set up camp in a protected canyon, tended our wounded, buried our dead and counted our loses. Numerically, we had done well. We lost five hundred dead and had over a thousand wounded bad enough to side line them. Most of the casualties were from the two cannon volleys that hit my pursuit team and from the one successful incursion into Ivanov's camp.

The Mongols had started with perhaps forty thousand men. They had lost the entire bait team, maybe around ten thousand men, and most of the men who had attacked our supply wagons, perhaps as many as ten thousand more.

Twenty years before, they had defeated the Hungarians by being on the other side of figures like that.

It took two days to stabilize our wounded, repack our gear, and start again for Karakorum.

Karakorum at Last

Our guide told us that Karakorum sat in the Orkhon River basin, on a flat plain about thirty miles wide, surrounded by steep mountains. Three major roads converged on it. From the west the caravan trail from Europe wound through river gorges and mountain passes. The road to the south was flatter, wider and ended up in what is now Beijing. To the east, a third caravan trail led to Eastern China and Korea. When we resumed our march, I decided to follow the caravan trail to the city. The mountains left us little choice. The trail was not designed for forty thousand men. Despite our best efforts, we were scattered along a twenty-mile long path.

Sir Grzegorz rode beside me for a moment as I made my way to the head of the column. "How considerate of you, your grace", he said, "to relieve the scouts of the tedium of their work. Shall I inform the cook tents that you will be by later to prepare dinner for us?"

"No." I answered, "But I intend to be one of the first to see Karakorum. If you've run out of sarcasm, you're welcome to join me."

"I'll gather up a couple of lances and catch up to you. We can't afford for you to be too exposed out here."

We traveled long the Orkhon River for about an hour. Some time during the trip I moved close to Grzegorz. "Your concern is appreciated, but your comments now border on the insubordinate. I know what I am doing."

He kept his eyes ahead. "I was with you, my lord, twenty years ago when you forbid your liege lord, the king, to enter a fire pit. You insisted that, as his liege, you could not allow him to injure himself trying to walk on fire like the recruits.

"I now ride beside my liege lord, who is endangering himself, and I will continue to remind you that if you should get killed doing someone else's job, forty thousand men will have wasted a year of their lives and given your their loyalty for nothing. That is my responsibility."

The insubordinate bastard really pissed me off, by quoting my words back to me, but I'm the damned hetman and I go where I want.

The plain was broken by hills to the north and west of the city, as we were riding by one of them, I heard gunfire from the top. Before we had time to look for cover, we realized that most of the gunfire was from Sten guns with only a few reports from the larger caliber Mongol weapons. We were still looking up to see the source of the gunfire when two troopers came riding down the side of the hill. When they reached us, the one in front gestured behind him and said, "There's a good place to see the city from up on top this hill, your grace."

I asked, "What was the fight about?"

"Oh, some Mongols were sitting in your seats. We had to move them over."

It was a perfect observation post. It had protective walls, a roof overhead, and a glorious view of the valley. The troopers had moved the Mongol bodies away and thrown dirt over the blood they had left behind. We seem to have lucked into the closest observation point as the flat tundra surrounded the city for miles in every other direction. At that we were at least a mile away.

At this distance the impression through the field glasses was there was a lot of empty space. I could make out the palace complex at the southwest edge of the city and even that had a lot of green inside the walls.

Speaking of walls, they weren't very impressive either. The gates, like the buildings, had a Chinese look to them, but the walls couldn't have been over thirty fifty feet high and they looked flimsy compared the standard thirty foot thick rubble filled walls in Europe.

As my retinue spread out on both sides of me and we sat in our saddles gazing at the Mongol capital, there was only one thing to say, "That's Karakorum? That village can't be two miles square, and the walls are a joke!"

Ahmed shifted in his saddle, "It's closer to three miles on a side, but lord, remember that they have not had a thousand years to build walls like Constantinople. This place has only existed for less than a hundred years, and the Mongols do not like cities anyway. The khan is only here for a few days a year. This time of year he is usually at his camp about a hundred miles north of here. He is also only the Khan of the Golden Horde. His brother, Kublai, has his capital in Dadu in China. It is much bigger."

I shook my head in wonder. "It seems that we have spent six months traveling two thousand miles to attack a city used by a junior khan as a party pad."

Ahmed raised his palms and shrugged. "I thought that you knew what was here. You never asked me about it. However, it is much more important that it looks. The Mongols revere it as a symbol of their power. There is great prestige in owning Karakorum."

Ahmed pointed to the city and nodded as he added, "And I think that you should look closer before you decide how big it is, particularly that row of barn like buildings that hold the royal treasury."

There seemed to a lot of activity around the city. Ant-sized figures scurried about the walls and the surrounding fields. It looked like they were working on a moat and I would guess that they were placing stakes and mines in the fields.

As with many Mongol cities, most of the population was transitory and lived in yurts erected both inside and outside of the walls. Those yurts were now in motion, leaving the area in yurt wagons going in every direction except ours. There were none left outside the city, and a steady stream of wagons was leaving the gates.

The most disturbing thing was the train. A damned train! A steam train was entering the city through massive gates on the south wall! Whatever it was carrying had to be trouble for us. What the hell were they doing with one of my damned trains?

"Ahmed, you might be right. This may be an important city, but important or not, we are going to burn it to the ground."

I called a messenger over, "Find Kolomel Ivanov and tell him to establish a camp in the best spot he can find near here. Tell him that we may be here for a while so the camp should be very defensible." I turned to Sir Grzegorz. "That railroad belongs to you and your men. Have the airships find someplace you can cut it and send out a crew to cut the line."

He was still looking at the city. "Maybe we should make a quick sortie along the walls to disrupt their work. Scattering them now could save trouble later."

I handed him my field glasses, "They probably have swivel guns in those towers, and they certainly have artillery somewhere on that wall. Charging their artillery was expensive last time so let's let Baron Kowalski soften them up first."

It was nearly dark when I arrived at the new camp. As we were no longer in the grasslands, there was no chance of building our often used sod walls, and there wasn't a forest in site to provide lumber for a palisade. Kolomel Ivanov had established our camp along the banks of the Orkhon River in a place where there were hills to our back, a river in front of us and defensively narrow spaces between them. It took me almost half an hour to get to my tent after I reached the camp. I realized that the camp probably stretched fifteen miles along the river banks, making it larger than the city we were attacking. Among the messages awaiting me was one from the captain of the *Flying Cloud* informing me that my big gun had arrived. Despite my fatigue, I met with Kowalski and a couple of his engineers. I decided that that right beside the camp was as good a place as any to drop the gun. The river banks here were hard rocky material and the carriage was already here.

Captain Stanislaw's Tale

Before dawn two lances of Wolves scoured the hills around us for enemy spies and then took positions giving a clear view of the area. When they were done, *Flying Cloud* made several passes over the area, looking for any enemy gunners. It was almost noon when they were satisfied that the area was secure, and they dropped toward the camp.

It's always majestic when an airship lands. It's a slow motion ballet of engines and wind, lift and ballast, but this time, *Flying Cloud* had a new trick. She flew slowly down the river dropping lower and lower until she could put water pipes in the river, then the captain reversed the engines and gunned them to slow her. As she stopped, he swiveled two engines and drove her sideways over the bank. When the ballast tanks had filled enough to bring the ship to a stop on the bank, her sides began to roll up like Venetian blinds. She settled down as a bare aluminum statue, unaffected by the wind. Her captain and cargo master were the first down the ramp. They must have noted my amazed looks. I was still trying to see how they kept the cloth taut when they rolled it back down, when he approached. Instead of the usual military greeting he said, "Hell of trick, ain't it. We learned it from *Vagabond*."

I was too focused on the ship to notice the lack of military courtesy. "That was the ship that crashed a few months ago."

They must pick airship captains from the people who model for recruiting posters. As usual, this one was trim, handsome, with a killer smile and an easy, graceful way of moving. "They had several old blue water sailors aboard when it went down. They complained all the way home that 'of course we crashed, you idiots! We couldn't reef the sails. If you can't reef the sails in a storm, you sink. Any idiot knows that.'

By the time they got back to Gdansk, the engineers did know it. When they rebuilt *Vagabond*, the envelope covering was replaced with twenty slightly heavier cloth panels that could be manually reefed up like the sails on an old ship.

When we were in port last month, they installed this new system for us. You notice that we have three rows of panels the length of each side with electric spoolers. It slows us down about eight knots, but we can ride out a gale by going to ground, reefing the covering and blowing the gas. We're just a heavy metal statue when we do that. It's also easier when we're maneuvering near the ground and having wind problems."

I was so fascinated by the rigidible that I almost forgot we why we were there. I noticed there were now leather caps on top of the hydrogen cells so that they could be battened down when they were grounded in rough weather. In my own time-line, virtually every airship except the *Hindenburg* had been killed by bad weather. These people seemed to have solved the problem the first time they saw it.

The informal moment passed when the captain snapped to attention and saluted, "Captain Stanislaw reporting, your grace. I have a large cargo for you. Do I have permission to offload at this location?"

"Permission granted. I believe that my quartermaster and your cargo master can handle the unloading. Do you have any cargo besides the new gun?"

"Sir, I am carrying the five-inch naval gun and three hundred rounds of powder and explosive shot. We brought all the ammunition we could carry and left no margin for additional cargo. As it was, we had some difficulty in maintaining altitude and directional control."

"Captain, neither of us is needed for the unloading and I'd like to catch up what's happening in the dirigible corps. I suggest that your off duty men stretch their legs and get a little fresh food while you and I confer in the officer's tent. We've got one of the best commissary corps in the army."

As usual the cooks had laid out a feast of fresh bread, roast mutton, rice, cheese, whatever vegetables they had been able to find – and standard canned lunches for those who like life plain and simple. There were folding chairs for the men and a small tent for conferencing out of the sun."

By the time we sat down without plates, curious officers filled every seat in the tent, pretending to eat, hoping for a story. If you ever want to start a successful carnival, include a tent with dirigible. Everybody loves them.

It didn't take much to get him talking. "Are all of the airships configured like yours now?"

"No, sir. Just the overland ships. R7 and R9 are Atlantic Clippers. They have auxiliary sails, and then there's *Sea Sicker*. I don't know how you describe that one."

"I thought that you were only going to build four ships?"

"That was the plan, but an empire as large as ours needs fast, long distance travel. They already had the jigs, the plans, and the docks, so they just kept on building. We're up to nine ships now and the plans are to have regularly scheduled service everywhere in the Empire by late next year.

"Oh, you asked if they were all the same. I was about to explain that R7 and R9 are different. They were built to take advantage of the trade winds between Europe and the new world. They're a little bigger than my ship and they've got two sails on each side. When they're extended, they look like the fins on a fish. Their route takes them south out of Gibraltar, down the coast of Africa to where the winds change, across to the southern continent and then north up the coast to our colonies and trading posts. They go back by the northern route, south of Greenland and north of Poland.

"They have the wind at their back all the way and a skillful captain with a little luck can do the whole trip and come home with full fuel tanks.

"'Course, it don't always work that way."

What a great line. There wasn't a fork moving in the entire tent, while we waited for him to go on.

"Captain Morrison had some difficulty on his second trip. He was on his homeward leg just south of Greenland when he hit a terrible storm one night. The winds weren't strong enough to damage his ship, but ice formed on the canopy, a lot of it. Even after he dumped all of his ballast, he couldn't maintain altitude. He sent the crew down to dump cargo but it was bulk stuff in big sealed containers, and they didn't have equipment on board that could move containers that size.

"I can tell you, that was the last time any airship will rise with a cargo she can't dump herself. He had about twenty passengers on board, so he set them to breaking into the containers and dumping the cargo piecemeal.

"He sent the crew up the canopy to start breaking ice loose. They tried climbing the ribs and pounding on the ice from inside to dislodge it, but they mostly just put holes in the fabric. When they got down to wave height, he reefed the top section of the envelope. Most of the canopy motors burned out but with sledge hammers and pry bars and the ones that worked, he got the fabric rolled up.

"That knocked enough ice loose to gain some altitude. Unfortunately, half the damned ice fell on the deck and had to be manually thrown overboard and he still didn't have enough altitude to get out of the storm. Ice started to form on the exposed ribs and the interior structure and threatened to bring them down again. While the passengers tried desperately to dump buffalo meat and bales of rubber overboard, the crew had to climb the ribs with fire axes, hammers, pipes and whatever else they could find to bust loose the ice and get it overboard. Half the crew had to stand on the upper deck and dump snow and ice over the side with a few shovels, a few boards, and their hands.

196

"They had to cut the rear sails loose and jettison them, but they kept the two front sails out to keep themselves pointed downwind. The log says that it went on for over four hours. I'll tell you, I sail one of these and I'm not a bit afraid of heights, but the thought of climbing those bare ribs in the middle of the night, pounding ice loose during a storm – with the wind shaking you around and nothing but ten thousand feet of air between you and the ocean gives even me nightmares.

"By the time they got to warm air, they lost two men. One slipped off the ribs and was thrown overboard. Another lost his grip and fell to the deck. The fall killed him. It was one Hell of a night.

"Well. We'll never fly again with a cargo we can't jettison and the engineers are working on plans for de-icing heaters for the canopy, but things still go wrong."

We were still listening to him when the gun and ammo had been unloaded and his crew fed.

I almost forgot to have our conference. Eventually, I excused everyone from the tent except the captain, myself, and a few of my staff members. "Captain, I need to know more specifics about your current mission. I have the feeling that we are not well-coordinated."

He opened a leather folio and pulled out several maps. "You are correct, your grace. When we only had one ship overhead doing scout work, casual communications were adequate, but now we have a squad here and we need to liaison better if we are to be integrated into your campaign.

"As to our situation, *Wanderlust* has returned to Poland, but in addition to my ship, *Zephyr* is overhead, scouting out the railroad line for the Wolves. *Vagabond* is due on station late tomorrow. She's been rebuilt, refitted, and she's carrying some kind of anti aircraft weapons to protect us from the Chinese planes.

"We're all prepared for extended duty. We plan to be here for the duration.

"We actually arrived almost in the area about forty-eight hours ago, but we were told to limit radio communications until the problems at home sort themselves out so I waited until you got here to announce ourselves, and spent some time mapping out the area.

He selected a map and set it between us. "If you look here, this is where you and I are now. This camp is on this river bend. Now look about fifty miles north. This spot is a narrow river canyon. It has very steep walls, and a narrow opening at both ends of the canyon. It's only easy to get to from the air. It's protected from the worse weather, has a river to replenish our ballast, and the narrow openings at both ends make it easy to defend if anyone figures out we're there. We didn't see any human habitation for miles so we hope to go unnoticed there.

197

"We've already set up our base there. We wanted to coordinate the location with your people, but you've been too busy to be bothered the past few days. We brought in several hydrogen plants and dropped them down on the riverbank. *Zephyr* brought a couple of squads of marines with their gear, but frankly we could use a company out there, and we're a little short of supplies since we sent everything over to your people. We don't even have any Big People with us."

"I'll have Baron Krol break loose a company and assign it too you. If this map is accurate, they can be at your site by nightfall with a couple of weeks of supplies, unless, of course, you want to take them yourself in the *Cloud*."

"We can take their wagons and supplies, but Big People don't like air travel much so I suggest they ride out on their own."

"Is there anything else you need?"

He reached for another map. "As I said, better liaison. I've got a map here of the current Mongol positions, and I don't know who to give it to."

"I'll set up two staff members to keep in regular communication with you, but right now, show us the map. We're trying to plan a campaign."

He spread the map out on the table and started to brief me while the others crowded around. It was gold, simple, pure, premium gold that any commander would kill for. "This map covers about a hundred miles in all directions, so the scale is a little small. However, this is Karakorum."He pointed to a spot near the center of the map, "and about fifty miles north this is the khan's winter camp. Our guides say that it should be empty this time of year, but there hundreds of Yurts there. There are only a couple of permanent structures, but the whole camp is dug in and defended pretty well. They have a moat, small walls, and some cannon and they just happen to straddle the only road north.

"South of us, there are several more small towns along this river. Our chink guide says that they are built around the palaces of some high officers. Damned near every officer is called a 'khan' so sometimes it's hard to sort out who's who.

Most of them are empty now, but this one is an exception. They're set up like the other camp. There are lots of yurts, lots of horses, lots of activity. Several groups seem to be consolidating there, and its close to where you were ambushed on the way in. "

He reached for a third map. "I spent part of the day yesterday looking down at Karakorum though a telescope. This is a map of the city, and I have to say that is isn't much of fort. From what I've heard, I expected Sarai to be better defended. Frankly, it looks like you could send in the quartermasters to serve lunch and they could clear out the Mongols while they're setting up the tables.

"The place is about two and half miles east to west and about a mile and half north to south. It has the usual four gates at the compass points. The main gate is in the south wall near the khan's palace – and it's a palace, not a fort. A large single story brick building with columns running on three sides.

"Now, up in the North West corner is the Saracen quarter. That's where the merchants have their houses. Our guide says he stayed in a home there on his way to Sarai. The other northern corner is for craftsmen and small businesses. Aside from the craftsmen and a few officials, our guide says there aren't many Mongols in permanent residence. Most of them still don't like cities.

"That doesn't mean that they are going to let you have the city for free. Between the palace and the rest of the city, there's a lot of empty space. There's a huge flat area east of the palace that's usually packed with yurts and vendor stands and temporary businesses. Part of that's taken up by a small rail siding. Now it looks empty, but if you look carefully from above, you can see that it's been crisscrossed with concealed trenches and spikes.

"They're also reinforcing parts of the city. Some of the civilians are dumping dirt on their roofs to protect from cannon balls and digging shelters under their homes. Over by the treasure houses on the East wall, the warriors are doing the same on a larger scale.

"They are also blocking major intersections with spiked tree trunks. Some are already in place, and others are hanging on tackle, ready to drop on soldiers. They're got laborers digging ditches across some of the roads and it looks like they're sandbagging the treasure houses.

"Two other things, lord. The walls are a joke. The best ones are less than thirty feet tall and not more than six or eight feet thick. I even think that some of the walls on the Eastern side might be mainly mud walls. Or course, they do have swivel guns mounted at intervals on the wall and there thirty or forty cannon scattered around, but those walls are obviously for population control, not war.

"The last important thing is something I can't tell you. I have no idea where the defenders are. I can tell you that there seventy or eighty thousand Mongols in the camps outside the city, but that damned city couldn't hold ten thousand people on the best day of its life. I don't see any big barracks. I can't tell you where the defenders are."

And then my "million man Mongol army" vanished in front of my eyes.

199

Komander Jazinski leaned forward at the end of the table, "Your grace, there's even more mystery here than you've mentioned. We're always hearing about millions of Mongols, and we certainly got hit by a lot of them when they invaded us, but most of those troops were Chinese or Turkish or some other kind of auxiliary troops. My family was in agricultural businesses. Take my word for it. This is a dry, cold place. Their main food is meat and the grass is terrible for grazing. They must move their herds constantly, and even if they import half of their food, there can't be over a hundred, hundred fifty thousand adult males in this county out of a population of maybe a million. Even if they're all home, all mounted, and no one has a cold, after the number we already killed, there can't be eighty, ninety thousand effectives left.

"If this report is correct, it looks like Karakorum's almost empty."

I decided to step in. I was a little uncomfortable that they might realize the 'million man Mongol army' that I had been touting might actually be a little smaller than that. "Whatever their numbers are, their plan is obvious. They want us to attack Karakorum and they don't really care if we level it. Their plan is to bring those two reserve forces and hit us from behind while we are bogged down there, fighting street to street. That defensive work is just to slow us down until the cavalry arrives. Mongols don't defend, they rope-a-dope, they trick, they sneak and they attack when they want to.

"That's handy. If they come to us, we won't need to go looking for them. We will make a few changes in their plan. Instead of fighting street to street, we'll level the city with artillery and walk in over the dead bodies of the defenders. When the other two armies show up we'll be ready for them."

I was delighted with the report. If we were going to face a Mongol army not more that twice our size with our machine guns, rifled cannons and twelve shot rifles, this was going to be a cakewalk. We'd be home before the end of spring. You know, someday I will stop thinking like that, but when that day comes I will probably have an arrow sticking out of my chest, be shot in both legs, and have a barbarian axe buried in my skull. Of course it wouldn't be that easy, but some things, I just learn slow.

Outside, Kowalski was walking around the naval gun with a look of admiration. He was patting the carriage and almost crooning to it. I had to slap him on the back to get his attention, "We, baron, where do you plan to put your new toy?"

He never took his eyes off of it. "Put it? Hell, we're less than fifteen miles from the city. I could just leave it here and blast the piss out of them. I could level that city and never leave this spot.

"However, their best cannon can't reach out more than three or four miles, so we'll move downstream until we're maybe five miles from the city and set up wherever it looks good. We'll just have to use a lighter powder charge.

"We've got three hundred rounds that the *Flying Cloud* brought in and another seven hundred rounds they delivered with the carriage. A thousand rounds won't actually level nine square miles of city, but it'll punch some damned big holes in it.

"We'll have her secure on the carriage and all of the ammo loaded by tonight. We'll set up a fire base and move her tomorrow. Morning, two days from now, you can start using her."

The next day was a watch and wait day for us. *Zephyr* continued to scout for the Wolves sabotaging the rail line. *Vagabond* radioed that she wouldn't arrive until morning, and that she would deliver her supplies directly to the main camp. *Flying Cloud* did a circuit of the other two Mongol camps and by noon was parked high over Karakorum.

That's when the fun began. The *Flying Cloud* was on station for less than an hour when two rocket planes took off from a runway inside the city. They both looped over our camp and then circled off one of the mountains looking for thermals. When they rose as far as they could, one of them took off down the rail line. The other went *Cloud* hunting.

She coasted in from the mountainside picking as much speed as possible and then turned nose up, blasting her engine as she headed for the dirigible.

Stanislaw was ready for it. He had mounted a couple of machine guns to fire through the floor of the cargo bay. He blasted out tracers while the attacker clawed for altitude. As the plane started to fall off her climb, her pilot fired a missile – which fell short by a thousand feet.

The ballet went on most of the afternoon. There was no way Stanislaw's crew could hit a tiny plane moving a hundred miles an hour thousands of feet below them, and try as he might, the Mongol pilot couldn't get to the dirigible.

He sure tried. He landed several times to re-arm and refuel. He tried again and again to get more altitude. He rode the thermals until they died and then fired off one or more rocket motors to get more altitude before he left the thermal. He would fire a rocket motor during his high speed run back to the dirigible and then another one during his ascent. The men started betting on when he would tear the wings off his plane.

The closest he got was one missile that exploded at the same level as the dirigible but hundreds of yards behind it.

Eventually, about a thousand troopers found reasons to "do observation" near the front and even the Mongols working on their walls would occasionally take a break to watch the fight.

On the morning of the second day, I met with Sir Grzegorz, Sir Wladyclaw, and Baron Kowalski in the chilly darkness before sunrise. We stood around Stanislaw's map of the city and gulped down hot chocolate and coffee against the morning cold. Kowalski pointed down at the east wall. "If you want to do serious damage to that wall, I'm going to have to move artillery around the city. As it is, we can only really damage the western and northern walls. We'll need to move the camp up to the city walls and surround them like the Vandals attacking Rome."

Sir Wladyclaw agreed. "We've got an unbeatable defensive position where we are, but we're not here to defend, we're here to kill. It's time to step out and fight."

They waited silently, if not gracefully, while I pondered the map. "Prepare to break camp. It's time to play a game of *barbarian*. If we don't get more aggressive, we'll be here until Christmas.

During our move out to the tundra, *Vagabond* showed up with Komander Edmund's idea of "anti-aircraft" weapons. I was sitting on Silver watching the men pack up the camp when I heard the unmistakable whir of a dirigible overhead. A few minutes later, my radioman ran over with a message. "It's the *Vagabond*, sire. She wants to know where the antiaircraft equipment should land." I missed the strange wording for a moment until I looked up though my field glasses. The dirigible had six of our old wooden biplanes hanging underneath her.

"Get me the captain of the *Vagabond*." The captain was waiting on the mike when I reached the radio wagon. "Captain, we're grateful for the equipment, but we could have used a little more warning. We're in the middle of moving our camp."

"I'm sorry, sire, that we didn't give you more warning, but we have been ordered to limit long distance radio due to the tense situation between Hetman Piotr and the King. The Hetman doesn't want this mission to distract them right now.

"I think you'll find the planes worth the trouble, your grace. They're listed as scrap on the army books, but they've got new engines and upgraded guns and they're years ahead of anything else within five thousand miles of you."

They put a nasty drag on us, but I can hold them onboard for a day if I have too. The biggest problem is that the pilots are bugging the Hell out of me to let them shoot some Mongols. Well, that and the fact that we're useless for other work while we have planes hanging under us. "

I left Baron Krol with the job of deciding where to put the planes. He had them land on a section of riverbank that had recently held tents. The planes were another media event. Unlike the failed US Macon, *Vagabond* was not a true carrier. It could not recover planes in flight and was simply a transport that could carry aircraft one way. However, watching as each plane's pilot revved up his engine and dropped away from the carrier brought cheers from the troops that they buzzed before landing.

The *Vagabond* then landed near them and unloaded hundreds of gallons of fuel and spare parts. After her crew enjoyed a few hours of much-needed ground leave, she took off to start patrolling the southern skies. It wasn't until much later that I realized that I hadn't asked, "What situation between Piotr and the king?"

Life was good. Unbelievably good. I had gone from having an undermanned, underfed, under equipped little army back to having the most powerful army on the continent. I even had airplanes – with machine guns on them. I had more ammo than any general in history and better weapons than anyone else in the world.

I was beginning to think that this would be a replay of the Africa campaign. All I had to do was take one small city and wipe out a couple of armies from long distance and we were home free. The only problem was that I was not certain where "home" was. Well, that and the fact that I was absolutely and totally wrong about the war.

From the Secret Journal of Su Song, Part Six

With Korea now part of the Mongol Empire, Kublai decided that it was time to take the Song capital and integrate them into his empire. To assure that the city would fall, we prepared to cast the two largest cannon in history.

Now the Poles have changed all that. They have begun a winter campaign against the Kipchak Khanate. They have destroyed the administrative center at Sari and have moved toward Karakorum.

We have even been ordered to stop work on the Fists of Heaven. They would have been thirty feet long, firing a thirty inch ball up to ten miles, and would have been our greatest achievement in weaponry. The barrels would have been large enough to let six men crawl inside and sleep comfortably, but now they will have to wait. Perhaps next year.

The Kipchaks have not been able to respond to the Polish invasion due to a mysterious ailment that has wiped out most of their horses. Kublai's administrators have spent the entire winter scouring the countryside for one hundred fifty thousand new horses and sending them to Karakorum. Most of the horses are untrained and require additional work once they reach Mongolia.

I was told to juggle the railroad schedule to free up enough cars and engines to move the entire force and its supplies to Mongolia in the early spring. During the winter, I established supply depots along the line to Mongolia and stocked with them food, ammunition, weapons, and clothes for the men. As the khan's plan involves surprise, the northernmost depot is one hundred fifty miles south of Karakorum, close enough to supply the army but far enough way to avoid detection. There has been considerable disruption of the economy and even famine in some areas as the rail equipment has moved north and been parked, But the khan is adamant.

The exact date of the final northward march depends upon the Polish army, but I have been warned to have enough cars available for the entire army on three days notice. Just finding a place to store twenty five miles of cars is a challenge.

The Kipchaks have been ordered to delay the Poles in Mongolia. The great khan has ordered that they avoid pitched battle and draw the Poles into an attack on the capital. Once the Poles are fully engaged, it will be my job to move the largest army in Chinese history the final one hundred and fifty miles onto the Mongolian plain and end the Polish threat forever.

Visitors are Coming for Dinner

After I had relaxed with little horizontal exercise, I tried to plan out the battle strategy. It was hard. I was bored stiff. How many leaders have to plan out a battle that both sides know is a fake? The Mongols obviously weren't going to try hard to hold Karakorum, and aside from its symbolic value, we didn't really want it.

After a lot of well lubricated thought, I decided to continue my "stand off and kill the bastards" policy. We could probably smash our way into the city and back on the road to Poland tomorrow, and the idea was very tempting, but I reminded myself over and over that there were no extra points for playing war the hard way. We had the time and ammo to soften them up nicely before we attacked, so I stuck with the plan I had given to Kowalski.

We had thousands of artillery rounds with us and one small city to take. We had a thousand rounds of ammo for a five-inch gun that that I didn't want to move after the battle, so we would do our best to use up that ammo here. That was almost enough to put a five-inch shell though every door in Karakorum.

There would be a few surprises. Even though the Mongols were preparing for an artillery siege, I doubt that they realized the power of modern shells. We weren't firing stone balls or grape-shot. It was late when I got to sleep.

The first surprise, however, came from the Mongols. At first light I was awakened by a committee. I was used to being awakened by gently massage from my delectably naked bodyguards and instead my aide, Baron Kowalski, one of our Chinese translators and some other people I was too bleary to recognize insisted that I had to get up, now! I managed to rub my eyes, look at Kowalski and ask through my dried out lips, "Aren't you supposed to bombing a city this morning?"

"Yes, your grace. But I had to delay it. There's a Chinaman in the way."

"Well. Shoot him. Then he won't be in the way. Let me sleep a little more."

"I can't shoot him, your grace. He's sitting under a canopy flying white flag. They want to negotiate."

"Well, shoot him anyway and then we won't need to get up so early and talk so much."

"Your humor is appreciated, Sire, particularly at this early hour, but when you are fully awake, you will realize that we have to meet with him first, and kill him later."

I was still in pain when we reached the observation post. Sure enough. There was a Chinaman sitting under a little tent about halfway between ourselves and the city. He was dressed like a rich version of Fu Man Chu and flanked by four assistants, two sitting at his side, two standing behind him, and all richly dressed but apparently unarmed.

By this time Sir Wladyclaw and two Chinese looking translators had joined us. I wondered only for a moment where the translators came from before I remembered the Chinese that we had recruited in Sarai.

I straightened up in my chair and said, "I'll go down to meet him. Get me a lance to go along. Make certain they're polished up and presentable."

One of the translators cleared his throat and bowed very deeply. He said in very bad Polish "Excuse me, Lord, but must tell that is not how it is normal done. You are a king and kings only speak with kings. One send messenger to find his rank. Then send right size man to speak."

I motioned for some hot chocolate from the sideboard someone had thoughtfully set up, and tried to think clearly. "Okay Sir Wladyclaw, You're as handsome as any of us. Take this translator and a lance with you. Find out what they want, and then don't give it to them." Looking at the translator who had spoken, I asked, "Do you think you can understand the Chinaman?" He bowed so deep I could barely hear his answer. "Yes, your grace Sir, I study Polish all winter with Baron Sir Ivanov, and that man speak Cantonese or Ubuntu. I speak both."

We brought up a couple of snipers to cover the party and then Sir Wladyclaw made a properly pompous approach to the Chinaman. He left his knights about thirty feet short of the canopy and went ahead with only his two translators. There was a lot of bowing and talking that I couldn't make out and after about twenty minutes he returned to our position carrying a scroll. The Chinaman sat passively awaiting his return.

He handed me the scroll and motioned to the translator, who took so long to praise me, flatter my talents, and praise my ancestors that I damned well nearly made him an ancestor before he got down to business. "Your grace, the Chinaman he wants two days."

I was still digesting that comment when the translator continued, "He say he not know why you want Karakorum, but he will fight you if you want. But city have thousands of your people in it. He want time for them to leave."

"My people are back in camp. Who is he talking about?"

He gestured to the scroll, "Paper list this. Four thousand Muslim, nine hundred Christian, Ambassadors from your countries, other people. He want time for them to leave the city."

"Why the Hell aren't they already gone. We haven't exactly tiptoed up on them?"

The translator I was talking to looked confused and exchanged a couple of sentences with his companion.

"They not left because they know you kill everyone. Traders have friends in Sarai and Africa and they know when Christian Army march, everyone die. They afraid leave unless you swear they not be killed on the road."

There it was again. I was so angry my vision went red, my fists clenched, and I had to hold myself back from killing the damned translator. We were facing Mongols who made mountains of skulls at some cities, massacred other cities just because they didn't want to leave anyone in their rear, and killed so many people that some areas were depopulated for hundreds of years – and they were accusing me of war crimes, making us out to be killers.

I was already haunted by a little girl's eyes and now I have to listen to charges of wanton murder. It was too much.

"Fuck 'em. They chose their friends. Let 'em die with them. Negotiations are over!"

No one moved. No one spoke or moved for a long time. I concentrated on calming down and tried to stop pacing around the observation post. Finally, Sir Wladyclaw motioned to everyone to leave, "Wait outside until we call you."

When we were alone, he turned to me and said, "Your grace, when you calm down, I think you will change that order. Your reputation has already suffered grievous harm from the battles in Sarai and in Africa. How would you explain knowingly slaughtering thousands of innocents?"

I still couldn't stand or sit still "I am the Hetman! I explain to no one, and I don't care what anyone thinks. These people are Mongol sympathizers and they deserve what they get."

The bastard just wouldn't shut up. "Your grace, you are so angry at merely being accused of such a murder that you almost cannot speak. Do you want to meet your maker someday and tell him you were so angry about being accused that you made the accusation truth?

I'll be outside waiting for your final decision."

It must have been an hour. I paced. I cursed. I drank hot chocolate and pounded my fists on a table. I wanted booze, but I was too stubborn angry to tell someone to fetch it for me. I sat on a bench and fumed. The bastards had me. The Mongols didn't give a crap about the people in Karakorum. This was just a delaying tactic, but it would work. Sir Wladyclaw was aggravatingly right. Murder wasn't Christian Army tactics. I dreamed of someday thanking Sir Wladyclaw by putting a knife in his ribs, but I gave in.

When I left the outpost, the Chinaman was still sitting patiently waiting. I gestured toward him and told no one in general. "One day. Tell the bastard we will give the civilians one day, from now until this time tomorrow, to leave the city. They can leave by the southern road. We'll have a checkpoint set up to verify that they take no modern weapons with them. They have my word that they will not be harmed.

Someone make it happen. I'm going back to bed.

Someone tell Ivanov to get his cannons ready. He'll need them tomorrow."

And I did go back to bed until noon.

By noon my anger had cooled and my mind was working clearly. By the time I did my morning rituals and finished grooming Silver my head was crystal clear.

First, I needed more information then I needed a staff meeting. I trust my own decisions more than anyone else's, but I wanted people to bounce ideas off.

I called terry over to take message to my radio cart. "To Captain Stanislaw: You are promoted immediately to commodore and given command of the Easter Flotilla. Your choice of officers is to be promoted to captain of *Flying Cloud* immediately. Your command will consist of all airships and aircraft in this theater of war. Your first order as Commodore: Determine the status of both detached Mongol armies, with particular attention to any defensive measures currently under construction. Acquire all possible intelligence on Mongol activity as far as two hundred fifty miles south with emphasis on the rail line.

If your schedule permits, you are invited to a staff meeting at nine hundred hours. Will understand if you are unable to make it. "

Then I gave her a list of people to invite to the staff meeting. Some people were entitled to come because of their status, but there were others who's thinking I trusted, so it was not the usual top officers only meeting. "This will not be the usual staff meeting. We will need a few tables to sit around during the first part of the meeting, but I want a big buffet waiting when they get here and I want cushions and pillows set up for after dinner along with some cigars and some of my private stock of whiskey."

Everyone except Captain Stanislaw was waiting respectfully when it was time for the meeting. However, as my adjutant was escorting the men in, there was a whooshing sound outside. We all ran out to be greeted by the sight of a man swinging down the road in a sedan chair. He seemed to be having some trouble stabilizing himself because the chair was on the end of a thousand foot cable running up to a rigidible overhead. On his second swing past us, he released the bar holding him in and stepped out at our feet. Well. Close to our feet when he was able to stop hopping, stand upright, and do a snappy salute.

"Captain Stanislaw reporting, your grace. I hope I'm not late. It's actually easier to be picked up than to be dropped off."

I couldn't help it. My engineer side took over as we walked back into the tent. I looked back the rapidly rising gondola and commented "Maybe you should add some control surfaces to the basket. A simple rudder would make it more controllable."

"An excellent idea, your grace. I'll pass it on to the crew."

It wasn't until later that I realized I had been so impressed with Stanislaw that I gave him a suggestion instead of simply ordering a rudder. Either I was slipping or he was one Hell of a soldier.

I deliberately waited until everyone filled their plates with mutton and beef and roasted vegetables and their cups with cold water or beer. "You probably all know that we are not bombarding Karakorum today because of an unusual treaty request by the Mongols. For those of you who are not on the grapevine, the Mongol administration of the city told us that there are several thousand Europeans in the city who are craftsman, traders, priests, ambassadors and their families and even a Jewish rabbi. They requested two days truce so that the bystanders could leave the city. We gave them one."

I looked at the Chinese translator who had met with the Chinaman, "You served in the Mongol army at Sarai. Do you see anything unusual about what they wanted?"

"I never in battle with Mongols, but my father say when they attacked our city, they put Chinese people in front of their army to protect themselves. Men, women, even children pushed out in front to die and then bodies ridden over by Mongols. I hear they do that every time. No way they care a turd about Europeans. Sorry, no know how to say it polite."

Gentlemen, Ahmed is here because he has traveled these lands for years and has seen what the Mongols do. "Ahmed, from what you have seen and heard about the Mongols, what would you expect them to do with the Europeans in the city?"

"My lord, the history is clear. They would either chain them to the walls to die as padding or they would put them behind the gates to take the first arrows from invaders. In no case would they let them live. I heard that when they were besieging one city, they took living captives, covered them in oil, lit them on fire, and catapulted their burning bodies into the city."

"OK, we know that the Mongols don't give a rat's ass about the Europeans, so we now know what they wanted. They wanted the two days. They wanted us to sit here in front of this city for two more days. What's going to happen two days from now? We've been working on the assumption that they wanted us to attack a worthless city so that their reserves could flank us while we were bogged down in the city. Unfortunately that doesn't make sense now. They're maintaining a huge army in the field waiting for us to do something and the best thing for them would be for us to move as soon as possible.

Commodore Stanislaw, are the reserve Mongols moving our way yet?"

"No sign of movement this way, your grace. Zephyr overflew the easternmost camp this morning and she was able to reach the khan's camp about an hour after sunrise. The Mongols aren't moving this way, but both armies are bee hives of activity.

The khan's contingent has been on the move down one of the silk roads, but he isn't coming this way. He's headed south and slightly west with his entire force. They're moving fast as they can go with a caravan full of yurt wagons. It looks more like his annual vacation trip than a move toward war.

The western group of Mongols is still digging in, but Zephyr says that the work has intensified. They've are trenched clear across the pass that we took to get in here, and they're rolling big boulders down from the hills to line up in front of the trenches.

It doesn't look like they are moving on us anytime soon."

I had my aide attach a large map of Mongolia to the blackboard. "I think that I do know where they're going. This is a map that Ahmed drew up showing the Silk Road routes around Karakorum. Of course we all know that there is no one Silk Road. It's like a patchwork of roads, but you'll notice that there are only two easy routes going west. The Western Mongol force has just blocked off the route that we took to get here. If the khan's army keeps moving in its current direction, it will be at the junction of the other pass leading west by the end of today.

All of the other useable routes out lead either south or southeast into China. They're big roads all going the wrong way.

They haven't been waiting for us to attack Karakorum. They've been buying time to block the passes. They want to keep up here.

We should all have realized what was happening as soon as we saw the railroad. The rules of war change when you can move men two or three hundred miles a day. Big brother Kublai is coming. Karakorum is the hard place and Kublai's army is the rock.

If I'm right, we should be hearing something from Vagabond by morning."

Stanislaw leaned forward in his seat, "Your grace, Gentlemen, we are getting hourly reports from Vagabond. She's penetrated almost two hundred miles south and she hasn't seen a large army yet, but, at the hundred and hundred fifty mile marks she did find large storage yards flanking the rails. The Captain says they are each about twenty acres in size and surrounded by palisades. In his first fly over about four days ago, he thought they were rail yards or commercial warehouses but this time he looked closer. The workers seem to be a mix of slaves and men in military uniform. He can't tell what is in the warehouses and wagons, but he thinks the places may be military storage yards.

He hasn't seen an army yet, but he's still traveling south."

I looked around the table, "I'm convinced that Uncle Kublai is on his way. We'll know for certain soon enough, but in case I'm right, we can't wait until the last minute to plan how we'll introduce ourselves to him. We have a lot of plans to make."

In the lull, Baron Ryszard spoke up, "Your grace, everyone here knows that I am no coward and I enjoy a good fight as much as any man, but Kublai's army could easily be twenty or thirty times our size. Perhaps this would be a good time to retire from the field."

I tried to keep my voice as respectful as possible, "Baron Ryszard . You have the respect of every man here and your advice is valuable, but we may not have an option. We have forty thousand men and thousands of carts going the wrong way."

In fact, I was happy he had brought up the idea of retreat. Discussing the possibility was the only way to get the men to see we only had one choice. "We have the expert here. Baron Ivanov is there any reason that we can't go back to Poland tomorrow."

The Baron took time looking into the distance, rubbing his hands together and sighing. Finally, he said, "As I see it, our biggest problems would be starvation, pain, and death. We're sitting in the middle of the toughest, fastest, meanest best trained army in the world. They could move out in good order by midnight, kick the crap out of any Mongols in our way, and most of them would be dead in a month.

If Lord Conrad is correct, and he is not often wrong, the Mongols here are not going to attack us. They're going to fortify the passes and try to keep us from leaving. I have no doubt that either Count Grzegorz or Count Wladyclaw can smash through any Mongol line, particularly with the help of Baron Kowalski's excellent artillery, but it won't matter if we can't get our carts through before Kublai gets here. We need to reach the steppes with at least five thousand carts if we're going to fight our way home and that's what the blockades are for. Trenches, boulders, stakes, and harassment to stop our supply train, not our soldiers. There are a few thousand miles of starvation between here and civilization."

I took over the floor again. "That's also the way I see it. They'll try to hold us for a few days. If we attack one pass, the other army will hit our rear. If we get through one pass, they'll concentrate on the baggage train and try to delay us. We know about the trenching, but they probably have the passes mined too. Nothing we can't handle, but if were still clearing a pass when Brother Kublai gets here, the game is over.

Until we know different, we're going to assume Kublai is coming. That means we have very little time to get organized. We can't fight him here and we can't fight him tomorrow. We need to find a place to stand where we limit his access to us. We need a canyon, a peninsula, something constricted and we need time to find it and move.

This meeting is to figure out what we are going to do. We have the toughest army in the world and enough ammo to kill all of Asia. We just need to avoid getting overrun by sheer numbers.

A few things are obvious. At first light, Count Wladyclaw will send out a company of wolves with a company of engineers to sabotage that rail line. A Chinese army can't walk more than twenty miles a day, so we need to put them on foot.

Count Grzegorz will be in charge of finding a place to make a stand. I'll be working with him as will Commodore Stanislaw.

Baron Ryszard , you get charge of Karakorum. We know it has to be lightly defended, but we can't afford to leave it behind us, and there may be supplies that we can use. Forget any plans I made. Find a way to kill it quick and simple. Tell Wladyclaw and Kowalski what you need to get the job done.

The rest of you figure out what I've missed. We haven't heard from the pilots. Can we defend their base where they are, or they need to move? There are a thousand things to discuss.

You've got food, cigars, and soft places to sit. There are runners outside who can summon anyone else you need.

Get to work."

One long army hour later, a half hour after darkness fell, we got a message from the Vagabond "Campfires sighted. From horizon to horizon. Three hundred fifty miles south."

We had found Kublai.

About the same time, a full company of engineers left camp with their escort of Wolves. The men would sleep in the saddle and be ready for railroad demolition in the morning.

An hour before midnight I broke up the meeting. Everyone would need some rest before sunrise. My last order of the night was for the radio corps to set up a camp wide broadcast to take place after morning rituals. As tired as I was, I had a hard time sleeping. Even with Terry and Shauna massaging my sore muscles my mind was full of images of Chinese catapults and Mongol horsemen.

Rumors of the size of the Mongol army were certainly circulating through the camp, and some warriors were going to be fearful. I had to replace those fears with a sense of pride and determination. In the dim light of early morning, I climbed to the highest point in the camp and took the microphone the communications corpsman handed me. Most men would just be finishing their morning rituals. At my first word, the camp went silent, "You may have heard that we have company coming. In fact we have learned that we are surrounded by three Mongol armies. The armies of Mongolia have fortified and blocked both roads back to Poland, and a large Chinese army, led by Mongols, is approaching from the south.

They think they have us trapped, but we are the meanest, toughest, fastest army in creation, and we go anywhere we want. Moreover, six months ago, standing on the plains of Mongolia, each and every one us made the decision to kill Mongols and end forever the threat to the civilized world.

So we will fight. That is what the Christian Army does. We kill the enemies of Poland. We annihilate those who would threaten our families and our friends. Today that means we kill the heathen Mongols.

The Mongols will help us in this. They are bringing a lot of Chinese friends. They will line them up in close order from horizon to horizon, to make certain that we can't miss hitting one, no matter where we aim.

Months ago, I promised you the wealth of Karakorum. Tomorrow, we will take it, and then leave to prepare our welcome for the Mongols. In a few days, we will see our enemy's campfires stretching to the horizon. Before we leave, their funeral pyres will be even larger.

We fight for Poland, for God, for our families. God Bless us all."

Second Interlude in Uncle Toms Control Room

I pushed the pause button again. "He actually did it! He convinced them they have to stay and fight a useless battle. That's either suicidal or just plain stupid."

"I know"

Uncle Tom look unconcerned but I went on, "They can leave anytime they want. They could walk through either Mongol blocking army and have plenty of time to get the carts that they really need across any Mongol blockade, or they could just load the bare essentials and the booty onto panniers and high tail if for home. Without dragging the baggage train they could be back in Poland in a few weeks, and the Mongols could never catch them. They could even take time to loot Karakorum and still get away clean. If they run short of food or want to ship booty home, they have a fleet of airships to help them."

Uncle Tom looked amused. "Don't sell the warrior's intelligence short. They aren't used to aerial re-supply and even Ivanov didn't think about it. They're also blinded with gold fever and adrenalin, and they're warriors who think in terms of glory and booty not retreats and running. Most of them don't really want to go home that way.

And, remember they can't all go home. Conrad can't."

"But he has to know it's stupid. Why is he doing it?"

"The slavery. Remember he spent a year as a slave. Not a well treated household tutor slave or well fed kitchen slave, a subhuman animal slave. A piece of machinery. He was in Hell for months and I still don't understand why he never once asked me for help.

Now he's consumed with anger. The old Conrad would never have allowed the slaughter of women and children and there's enough of old Conrad left in him so that he still lets his men talk him out of it. He tolerates the insubordination because deep down inside he doesn't like his own orders. He can't go home, but maybe if he kills enough bad guys he can rid himself of the anger and let the old Conrad out again.

For now, I'm with Conrad. Thousands of people have invested countless man years of effort and busted their butts to get this army to this battle. It would be a shame to go home now."

The Battle of Karakorum

The cannon fire began about an hour later. The truce was over, and Ryszard was beginning his bombardment. At breakfast I learned that I had missed Stanislaw's return to his ship. Apparently the airship dropped the sedan chair on the empty space in front of my tent and continued to drop until there was a lot of slack in the line. Then Stanislaw stepped in, fastened his safety belt and rose into the sky.

He left a message that he was on his way to confer with the fighter pilots. When he was dropped there, Flying Cloud would continue to search for a place to make our stand.

I breakfasted on bread slathered with soft white cheese and a tumbler of cold well water. I was still licking my fingers while my bodyguards dressed me in armor. Except for a few weeks in our winter camp, I had been wearing armor almost every day for year. My body was wearing calluses where the straps wore on my shoulders and the chafing on my calves was permanent. I dreamed of living in my favorite silk bathrobe or, better yet, in my favorite bare skin, but today I would ride forth in full golden glory – again.

Ryszard was at the observation point with of his personal lance, watching shells landing on Karakorum. As we watched the bombardment, he explained what he had decided to do. "I'm going to burn all the residential and business areas with incendiaries. It doesn't take very many of them to get a good fire going, and I want to save as many shells as possible for the main event. They're supposed to be empty anyway. Then we'll flatten that palace and the meeting hall with the five incher. The khan's treasure warehouses are those buildings by the far wall. We'll spare them until I see what's inside.

We'll punch some exit holes in the north wall early in case there are Europeans stuck in the city. Count Wladyclaw is stationing several companies near that wall with instructions to kill anyone leaving the city with a weapon or wearing armor, or just looking like a Mongol, and let women and children pass. When the fires die down a little, Kowalski is going to punch some holes in the wall, and then he'll clear a road for us from the front gate to the warehouses."

He always pissed me off with his bleeding heart crap, but the plan was basically sound, "My Liege, you seem to have things well in hand, but I must remind you that we have no facilities for prisoners and it is much to dangerous to leave them behind us. Do not take prisoners.

Keep me informed. I want to know when you launch the attack."

By the time I got back to my tent, there was a lot of news waiting. The radio crew had run a microphone and speaker into the tent so that Sir Wladyclaw and I could conference with Stanislaw from my desk. He told us that the Chinese Mongol army was on the move. They began breaking camp at first light and were moving to the rail cars. They were also moving with air cover. Zephyr needed to stay at high altitude to avoid the two Chinese rocket planes that circled the camp. Unless we neutralized the planes, there was no chance of surprise on either side. I put it on my todo list. Well, Stanislaw's todo list. The more important thing was choosing a place for our stand. I was anxious to finalize the decision, but the air corps needed time to finish their survey. Zephyr was flying a forty mile grid pattern that would take several more hours to finish while Flying cloud was following caravan trails and working the guides for suggestions. I set a meeting for nightfall to make the final decision.

The rest of the day was a steady parade of conferences. When will we make the move? Answer after we take the city. We didn't need the entire force to deal with Karakorum, but I didn't want to spit our forces in such hostile territory. The last time we did that Captain Ivanov earned a promotion to Baron, so I decided that the column would pack up and prepare to move, but stand in place while Ryszard handled the city.

Kowalski and I debated whether to take the naval gun with us or disable the monster. It was powerful, but we'd have to remake The Pride and the Passion to move it. We decided to drag it along. We had more ammo than any army in history and plenty of cannon, Sten guns, machine guns and rifles to shoot it with.

I was surprised that we had over three months of food with us. We could probably outlast the Chinese in a siege. Just to make certain, we'd shop a little in Karakorum before we left.

Late in the afternoon, Ryszard sent word that the fires were still burning in the city and that he would carry out his attack at first light.

At dark, our move team showed up. All the barons, both counts, and, not surprisingly, Captain Stanislaw were there. This time the sedan chair had a rudder on the back and springy skids in place of the legs.

I began the meeting with a good old fashioned pep talk. "All we need is a good place to fight in and a little time to get it ready. Komander Jazinski has already pointed out that there aren't all that many true Mongols in Mongolia. There aren't more than sixty or seventy thousand fighting men left here. We've already faced them a couple of times and kicked their asses.

The Chinese army isn't going to be much different. It's bigger, but no better. They've been doin' a lot of raping and they all have slave girls, but there still can't be more than a hundred thousand or so more Mongols in the entire Chinese Empire. We learned this winter that the Turks have joined the Mongols so enthusiastically that you can't tell one from another, so add another sixty, seventy thousand Turks. The rest of the men sitting around those campfires are Chinese or other subjects. We already know that they don't want to fight us. The Mongols will push them forward as cannon fodder but they will fight only as hard they have too.

It doesn't matter if there are a thousand of them or a million. They are just targets, and we have lots of ammo. This won't be a stroll in the park, but we can beat them.

Now let's choose their graveyard."

The first suggestion was that we use the pass that we came through on the way in. True, it was now full of Mongols and trenches and boulders, but the Mongols were never a major problem, and after we cleared them out, we would have a ready made defensive wall left behind.

I gave the idea five points for creativity and ten points for dumb. The Mongols there could refuse battle and vanish into the hills until we were under attack and then jump us from behind.

Our second choice had a similar problem. The rigidibles had found a glacial canyon about thirty miles north. The mouth of the canyon was perhaps fifteen hundred feet wide and the steep hills protected the sides. Once we were dug in, we couldn't be dislodged by anyone. Unfortunately, the Chinese could decide to simply blockade the entrance and keep us there until we came out to fight against their prepared positions.

We settled on a canyon about twenty five miles east of us on the Silk Road segment that led to Korea. Both ends of the canyon were narrow and it had relatively high hills on both sides. The surrounding mountains would make the Chinese Mongols take days to ride around if they wanted to attack our back door, and the second opening gave us room to run if things went wrong. Before we broke up the meeting, I asked Sir Grzegorz for any news on the troops delaying the Mongols. "After a little consideration, I sent an additional party with Wolves and Engineers south. The original party didn't start destroying tracks until they were almost two hundred miles south, and they're looking for big things to wreck. They're searching for bridges and viaducts. They'll keep going until they meet the Chinese. Then they'll do some damage to the rolling stock and depend on the Big Peoples speed to get them out of there.

The second party is pulling up rails and twisting them starting about one hundred miles out and they aren't necessarily looking for big targets. Any bend in the road or any switch that can be twisted up quickly is a target. On the way back, they'll pull up track all the way home.

However, Captain Stanislaw has come up with a good delaying tactic. " Stanislaw tried to look surprised and then humble and failed at both, "Your grace, when the captain of Vagabond realized that it would be handy to put bullet holes in the steam engines - if the planes could reach trains, he remounted two of the fighters and flew them south. He'll drop the planes over the trains and provide the Chinese with some holes to patch."

"The plan, Captain, is ingenious, but you said that the planes can't re-hook to Vagabond, so how do you get them home? Those trains are way out of range."

"Vagabond can't take the planes back on board, but she's carrying extra barrels of fuel. They'll attack at first light and after the attack they'll all fly north. When the planes are low on fuel, they'll all land and Vagabond will refuel the planes for the flight home.

It's slightly risky. We know that those wooden planes can be brought down by ground fire, but the Chinese have never seen a real fighter plane so we figure they can do two or three passes before anyone thinks to shoot at them."

One of the interpreters bowed to Stanislaw, "Pilots not have trouble finding engines. Kublai so proud of new engines he have them painted bright red with yellow smoke stacks. Tell warriors easy to see."

I spent the rest of the evening hours touring the artillery emplacements, encouraging the men, congratulating them on their work and occasionally dismounting to share little food or a hear a few jokes. The men were polite, respectful, grateful, and, as usual, a little uncomfortable with having the boss around. Being the boss was not a path to popularity.

The next morning I was up early. The day started badly.

I decided to give a hand to Baron Ryszard. Actually, I decided that I was bored out of my mind from planning and paperwork and that I was not going to miss another battle. While they were dressing me, I told Terry and Shauna that they would not be riding with me today. They were the world's best bodyguards but I had decided that modern warfare was not a place for nymphs. This was no longer medieval warfare. We now had bullets flying around, lots of them, and my bodyguards absolutely refused to wear armor.

They wailed and whined and cried and clung to me and begged me to let them come. When I ordered them to Shut Up, they choked back their tears and sobbed silently. That was worse than the wailing and whining. Terry finally promised to wear greaves on her legs and arms and convinced me she could shelter between my body and my shield. I refused to relent on Shauna, but I finally promised she could ride in the future if she could find some way to protect herself on Silver's back.

I was already in a foul mood when Grzegorz rode by my tent. He gave a snappy salute from horseback, donned his most respectful face and said, "Your orders conspicuously failed to specify from where you will observe and direct the battle. I assume you will have a radio cart, but on the eave of a battle, we don't know where to send messages?"

"You know damned well that I'm not putting on this tin suit to be an observer. We've come a long way and now I'm going to lead a column into that city."

"Most odd, Sire, Baron Ryszard has also ridden far this last year and shown great courage in every battle. One might think he has earned the right the lead his men into battle." Before I could skewer him, he shrugged and turned his horse to leave, "But, the Hetman knows best."

I do not like it when subordinates question my decisions, but I just gritted my teeth. He knew that the Wolves were as loyal to him as they were to me and I wasn't going to punish him. It didn't help that the bastard might be right. Maybe my proper place in this battle was on a high hill next to a radio cart and a bunch of runners.

I always thought that one of the reasons that Alexander beat the Persians was that Alexander led the Greek side from horseback in the middle of the battle and Darius led the Persians from a sedan chair sitting on a hill surrounded by guards. Sooner or later, however, we were going to stop being a medieval army. Now that we had radios and observers flying over the battle, and a well trained force, it was probably time to stop being Alexander and become Eisenhower – but not today, damn it. Today, I'm going to kill something in Karakorum with my own hands

Baron Ryszard was clearly not happy when I showed up with three companies of mounted infantry. As I drew up beside him, I gestured down to the city. "Baron, you are doing a good job. The plan is yours and the battle yours to lead. However, I am going to make one small addition. I will take a small force and lead a distraction. These laggards were lounging around with nothing to do, so I will take them through the railroad gate and perhaps draw off some fire from you and strengthen your flank."

Ryszard was a little happier when he realized that I was going to let him lead his own men. He would charge through the western wall, opposite the khan's treasure houses. The artillery had cleared a path for him all the way through town.

I had decided to make my assault through the railroad gates because if we went through the gate, we'd be right next to the khan's palace. A good place to start killing Mongols. There was also a large empty area just beyond the gates that was usually filled with Yurts that would give us a lot of maneuvering room inside the walls. It was staked and ditched, but neither would slow up Big People.

That maneuvering room also meant that we would be very exposed, but I had a shock tactic that should give us plenty of time to find cover. When Ryszard signaled the charge, I signaled to a lance of wolves who had loaded a boxcar with a hundred fifty pounds of black powder and parked it about a half mile down the tracks. A few minutes later a flaming boxcar appeared from the south, pushed by two Big People. Less than a quarter mile from the gate, the Big People pealed off and we began our charge, sweeping around behind the boxcar, but giving it lots of room. I lowered my shield around Terry as we approached the wall.

That much black powder makes a spectacular explosion. The gate and a big section of wall around it disappeared and we were through before the dust settled. I doubt that anyone in this century had seen an explosion that big. There wasn't much resistance inside, but there also wasn't much cover. We were depending on surprise to get us across the quarter mile of empty land between us and the Palace before they could open up. The Mongols had trenched the area just inside the walls with trenches wide enough to stop any normal horses, but the Big People just stepped over them. The same would happen to the fence at the far side of the field. Any place that it hadn't been smashed by our artillery, a Big Person could jump. Ahead of us and to the right was a small rail yard holding mostly burned out cars. There were perhaps twenty or thirty yurts still standing, but I doubt that anyone was riding out our artillery barrage in a yurt.

Baron Gorski led one company on a wide sweep to the right, clearing the wall of defenders and sweeping any defenders from the rail yard to make certain we weren't going to be hit from behind while I charged across the open space toward the Palace. Our first objective was the inner palace wall. The plan was to get there, dismount, establish a base, and then move forward under artillery cover. Before we could do that, we needed to get a radio into a safe position

We made it almost to the palace wall before we hit any serious resistance, then the trooper beside me dropped out of his saddle. I glanced over long enough to see that another trooper was slumped over his saddle, but still riding. More men began to drop.

The bastards were using my swivel guns! Unlike their usual black powder guns, those swivel guns could go though chain mail like newspaper and even drop a knight from a hundred yards. We moved even faster to get over under the cover of the perimeter wall and I began to wish we had left more of it standing. We dismounted, found cover, and looked over the wall. The palace was a lot shorter than it had been three days before, but it was built on a large earth and masonry foundation that extended out in every direction. The Mongols had moved their guns to the foundation and shielded them behind mounds of rubble.

We were still pinned down when a line of artillery fire suddenly marched across the base of the palace, taking out the gun emplacements, the guns, and considerable pieces of palace. That's when I realized that I was in a modern war. The Flying Cloud was watching the battle from overhead. She must have seen we were pinned down and told the artillery where to drop shells.

It seemed like a good time to leave. I raised my sword, yelled "For God. For Poland. For plunder!" and charged at the palace. Fortunately my men took the hint and followed me. It wasn't until I ran into my first Mongol that I realized that I was still holding the useless sword in my right hand and switched to my Sten gun. Stens are fast, but it just isn't as much fun killing a Mongol with a bullet as it is with a good sharp sword.

The palace was pretty much flattened along with most of the defenders. We spent an hour scouring the base looking for a basement or underground bunkers, but we found nothing. I suppose it made sense. The khan was probably at his summer camp and with him gone, this was just a big flammable building barely worth defending.

There were several mansions spread out between the palace and the rest of the town. Baron Gorski rode his men through each of them, but there didn't seem to be anyone left alive in the wreckage. By the time I left the palace, he was already past the interior walls and into the commercial area of the city.

As we swept though the small rail yard, my men formed up on both sides of me and we jumped to wall into the inner city in one long line. I heard gunfire on both sides of me as the troopers exchanged shots with scattered defenders. There was no serious resistance as I led them down a burning valley that was once a street. Most buildings were already reduced to smoldering ruins, but occasionally one would still burn brightly. When we reached the main east – west artery and turned toward the treasure houses, I saw that Ryszard had dropped machine gun wagons and squads at each of the major intersections. There were a lot or dead Mongols behind the barriers in the streets. They had ditched and blocked every major street, but hadn't known just how big a tree trunk a Big Person could jump. It looked like the troopers had just galloped through, surprising and killing everything they met.

Any wounded troopers had been evacuated, but occasion pieces of discarded armor and saddles showed the battle had not been all one sided. Some of that blood was ours.

Ryszard had set up his headquarters in a plaza set between two warehouses. He was sitting on a salvaged desk dropped between two hedges, taking messages from runners and sending out orders. His face and clothing held the bloody marks of a warrior who does more than give orders. Above the message he was reading, a corpsman had already stitched up a wound on his bicep.

As I approached, he looked up, "Hetman, Sire. I just sent a message to Ivanov telling him to start bringing in his wagons for the khan's inventory." About then, an explosion behind him made us all duck, "I guess the troopers couldn't find the keys to the gate. Your grace, you may want to look over the treasure houses yourself. Your plans leave us very little time to loot what we need and burn the rest. Tread careful, sire, there are still some mad Mongols lurking nearby."

"I think I will take a quick look at the fabled treasury, but how is the rest of the battle progressing"

"Its about over. The Mongols seriously underestimated the mobility of a man on his Big Person, so we just powered through. Caught most of them by surprise. Of course we don't have enough men to search five square miles of burning buildings, but there can't be many alive in the ashes. We'll do as much damage and steal as much plunder as we can and leave before dark."

The sound of gunfire in the distance promised more adventure, but who wouldn't want to see a khan's fabulous treasure. Problem is that it wasn't all that fabulous. When you got past the foyer and entered the warehouse it was just a warehouse. Boxes and bundles were stacked everywhere on shelves and the floor. The warehouse was full of blankets and robes and bolts of cloth. It held crates filled with pots and pans, stacks of rugs, fancy dishes from China, saddles, and household goods. I should have realized this was treasure that the khan used to reward his people for their loyalty, and they didn't need golden idols and trees of silver in their yurts

By the time I left the first warehouse, the Quartermasters corps had already started inventorying the other four warehouses. With smoke from a burning city swirling around us and the occasional artillery round falling, the Christian Army was already shopping.

I was still sitting on the warehouse steps reading the reports when Ivanov led a line of wagons through the recently opened gate and a company of mounted infantry fanned out to make certain that his boys weren't distracted. By the time the first wagons were lined up at the loading docks, quartermaster troops were coming out of the warehouses with lists of supplies to be loaded. It turned out that one of the warehouses stored food from China. Ivanov was already loading up wheat, rice, oranges and dried fish for our own use. One of the remaining warehouses was actually a treasury, and even though it had been partially emptied before we got there, we were able to confiscate several wagon loads of gold and jewels. We left the tons of Chinese money, because I had no idea where we would spend bronze coins.

The report on the last warehouse got my attention. It held personal weapons for the Mongol citizens. The muskets and bullets were mostly gone, as were the swords. There were however, a substantial number of bows left behind and thousands of arrows. In fact, there were tens of thousands of arrows. Apparently they became surplus when the Mongols got rifles. Most of it would burn, but I sent a note to Ivanov to save as many of the arrows as possible. I had an idea that might make them more valuable than gold.

As the wagons were filled, they joined the steady stream of men and equipment moving out to our new camp. As it became obvious that my presence was totally unnecessary in Karakorum, I turned over my command to Ryszard and joined the twenty mile long formation again moving out to our new camp.

Waiting for Our Visitors

Letter from Sir Polanski, Knight Banner in the Eagles to his fiancé. Never delivered.

We finally have some excitement. Leon and I were intercepted on our way to bed and told to get our flight gear together and report to the flight line. We grabbed our gear and then had to weave past campfires to get to the flight lines. Our ground crews were already fueling our planes when we got there, and as we began the preflight checks more mechanics and staff began to stumble into the light.

Unfortunately, the model threes are not night fighters and we didn't even have a single light on the runways, so no one had any idea of why we were there. Then I heard the sound of motors overhead and looked up to see the stars go out over one of canyon walls. Suddenly a bright light poured out of a door in the sky and ropes holding seamen dropped from above. One of the men landed next to me and gestured for me to raise my arms. He looped a rope under my armpits and yelled "hang on" as someone jerked me into the sky.

When we reached the cargo deck, a sailor that I recognized pushed me toward the front of the ship, "Your old bunks are waiting. Get some sleep. You'll need it."

We took the hint and got out of the way while the crew dropped through the hatch to lash up our planes. They had used a special cradle to load the planes in Poland and they must be having a hell of time doing it in the middle of a battlefield.

No one had time to talk to us but the beds were as good as ever. You know I've been able to sleep anywhere since basic training, but sleeping on a rigidible in flight is pure Heaven. About half an hour later the engines started up and the steady hum of the engines and the floating motion of the ship makes it better than sleeping in the womb. I didn't even worry about where we were going.

'Course the problem was that it was still the damned navy, so they got us up before dawn. A sailor handed us loaves of cheese filled bread and canteens of hot tea and then took us to the forward observation bubble. The captain looked over briefly and then pointed down at a row of lights moving like a giant caterpillar, stretching out to the horizon. "Those are Mongol trains. The lights are the engines. Think of them more like high pressure steam kettles that will react poorly to bullet holes. If we can cripple the lead engines, that turns into fifty miles of parked rail cars and gives the boys up north a little more time.

Mongols have never seen a fighting plane, so if you work fast, you should be able to cripple a dozen or so engines before anyone gets around to shooting back.

If it gets hot, get out. We might be able to live without your skins, but we're going to need those planes later."

The navigator unrolled a map and pointed to a spot. "You're about 275 miles south of Karakorum. Home base is not straight north, but if you follow the tracks north they'll lead you home. Stay above the tracks! We'll be behind you so if you run out of fuel we'll find you and drop a barrel of gas. However, that's not friendly territory down there so we'd prefer you made it all the way home on your own.

You're at the extreme limit of your range, so, if you're going to make it home, you've only got about fifteen minutes before you have to start heading north. Make the most of them.

We'll drop you as soon as it is light enough to make out a target. Oh, I'd also advise you to make your attack runs from the west, to keep from being silhouetted in the sun. With luck, you might be invisible for a little longer."

So, with the happy thoughts that the planes were more valuable than the two of us, and we'd probably run out of gas on the way home, and that we were going to attack a few hundred thousand Mongols with four machine guns, two planes, and pluck, we headed back to our planes.

It was pitch black when they handed me my rations bag and lowered me down into my plane, but by the time stored my supplies and put your picture on the dash, a slight glow formed in the east. They dropped us due west of the lead engine as soon as it was light enough to make out forms in the gloom.

You know I love that sudden drop when the hooks let go and the plane heals over into a slow dive. We let our engines idle and dropped almost silently down to the shadowy treetops. Then we made our first pass slowly to give us more time to punch holes before we climbed out. I took the lead engine and Leon was a quarter mile on my right headed for the second in line. It was still too dark to see color, but the shiny golden chimneys on the engines and the fire leaking from the stacks made easy targets. I held the trigger down until I could see steam escaping, so much steam that I felt the wet heat as I flew over.

Then out, bank right, and head for the third and fourth engines. By this time doors were opening and men were pouring out of the cars, but none of them even knew what direction to look. By the time we made our third pass, the light was good enough to show the bright red paint and gold trim on the engines. Made them easy to find.

I skipped the next engine because there wasn't much point in putting bullets into a train that was already firmly stuffed up the butt of the train in front of it. I hope he wasn't only one who had a hard time stopping. At the end of the next pass, we were low on ammo and really low on time, and I think that some of them were actually starting to shoot in our direction. I motioned to Leon to follow me into a steep climb.

I decided that there was enough confusion down below to make a final pass safe. They were probably still paying more attention to getting the trains stopped than looking for us, so we each made a long pass from the back to the front of a train, putting a few rounds into any car that looked different, trying to spread around the wealth.

I was lucky enough to hit a powder car, and unlucky enough to be just about over it when it blew. The concussion would have thrown me through the upper wing if it weren't for my seatbelt. The explosion put a rip in the fabric near my right foot and a couple of rips in the lower right wing, but I was still airworthy. Poles make tough machines.

We passed the front of the train, climbed to comfortable altitude, and relaxed. There was nothing around for miles except rolling hills and the railroad track winding below. All that was left was to adjust my speed for maximum range, settle back in my seat, and start a letter to you. Remind me to suggest a reclining seat as the next improvement for planes. My back is starting to ache.

As I write this letter, my mind is on our future. It should be a good one. Of course, I'll get my combat pay and a promotion for volunteering, but the word is that all of the flyers will get a small share of the booty the army has already picked up. The grunts tell me they picked up literally tons of gold from Sarai. They're looting Karakorum today and we should soon have a share of tons of brass and steel when we dispatch the wearers to Chinese heaven. Now that Henryk won't be getting the Royal Third, our shares could be even higher. The Hetman has always been generous with his men.

I know you like life on base, but we won't be in the Christian Army forever and this one trip should pay for a county estate.

I arrived at the new camp as part of a miles long stream of men. My personal lance was preceded and trailed by men in clanking armor, as we rode past cart after creaking cart. Entering the camp was like entering a medieval city. The air was already filled with the odors of cooking food, sweaty men, hot leather, and horses.

Our new home was well chosen. The west end, closest to where the Chinese should appear closed down to less than a half mile wide and the east side opening was even smaller. The side walls could be climbed from either side, but it would be a slow and difficult ascent. There was river down the middle of the canyon and a lake for when the Mongols damned the river. When I arrived, the work was already well under way. In a half a day, the grunts had dug a ditch and raised a defensive embankment across ninety percent of the opening. By the end of the day, a second ditch would be in place and fighting towers would be appearing. The ditches had to be deep to prevent the Mongols from filling them with dead Chinese troops and waking across the dead bodies.

The camp was set up more compact that usual but, even after we crossed the boundaries, my tent was two or three miles down the river. It was set up right next to a large but deserted county house. The Polish flag flew from the top of the building and the word "Headquarters" was painted over the door. Megan was waiting for us, "Welcome, My Master. The building is good enough for meetings, but not very comfortable, so we set your tent up here and heated your bath." I was grateful for the bath, but it was a little uncomfortable. Although she smiled and bowed as friendly as ever, Shauna damn near took my skin off when she scrubbed my back, smile or no smile. I decided she would have to have a little extra attention that night.

It would have to be later, however, as the evening was filled with plans, drawings, and meetings. Since I couldn't be certain when the Mongols would be here with their Chinese army, I had to plan in order of importance. We'd start at the top of the list and keep working until people were shooting at us. First thing was to ditch the entrance to the canyon. I was certain that the first two ditches were done on the western end, but I had not asked about the eastern end of the canyon. When the first two ditches and embankments were done, we'd have to a line of elevated firing platforms behind them and a line of machine gun foxholes actually at the top of the innermost embankment. Caesar's troops did something similar every night, but the lucky bastards were fighting in a forest. We were going to have to use dirt and rocks for most of our defenses.

As soon as the ends were sealed, we had to secure the walls. The first people on top of the hill owned it, so we would start sending lances with machine guns up the steep canyon walls in the morning. They would have a Hell of an advantage over anyone trying to climb up from the outside, but only if they were already dug in. They would also need some good sharpshooters with them.

I was certain that the Mongols could eventually get past the first barricades. We had lots of ammo, but they had a lot of cheap soldiers they didn't mind getting dead, so, if we got another day, we'd build another set of ditches and walls about a quarter mile inside the first one. The second set would be a saw tooth pattern like a snowflake fort. Each wall would be able to give supporting fire to its neighbors. We'd clear out that quarter mile stretch between walls to make certain that there wasn't a tree or a rock for the Chinese to hide behind while they crossed it.

That would give us an outer defensive line, an inner defensive line and a killing field in between.

Kowalski would place some of his more mobile pieces right behind the first wall so he could reach out further and harass the enemy rear, but he wanted to place most of his artillery behind second wall, where he would be able reach out to the enemy and still stay out of reach if the wall was breached.

We also needed crews up in the hill as artillery spotters. I figured that we could dismount two radios from their carts and manhandle one up each hill for the hill watchers, but we weren't going to be able to get a radio up to every watch stand. The first idea was to use naval flag codes but we immediately realized that anyone waving colored flags would be nice target for snipers and artillery. A few more ideas came and went before one of my radio techs said that they probably had enough wire, batteries, and spare parts to put together a half dozen field phones. It worked in WWI, but they didn't know that.

There were a hundred other details, but our Achilles heel was the other end of the canyon. We had a little more time there because it would take the Mongols at least another day to reach it. Of course, we'd protect it, but we couldn't afford a full defense on both ends. Kowalski had the best idea. His suggestion was that we put enough force at the eastern end to delay any invader for an hour of so and concentrate on marking out and smoothing roads from one end of the canyon to another. Big People could get a force there in less than an hour. They were fast. If there was a smoothed out path, the artillery could be there less than an hour later.

Despite the late hour and my overwhelming fatigue, I did do my best to comfort Shauna when I finally got to bed. It took longer than I could afford.

My night had been filled with dreams of battle and nightmares about what could go wrong. I rushed through my morning rituals and met with Count Wladyclaw and Kolomel Eikmann over breakfast. They must have been less nervous than me, because they were eating while I drew a diagram of our valley on the table and started talking. "We're going to have a fighting front of thousand yards on this end of the valley, and not more than about eight hundred on the other end. We've been talking about how this is good because the Mongols won't be able to use their numbers to overwhelm us, but that also gives us the advantage and the problem that we can't get much more than fifteen or twenty percent of our people on the line at one time.

We have two problems to address today. Sir Eikmann, you've done a good job getting our first two barriers in place. However, we need to give special attention to stepped firing positions. We need to get as many guns on target as we can without shooting our own men, and that means setting up one or two gun platforms higher than the front line and shooting over their heads. We also need to start practicing a Roman rotation move. The Roman Army used to set up a tight front ten men deep and then rotate soldiers from the front to the back position every few minutes. That way, they always had fresh hacking arms facing increasingly tired opponents. We don't have the problem of sore sword arms anymore, but battle fatigue is still real. If we can keep the time on the front line down to thirty or forty minutes, we'll always have fresh troops doing the fighting.

However, rotating seven thousand men on two or three firing lines without stumbling, loosing focus or shooting ourselves in the foot takes practice. We need to get that practice in sometime before the Mongols get here.

I know you've already set up drills for moving men from one end of the valley to the other and now you're going to have to squeeze these in too.

I expect to hear from Commodore Stanislaw within the hour. That'll tell us how long we have. I'll send messengers to you when we know.

Early the next morning, Stanislaw sent in his first report on operation "slow the Mongol". Vagabond had loitered over the Mongol train long enough to see them get hundreds of soldiers together to push and pull the most damaged engines off the tracks and onto their sides. Mechanics were already swarming over the other engines when she left to follow her fighters home. The Mongols were stopped for the day, but would be back on the road by tomorrow morning.

On the way home, the rigidible was able to verify that the wolves had made at least twenty gaps in the rails and destroyed two small bridges.

There was other, less promising news. The local Mongol armies were on the move. They had broken camp within hours of our assault on Karakorum and started moving in our direction. Stanislaw reported that they were moving in three columns. Two cavalry columns were moving at high speed and they were followed by a slower group escorting cannon and what appeared to be siege equipment.

In fact, Zephyr warned that we would probably have visitors by the end of the day.

Apparently, they had decided that there was no point in letting us build defenses in peace.

I spent the day riding around the camp watching, encouraging, ordering, and definitely not looking worried. Eikmann's men and every grunt in camp were working on a series of defensive walls and ditches that he laid out. We had no ready source of lumber, so the defenses were built with shovel and pick and boulders rolled down from the hills. Ivanov's kitchens were working constantly baking bread, filling it with vegetables and beef or cheese and running the cooked food and baskets of fruit out to work parties. Men ate and drank where they worked.

When I found Eikmann, he was riding the riverbank searching for a place to put a landing strip for the planes.

The men on the first line of defense at each end of the valley continued to improve their foxholes with guns at hand. Half worked while half watched the horizon. A quarter of the artillerymen were stationed at their cannon while the rest worked on improving the paths that would be used to move the artillery if needed.

It was two of our long army hours after noon when the Mongols made camp about five miles upriver from where we were. I decided to keep the fact that we had a gun that could reach them from here a secret for now. Maybe the khan would be nice enough to put his headquarters in the middle of such a nice place.

An hour before dusk, they made a probing attack on our front door. It was just their polite way of saying "Hi. We're here. Don't sleep too well tonight, and, by the way, be a little nervous while you're working." Our troops held their fire to hide the real range of our guns, and only dropped a few Mongols for target practice.

The work went on, but the next morning we had a Mongol infestation worse than mosquitoes on a summer lake. I had decided not to put out a picket of Big People in front of out lines that night, so we missed the small groups of Mongols who sneaked over the tundra and climbed up the outer walls.

By midmorning, arrows were dropping into the camp. From their spots on the canyon wall, the archers could reach clear across the camp with armor piercing arrows. Of course they used arrows because they didn't have a muzzle flash and they were damned hard to spot. Thirty or forty archers couldn't do serious damage if I lined the men for them to shoot at, but they were disrupting work. More men were wearing armor even when they were moving dirt and boulders and they spent time looking over their shoulders I set up a couple of squads to scan the walls with field glasses and sent a note to Kowalski telling him that if the machine guns didn't get a sniper, that it was worth using an artillery shell or two to get them. The squad played hide and seek with the snipers all day without any visible results.

Eventually my bodyguards took care of them. When night fell, the girls climbed the hills, found the Mongols by smell or sound and quietly cut their throats.

The real action was happening over a hundred miles away where the Wolves were still delaying the Mongol army. Reports from the Vagabond showed that the Wolves and the Air Force were doing a good job. The air attack had halted the trains for over twenty four hours and they were now moving at reduced speed. The Chinese engineers had used their enormous manpower to muscle the unrepairable engines and some cars off the tracks. While they did that other soldiers carried new rails forward from somewhere in the train and stacked them on cars near the front of the train. The trains were creeping forward with rail repair crews and rails in the first section.

Mongol cavalry was now sweeping out ahead of the trains looking for the Wolves and protecting repair crews who were dragging rails on carts and fixing tracks. The Wolves were moving too fast to carry radio carts, but by the third day there was evidence from the air that they were doing their jobs. Dead rail crews were lying next to their burned carts and Mongol horses roamed the rails without their riders.

Despite all of the Wolves work, the Mongol army was moving forward as inexorably as army ants.

For me the bad news was that it was going to take a week for the Mongol army to get to us. If I had known that we could delay them that long, I could have led this army past the Mongol blockades and been well on the way home by now. Eventually I decided this fight had to be done someday and it was best done when we were flush from success and well stocked with ammo.

From the Secret Journal of Su Song, Part 7

I sit here wrapped in the comfort of a warm cloak and sipping my favorite wine thanks to my eldest wife. When I decided that I would accompany my trains north, I intended to travel with a single trunk holding a few changes of clothes, a few books, and my writing materials. When I arrived at the station I learned that my eldest wife had ordered a private rail car filled with clothes, my favorite food and wine, writing desks, plush rugs, a soft bed, and my two newest concubines to share it. "My husband, you cannot concentrate on your job if you are tense or lonely. The girls will massage your painful muscles, make certain you are well fed, and relax you at night." My wife is a very intelligent woman, but she cannot understand that I would prefer that it were her grey hairs lying on my shoulder.

I am now convinced more than ever that the "Conrad Guardian of the Heavens" character is a fictitious front for a huge school of engineering. This morning, my train was attacked by aircraft mounting guns capable of firing multiple rounds at very high speed. I estimate their rate of fire to be at least 150 rounds per minute. Twenty years ago, the best weapons they had were breach loading single shot rifles.

There is no conceivable way that much progress could be made in only twenty years by one team led by one man. My laboratory has the best minds to be found among forty million people and we could not reproduce those guns in my lifetime.

The khan's fears may be well founded. Given a few more years the Polish army will be invincible, and while I disapprove of my masters occasional cruelties, we all know that the Poles take no prisoners – ever.

General Obedai is in charge of the army, but the train is my responsibility, and the aircraft did considerable damage in only a few minutes. I sit here wrapped in a heavy cloak because they even put several holes in the roof of my private car, letting in the draft and scaring my concubines nearly to death. Thirteen engines were disabled due to the guns or subsequent collisions and random cars were attacked. My engineers have repaired six of the engines and removed another seven from the tracks, and we are moving again, but the loss of engines has us moving at a crawl.

It probably doesn't matter. The Polish have railroads of their own and certainly know the importance of removing rails, bridges, and culverts. At my suggestion, Obedai has sent mixed teams of soldiers and laborers ahead with rails and repair tools. We have heard gunfire in the distance, and I do not expect all of the teams to return.

I feel a constant pressure to impress on the General the need for speed. He is a competent and fierce leader, but the fact he has an overwhelming force is taking the edge off of his leadership.

His force is overwhelming, but the cost is high. We have brought almost ninety percent of all the Mongol warriors in China with us, a total of over one hundred thousand warriors, including all of the Turkish soldiers. The khan also demanded twenty thousand warriors from Korea and has gotten most of what he demanded.

When we arrive in Mongolia, the General will also assume command of all the Mongolian armies, perhaps sixty thousand mounted men. Even without the Chinese crossbowmen, engineers and foot soldiers, this is by far the largest army ever assembled, and we have more Chinese cannon fodder than we have Mongol warriors.

Speed is of the essence.

No khan has ever assembled a force a third of the size of this one, and I can't feed them. During the last year, I stockpiled supplies for a large but normal army, perhaps one hundred thousand men for a siege of three or four months. This horde will be hungry in about six weeks.

The other reason for hurry is that the khan has stripped the county of troops. He has the largest army the world has ever seen and he is sitting in a county left defenseless. If the population realizes how few troops are left in the county, we may return to a burned and dead city.

General Obedai would have abandoned that train this morning and continued on horseback, but we only brought a few hundred horses with us. When the Great Khan replenished the Mongolians stock of horses after the great die off, they sent enough to give every warrior the traditional three or four horses. As this would not be a long campaign, the Mongolians had enough spare horses to provide for all of our cavalrymen.

This morning, I had a rocket plane assembled and sent to the Khan of Mongolia, with a letter from General Obedai ordering him to drive the herd south to meet us nearer our current location. It will still be at least three days before they arrive.

I will still need to get the tracks repaired and then move the train through to Karakorum. Most of our supplies are in the two storage yards ahead and we still have thousands of infantry troops to move.

My Guests Arrive

It took them five more days to get to Karakorum. Eventually they abandoned the train and came on horseback and foot. They camped where they believed they were safe from our artillery and their campfires, as expected, really did reach from horizon to horizon.

The first serious attacks came on the seventh day. They began by moving artillery into range of our embankments and preparing to knock on our door. They actually got off one ranging volley before our artillery opened up on their positions. It was an uneven contest. It was cavalry observer against aerial observer and smooth bore against rifled barrel. They didn't even get off a second volley.

We listened to the customary hour of hooting, hollering, drum banging and bell ringing before the first ground attack began. It gave me plenty of time to join the men on top of the first embankment. They didn't need me for anything, but moral insisted the boss had to make a show in his fancy armor, and I was too curious to miss it anyway.

Eventually the hollerin' and hooting died down and was replaced by a slow rhythmic drum beat. In time to the unseen drums, small groups of Chinese crossbowmen formed up behind the type of mobile barrier we had seen on the tundra. It was as well rehearsed as the changing of the guard in London. Boom. Seven men stepped forward. Boom. Three of them lifted a wooden slab about as tall as they were up from the ground. Boom. Four of them unfolded the skids that held it upright. Boom. Three men stepped forward to grasp handles on the back of the slab. Boom. Four crossbowmen stepped up behind them and waited.

This was definitely not a Mongol way to fight. Screaming, yelling, and charging were Mongol tactics. They must have picked this one up from the Chinese.

When they were about twenty rows deep, the horns and bells and yelling started up again and they began a slow march toward us, pushing the wooden barriers ahead of them. In the rear, we could see Mongol horsemen making certain that no one went the wrong way.

We still didn't want them to know how good our guns were, so we waited until the first row launched crossbow bolts on a high trajectory, then the machine guns opened up. The Chinese started to double time, pushing the barriers ahead and shooting from behind them. I was surprised that the barriers stopped some of the fifty caliber rounds. Somebody had improved them. The Chinese got off two more volleys before our artillery opened up with grapeshot. Even the Mongols couldn't stop the retreat, but the soldiers left their barriers standing in the field, ready for the next fight.

Several of our troops, who had failed to raise their shields, learned the hard way that the crossbow bolts were poisoned.

Things were quiet the rest of the day. I noticed that the Mongols made no attempt to help the wounded Chinese stranded on the field. After dark, a company of Wolves snuck out onto the battlefield and burned most of the barriers.

The next day started the same, but this time, the Chinese rolled up four story siege towers to a line about a quarter of a mile from us. They were carried into sight lying down and were pulled upright. It must have taken a Hell of a pull. The towers were sheathed in bronze and had real cannon sticking out of the ports.

They filled in the gaps between the towers with more poor suckers pushing barriers in front of them. This time most of the poor suckers had guns instead of crossbows.

This time the Mongol artillery opened up when the towers started creaking forward. That meant that our artillery had to handle both the towers and the Mongol artillery at the same time. We soon learned that the siege towers also held men with competent copies of our swivel guns.

I had a swivel gun set up in front of me and, with Terry feeding me clips, gleefully shot at red uniforms until I heard the command "rotate!" coming from behind me. That was the command to change front line troops, so I must have been there almost an army hour. Time flies when you're having a good time.

When I stood up to move back, a horse kicked me in the chest and I got to see a nice light show before the world went black.

I woke up in an aid station surrounded by corpsmen and four of my bodyguards. I could see my breastplate standing on a table nearby. It had a nice big dent about six inches below the collar line, about where the pain in my chest was centered. The corpsman placed a hand on my shoulder, "Sire, you've got a couple of broken ribs. If you move abound before we get you taped up, you could puncture a lung and bleed to death. I'm going to have the aides slowly lift you to a sitting position so we can get tape around you. It's going to hurt like Hell, but if you move on your own, the results could be very bad."

He kept talking to distract while the pain lanced through me, "It looks like you were hit with a fifty caliber ball from a muzzle loader. It must have been spent because you're still breathing."

When they had me taped up, they transferred me to a litter that held me in a sitting position. "The baron said to carry you sitting up so that the men can see you're alive, but don't wave at anyone for the next couple of days. I suggest that it is safest to stay sitting up until the bones start to heal."

There was a great cheer as I was carried out of the tent. Men yelled, waved, and stomped in celebration of my continued breathing. I guess that nothing makes a grunt as happy as seeing the boss take a bullet. As gently as they carried me, every step was source of pain.

Sir Grzegorz was at my tent before I was. He was so angry that I was afraid one of my bodyguards would cut his throat. The pain killers were making my eyes a little glassy, but I could see every vein in his forehead and count his pulse without leaving my bed.

He sent everybody out of the tent before my befuddled mind could even recognize them, though I thought I saw a scowling Baron Krol exiting the door.

"Your grace, it is now my most unpleasant duty to remind you of your oath. Each man here has sworn to you as liege, but you should remember that the oath binds you as well as the men. You swore oath to lead them well and care for them. You can do neither if you are dead."

He picked up my breastplate and shook it in the air. "If this bullet had been six inches higher, you would have been decapitated and would have needlessly abandoned your army three thousand miles from home.

This army, and myself, have followed you faithfully for years. We have followed your orders without question and have marched thousands of miles into unknown lands for you. We have left our families and friends. We followed you when you were relieved of command, excommunicated, recalled, and fired. I personally have fought at your side in a dozen battles. I know that you consider yourself a warrior king like Alexander, leading your men by shear force of arms from a position in the very front of the army, but remember what happened to Alexander. He died young and his empire died the next day.

I doubt that the Christian Army will dissolve upon your death, but the heart will go out of this army if you die before this battle is over."

My anger was almost strong enough to reach through my pain and the drugs. If were not for the possibility that I would puncture a lung, I would have stood in spite of my pain and run the bastard through but I settled for clenching my teeth.

"Get the Hell out of here!"

"In a moment. I have met with other senior officers and we have agreed that your oath requires you to act a bit more responsibly. Fortunately, your current injuries will force you to avoid combat for at least three weeks, so our decision may never have any effect, but it stands for the length of the battle."

"I will see you hung for mutiny!"

"Mutiny? There is no mutiny. There is only a formal demand by a liegeman for the rights you guaranteed him under the oath of fealty. Despite this disagreement, I am a loyal servant who would give his life for yours, and I want no man to think differently.

By the way, the Mongol building next door has a rather high tower with a balcony on the top. The engineers have been enlarging and roofing the balcony for use as an observation post. As you are currently limited in your mobility, you may want to oversee the battle from there. In addition to the excellent visibility for yourself, the men can see you up there and take heart from your continued health and attention to their welfare."

And then the bastard was gone and despite my anger and pain, the laudanum kicked in and I was soon sleeping.

The next three days were almost a blur. I tried to resist the pain killers, but I spent most of the time in a daze. The Mongols launched two more attacks, improving their tactics each time. During one of my waking periods, I ordered that sharpshooters be stationed on the hillsides, to target only the Mongol horsemen driving the Chinese troops forward. Perhaps without the incentive of armed Mongols, the Chinese troops would not try so hard to move forward.

By the morning of the third day, I was able to stand with little pain and even to walk carefully. I held my normal morning staff meeting. Sir Grzegorz was pointedly not invited and he pointedly showed up anyway, knowing that there was no way I wanted our disagreement to be made public. The traitorous bastard was even cheerful.

I learned that the Mongols had made progress. When the wolves snuck out at night to burn the toppled siege towers, they found that the towers were booby trapped with black powder bombs. They learned the hard way and it was the last thing some of them learned. It cost us a squad.

The Mongols were using cheap Chinese lives to litter the battlefield with cover. Behind some of the barriers the Chinese dug foxholes. On some attacks they rolled boulders ahead of themselves and left the boulders when we chased them back. Slowly, they were moving shrinking the unprotected area.

I still held back on our air power and our biggest artillery. The troops being sent forward now were just cannon fodder. I wanted to use our big guns on the Mongols.

As angry as I was at my own army trying to keep me away from combat, I was in no shape to ride Silver anywhere and unable to walk more than a few feet, so I finally relented and went to the new observation post. I tried to put on my repaired breastplate, but the pain was teeth gritting, so I settled for my golden helmet, greaves, and a bright gold cape. I walked proudly from my tent to the Mongol mansion behind it and then collapsed into the arms of four strong corpsmen who carried me up six long flights of stairs.

The balcony had been extended around all four sides of the tower. The engineers had done an excellent job. It was roofed over to avoid glare and there were telescope stands on all four sides. One of my desks was there with a comfortable chair, a box of cigars, and a phone connected to the radiomen on the first floor. There were other chairs and small desks for observers and a machine gun mounted on each side, "just in case." If it had an elevator it would have been heaven.

A cheer went up from the men below when I appeared at the railing, forcing me to spend a painful minute waving my arm and smiling.

Our soldiers below were working like Roman Legionnaires. I read where a Roman soldier might go his entire life without a battle in some periods, but he rarely went more than a few months without building something. Since we couldn't get more that twenty percent of our men on the front lines, at one time, the rest were working off their tension by improving the compound, There was too much going on to take it all in. I saw men digging foxholes and latrines, putting dirt walls around cooking tents, and building dirt embankments around artillery pieces.

Kolomel Eikmann had been as busy and competent as usual. To the east I could see a single runway cut alongside the riverbed. He had tested the riverbed and found it to be mostly gravel for its entire length, making it a good road for Big People and passable for our carts. Along one side he marked out a wagon trail and posted orders to keep it clear.

That gave us a rapid road between the two ends of the valley or a rapid egress if we had to leave in a hurry. It fit the plans I had made while drifting between sleep and wakefulness. I now knew how the battle would end.

It was time to fill in the senior staff. I sent runners out for Count Sir Grzegorz, Count Sir Wladyclaw, Kolomel Eikman , Baron Kowalski, Commodore Stanislaw and Baron Ivanov. As it was still early, I set the meeting for noon. I decided to hold the meeting right where I was, overlooking the valley, and taking some glee in the fact the Grzegorz would have to climb all those damned stairs.

Then I sat at my desk for the next few hours, basking in the early sunlight, and went over my plans.

My aides had set up a simple sideboard by the time the last of them huffed and puffed his way up the stairs. The balcony was only about 8 feet wide, so it was close quarters.

When they had their drinks and were balancing their sandwiches on their knees I opened the meeting. "Gentlemen, I now know how this battle is going to end, but I'm going to need a lot of help to pull it off, so you're all going to be busy for next few days.

Most of you expected that we would sit here behind our defenses while the Mongols threw themselves on our swords until there were only a few Mongols left, and then we would ride out and kill the leftovers. The odds of this diminish every day. The Mongols have been cautious so far and they've only used their Chinese troops to attack us. They're moving slow, looking for a weakness, and trying to compromise our fortifications.

There is a time limit here. If the Mongols don't get through our defenses in a few months, they'll run out of food and cannon fodder, and retreat south. They can afford to wait for another day or another year to fight us.

If they scatter and move out, we will never have a decisive battle. We won't be able to do anything but harass them as they leave, and, frankly, our men would be very unhappy if we decided to take more months of their lives following Mongols around.

So, we'll take a page out of the Mongol battle plan. We'll make them think they are doing well. We'll encourage them to keep letting us kill their men the easy way, by shooting them while they run at us. If they lose heart, we may even need to let them have a little success, like taking the outer defense ditches. The more of their men we can kill from home, the less we will have to handle on the tundra.

To encourage them, we're going to hide our assets and minimize what we can do. I know that our artillery could take out the center of the Mongol camp without moving an inch from where they are and our planes could wipe any attack without breathing hard.

As long as they keep trying, we keep it low key.

Before they get too discouraged and stop sending us targets. We're gonna kill them where they stand.

We'll send out half our force through the back door, ride like Hell and get ready to flank the main Mongol force. The other half of the force will boil out the front door and head for the main camp. We'll have a pincer on the Mongols.

At about the time they're in position, we'll open up with everything we have. We'll throw in enough artillery to clear our front door, and then open up with the big gun on the center of the main camp. The rigidibles will drop the arrows we liberated from Karakorum and whatever bombs we can jerry rig. The airplanes will block the way south by blasting anything that moves that way. We will unleash Hell.

I know that each of you sees problems and complications that you have to handle, and I'll give you time to consider the plan before we discuss it further, but a few things come to mind. Sir Eikmann, you'll have to prepare our egress. We need a way to get past out own defenses with fifteen thousand or so men without slowing down."

"We considered that when we prepared the defenses, Sire. From the top of an embankment, a Big Person can jump the ditches without slowing down. If we add some charges in the right places, we can probably improve that by blowing some of the embankments down into the ditches. I'll get back to you on that,"

"That's a good start, but be certain we can do it. Sir Stanislaw, your job is one of the most important. There will be Mongol force of some sort at both ends of the valley. I'm hoping the back gate will be more lightly defended so we can go out that way. However, the entire plan will fail if the Mongols at the east entrance can tell their friends in the main camp that we're on the way. So, you have to cut then off. Kill the rocket planes, find any messenger stations between the two forces and take them out. We'll also need a good map of the best path for an army from the east end to take around to the main Mongol camp.

It took the Mongols almost a week to move that distance, Big People can do it in less than two days if you can find us a path.

Sir Kowalski, you are going to have to plan and execute a ballet. We need artillery at the east barrier until the force gets through, then most of the pieces need to be re-positioned to support the main break out.

When the main force breaks out, they will need artillery support and you may need to move the smaller pieces closer to the Mongol camp.

Unfortunately, my injuries keep me from being involved in most of the planning. In a few minutes, I will need to go back to my tent and continue to heal. Tomorrow noon we will convene again and go over our preliminary plans.

Please enjoy the wine before you leave."

Then I carefully and slowly walked to the stairwell and, as soon as I was out of sight, collapsed into the arms of the waiting corpsmen,

The Waiting Game.

Doodles done by Su Song – and immediately burned.

The end is near. Now all I have to do is wonder whether my notebooks have reached my friend and whether the true Emperor has taken action. I have informed the general that I must leave tomorrow to coordinate supply shipments from the south. He was unable to hide his glee at losing me.

Thanks to Uncle Tom's modifications, my body heals amazingly fast. I was mobile again in a week. I wasn't completely healed, but the ribs were mending quickly, and I would be completely healed in another week.

The Mongols didn't need encouragement yet to keep attacking us. They literally stacked up the bodies in front of us. They made no attempt to recover their wounded or dying and when the wind was from the west, the smell was nauseating.

They managed to reach the outer ditch just once. The sent in Chinese soldiers rolling boulders, intending to start filling in the ditch with boulders and bodies. We were still holding back on our full firepower in an attempt to get the herding Mongols in range, but the game was getting dicey. Our losses were small compared to the Chinese, but not negligible. The med tents were getting a lot of business and the graveyard was growing.

Baron Ryszard pitched a tent close to the outer embankment and assumed twenty four hour command of the western walls. Baron Krol did the same at the eastern defensive wall.

About two weeks after the first attack, I was taking a careful ride around the camp when several medical wagons charged by. I couldn't keep up yet, but I followed them to the eastern defenses. A mounted Mongol force had reached our eastern side charged right in. No bells, no whistles, no chants, no hesitation, just charge!

A less experienced commander or a cowardly one might have been unnerved by the speed of the attack, but Krol already had cannon loaded with grape shot aiming outward and camouflaged machine gun wagons on elevated platforms. His men held fire until they could almost smell the leading Mongols and then unloaded with everything.

Half of the Mongols died in the first few minutes, but the other half kept coming. They were still coming when I reached the embankment, but it didn't last long and nobody saved one for me.

Krol and one of his aides were looking over the battlefield from the top of a embankment as I drew up. I just opened my mouth to warn Krol about "dead" Mongols when a shot rang out and his aid dropped where he stood. Machine guns raked the area the shot had come from.

Krol grabbed his aid under the arms and pulled him down to where the corpsmen could get him on a stretcher. There was a lot of blood and I doubted that he would reach the med tent alive.

He stood there for a moment with his aides blood spattered on his left arm and chest. He was breathing heavily and his mustache dripped sweat. When he saw me he grunted in my direction, gave a minimal salute and said, "My mistake, Sire, but I'm afraid that Albin has paid the price."

"It was a mistake, Baron, but Squire Albin could have warned you about dead Mongols, or discouraged you from standing where you were. The error was also his. You had better send out a mercy crew to make certain that none of the other 'dead' Mongols are still suffering.

Is there anything you need? Do you need more men or anything that I can send you from stores?"

His voice was higher than usual and he seemed distracted, "No, they're going to rotate in about half an hour. I'll have plenty of men and we barely touched our ammo supply. We're good."

"Sire Krol, you have done a good job here. I will not worry about this barricade while you command it. Perhaps you should have a little rest now and let one of your captains organize the mercy squads."

I stopped by the med tent on the way back and learned than Albin had, indeed, paid the ultimate price for his mistake. As Christians, we were required to inter our dead. Since there was little space in our crowded camp, the Chaplains had dug a cave into the valley wall. Albin would be placed there and his name added to a plaque. The last act of the Chaplain when we left this valley would be to collapse the cave and place the plaque over the entrance. May God have mercy on their souls.

I figured that the Mongols would stay for three more months. The medieval world was governed by seasons. There was a hunting season, a fishing season, a harvest season, and a war season between the planting and harvest seasons. In my old time-line, the Mongols had shocked their opponents by fighting in the winter season by using the frozen rivers as roads into Russia and the Middle East, but generally, there was a war season.

I'm certain that my own men thought that the plan was to sit out the war season in the valley and then head for home when the game was called on account of weather. I guess I should have told the Mongols what they were supposed to do.

About four weeks into the siege things had been quiet for several days, when we got a message from Zerphr. Apparently the Mongols were moving more troops east for another attempt at that entrance. They had moved about half way and were camped at a site where the trail came close to the mountains that ringed our valley. The next day, the observation post at the ridge reported that the Mongols had brought up artillery and fired several volleys at them. However, all the shells fell short, very short, so the post wasn't particularly worried.

When the ridge post failed to check in the next morning, we sent squad scrambling up the hillside to check on them. They didn't get very far.

In was barely dawn when I was awakened by battle sounds. I felt no need to move fast or soon. This attack wouldn't be any more exiting than the last.

Terry was spooned next to my stomach and Shauna cuddled up behind me. It was a warm, soft, drifting sleep that stole away quietly – until the explosion happened in front of my tent.

The three of us were out of bed, covered enough for decency and astride Silver in less than a minute. We sped toward the front and arrived in the middle of the biggest battle yet. I stopped at the headquarters bunker for the inner barricade to get my bearings.

Beyond the outer barrier, the Chinese and Mongols were moving forward, but this was no probing attack, no march of the cannon fodder. The siege towers were back, shortened, better armored, and mounting swivel guns. The foot soldiers pushed barriers ahead of them again, but moved from cover to cover, using the flotsam from prior battles for shielding.

The Mongols were all on foot, no longer willing to give us easy targets by standing tall in the saddle.

As I watched, machine gun fire raked our own men – from behind. It wasn't very accurate, but it didn't need to be. Half a dozen men took fifty caliber shells in the first thirty seconds. I looked up to see firing from the ridge top and thirty or forty Chinese troops manning a captured machine gun, swivel guns, and a couple of small mortars. One of those mortars had been my wake up call.

The bastards had flanked us.

We were in serious danger of being overrun, but the army was already fighting back. From somewhere, ten men dislodged a wooden footbridge and carried it up onto the embankment to cover the defender's backs. Big People were pulling wagons up the hill and leaving them behind soldiers for cover. Reserve warriors were grabbing shields and throwing themselves on the ground next to the defenders, holding the shields up to defend from the guns on the ridge.

243

The machine guns on the front line were busy stopping the attack, but on the inner defensive line and in the camp, several level headed officers had turned their guns around and started firing at the ridge line. It was a long shot, over 1200 yards straight up, but doable.

It wasn't enough. We were being pushed back. Despite the spirit shown by the men, confusion was crippling our front line. It's hard to concentrate on killing the man in front of you when the unseen man behind you is shooting at you.

Fortunately, my runners and my aids had dressed almost as fast as I did, and there was a radio cart in the bunker. I grabbed one of the radio men and told him to get a message out to the Eagles. "Time to fly. Kill the bastards on the ridge. Now!"

Kowalski had already swiveled some of his artillery in that direction, but dropping a shell on a crest that far up was damned near impossible. Still, it might keep their heads down. Didn't seem to help much. The Mongol mortar men kept dropping shells onto random areas of the camp as often as they could reload.

In front of me, the Chinese had reached the forward ditch and they were throwing ladders over it. Most of them were dying, but a few had picked spots where the machine guns had cleared away the defenders and they were getting though. The machine gun platforms could hold them, but Baron Ryszard apparently thought it was time to call it.

He signaled for a retreat to the inner defenses. Big People raced by me on both sides to recover the wounded and dead, while others hurried to man the carts parked under each elevated gun. As the machine guns in the inner line took over defense, the teams on the forward line began dropping their guns into the carts and racing back in my direction.

Ryszard had trained them well. The movement was smooth. Five thousand men in a half mile long line raced on foot across the empty stretch between the walls and took positions among the men already on the inner line with virtually no confusion and very few losses. The machine guns were reset before the Chinese got half way across.

Ryszard ended up on the ground between me and his radioman. "I needed to get the men out of the way before our next move. I hope you approve, Sire." He pointed at a line of white stones across the killing field. "Kowalski has pieces ranged in on that line. He'll let loose when they reach it."

Above us, I heard airplane engines, but I was too busy to look up. Eventually I heard several long bursts from the thirty cals on the planes and I stopped worrying so much about my back.

The machine guns slowed the enemy advance, but didn't stop it. We didn't want it stopped. When the first Chinese reached a white stone I heard whistling overhead. Baron Ryszard tugged on my arm, "Time to duck, Sire, and plug your ears."

Then the ground started shaking and the earthquake went on forever. For the next twenty minutes, all I heard was whistle, boom, rocks and debris falling, whistle, boom, ...

When we looked up, the killing field was a montage of body parts. There were a few bodies lying around, but it was mostly dirt covered hands, heads, torsos and feet, most with shreds of red uniforms hanging on them. There were so many that your mind blocked it out and you didn't even feel nausea. It was just pieces, not pieces of people.

A few shots rang out up and down the line where troopers were making certain that none of the survivors, if any, suffered.

Up on the ridgeline, the fighting had stopped. The planes were still making passes, but not finding anything to shoot at. From both sides, squads from the other ridge emplacements were converging on the Chinese squad, prominently displaying Christian Army flags so the pilots would know which side they were on.

It took a day to find out what had happened, and it was a story that would have made a ninja proud. The ridge troopers had become careless about watching the outer wall because it consisted of steep walls that would be almost impossible to for the Chinese to climb, particularly impossible in the dark.

The Chinese had waited for a full moon and then used cannon fire to create a ladder for their troops. The cannon fire the previous day had not fallen short of its mark. Instead, it was always planned to form cracks and footholds in the cliff face. Probably starting a few hours before dark, a small group of mountain climbers had scaled the cliff in the moonlight and lowered ropes down to their companions. By morning a sizeable squad had climbed the cliff.

Just before dawn, they attacked the observation point and took control of two machine guns and a handy place to shoot them from. I doubt that many of my men could have climbed that cliff even in the daylight and I vowed to never underestimate our enemy again.

The Chinese attacks stopped. I didn't know if they were waiting for a better plan, executing a better plan, or just taking a break, but it gave us a chance to finish our preparations. After we reclaimed the outer defense line, the engineers planted charges in several locations on our side of the embankments. The charges would drop the embankments into the ditch and create a quick exit ramp.

The machine gun carts were inspected, greased and prepared for rapid deployment. Kowalski selected his most mobile cannon and set the men to greasing the wheels, loading the carts with grape shot and tightening every bolt and band. Half the pieces would be left in camp, firing high explosive shells from a distance, but the other half would go with us when we charged. Stanislaw's men scavenged explosives and shells and improvised bombs for the rigidibles. Flying Cloud was carrying thousands of liberated Mongol arrows that would be simply shoveled out the hatch over enemy troops. Zephyr finished its survey of the terrain around the valley and sent down maps of the possible routes. It turned out that the best route from our eastern barriers around to the western side ran north of us through difficult but passable terrain. The Big People had excellent night vision and great stamina, so they could make the normally seven day journey in less than two non-stop days, but Sir Grzegorz argued that the men should stop for three hours of sleep during the night. "The men can sleep in the saddle and we can make a grand dash into battle. Hell, we've all done it before, but they can't be at full capacity that way. Better the trip should take a few more hours and they should hit the battlefield refreshed. We know that we want the battle to start at dawn, so we'll try to arrive near the battlefield early and let the men sleep the rest of the night, and stop for a few hours of sleep during the first night." The nine thousand wolves that would be the flanking movement were issued enough of our remaining stock of canned food to make the trip, and loaded up with ammunition.

They couldn't take a radio with them because it would be pounded to death at their speed, so we'd have to coordinate through the rigidibles overhead. As the rigidibles would have to stay at a safe height, a code system was devised using colored flares and large mirrors. For detailed messages, the rigidibles would drop a canister trailing a long ribbon.

The details went on and on, but eventually we were down to picking the actual day for the attack. Good thing, since the day was chosen for us.

We were in our morning staff meeting and Baron Ryszard was making the case for telling the Chinese troops they could surrender. "Every time we have faced Mongols, we have been unable to take prisoners. That is not unusual, but our reputation is hurting us in this battle. The Chinese are half hearted at best in their support of the Mongol emperor, but everyone 'knows' that the Christian Army takes no prisoners, so they might fight on just from fear of being killed if they quit.

If we could convince them that they could throw down their weapons and leave the field of battle without us killing them, we would have a lot less people shooting at us."

His idea was not a bad one. Frankly, I was getting tired of people screaming in fear when they see us, but we didn't have a chance to talk about it because Stanislaw's aid entered the tent making the worst attempt in history to be unobtrusive and furtively handed his boss a sheaf of papers. Stanislaw scanned the first page and then cleared his throat "Gentlemen, I am sorry to interrupt the chain of thought here, but we have important news from Vagabond." When he had everyone's attention he continued, "Captain Orbitz is reporting troop movements up from the south. This morning, I sent him to check the rail line for signs of supply trains coming this way.

He reports that he sighted trains stretching over several miles of track and all headed this way. He thought that they were a large supply operation until the trains made water stops. When the trains stopped thousands of troops jumped out for 'sanitary needs'.

Once he realized he was looking at a troop train, he scanned the area twenty miles on both sides of the track. He encountered additional thousands of mounted troops traveling parallel to the tracks and large herds of horses. It looks as if we scared our enemies into sending for help."

Things weren't adding up for me. I asked "Does the report describe the troops, Chinese, Mongol, uniformed, armored? What do they look like?"

He scanned the second page of the report. "He says that they are similar in appearance to the Imperial troops already here except that they are wearing green and black uniforms rather than the red uniforms we have seen. They appear to be mostly cavalry, lightly armed. He doesn't mention armor or specific weapons and there is no mention of Mongols or Turks on the train."

I decided we had to speak to Orbitz, so I sent an aid outside to the radio cart. "Get Captain Orbitz of Vagabond on the horn and then run a speaker and mike in here."

It didn't take long. "Captain Orbitz, do you recognize my voice?"

"Yes my liege. I can verify your identity."

"Then know that you can speak freely. We need additional information about the troops you have spotted. Do you see any Mongol or Turkish troops with them?"

"I cannot say for certain. We dropped down several times for a close look, but looking down from two thousand feet through a glass is not the best way to judge troops. However, I can verify that everyone we have seen is in uniform. There are several types, but all in uniform of one kind or another. As the Mongols and Turks purchase their own clothing and armor, they stand out from the Imperial troops, and I have seen no one like that below.'"

"Thank you, please describe the any arms and armor that are wearing or carrying."

"The men in the trains are not dressed for combat, but the mounted troops driving the herds mostly have leather armor and metal helmets. I got the impression that they also had chain mail. I did see a few guards on top of the trains who were wearing steel breastplates clearly showing mail underneath. The train guards were carrying swords and rifles. The cavalry had crossbows slung on their saddles and rifles over their shoulders. They were very visible even from our height.

As to heavy weapons, all I can say is that they aren't carrying anything too big to hide inside a rail car."

"Thank you again. Two last questions. What is your best approximation of the number of troops coming and when should we expect them?"

"Any count would be only a wild guess. At least a hundred thousand, maybe more and they are on your doorstep. Now that the tracks are repaired, the trains move fast and they could begin to arrive in Karakorum before the end of the day. Depending upon how organized they are, you could see them as early forty eight to seventy two hours after that."

I thanked Orbitz and resumed the meeting. "Since I doubt that an unfriendly force could travel though China on Mongol rail cars, we have to conclude that they are simply Mongol reinforcements. A lot of them.

We need to conclude this battle before they get here. Count Grzegorz, sir. When can your troops leave?"

"We're ready. Have been for days. We can get under way within the hour."

"Make it so."

The Count was as good as his word. In less than one of our double length hours, he had nine thousand wolves mounted and waiting by the eastern ramparts. By that time, artillery had been pounding the Mongols for over half an hour. The wolves could probably have ridden right through the Mongols with minimal losses, but I insisted we up the odds with well dropped explosives.

All of the Big People had been shown the route and had the mission explained to them. They would do the navigation, leaving the wolves to watch, rest in the saddle, and fight without sweating the small stuff.

Despite the artillery firing behind us and the shells landing a mile away, the formation was quiet compared to conventional cavalry formations. Big People don't jostle around or snort and they knew their place in line. The wolves were all proud sons of nobility, too proud to be nervous and too nervous to chat.

I sat on Silver overlooking the formation, but Count Grzegorz was in the lead and in command. He raised his Sten gun over his head and bowed his head in my direction. I saluted him and as my arm fell, he charged over the ramparts.

The columns were almost two gross men wide, and they were over the ramparts in less than ten minutes. A few minutes later, another thousand men from the mobile infantry followed them. These men would be returning. There would be casualties when the column bashed their way through the Mongols and this last group of men was there to get our casualties back behind our lines. The Christian Army never leaves a man behind.
I waited an hour until the rescue column returned with the wounded and dead. There were too many of them.
We had forty eight hours to kill.

The End Game.

By the time Zephyr confirmed that our flanking column was in place, the second Chinese army was closing on the enemy camp. We needed to end this before we had to fight more men than we had bullets.

The main force that I led was much larger than the flanking force. I was going to lead almost thirty thousand troopers and artillery men into the battle, and the enemy knew we are coming.

I had Baron Kowalski start his bombardment just before midnight the night before. All three rigidibles were overhead, dropping illumination flares and calling in target corrections. The Baron gleefully started the bombardment by dropping shells from his five inch cannon into the center the camp. Our artillery could reach over half of the Mongol camp. They pounded the camp and the troops between us and the camp all night. It was impressive as Hell, but it takes a lot of ammo to kill a half a million men.

Our column was very different from the flanking column. We would be moving fast only by medieval standards. We would move slowly enough keep to ammo wagons, radio wagons, mobile artillery, and surgeries with us. We were an army on the move.

Behind us, we would leave about two thousand men as a rear guard. They would man the barriers behind us. They job was to protect the rest of our baggage train and wounded warriors. Two planes were in the air scanning for Chinese planes and four more were waiting to strafe the Mongols.

As dawn broke, twenty charges laid by Kowalski, noisily dumper the embankments into the ditch ahead of them, and we moved out. This time I took the lead in my golden armor with Terry riding behind me protected by the new shield on her back. It felt good. Beside me two aids rode, flying my personal flag on staffs held high enough to be seen by all.

Holding my sword over my head, I gradually sped up, leaving the carts behind and preparing to hit the Chinese line with maximum power. The first Chinese defense line had been pounded so badly by the artillery that there was nothing left to fight. The Big People and the warriors had been told to ride down any armed opponents, but to avoid killing any Chinese who threw down their weapons or who were too wounded to be dangerous. We wanted them to know they could run and live. Mongols, we just killed.

We didn't even slow down and very few shots were fired. Most fighting was done by the Big People.

As we approached the Mongol camp, I sheathed my useless sword and took up my Sten. Here we hit intact defenses and had to fight. The Chinese had dug trenches and put up wooden barricades and it looked as if the massive artillery bombardment had spurred the sudden development of modern foxhole. Here I slowed down to let the machine gun carts catch up. Then we hung back a little while the guns raked the Chinese troops.

The shock of machine gun fire scattered the defenders. We jumped the ditches and brushed through the wooden barriers. The wooden barricades made good bridges to get our carts over the ditches, and we delayed long enough to gather all of our equipment before advancing.

The ruins of the Mongol camp were in sight. Our next obstacle would the Mongol kill zone. Like us, they had left a large clear area between their main camp and their outer defenses and had built an embankment on their side. You could be certain that they had cannon zeroed in on it and sharpshooters watching it from foxholes. If we didn't prepare well and move through it fast, we'd pay a heavy price. Unfortunately, our survival required we move soon. While I waited for our artillery to soften up the defenders again, I got on the radio. We were fighting over a nine mile long front, and I had no idea how we were doing.

The news was not a good as I hoped. Most companies had done about as well as we did. They were at final barrier. A few companies were so far south that they were past the end of the Mongol defenses and they were already fighting their way into the camp. The flanking force had begun their swing around the Mongols when we breached the first line. At least a few companies had taken serious losses from dug in Chinese who didn't run, but we were still in good shape for the final push. The best news was that a lot of the Chinese troops were running for China. Once they realized that we wouldn't pursue them, death from machine gun looked a lot more certain than death from angry Mongol masters.

On the other hand, the Mongols themselves outnumbered us four to one and they hadn't taken any loses and weren't retreating.

Our success depended upon keeping the blitzkrieg going. If we stayed in one place too long, we could be overwhelmed by sheer suicidal numbers, so I didn't have time to chat. In the twenty minutes if took to get organized, the gunners manning the machine gun carts reloaded from the ammo carts and then the Big People who had been pulling the carts turned around and got re-hitched so they could push the gun carts forward. It was a clumsy way to travel, but allowed the guns to fire on the move without hitting us.

I gave the order to move forward, and miles of men surged out. We were almost across when Silver stopped so fast that Terry was tossed to the ground. Beside us, another Big Person screamed in pain and dropped to his knees. When I dismounted to help Terri, I saw the reason. The ground was thick with caltrops. Hidden in soft dirt, under straw or just laying on the ground, the evil things covered the ground as far as I could see in both directions.

The caltrop is a four pointed metal star designed to land with one point straight up no matter how they fall. These were large enough to penetrate a Big Person's foot. They had been around since Greek times, but no one had ever been able to make enough to cover a battlefield. The Chinese had done it.

I turned Silver back, but as we headed for our own lines, I heard the creak of a trebuchet. In a few seconds, a bag opened in the air and showered the space in front of me with more caltrops. While we were picking out way through, I heard more launches up and down the line. While Silver handled the navigation, I stood in the saddle and looked back.

In addition to the trebuchets, the Chinese were using man powered launchers. The oldest form of catapult, they consisted of two A frames with an axle between them and a throwing arm mounted to the axle. The basket was loaded and then six or eight soldiers simply jumped up and pulled down on ropes tied to the shorter arm to launch.

Machine guns and rifles had longer ranges, so the simple throwers were going out of business fast. In a few minutes, the trebuchets began to disintegrate under artillery fire, but they had done their job. We were stuck in the open. At least I was. I could see that some units had retreated successfully to the last defensive line.

While we carefully picked our way out, thousands of Chinese and Mongol troops would be firing at us from foxholes and barricades, and doing a lot of damage.

The carts were just stuck. There was no way to maneuver a Big Person and two balloon tires past the caltrops field. The machine gunners kept firing from where they were, covering our retreat. I saw two troopers jump off their Big People and climb onto a cart to protect the gunners with their shields. Up and down the line people were coping.

It seemed like Silver had been tiptoeing forever, when I looked up to see troopers dragging parts of the Chinese wooden walls toward us.

Soon I was clear, but on the clock. If the flanking force hit the main Mongol camp with only nine thousand men and no main force, it would make the charge of the light brigade look like a cake walk. We had to get across fast.

I told my number two to grab whatever material he could and bridge the caltrops field. He was to get our men across as soon as possible and establish a base on the other side, but to wait until he saw the signal flares from the rigidibles before he advanced. We couldn't create shock waves in small groups. I gave the same orders to the radiomen to transmit and then sent messengers north to make certain everyone got the message.

I headed south with a small force to spread the word and keep the action going. It turned out the caltrops fields were not complete, so a few companies had gotten across with little trouble. Maybe the Mongols had deliberately left small areas clear of mines for their own horses. Other troops were reforming to use the clear lanes, and some were building wooden roads. In all cases, the Chinese and Mongol troops were firing from protected positions on their embankment and we were taking loses. The longer our men were in the cleared area, the more we lost.

I was over a mile from the southern end of our line when I saw Baron Krol behind the lines on the Mongol side of the field. His force had been so far south that he was beyond the Mongol defenses. He had just ridden by the defenders and turned north to clear the opposition. It was one of the few times I was able to watch a cavalry charge and see the grandeur because I wasn't being shot at. He and his men were running Hell bent over the bodies of the Chinese, firing and stabbing as they went, scattering or killing everyone in their path.

I decided to cross over and follow the baron north. Most of the fighting was happening ahead of me as the baron's men cleared Chinese troops from their embankment, but we took and gave fire from Chinese on the camp side. As I rode hard to catch them, I could see men in red uniforms streaming south, away from the battle. In the distance, I saw them overwhelm a mounted officer who was trying to stop them. Maybe we would only have to fight the Mongols themselves. I started with most of a company, maybe two hundred men, but I was losing a few men to gunfire and dropping off men to aid the wounded who had fallen from Krol's force

By the time I reached my own Komand with my last hundred men, they were across the ramparts and moping up the opposition. My first thought was that it was time to move on. We were short of machine guns and artillery, but some had gotten across and even the artillery left behind could give us support.

Fortunately my adrenalin dropped enough for rational thought. My radio cart was set up in a safe area and I took time to assess the situation before I leaped into battle.

My biggest worries were the green army reinforcements coming onto the field and what would happen to the flanking force if they moved ahead of us.

Zephyr was hanging over the green army, but the report was confusing. "The first red troops ran into the green formation about an hour ago, and they got a very unfriendly reception. The front line of the greens sprayed them with fire lances, and there was some fighting. Fifteen minutes later, the greens opened up clear lanes through their formation and began letting red troops retreat through them. Now I see that some red groups have stopped running and joined the greens. It looks as if they are letting the cowards run and leading the better troops back into battle.

I'm not even certain if they are friends or enemies or which side they're on but they aren't going to be a problem for another hour or so. They stopped moving toward your flank and they are now moving around to the back of the Mongol formation. Maybe they're going to interleave with the Mongols and reinforce their front line."

Flying Cloud was over our flanking force, trying to help out with drops of improvised bombs and the Mongol arrows that we captured. Commodore Stanislaw was directing the air war from there. "We're holding. We have four planes doing strafing runs on the Mongols and we're dropping everything we've got. Its close, but we're holding so ..... What the Hell is that?"

I was still looking down at the radio when the sun went out. Literally. I looked up to see the biggest damned airplane in this or any other world block the sun as it passed overhead. My first thought was "My God. I hope that's ours". Everyone else saw it too. The battlefield almost went quiet as necks strained to follow the behemoth as it rose into the northern sky and then suddenly nosed over and dove faster than anything the medieval world had ever seen.

I was still holding mike when the receiver came alive. "Hetman Conrad, Commodore Stanislaw, this is Captain Lawson on the White Dragon. I think we can be of assistance to your flankers." I could hear the roar of machine guns before he closed his mike.

I could see the huge rigidible buck and shudder when its machine guns starting firing. It seemed to almost stop in the air and I could see the huge white wings flexing momentarily. Then it smoothed out and headed for the clouds.

It was enough for the Chinese. A sea of red uniforms ran, rode, stumbled and scrambled to leave the field. By the time White Dragon made its second pass, all we had left to fight were the Mongols – a lot of Mongols – well armed.

I listened into Captain Lawson talking to Commodore Stanislaw on the radio, "My apologies for the surprise Commodore. Twelve hours ago we were two thousand miles away on a shakedown cruise and I doubted we could make the party. We were ordered to make the attempt but keep a low radio presence.

Should we make a pass at the green force approaching from the north?"

"Not yet. We think they are hostile, but we have no idea who they actually are. It's better to concentrate on more immediate threats. If we kill enough Mongols, there will be no battle for the greenies to join. Attack the Mongols wherever you see a target."

We still had time to soften them up a little more. I got on the radio to the Commodore. "Commodore Stanislaw, for the next hour, the primary job for your ships will be working with the artillery. There is no point in letting a Mongol get close enough to shoot at us when we have thousands of artillery rounds left. In an hour we'll evaluate the damage and decide whether to go."

I sent several riders out in both directions with messages for any artillery units out of radio contact. They were ordered to kill anything they could find for the next hour if they couldn't contact a rigidible for targeting.

Then I sat down for lunch with my men. It made sense. There was nothing to do for the next hour but listen to whistling shells and watch explosions.

The medical corps used the time to set up aid stations just behind the lines, where they stabilized the wounded and tagged dead before they were sent back to our main camp. Business was good, too good.

After I refilled my ammo supplies, I joined the circle of men sitting behind a dirt mound and opened a can of "lunch". It wasn't too bad. It had a separate container on the top for a thick chunk of bread and the stew inside was edible, sort of, even cold. If I had a cigar, the world would be good.

I would have loved to have swapped war stories and lie about women with the men around me, but, as usual, being the boss was a conversation dampener. I settled for lying back with my hands behind my head, wondering what I would do after the battle. My future plans ended with a sword point in the khan's neck.

The idyll ended when I remounted Silver, and signaled to the radioman to give the move command to the rigidibles. Green flares began to drop from the sky a minute later and we moved out.

We were about mile from the center of the Mongol camp and the ground in front of us was a mangled mess. My first impression was a lot of shell craters surrounded by pieces and parts of tents, bodies, and junk. There wasn't a living soul in site. The previous inhabitants had fled, retreated or died.

We started out at a gentle trot. There was, after all, nothing to charge. Above us, White Dragon began a strafing run. Unfortunately, the Mongols learn war faster than most. When the Dragon bottomed out less than a thousand feet over the camp, dozens of cannons fired straight up. It was the medieval equivalent of flak, and they got the luckiest shot in the history of warfare. As the ship rose, I could see a huge hole in the left wing and she began to roll over on to that side. The roll stopped with the ship hanging in the air at almost ninety degree angle and drifting very slowly back toward the Earth. As the minutes passed, the drop slowed and she seemed to lift very slowly. We were on our own.

There was no more action until we were less than a thousand yards from the edge of the camp, then all Hell broke loose. The bastards were supposed to be dead, but they must have dug in really well because there were a lot of them shooting at us from behind barricades and berms.

We were ready. We pushed up machine gun carts and cannon ahead of us all along the line. We slowed our advance while the cannon fired grape shot and the machine guns swept barricades. The progress was slow but steady. We were taking loses, but hurting them more.

As I expected, the last hundred feet was strewn with more caltrops. The carts slowed down, but kept up a slow but steady suppression fire as I and the troopers dismounted and walked our Big People through the caltrops field. Then we were over the line and surrounded by Mongols. Armed Mongols, armored Mongols, hiding Mongols, prone Mongols, mounted Mongols and mainly very angry Mongols. I didn't even need to aim. Behind us, the cart drivers were throwing down ground cover and trying get past the caltrops. The artillery was still falling on the middle of the camp and the troopers were struggling to get the ones we brought with us past the barriers. About one Big Person in twenty carried a machine gun strapped to his side. They stopped at the highest places they could find where the riders unpacked the guns and set them up on tripods while the rest of us kept the Mongols away from them. After a few minutes, I jumped down from Silver and gestured for the rest of my men to do the same. Now that the Mongols all had guns, it didn't make sense to sit up in the saddle and make a good target. I told Silver to get away from me and find shelter. He just snorted and refused to leave. If I could have caught her, I would have thrown Terry off the battle line, but she also refused to leave.

The next half hour was trudge and smash. The Mongols came out of trenches, fired from behind mobile walls, poked up out of foxholes and occasionally rode down on us. They came in groups from our flanks and, on one occasion, a small group of them got behind us.

We struggled over their dead bodies and killed them with Sten guns, grape shot, and occasionally good old fashioned steel, and they kept coming. I didn't know how we were doing, but every tine I looked around there were different troopers around me and sometimes fewer of them.

I think that I just caught sight of the general's tent when the lights went out and the world slipped away.

Post Game Highlights

When I woke up, there was a Chinaman in my tent. I was surrounded by corpsmen, two bodyguards, and a Chinaman dressed in glorious golden and purple silk robes. I seemed to have only one eye working, but I could see him sitting in a red and gilded chair near the foot of my bed. After awhile I managed to say, "I see we lost."

He gestured to a corpsman near him and said in the worst pigeon I have ever heard, "Get General." Then he listed to his translator and turned back to me. "No. No lose. I Su Song. Chinaman. We kill Mongols, you and me. No Mongols now."

That seemed to exhaust his pigeon and my strength so I drifted back to sleep. When I awoke again, the sun was going down and he was still there. I tried to lift my head but someone seemed to have put lead weights on it. I managed to croak, "How long."

The Chinaman leaned toward me and said, "General come. Rest now. Four days here. Was bad. Better now."

I couldn't wait for whoever The General was, I asked the corpsman, "How is Terry? Is Silver alright?" I felt the chill in the room. No one wanted to tell me. The Chinaman's translator spoke to the corpsman and then his boss. His boss thought for a moment and spoke through the translator. "Not all news is good. The girl with you died covering your body with her own. The horse was badly wounded trying to drag you back to the doctors. He is alive, but they do not know if he will live long."

He could see my agitation. He spoke through the interpreter again. "You did well. Almost half your men survived. They will see home and family again. It was great battle. There will be murals painted and stories will be told for a thousand years."

About that time Count Wladyclaw entered the tent followed by two of his aids. "It is good to see you awake, your grace. I see you have met Su Song." The name seemed so familiar, but I couldn't remember where I had heard it. "I've met him but I don't know why he's here or who he is."

Wladyclaw smiled and bowed slightly to the Chinaman, "This honorable Chink is the man who brought the army that saved our Christian butts. He says that we would have known that earlier if we hadn't shot down both of the messenger planes he sent to us.

He knew your name and was particularly keen to meet you. His official post now is liaison with us barbarians, and his tent is pitched next to yours."

"How did the battle go? I seem to have missed it again."

"You couldn't have missed much. You went down on a pile of Mongol bodies that you created yourself. You were almost out of ammo and your sword, your armor and most of your skin was covered with blood that wasn't yours. You didn't miss much.

The blow to your skull finally brought you down, but you've got one broken arm, slashes on both arms and one leg, and your body is one mass of bruises. When you went down, both your main force and the flanking expedition were holding their own, but we were unable to advance on either front. Apparently our reputation of not taking prisoners energized the Mongols to insane resistance. We were in severe danger of having a pyrrhic victory when Su Song hit the Mongols from behind with the Song Imperial army and a lot of Chinese who started the day fighting for the Mongols

He told me that his major fear was that we would attack him with our flying machines before he had a chance to fight. Fortunately, the planes and rigidibles were too busy defending us to bother with him. When Song hit the Mongols from behind they panicked and sent troops back to block the newcomers.

That relieved the pressure on Count Grzegorz and the wolves. He broke through and overran the Mongol command center in less than half an hour and they just keep going until all the Mongols stopped breathing."

There were a few tense moments when the wolves met the Chinese, but it didn't take long to realize we were both in the same business. "

"How is Count Grzegorz?"

He shrugged. "The doctors say that there is still hope. We lost a lot of good men. By the way, when I took temporary command, I had a couple of the coded messages you have been refusing to read decoded. You need to read this one. It's been around for several weeks."

From: Count Piotr, Hetman of the Free Christian Army in Europe.
You might notice the name change. We have completed our negotiations with King Henryk.
In your absence, his transgressions became intolerable. He demanded full control of our finances. He demanded that all Jews be allowed to hold only low rank in the Army and forbade intermarriage. He insisted that all Muslims be expelled from the Army and issued orders that we attack peaceful Muslim countries and kill every Muslim who refused to convert to Christianity.
None of this was allowed by our creed.
When he arranged his own coronation as "Emperor Henryk, King of Poland and the Middle East, King of Egypt…" and so on, it was obviously time to dump our medieval monarch.

However, oath breaking is a serious matter and we opted to negotiate his removal rather than simply declare that we no longer recognized him as our Liege Lord.

We agreed to cede several forts to him and to give him a one time payment of twenty percent of all funds held in Europe. There is also an agreement for annual loyalty payments to be made for the remainder of his life. Even in Poland, we retained control of all of our factories, ships, bases and businesses.

We now hold dominion over most of the old Arab states of the Middle East, the former Cuman Khanates, Sicily, Gibraltar and various small states that were without leadership and protection. The area formerly controlled by the Golden Horde is ours to occupy if we want it.

Most of northern Africa is held by our vassal states, and our close friends, the Byzantines, have retaken all of the territory on the southern shores of the Black Sea. Our relation with the remaining Muslim lands is friendly and a few of the smaller states have asked to taken into Army dominion.

We have agreements to keep all of our forts in European countries in exchange for taxes and border security. In those countries, we retain control over only our own estates and castles and demand only the right to do business under the laws of their lands.

I have thus far retrained the title of Hetman. The army needs a supreme commander and I serve in your stead while you are on campaign. As our supply efforts have shown, you are still in command of as much of the Free Christian Army as you want. Any title from Hetman to Monarch is yours to take.

Let us know your desires. I hope all is well with my loyal friend and Liege Lord.

The news that I had won everything I wanted in Poland without even being there made little impression. It was still a place where I had been betrayed and abandoned and I wanted nothing to do with anyone there. I admit that the thought of having my ex wife arrested for adultery and confined for life in a monastery was a delightful fantasy, but sticking King Henryk and her together for the rest of their lives seemed punishment enough.

I did not even retake full command of my army. Healing was taking all of my energy and Wladyclaw was doing a good job. I had faith that he could get the men home safely.

The men would be going home rich. We had done well in Sarai and added gold in Karakorum. They had stripped the bodies of the Mongols and discovered that the Mongols took considerable wealth with them on the road. Even the lowest ranks would have enough money to purchase a small estate when they returned home.

As there was no king to share with, I accepted my share as Hetman and split the king's share between myself and the officers. I ended up with enough gold to found at least one kingdom.

Wladyclaw decided that they would take two months to allow the wounded to heal and equipment to be repaired before they headed home. Su Song made certain that provisions were supplied every week and when they left, a company of Chinese engineers would accompany them to map out the route for the new Trans-Tundra railway. Perhaps Su Song felt that negotiating rights of way would be easier when his men were accompanied by a battle hardened army.

The first rail line would be a joint effort of the Free Christian Army and the Song emperor. Within a year, the first section would be completed between Mongolia and Constantinople. The Silk Road was about to get a lot shorter.

One bright spot was my friendship with Su Song. As soon as my head cleared, I remembered who he was. In my original time-line, he was never captured by the Mongols but he was remembered a thousand years in the future for designing the world's first accurate clock and writing books on everything from pharmacology to engineering.

He had decided to learn Polish in order to read technical books from Europe and his amazing mind could pick up two or three hundred new words every day. Within weeks we were able to have simple conversations without an interpreter.

The story of how he fooled his Mongol bosses for years was fascinating. While he turned out invention after invention for the Mongols, he kept his old students in the Song Empire informed of his progress.

His final plan will go down in history beside the Trojan horse. When he realized that the Mongols were going to strip the country of troops to fight us, he had his allies in Hangzhou throw together hundreds of quick and dirty flat cars, and sent as many engines as he could to the southern border for "maintenance". As the Mongols moved their troops north, the Song carried their cars over the border and jumped on the khan's railroad. They captured Beijing and the emperor weeks before our battle happened.

As soon as the capitol was secure, Su Song's generals moved north to finish off the Mongols with our help.

It has been a good life or three, but I have the feeling that this part of my life is over. I have instructed Novacheck to create a corporation to hold all my assets in Poland and have given instructions that he keep ten percent of the profit for his personal use. The rest is to be reinvested. Since there is no concept of joint property in Polish law, I have deeded my home and estates in Poland to the Army to be used as rest home for retirees, with specific instructions that my ex wife not be allowed on the grounds. The instructions have been radioed home, and the physical papers will follow with Wladyclaw.

I'm not certain what I and my wagons full of gold will do next, but Su Song has some interesting ideas.

For now, I'm going to take a nap.

This ends the journal of Conrad Stargard.

Last from the Journals of Su Song

He was asleep when I first saw him. His red silk robes were stretched around the bandages on both arms and one of his legs. His head was also bandaged and I knew that he had bruises all over his body.

I was surprised at his youth. I expected a man much older than myself, but he looked like a warrior in the prime of life, powerfully muscled everywhere and handsome enough for other men to hate. I was amazed just to know that he was a real person. I also checked to see that he had only five fingers and five toes on each appendage.

In addition to his own physician and bodyguards, I sat near the door, surrounded by my retainers and three interpreters. We spoke little that day.

The next day, he was alert and full of questions. "Su Song. I have heard your name. You are famous in my lands for a fabulous clock that you built for the Emperor and the books that you wrote. Are you that Su Song?"

"Yes, but the clock is not yet finished. We have spent far too much time on warfare. Your staff tells me you are the famous 'Conrad, Guardian of the Heavens'. If so, I have read your amazing books. We thought that you were a myth or a college of scholars writing under a single name. I am amazed to meet you.

Every scholar I know would sell his wife and firstborn son to have you explain some of the mysteries in the text."

It was several weeks before we were able to converse freely and even then we occasionally needed an interpreter.

Over dinner one night he said, "I am surprised that a scholar like you could make plans so devious. On one hand you pretend to help the Mongols and behind your back, you destroy them."

I was amazed at the lack of moral comprehension in my friend, "I pretended nothing. I served my masters well and kept my oath."

When he looked dubious, I explained. "Unlike your world, we believe following in the Will of Heaven. We have known of Europe for fifteen hundred years. But every time we send envoys, there is a different Europe. At first it was Greeks and Egyptians. Then it was Roman. Then it was Goth and Vandal. Eventually it became Catholic, Byzantine and Muslim. Each time the rulers changed, you burned down your cities, killed your civil servants, closed your roads, destroyed your aqueducts, fought to the death and started all over.

We do not do that. The same China that first sent silk to the Egyptians still exists, because it is considered a moral imperative to respect the Will of Heaven. When it is time for a change, you support the new rulers. You continue to collect the taxes and dredge the canals for the new emperor."

"How do you know someone has the 'Will of Heaven' on his side?"

"Well. Personally, I find it a convincing argument when someone has a sword pressed to my throat."

"But eventually you betrayed the Muslims. You turned on your bosses."

"I did no such thing. When the Mongols were foolish enough to strip the country of troops, it was obvious that they were no longer favored by the Heavens. I simply cooperated with the inevitable."

When the rest of the army left, Conrad and I traveled to Beijing in my private rail car. In appreciation for his service, the Emperor granted Conrad the estates of a rich but dead Mongol. He received a large land grant, a palace in the country, a rich townhouse in the center of Beijing and assorted slaves, wives and concubines. It was a rich reward, but it cost the emperor nothing as there was a sudden surplus of Mongol estates on the market.

He remained in Beijing for several years. He was never able to master more than a few hundred words of Chinese and the only phrases I heard him use were "More wine, bartender", "You are very beautiful.", and "Please take your clothes off."

Still he wandered the streets with his retinue of beautiful interpreters or couched in his sedan chair, visiting bars, restaurants, and music halls. His Chinese was terrible, but he still tried to sing when he had too much wine. As there were no distilled spirits in China, he started a distillery and became even wealthier selling concoctions he called "Vodka" and "Wiskey".

For all of Poland's scientific genius, polish physicians were unable to treat simple problems like diabetes and infection or provide good birth control. When Conrad realized how advanced our pharmacology was, he began packaging our cures, transporting them on the Trans-Tundra to Europe and made yet another fortune.

Eventually boredom set in again. He tired of his concubines and palaces and complained bitterly that he could neither find nor train a good nude dancer in all of China.

I think he really missed charging his enemies, sword held high, with a mighty steed beneath him. Some men are not bred for peace time.

Eventually he ordered a luxurious rigidible from Poland. He bragged about it like men brag of their sons. It was pressurized to thirty thousand feet and had luxury suites for him and his concubines. It could carry a staff of fifty crew and marines, and mounted the latest machine guns. It also came with a crew of twenty trained sailors and mechanics recruited from Poland. Years of peacetime had made it easy to recruit men who craved adventure more than home.

At our last dinner, he talked about possible destinations. He spoke of islands in the middle of the Pacific Ocean, a continent south of India, and destinations in the new world. He was particularly interested in a civilization he called the Maya. He felt that they might be ripe for some "enlightened guidance."

He promised to return after his journey, but as I watched the ship rise into the eastern sky, I knew that I would never see him again, and I did not.

The View from on High

It was like climbing into a cloud. *SeaSicker* floated less than fifty feet above us when we climbed the gangplank into her belly. The bright white wings stretched out forever on both sides of us and over our shoulders we could see the massive burners in the darkened hot air bay.

We'd all been warned to never call her the *SeaSicker* in front of Captain Lawson, but no one who'd flown in her called her anything else.

We all knew we were volunteering to ride a ship that had had its problems. I was on the beach the day she returned from a test dive running about fifty feet above the waves. Her gas valves all ran through one manifold. When it jammed, she couldn't restart her gas jets and damn near crashed before they valved more hydrogen into the bags.

We all heard that she ended one flight hanging straight up in the air with her nose to Heaven and her tail to hell, and no way to right her. Speaking of her tail, there was a rumor that the one she carried now was the third one they tried. One almost crashed her. One couldn't control her, and the current hawk like one was the first that seemed to actually work.

But when she flew right, she was faster than Hermes, and just looking at her took your breath away.

She was also a modern marvel. She was way bigger than a battleship but, for all her size, she only needed twenty common seamen, all warriors, to keep her aloft. Another fifteen officers came along and kept getting in our way. She was so big that every man, including our five squires had a cubbyhole all of his own, and there were common rooms for both enlisted men and officers.

Of course, outside of the pressurized area, you had to kinda walk careful because all that was between you and your God was the catwalk you were on and the canvas below it.

My battle station was outside the pressure, and I would be wearing an oxygen mask and fur lined leather while I did my job. I was a loader for the machine guns. There were eight guns in fixed mounts on each side of the hot air bay. There had been more, but they damn near shook the ship apart when they fired, so we ended up with sixteen total. I carried ammo up and down a narrow catwalk, reloaded the guns, and cleared jams. It was cold, noisy work but I didn't have to do it often. Mostly, I cooked.

Riding her wasn't quite as bad as I expected. The engineer would fire up the gas jets and we would start to slide up in the air. The wing forced us forward, picking up speed as we rose. When we were about five miles higher he'd shut down the jets and we'd start to glide down, trading height for speed. If he was in a hurry, he'd open the vents over the hot air bay and drop us fast.

What I hadn't realized was that when were just cruising easy, the ship had a glide angle of over thirty to one. While we rose or went down five miles, we went forward about hundred and fifty miles, so each cycle was over an hour long.

Of course, when the captain was in a hurry we went up and down like a pogo stick. That's when *SeaSicker* got her name.

We were on a test flight over the Black Sea when the captain opened the intercom to tell us we going to war. "This is the captain. We have received an urgent request for help from the Eastern Expeditionary Force. They will be going into combat against a numerically superior force in less than twenty four hours. All areas rig for flank speed. All non-essential personnel stand down.... And hold on." Rigging for speed involved clearing all the counters, locking all the cupboards, picking up tools and mops and anything else that bounces, roles, vibrates, falls over, falls off, or slips, and then strapping in wherever you were.

Ever watch a fish try to get away. You remember that high speed tail waggle that propelled it through the water? That was us for the next twenty hours. Jam the jets full on. Climb fast. Dump the heat and dive. Jam the jets. Climb fast. Dump... There was a debate among the crew members whether it was better to be in bed or standing. In my mind it was miserable either way.

I delivered coffee and sandwiches to the wheelhouse several times during the trip. There was no question of using standard platters or cups. The sandwiches traveled in cloth sacks slung over my shoulder while the coffee went in closed jars. All of the staff stayed strapped in except Captain Lawson. He relaxed in the captain's chair behind the helmsman drinking coffee and munching sandwiches, immune to the changing pressures on his body. Even among a crew off old saltwater sailors, he stood out for being totally immune to seasickness. I never saw him in his cabin that trip, so he must have slept in his chair.

The next morning we were over the plains of Mongolia, following roads, looking for Karakorum. We had a great view of the landscape out of the galley windows. The galley, like everything else, was enclosed inside the pressure vessel but there were clear observation panels in some of the walls. We watched as the captain brought her over a ruined city, still smoldering below. He turned north, northeast and then brought us to flank speed again.

A few minutes later, beat to quarters rang out on the ships bells. I was already halfway to the machine gun platform when the captain made the announcement, "Battle Stations. Battle Stations. This is not a drill. Our first run will commence in less than fifteen minutes."

The guns were mounted on the inner side of the heat chamber, so I was standing next to an open area the size of a stadium with nothing between me and the ground but air. My guts refused to trust the safety line I had clamped to a rail behind me and insisted on heaving a little, but I had a great view.

I checked all of the guns on my side, opening the ammo canisters again to verify they were full, making certain they were cocked, needlessly straitening out the ammo belts and checking the safeties. I had done it all before, but I was full of nervous energy. In the distance, I could see Boleslaw wearing his leathers and fur doing the same things on the other side of the bay.

We both stopped when the gas jets came on full force. The roar was deafening and my face burned from the heat as we rose into the sky. My feet felt the deck pressing up on me, and then suddenly the world dropped. The jets died and the huge roof vents opened up to dump the heat. We dropped like the proverbial rock. It took both arms to pull myself close enough to the open bay to see the ground. We sped past hills, then tents, and then armored men, then the guns opened up and ship shuddered almost to a stop. The vents snapped shut and gas jets opened up again as we sped over a battlefield spewing death below.

We went up slower than we went down. It was almost peaceful.

This time, the captain lingered at the top of our arc. He used the maneuvering engines to line us up carefully before we attacked again. This time we were attacking east to west and below us I could see Mounted Infantry being pounded by Mongol guns – until we silenced the Mongol guns.

We made one more pass before we took a break. The captain was waiting for something. We just floated for about an hour. The guns held enough ammo for maybe three strafing runs, so it was time to refill the ammo canisters. That took half of the hour, and I spent the second half of the hour wishing I had gone to the john before the battle started. I tried to figure out if I could get in a position to piss over the rail, but I was afraid that I would be unzipped and pants down when the captain decided to make another run. Eventually nature won the argument. I hope there was a Mongol below.

Then I heard the maneuvering engines running again. The captain lined up carefully and began another high speed run. Damned high speed. I was watching the guns chew up the ground beneath us when I heard a large crash behind me and felt the ship heel over. I could see sky through the canvas about half way down the wing. Something had punched a big hole in our wing.

We were still tilting when the load speaker came on, "Damage crew to the starboard wing. Hydrogen crews prepare to mount new bags. Move!"

I saw crewmen scrambling down the wing, holding onto a catwalk that was suddenly vertical. In fact, I was standing on the side of the rail and lying back on the catwalk floor. Above me, the other gun tender was hanging over the edge of hot air bay, dangling from his safety belt.

We were still sliding toward the ground. The gas jets fired several times, but we were so keeled over the hot air was escaping out the sides of the bay and not doing much good.

It did slow our fall a little, and the gas boys must have done something. Either they pumped enough gas into our good bags to lift that side a little or they got new bags fitted and filled or something because we came back to almost level.

Boleslaw was left hanging onto the wall of the air chamber – from the outside, feet dangling over death below. I will have to make penance some day for the delay. Fear glued my feet to the catwalk for far too long. It took every bit of courage I had to clamber around that tilted chasm and pull Boleslaw over the edge.

We sat down on the catwalk for several minutes, holding onto our safety lines and waiting for another disaster. The ship continued to rise slowly and finally settled down about ten degrees starboard.

Finally, the speaker barked, "All hands stand down from general quarters except for damage crews."

We stayed over the battlefield for the rest of the day. I suppose the captain was doing his best to be an observation platform for the men below, but the reality was that we weren't able to go very far anyway. I want back to preparing tea and sandwiches for the bridge crew and rehearsing the heroic lies I would someday tell my grandkids.

The next day, we were all pressed into service repairing the damaged canvas and shoring up the wing. Much of the work on the envelope had to be done from the outside, standing on the top of a wing that was five thousand feet above the ground. The new canvas had to be glued and sown at the leading edge and then unrolled back over the spars and glued as it went down. The job needed men all around the edges. The curved shape of the wing made footing uncertain, so I was constantly looking for a place to clip my safety belt or a way to work on the canvas with my feet stuck inside the envelope. Like all sailors, I got not one bit of fear of heights, but I was relieved to get back inside when that job was done.

We were level by then, but our airfoil shape was wrecked and the captain was afraid the repaired wing wouldn't handle the stress of high speed flight. Fortunately, we did have engines. There were the two rather weak diesel engines near the end each wing. They were only backup engines and normally only used for fine direction control, but if the winds were on our side, they would take us back to Poland.

269

It took a week, but the captain nursed us back to dock. After the repairs, we were mostly used for diplomatic missions to China and the new world. White Dragon became vital tool to impress people who didn't have to ride her. We only fought one more small battle during my service.

And that, my children is the story of your father's illustrious battle career.

The Final Interlude in Uncle Tom's Control Room

Uncle Tom hit the control button again.

"Well, aren't we going to keep watching him?"

"No. His part in history is over. He'll live for a long time if he doesn't get in the way of any arrows or bullets, but one time at the golden table is all any man gets.

"He's rebuilt a civilization and improved an entire time-line beyond belief, but he's done his part and retired

"Remember that in most time-lines, he ended up as the town blacksmith. This is the best he will ever be.

"However, we do have that chemist fellow that we dropped into Bronze Age England. He's making quite a name for himself as a wizard.

"If you'll push that yellow button, we can look in on him."

Printed in Great Britain
by Amazon